Dinnan Rocks

Alistair Hume

Published by Alistair Hume, 2026.

This is a work of fiction. Similarities to real people, places, or events are entirely coincidental.

DINNAN ROCKS

First edition. March 8, 2026.

ISBN: 978-1764587327

Written by Alistair Hume.

To Debra, my long-suffering book widow.

You can never leave the past behind if it refuses to be let go.

PROLOGUE

Dinnan Rocks 1978

The fibreglass boat lurched sideways, the currents pushing and pulling it in different directions making it hard for the three men to easily stay on their feet. A yellowed deck light shone from atop the central cutting table, illuminating two men still at the wheel holding on to the windshield and the younger one on the back deck bent at his grizzly task.

'Remind me why we're out here?' The young deckhand called back to the wheelhouse.

'We need fish. No one will believe us if we don't come in with fish. Keep chumming Anthony,' yelled the skipper.

The boat pitched and bucked even though it was out of the main swell, tucked in behind the small island. Waves pummelled the rock shelf, sending sheets of spray into the air, only for it to be whisked away in the wind. The sound of the surf crumped with every break. The moon was obscured by cloud, but when it broke through the fishermen could see the ships at anchor out at sea, and the distant headland crouched above the harbour and town lights below. Everywhere else was dark, their boat was the only small one out.

The deckhand returned to scooping fish offal from a bucket over the side. Underfoot, the deck was slippery, a plastic hand reel slid back and forth; he tried not to catch his foot on the bare hook.

'Heh!' called the skipper. 'Pick that up and bait it, will you. Put it over the side away from the prop.'

The engines were still running though not in gear, burbling as the boat rose and fell in the swell. The back eddies of current were keeping the boat in protected shelter behind the rocks – it was too rough to anchor, so the skipper stayed at the wheel, ready to engage the props and swing them away from danger at a moment's notice.

'Why can't he do it?' The deckhand pointed to a large man swathed in a yellow jacket holding onto the windscreen.

'He's sick!' yelled the skipper.

'Well, why the fuck did he come?' the deckhand sneered.

The skipper didn't answer.

Over the side, the water swirled and eddied, at times flattening the surface into an oily sheen in the glow of the deck lights. Beyond was black. Spits of rain and spray entered the light, and just as quickly left it.

The deckhand threaded a large steel hook through the bait, looking up to see where the two men were at the front. He flung the bait out over the side and let the line run from the spool, tracking the progress of the depth. Instantly, the line struck and pulled sharply at his hands, nearly jerking him off his feet.

The line ran out quickly, so he tightened his grip to slow the fish, and then he began the work of hauling it in. Retrieving the line was tough going; there was a big fish on the hook. He wound more line around the spool, concentrating on keeping it away from the props.

A large fish swirled and broke the surface in the glow of the deck light, just as suddenly, a large shark broached behind it, mouth agape, sweeping its jaws left to right, severing the hooked fish in half and hitting the side of the boat with its snout. The broad, blunt nose of a tiger shark sank back down, its long body sliding below the surface, the tip of its dorsal fin showing briefly before it was just another eddy.

Only then did the deckhand become aware of the two men behind him. He turned. A length of galvanised pipe hit him just above his ear. He fell to the deck unconscious, blood pulsing from his shattered skull.

'That'll do it,' the bigger of the two men said. He looked at the grey pipe in his hand and flicked it overboard.

Neither of the men felt for a pulse, it didn't matter, the deckhand was going over the side. The more blood the better.

They struggled with the body, lifting it up to the rail as the deck cantered and swayed beneath them. Finally, with a shove, the body flipped into the water.

The skipper turned back to the wheel, dragging the big man with him.

'Hold on,' he ordered him. The boat had drifted dangerously close to the rocks, so he gunned the motors and swung it in a circle, pointing the bow out from the shelter of the islands. The wind and waves stood up and belted the small boat as it headed for the harbour.

Neither of them looked back.

PART ONE

CHAPTER 1

Nerimbah 2001

Alex stood at the top of the stairs, looking out across the tarmac. God it was hot, Queensland in January, the only place hotter was Melbourne. He had just left there.

He sucked in a heady mix of eucalypt and salty air, a deep earthy smell with a faint whiff of jet fuel. To his left in the distance was the line of blue that was the ocean, while before him was the terminal and a backdrop of hazy green hills. He'd arrived. The passenger behind him nudged him gently in the back, he was holding up disembarkation, and that would never do.

Alex pulled at his sticky shirt and looked at his fellow passengers waiting patiently for their bags, wishing that this section of the new terminal was air-conditioned. The Departure Lounge was full of sunburnt tourists lining up to head home to Victoria on the same plane he had arrived on. Nerimbah was a holiday playground for southern families desperate for the sunshine and warm water without the humidity and box jellyfish of the northern tropics. Well, at least there were no box jellyfish here, but the humidity was another matter. He retrieved his bag as it clattered past on the conveyor belt and headed for the rental car counter.

Stepping out through the automatic doors of the terminal was an assault on the senses. He shaded his eyes against the intense glare and left the shade of the airport building to saunter across the road in front of a passing taxi, he could feel his shoes sticking to the bitumen. Alex stopped under a poinsettia tree, a row of hire cars in front of him. One of them was his.

A woman in a tight grey skirt and matching top stopped next to him, resting her wheeled luggage next to his. She had sat next to him on the plane. Kim, he thought her name was, she was his height, about forty years old, not too different in age. They discussed all the things strangers do when seated together on a plane. He didn't engage with the young girl in the window seat, she was far too engrossed in her magazine and headphones, but Kim was a different matter. She had been away for three days on business in Melbourne and was driving into Nerimbah before heading to The Breakers International resort up the road, on its own secluded beach. She was a Guest Services Manager, neat and personable.

'Are you sure you don't need a lift into town?' She held her car keys up in front of her. He held up his own set of keys and nodded toward the waiting cars.

'I decided to hire a car here instead.'

'Well,' she said with a tinge of disappointment.

'Plans change quickly don't they.'

'That they do,' he replied noncommittally.

She glanced down at her watch and turned to him

'It was a pleasure to meet you, Alan.' She grabbed at her bag and walked off toward the next carpark.

'Perhaps I'll see you on the beach,' he called after her.

'Perhaps,' she called back, but didn't turn her head.

He sighed. She got his name wrong, but then he wasn't so sure her name was Kim either. He surveyed the parking lot for the hire car.

'Now which one are you?' He mumbled and spied the car's rego plate in the furthest corner of the lot. 'Typical!'

Alex dropped into the front seat of a late model rental, mumbling the steps to start the car. 'Ignition on, windows down, aircon on.' He reached down and turned the dial up full, repeating his self-professed mantra in frustration, 'Never come to Queensland in January.'

With a blast of cold air, he began to cool down, flapping his arms, and pulling his sticky shirt away from his chest. There was nothing he could do about his jeans; they were glued to his legs and would have to wait. The Nokia chirped in his pocket; he flipped it open and checked his messages. Of course, the latest was from Megan, a missed call, she could wait.

There was a text from Beau. *Have you landed yet?* He pressed the call button and had only a few seconds before he answered.

'Alex, you're here!' Beau's voice squawked from the speaker.

'Yes, just in. I'm leaving the airport now. How about you?'

'Got here last night.'

'God it's hot. I forgot what it's like, this humidity is killing me,' Alex remarked.

'You've gone soft. You always were. You've been away so long you forgot what it's like. They reckon a cyclone is on its way and we'll start getting some of it later today.'

'Ah, thank God for that. I thought I might have missed it. I finally come home after twenty years, and the weather is going to piss down.'

'Sucker!' he said. 'Twenty years heh?'

'Well, nearly twenty,' he replied. 'A few quick trips to see the folks, but still too long.' He dropped his voice to a more serious tone.' Look, I was sorry to hear about your Mum. I liked her very much,' said Alex, referring to the passing of Beau's mother.

'Yeh, I know, I liked her too, more than my old man.' Beau replied.

'Nothing like a funeral to bring people back together. Do you need any help with the arrangements for tomorrow?'

'I don't know. I haven't done anything.' Beau confessed. 'Janice told me all the arrangements had been made by the church. All done, all paid for already. I just have to show up.'

Alex brightened up instantly. 'Is Janice coming to the funeral?'

'Yeh, she is. She arrived today as well, brought up the daughter with her.'

'She has a daughter. I didn't know that.' Alex felt a sense of excitement mixed with trepidation. He wasn't sure if he would ever see her again, but Janice was here, now, and with a daughter. 'Speaking of tomorrow, can you be seen at the church? Are they still looking for you? Surely after all this time....' Alex left the remainder unsaid.

'Don't know. I still must be careful. I don't want to be seen. It would be pretty dumb to get caught now.'

'Do you want to meet up this afternoon?' Alex asked.

'No. I'll come and see you tonight. Better that way, after dark.'

Alex nodded to himself. 'That's fine. It's midday now. I'll check in and go for a swim.' He gave him the address to the apartments on Nerimbah beachfront. 'I'll see you then Beau.'

'Mate, Beau's dead, remember. My names David Burton now.'

'Sorry...I'll try to remember that. I'll see you tonight.' He signed off. Beau couldn't really afford to be recognised after all that had happened. He had to decide about how he was going to attend his mother's funeral tomorrow, as Dennis 'Beau' Beaumont or David Burton, either way, changing names can only fool people for so long.

Alex pocketed the phone and started the car, heading for the exit, swinging past the terminal and its overlarge sign, *Welcome to Nerimbah Airport*. Above it, ponderous heavy-laden clouds stretched to the stratosphere, while in the sweltering heat below, shimmied the tail of a jet poking up from behind the terminal roof.

He drove south to Nerimbah, house blocks and new estates had replaced the cane land that he remembered had once stretched from the mountains to the sea. So much had changed. Casuarinas and tea trees followed the coastline and the glisten of blue water flickered between older two-storey houses nestled in the dunes. The sea beckoned, drawing his eyes away from the road, his head darted left, and left again, straining to catch a glimpse of the ocean.

It was good to be home. Alex hadn't seen an ocean this colour and so inviting in a long time. Sadly it was the price he paid for living in Melbourne. His phone shrilled. Somehow, he knew it would be Megan. He picked it up off the seat and flipped open the cover.

'Yes Megan,' he answered, juggling the phone while he drove, trying to concentrate on two things at once.

'You've landed!' She stated, her voice abrupt and tinny through the speaker.

'Yep! 'He said. There were no pleasantries about how his flight was or if it was comfortable. He had been away enough times that he knew how this would play out.

'You didn't call. You said you would.' The receiver was silent as she waited for his answer. He didn't have one, so she continued. 'You always say you'll do something but never do.'

'Please don't start that again. I've just got in; I haven't had time to call you. I'm driving from the airport as we speak.' He looked around, confirming he was heading in the right direction. It had been a lot of years, and it had changed so much.

'You could have let me know earlier that you were going up to Queensland. I could have come too.'

'It all happened in a rush; Beau only rang me yesterday. I told you he called me out of the blue. I didn't even know where he was living. I said I was sorry about that last night.'

'You were drunk again,' she said.

'Well, you weren't exactly sober when I came in either, you finished that bottle by yourself.' He fired back.

'You wouldn't know what I did. You barely said anything to me this morning, not even a goodbye.' Her recrimination was palpable. He did peck her on the cheek and mumbled that he would be back in three days, but secretly he didn't really check that she had understood what was going on. He wanted to get out of home with as little fuss as possible.

'That's not true, I did. You just didn't want to hear it,' he retorted.

'Well, it may as well have been true.'

'Look, this is going nowhere. I'm up here for Marjorie Beaumont's funeral; can we talk about this when I get back?' Alex pleaded.

'You never want to talk Alex, never want to talk to me here and now.' Alex could hear her winding up, her voice raising an octave, 'You always run away, same old, same old; got to go to work,' she mimicked his voice, 'weekend on set...'

'I'll talk when I get back,' he interrupted.

'Got a meeting, going to be late home you always whine... God I'm sick of it!' she said. The phone went quiet. All he could hear was her heavy breathing.

There was nothing to say to that, he knew he should reassure her, but he didn't. He ended the call and threw the phone onto the passenger seat. She made him so angry. It wasn't like this for the first few years while he was establishing his media company, they worked well together, but her motivations were a little different than his. She fell in love with the idea of owning a film and media production business, while he began fell in love with working in it, away from her. Although there were plenty of opportunities to stray from Megan, he never did. He doubted that she believed in his fidelity, but to be fair, she never accused him of unfaithfulness, more a lack of attention to her needs. It must have hurt her, but then she had ways of getting her own revenge.

Ahead was a small shopping village. He swung the car off the main road into the carpark, turned the engine off and sat silently for a while. In front of him was a liquor store advertising its good value wines, but that wasn't what he craved.

Back on the road, a bottle of scotch and a six pack of beers nestled on the seat next to him, he began to hum the tune from his latest TV series. He had liked the song to begin with, he heard it so often during production, now it just annoyed him when he found himself humming it all the time. He'd broken his cardinal rule, never pick a favourite tune to headline a production that you created, you end up never wanting to hear it again. The company had just wrapped up a second season of *The Cold Cases*, a very successful docudrama series for television and he could afford to take a break from work for a few days. A break from Megan wouldn't do him any harm either.

The original International Hotel flashed passed him on the left. Its rounded architecture was famous in its day but now had been made over to a bright white soulless façade of its former self. In the 80's, American mafia bosses had thought it was quirky, a place to hide money and a retreat for their loud wives from the flashy Las Vegas nightlife. However, it turned out to be too much of a retreat, and not enough flash. It was more a beachside haven for locals who thought that its presence added a touch of other world elegance to their lives. When he first got his licence, he and Beau would drive up there to see live bands on Saturday nights. It was chaotic, the noise, the alcohol and drugs, a packed beer garden of surf culture. When the night was done, they drove home half drunk, cocooned in the glow of headlights bouncing off the melaleuca trees, laughing at inane jokes and singing The Angels line up or trying to sound like Billy Thorpe. They struggled to keep the car on the bitumen in a haze of alcoholic stupor. Wouldn't get away with it today, he thought.

He drove into North Nerimbah and could only recognise some of the original houses that lined the main road, the fibro and weatherboard ones, where tall grass and vines strangled the wooden fences running down the side. The backyard swing sets had all gone. These were the houses of the old, the grandparents. Some neat and maintained, some running to disrepair, waiting to die and be knocked down for renewal, as life does.

He turned left into Wurung Street off the main road and slowed as he came closer to the beachfront. The houses were newer here, concrete and glass with holiday rental signs out the front. Architect designed unit blocks were scattered between clothing boutiques along the beachfront, alternated with cafes that wouldn't be out of place in Melbourne's Lygon street. Beachgoers, families with kids and backpackers filled tables on the footpath under bright umbrellas. There was an energy here that wasn't present twenty years ago. Alex liked it, the familiarity of the buzz as he drove past, reminded him of the city. Another part of him hankered for the past, when there were fewer cars, fewer people and less concrete. He drove over Georges Headland, and the bay stretched out before him. He would never tire of that view. Apartments lined the foreshore of the old fishing part of town, where the river swung out into the sea. The bay was a languid turquoise, edged with a crescent of scorched yellow sand. Fishing boats and yachts dotted the river, and the newer buildings reflected the sunlight in a blaze of white.

Alex slowed down in front of the swimming beach, leaning forward to watch brown bodies in bikinis skipping down the steps to the sand. and nearly ran up the back of a sedan reversing out of a car park. He swung the rental into the newly vacated spot. Just ahead was the high-rise units he was booked in to, *Sailfish Bay,* pristine and white, clad in reflective glass, bland chic. He shook his head, at least the ocean hadn't changed, it was hard to change that.

The third-floor unit overlooking the main beach was all pastel decor and characterless. He dumped his gear on the couch and opened the double sliding doors that led on to the veranda, sucking in the hot salt air. Below him, tourists swarmed the beach and ate their lunchtime takeaways on the grass. Gulls screeched and strutted around their legs, darting in to get at fallen chips. The summer holidays were nearly over, but no one had told them that. As much as the air conditioning was deliciously cool, he couldn't help but leave the doors open to what little breeze there was.

The phone rang, vibrating as it danced across the kitchen Laminex. Megan's name flashed up in the display.

'Yes?' Alex answered, standing looking out at Nerimbah bay, a world away from Melbourne.

'I thought I'd tell you; I'm going up to Mansfield to stay with my sister for a few days, maybe longer.... I might not be here when you get back.'

'OK. When will that be?'

'I don't know.' She answered briskly.

'What... by next weekend?'

'I said, I don't know! She's going through a hard time at the moment, and I might need to stay a while,' she explained.

He didn't point out the irony of attributing that remark to their own situation.

'I hope it all works out for her.' There was no conviction in his voice, his sister- in-law's troubles were numerous and long standing. He had tried to distance himself from them for a while now, but he wasn't so sure he wanted Megan to be around her too long.

'I thought I'd let you know, when you come home and there's no one here...' Megan murmured, her voice trailing away.

'OK. I understand. I'll see you when I get back. Love you.' It was bland, soulless, simple words by repetition. He flipped closed the phone and shook his head in self-recrimination.

He was tired. Megan could do that to him. He didn't know how to fix their relationship; a few days apart might do them both good. It seemed that she was just as eager to be apart from Alex as he was from her, and he didn't expect that. The mobile phone vibrated on the table, Megan again, he wasn't going to answer it. Love? What was that about? He hadn't had sex with Megan for weeks. He wasn't even sure if he still loved her. He wanted to blame it on long work hours and poor sleep, but he knew it was more than that. their relationship had been in trouble for a while. He opened and finished a beer in one hit, then poured a scotch, collapsed on the couch, and drank it. He looked at the empty glass and reached for the bottle to pour another.

When he woke with a dry mouth, he knew what it was, he'd been here before. It was mid-afternoon and the scotch bottle on the floor was half empty. The veranda doors were open, the air con still burring away in its fight against the humidity. He needed to go for a swim to clear his head. He staggered to the bathroom, wiping at the spittle in the corner of his mouth and feeling the rasp of his cheeks. At 41 years old, he was still relatively fit from cycling and the odd game of squash but when he stripped off and stood in front of the bathroom mirror, he had to admit that he was a mess. His green tinged eyes were red, his short dark hair was flattened from sleep, and the first hints of too much alcohol in the last month were showing around the waistline. He turned away from his reflection in disgust and hunted for some board shorts.

Above the high-water line, the sand was hot and squeaked underfoot. The first wave washed around his ankles, soothing to the skin, and he stopped to soak in the magic of its healing power. Pushing against the foam he strode into deeper water until he could dive under the first wave and let it wash the day away. His head broke the surface; he flicked the water from his eyes and scanned the horizon. The alcohol seeped from his body as he stretched his arms and back under the water, letting the swells lift him on to his toes and bounce him off the bottom. With a lazy stroke he turned and pushed on to a small wave about to break. He flung an arm forward, propelling him into the lip, and then the power of the small wave took over and sucked him forward down the face and out in front to easily glide ahead of the broken foam toward the beach. He was home. As the water shallowed, he pushed his palm into the sand as a brake and let the wave spin his body around to face back out to sea again. You never tire of that feeling. He jumped to his feet and briskly waded back out to the deep, legs pushing at the sweep, anchoring his body and soul in the ebb and flow of the swell. The next wave came, and the next. He surfed them all.

Back at the apartment, dry and refreshed, he put the scotch bottle back on the bench and took a swig of cold water instead. His muscles had worked hard in the water, it was a welcome change, his body had not felt this way in a year. Dressed in clean shorts and a T-shirt, he picked up the car keys and headed out to explore his past.

Chapter 2

Alex checked his phone in the lift on the way down to Reception, no more calls from Megan, and none from the office, thank God. There was one more he searched for, but she hadn't left any message or text either. The doors opened and he immediately smelled food.

The ground floor of the apartments was ribboned with take away shops, the most brightly painted was Mexican. He settled on a fish taco and took a stool at the bench overlooking the main beach. Nerimbah had never been a particularly large place, but it had been a great place to grow up, perhaps because of its size. Apart from the bay and long stretch of sand spit, the curve of the river inland behind him ended in mudflats and tea tree swamp, stifling any real westward expansion. The roof tops ended there, where the tidal flats morphed into a wetland. It was safe for the moment, but he wouldn't put it past an opportunist council to approve draining of the wetlands in favour of a canal subdivision.

Alex finished the taco and wiped his fingers clean. He drove south toward the boat ramp at the end of the spit where the rock wall jutted out below Bayman Heads. It was a valiant attempt to tame the river mouth from breaking seas, which mostly worked for the fishing fleet, but could still be treacherous in big surf. The original huts and pilot houses along the sand spit had long gone, but the riverbank was still home to the fishing fleet, anchored against pylons and small timber wharves that jutted out into the current.

He pulled into the concrete apron running next to the riverbank, notching the car into a space between two utilities. The detritus of old fishing nets and rusting steelwork littered the tall grass. There was no romance in this industry. It was a business, and the riverbank was the ocean farmers shed. Like farmers everywhere, the fishermen were constantly tending their machinery. He walked to the edge of the river, and stood on the rock wall, taking in the warm smell of salt and oil in the air. The river was not particularly long, or very deep. Once it was clear and pristine, where fish foraged around the rocks and sandbanks, easy to see from the wharf at the old Ice works on the corner of the esplanade. As a child, he would swim over to Bayman Heads to chase whiting in the shallows. But not anymore. No way would he willingly swim that river today. Its colour had changed to a dark, silty brown; the river water hid more than just small fish.

The heavy steel boats moved on their moorings, tall gantries jutting into the air, giving the hulls a powerful, squat appearance. Skippers and deckhands were moving among them, circling the decks, attaching extra lines ashore, and securing equipment in preparation for the coming bad weather.

On the far boat, he recognised Steve Henderson, an old school mate, on a relatively new looking trawler, the *Nerina Pacifica*. It was hardly surprising that he would recognise someone, most of his childhood friends were from fishing families, and if there was something that he knew, fishing, like farming, was a family business, passed from one generation to the next. He waved at Steve, who promptly waved back. At this distance, neither of them could be sure who they were waving at, but it didn't matter. Steve had the same build and mannerisms of his father Ron, tough and resilient but he had brought an honesty to a demanding business.

There were few gaps along the riverbank, all the boats were in, the berths full. Most of the older boats were adorned with the names of wives, personal attachments to the owners and skippers, bound to the port by their heritage and smaller size. The larger, newer boats bore more corporate, symbolic names, ones that befitted their departure from the usual hull shape and design. There were catamarans and mono hulls with clean lines, tuna boats with wheelhouses aft, and names that included Star, Ocean, Pacific, or their home port wherever a living from the ocean could be made. Before the river mouth was rock walled, there were only a few boats in the fleet, shallow drafted, built of timber, only able to cross the bar at high tide. But since the walls had changed the river mouth to an all-weather port in the 60's, the Nerimbah fishing fleet had exploded, and with it had come new families, like his own.

Upriver, in the distance, the riverbank was less crowded. Once they used to build timber trawlers on that riverbank. Whenever a new hull was launched, the whole school got a morning off to watch it being pulled into the water. It was that kind of town that he grew up in, he knew everyone, and everyone was from a fishing family in some way or another, and a few hours sitting in the sun on a riverbank beat sitting behind a school desk any day.

. A short, sharp gust of wind flicked at his back and rippled the water around the boats. A low, tortured squeal of tightened ropes came from the boats bumping against their moorings and straining against each other. As quickly as it came, the gust disappeared. The sky was still clear above, but to the southeast, thick clouds menaced the horizon, a sure sign that the weather was changing. Alex walked back to the car and headed to the river mouth.

The boat ramp was deserted. Most of the dinghies were gone from their moorings, already hauled onto the bank and tied down to rocks in the grass. There was no sense of urgency yet, but out on the river a few yachties were setting extra anchors and lines. He looked in the corner of the carpark, behind the front dune, at the spot where it had happened.

Alex got out of the car and approached the corner where the dirt carpark met the start of the rock wall. Nothing had changed much in twenty years. Kicking at the dirt, he expected to see burnt metal, or shards of glass and bullet cases. But there was nothing. It had long gone. There was no remorse, no sadness, He didn't feel anything. Alex had been over it so many times before in his mind, there were no surprises left. That arsehole had deserved it, but then you don't kill someone just for being an arsehole.

He started the car and drove back toward Nerimbah beach. Ahead was a name on a riverfront shop façade that he recognised, he slowed down and pulled into the carpark of 'Villi's Chandlery and Fishing Supplies'. The window artwork showed a stylized marlin launching from the water, and a man on its back riding it like a rodeo cowboy. It didn't look much like Villi Tanoa, but he was clearly a Pacific islander, complete with tattered shorts and what looked like a Kava bowl in his left hand. Very cheesy. Alex couldn't help but smile, he had to go inside.

Chapter 3

Villi wasn't his real name; it was only part of it. He really was Kai-Villi Tanoa, but for as long as Alex had known him, he had been called Villi. His imposing Fijian physique was matched with dark eyes and a deep, resonate voice. He had a habit of finishing each line with a short laugh and shake of the head, as if the world around him was some sort of stage and he was a spectator to it's constantly performed comedy. Villi slapped the counter when he recognised Alex.

'Alex Holmes... man, it's you. Where have you been?' He laughed and shook his head as if he should have known but it had escaped him for the moment.

'Villi, how are you?' Alex reached across the counter and returned Villi's big, outstretched hand, steeling himself for the vice grip about to crush his fingers. It wasn't intentional, Villi was big and strong, and his handshake honest, he just never knew his own strength, not even when they were in Grade Nine together and played football on the bottom oval at lunchtimes.

'You're looking good.' Alex said, retrieving his hand

'You bet ya. What's it been Alex? Fifteen years?'

'Longer Villi. Longer. I couldn't help but notice your front window, not a very good likeness, but I recognise the Kava bowl. You used to bring it to parties and fill it with rum and get very badly pissed.' Villi chuckled and took a quick sidelong glance at his young assistant and lowered his voice.

'I don't do that anymore Alex. Bit older now.'

'Is this all your chandlery?' Alex added, sweeping his arm behind him at the chandlery items piled up on shelves.

'You better believe it. Best one on the esplanade,' Villi chuckled. 'The only one. What are you doing back here? I heard you were a Melbourne boy now, gone soft in the city.'

'I am, but nothing like seeing you to remind myself of why I left.'

Villi guffawed. Like all his family, he loved the banter. Alex remembered him for his lazy fluid gait that bespoke of an athleticism that Alex could only envy. The family had come from Fiji as indentured labour at the turn of the century, 'Black birded' into North Queensland to work the cane farms. When the Tanoa family moved south to the Nerimbah coast in the 60's they mostly stayed inland around Dunoonan, but it was Villi who took to the water.

When they were both in Yr. 9 at the local High School, Alex spent the summer break trying to teach Villi to surf, but it was generally a failure. He was more at home on the boats, any boats. He used to joke that he was channelling his ancestral spirits. He could handle any boat, large or small. When Alex finished High school in 1976, Villi was already studying for his Masters ticket and was well known among the fishing community.

Villi turned to the young assistant next to him at the counter and nodded in the direction of a customer rifling through the marine paint tins halfway down the aisle. The assistant left immediately.

'You seem to be doing well.' Alex observed.

'Of course,' he beamed, 'Fishing is still good. Mostly gear for trawler and fishing boats, but plenty of yachties coming in now, they love the new stuff I'm getting in. What about you, what are you doing in Melbourne? What are you doing up here? Come to see your family?'

'No. Yes,' Alex paused,' I've come up for Marjorie Beaumont's funeral, she died last week, Beau's mother if you remember. I had a few days off, so I thought I'd come back to pay my respects and have a look around at the old stomping ground.'

'Beau's mother heh? She was a good woman. My Mum saw a lot of her at church after Beau was drowned. Didn't deserve what happened to her.'

'Beau didn't deserve what happened to him either,' said Alex quietly.

'Heh. I'm not saying anything. I'm not judging. Fijians don't judge, we have enough of our own shit,' he chuckled.

'So why aren't you out skippering a boat? You were when I was last here.'

'I did. For a lot of years, but...' he pointed to his left leg, 'Gantry accident, wrecked my ankle, tore all my tendons. I can't really go in boats much anymore, but I'm doing well selling stuff to people that do and I'm still half shares in a trawler, the *Nerina Pacifica*. Named her after my wife. Get it?'

'What? You call your wife Pacifica?'

'Nah, Nerina, ya idiot. What do you think!'

Alex was enjoying the wordplay. 'I saw her. She's moored up near the boat ramp now... the boat I mean, not your wife.'

'That's the spot. They're not going out, Steve's strapping her down for the big blow.'

'So, was that Steve Henderson on the deck that I saw? Is he the other owner?'

'No, Ronny, his dad owns part share, and Steve's the skipper, and he's good. Makes us all good money when the prawn seasons on. He's saving for his own boat.'

'Do you miss going out?' Alex asked.

'Of course. But truth is, the shop is a lot easier on the family. No long weeks away, and my Nerina would skin me alive if I was missing for more than a couple of days now. Do you remember Nerina Bati? We've been together for 18 years.' His voice was filled with pride.

'No. Sorry mate, I think I'd left the coast by then.'

'When was that, 1981 or 82?'

'Early 81. After we lost Beau.'

'Yeh, now I remember. What a mess that was. A few people lost in that storm. Beau was one of them.'

'What do you remember about that night?' Alex asked.

'Jeez, it wasn't that different from what's happening in the next few days. Cyclonic winds and seas. Why those blokes were going fishing in that weather, I don't know! Three of them idiots, and they paid for it. I respect the fishermen of this town, it's a dangerous job, we all know that. But nothing can account for stupidity, and your mate Beau was one of them. Sorry he drowned, but he shouldn't have been on that boat. If they had been caught out by accident, then that is another matter, but they went out knowing what they were going into.' He shook his head. 'And that Reggie Bishop, what was going on there, shooting at Police at the boat ramp? What was Beau doing hanging around with someone like that? Sorry Alex, I know he was your friend, but.... Sorry.' His voice trailed off, and he shook his head again.

Alex could tell that even now Villi seemed bewildered by events that happened twenty years ago, unable to make sense of the loss. It seemed that Fijians did make judgements after all.

'It's all right, I've moved on.' said Alex. He could hardly tell Villi that Beau was alive and well and staying on the other side of George's Headland.

'But what happened to you? You left the place quickly after that, heh'.

'I had a job in Melbourne I had to get to. I started almost straight away.'

'Yeh? Doing what?'

'Some writing and editing. Worked on a few small projects for TV, but I got a break working for a mini-series, *Vietnam*.'

'I remember that, with that new actress...' Villi paused. 'I'll think of her name in a second.'

'I got a lot more work after that.' Alex continued. 'Did you get to see *Blue Murder*? Came out five years back? Since then, I started out on my own, producing *The Cold Cases*.'

'Is that your show?'

'Yep, TV's unsolved crimes. There's a big market for it. I've just wrapped up a new program coming out soon, *The Great Bookie Robbery of Melbourne*. Fifty-minute docudrama.'

'I'll tell Nerina that, she loves those things. Excuse me a minute,' Villi said, as he turned away to help a customer.

Alex swung around and took in the expanse of the chandlery. It may have looked a little messy when he first saw the gear piled on the floor and shelves, but a closer inspection showed it was all labelled, arranged in like sections, and stocked for easy access by customers. Villi was doing well; he was glad he stopped by on his way back from the boat ramp.

'You married?' Villi asked him when he returned.

Alex started from his musings. 'Yeh. Megan... eight years now'

'What about kids heh?' Villi beamed as he asked.

'None yet.'

'You're missing out. I got four. Three girls, one boy Xavier. I'd have another one, but Nerrina's not keen.' He went on as if marriage and children were the most important things in life, which to Kai Villi Tanoa, it was. There were no arguments, no compromise, there was his wife, his children and him. Straight and true as a navigation beacon is to a safe anchorage.

It startled Alex to realise that was missing out on something that Villi had. He decided not to tell him about his own marriage difficulties, and he definitely could not tell him about Beau.

Another yachty came into the shop, making for the far corner where he started picking through ropes and mooring lines.

'You're getting busy, I'd better leave you to it,' Alex remarked.

'We're going to get busier when this weather breaks. Especially when they realise, they haven't got enough lines out. It's going to be big, plenty big. How long you here for?' asked Villi.

'Only a few days. Maybe I'll miss the storm.'

Villi turned and leaned across the counter to look out the door at the gathering clouds. 'Not likely,' he said. 'I'm going to have to tape that widow up'. He pointed at the large expanse of painted glass behind him, 'Stop the wind from breaking it and ruining my paintwork, or it will be my last ride.' He laughed at his own joke.

'It's been great to see you Villi, I'll drop in before I go.' Alex shook his hand with genuine pleasure.

'You do that and look after that wife of yours. Don't stay away from her too long. I did and look what happened to me!' He held up his stiff left leg and laughed at his own joke.

Alex grinned and stepped outside. He was glad he had come up, even if the heat was oppressive. He looked eastward at the whisps of cloud in the sky signalling an overnight change and thought that Villi might be right.

Chapter 4

The banging on the door startled Alex. It was getting dark, he glanced quickly at his watch, 7.15 pm. It was that late already. Night-time hadn't lessened the humidity, the outside noise had quietened, and floodlights now lit the beach and park below. A few sunburnt beachgoers were packing up their towels and bags and heading for their cars, weary gaits but all smiles and banter from a day in the sun. The door thumped again urgently. He jumped up from the verandah chair and hurried down the hallway. The banging came from an open palm, not the discrete knocks he expected. He stopped at the spyhole and checked it before reefing the door open.

'Shit! Beau,' he cried out.

Beau stood swaying on his feet, seemingly trying to gain purchase on the door jamb. His left eye was crusted with blood that seeped from his hairline.

Alex grabbed at him, but Beau pushed his hands away and he staggered into the foyer. Alex stepped to the side and had a quick look over Beau's shoulder to check that he was alone before closing the door.

Beau stumbled down the hallway and straight onto the couch and slumped into its folds, leaving gelatos blood smears on the armrest. He was breathing steadily, but small bubbles of blood kept popping from his crusted nostrils.

'Are you alright?' Alex asked.

'What do you fucken think?' Beau wiped his forearm across the base of his nose and top lip. He stared at it, then looked around for somewhere to wipe it. Alex grabbed at a tea towel from the kitchen and tossed it to him. Beau caught it and clamped it over his mouth and nose.

'What happened to you? Did you get in a fight?'

'Got bashed!'. His answer was muffled; he concentrated on pushing and dabbing at the blood. Alex stepped back to let him get on with it. Beau was smaller than Alex remembered him, not smaller, just lost the physical presence from when he was younger. Now he was just lean. He slumped in the couch, gone was the long unruly mop of blond hair, replaced by a short cut that revealed a blood trail across his scalp. Alex reached out and felt the first of two wounds, one at the front of his scalp, the other at the back. Beau winced in pain at the touch and pushed his hand away. The skin was broken and both wounds were crusted.

'When did this happen?'

'Hour ago.' Beau's eyes were wide, and unfocused.

Alex reached for his mobile and began to search the Hotel Information folder on the coffee table for the number of a 24-hour clinic. He stood looking down at his friend and paused. Beau was still wanted for questioning by the authorities, even after 20 years. There was no statute of limitations in an open murder investigation and any brush with the local medical fraternity would result in questions being asked. Beau had clearly been assaulted, and the police would be notified and would want to know more. Neither of them could afford that. Alex stopped looking. Beau was busy wiping away as much of the blood as he could feel without putting too much pressure on the swelling. Alex half-filled a glass with whiskey and passed it to him.

'Here, have a go at this. I think you need a doctor, or stitches at least.'

'Fuck off Alex. Not doing that,' he moaned, struggling to push himself up on an elbow and not spill the whiskey.

'You're going to need more than what I can do for you.'

'No doctors....no ambos!' He felt the top of his head and pulled his hand away to inspect the smear of blood on his fingers. 'You look after me... No one is to know I'm here, OK?'

'I think you need some help.'

'I fucking got here on my own didn't I? I don't need any other fucking help!'

'Settle down mate. You're a mess, that's all.' Alex disappeared into the bathroom, retrieved some pain killers from his toiletry kit and presented them to Beau. He swallowed them with a gulp of whiskey.

'Who did it?'

'I don't know, I didn't see him. Must have been waiting outside the motel room for me. I ducked out about five, for some beers, and when I came back, he got me from behind as I unlocked the door.'

'You didn't see him at all?'

'Didn't even hear him...could have been more than one, but I couldn't be sure, I dunno... maybe. I woke up just inside my door. Jesus, what a headache.' He felt his head again and discovered more than one injury. His eye and jawline were starting to change colour under the swelling, a purple hue beginning to tint his right cheek. He wiped at his bloodied nose again.

'How did you get that if you didn't see them,' Alex asked, pointing at his nose.

'Must have smashed it when I went down.'

'You've been hit hard Beau. More than once.'

'Shit, and don't I feel it,' he said with an attempted grin. 'Does it make me look any better?'

'It's an improvement. It's been twenty years, who am I to know that this isn't normal? No-one's going to recognise you now. Add a pair of sunglasses and you could be anybody.' They both chuckled, it made Beau clutch at his side. He swallowed the scotch in one gulp, then he sat silent for a minute, obviously deep in thought. Alex waited.

'They trashed my room. Upended my bag and pulled apart all the furniture,' Beau said.

'Were they looking for something?'

'Fucked if I know. I don't think anything was missing. I got nothing anyway. I've still got my wallet!' He pulled it out with some difficulty and looked through it 'Nothing gone. Still got my cash. Rookie mistake not getting that.'

Alex was not so sure it was a rookie who had rolled Beau.

'What about your cards?'

'Don't have any. Cash only. Can't leave a trail if I don't have cards.' He flipped the wallet onto the coffee table.

'Did you have any drugs on you?'

'None. So, I don't know what they were looking for. Maybe they thought I had some. I only brought some cash and clothes with me for the funeral. Living cheap. I'm a wanted man, remember'.

'You said you thought they were waiting for you. Do you think they knew you? Knew where you were staying?'

'Fucked if I know Alex. I'm careful. Remember, I found you, you didn't find me.'

'Where are you staying anyway?' Alex queried.

'North Nerimbah, *The Breakers*.'

'Not that old motel, don't tell me it's still standing.'

Beau looked reproachfully at Alex. 'Not all of us are made of money you know.'

'How did you get here?'

'Train. My car's rooted.'

'Not to here, on the coast, but to this unit, tonight, after you woke up.'

'Walked. Kept to the backstreets, behind Georges Head so no-one would see me.' He felt down at his ribs and lifted his shirt to inspect them. A dark bruise stretched around to his kidneys. 'I don't remember them giving me that.' He groaned and dropped his head back.

'Might have been after you were knocked out. Are those pain killers making a difference yet?'

'Yeh, a bit...more whiskey, I'll be right in the morning.'

Alex poured him another which he gulped straight down, then closed his eyes and settled deeper into the cushions, mouth open, his breathing returning to a steady rhythm.

Alex leaned across and shook his shoulder. 'Come on, go and have a shower. It'll clean you up.'

'Don't want one.'

'Do as you're told. Shower. Wake you up a bit, get rid of all this blood. I've got some spare shorts and a T shirt.'

'Fuck you're a bossy prick.'

'Stop whinging'

'I wasn't the whinger.' Beau shot back at him.

'That's better', said Alex,' that's what we want to hear. Just like old times.' Alex lifted Beau to his feet and gently propelled him into the bathroom. Beau began to gingerly strip his shirt off in front of the mirror. His back and sides were mottled with blue and purple bruising.

'Looks pretty.' Beau inspected himself, prodding and poking at his skin.

'You always did fancy yourself,' said Alex, 'Soaps there mate,' Alex pointed to the shower cubicle.

Alex backed out and left him to it. He washed out the tea towel in the kitchen sink, saw the scotch bottle on the bench, but passed over it in favour of a beer. He could hear the banging of the shower door from the bathroom, and various groans as the shower spurted into life. There was nothing more he could do for Beau for now. He rearranged the lounge chair in front of the verandah doors so that he could keep an eye on the hallway and the floodlit beach carpark at the same time.

'Heh Alex. It's good to see you mate!' Beau called from the bathroom.

'Yeh, you too.' He waited till he heard the shower water running steady, glanced down the hallway, then reached across for Beau's wallet.

Beau's wallet was thin and compressed around the edges. He had just short of $200 in smaller notes folded inside, and true to his word there were no credit cards, though that didn't mean he didn't have any, only that there were none on him now, in his name. There was a NSW drivers' licence in the name of David Burton, the photo showed Beau, thin faced, dark short hair, not blond like he once had, and wearing glasses. Good enough disguise from a distance. There was a receipt from The Breakers motel. He looked closer; the name of *D Burton* was faintly imprinted next to the sum of $110. So, Beau is staying here under another name after all. There was a receipt from a Murwillumbah grocery store, and an old membership slip from the Condong Bowls club dated 5 years earlier. Northern New South Wales he thought. He'd obviously been living there under another name, probably since he left the coast. He threw the wallet back on the table.

Beau had come up for his mother's funeral, had been here only one day, got himself bashed and had his room searched. Why was he not surprised. Beau thought the attack was random, but what if it wasn't? It could have been a coincidence, a junkie, kids looking for quick money, but Alex didn't believe in coincidences.

He looked out over the verandah. Most of the holiday makers had left the park in front, it was quieter now, a gentle babble of voices rising from the restaurant strip below. A cars headlight slowed and turned into a vacant space. A lone woman got out of the car, slim, dark haired, he couldn't see her clearly, he thought the way she walked was familiar. He turned away, distracted by noises from the bathroom as the shower ceased.

'Where will I put my shirt?' Beau called out.

Beau appeared in the hallway holding up his bloodied shirt, a towel wrapped around his waist, steam billowing behind him.

'Leave it on the floor. There's some stuff on the bed, at least a change of shirt.'

Beau sauntered into the bedroom leaving the door ajar. A minute later he was standing at the fridge wearing one of Alex's T-shirts, drinking heavily from the cold-water jug. He moved in front of the big loungeroom mirror, surveying the damage to his head.

'That's better,' he said, 'No more blood, a bit blue though. This shirt's too big, you've been putting on weight.'

'It's not that big, you must have concussion, can't see straight,' retorted Alex.

'I feel pretty good now.' Beau scoffed and eyed off the couch.

The knock at the apartment door was different this time, more discrete, a questioning knock, as if they weren't sure there was anyone on the other side. It startled Alex. He immediately lowered his voice.

'You expecting anyone? Were you followed?' asked Alex.

'I don't think I was.'

Alex looked around. 'Go in the bedroom, close the door. I'll let you know if it's OK to come out.'

'I'll take a beer with me.'

'Sure, just don't spill it.' Alex shook his head as he walked down the hallway and approached the entry door with a lot more caution than before.

Chapter 5

There was a spy hole in the door which Alex checked before he stood back, smiled and opened it. He recognised her straight away, twenty years couldn't change that. Janice looked flustered, uncertain, her dark hair was a little shorter now and unruly. She was still slim, in dark jeans and a loose-fitting white cotton shirt. Her strong face and green soulful eyes were still beautiful to Alex. When she spoke, her voice stripped away the years, and the words tumbled out.

'Thank God it's you Alex. Beau told me you would be here. Is he here? I went to his motel room, but it's been trashed. There's blood on the floor and I can't find him,' She held her arms out in concern, but no there was no real panic in her voice. She had been there before, looking for Beau. She was always in control; it was what he had loved about her.

Alex took a little time to react, finally he said. 'He's here!'

He pulled her gently into the apartment.

'Beau's here? Now?'

'He's been hurt; he was bashed.' A look of alarm flooded her face. 'He's a bit battered and bruised, but he'll be alright.'

Alex guided her up the hallway past the bedroom door. 'He's in there changing, but he can stay there for the moment.'

'Are you sure he's alright?'

'He's fine now...to a degree. I gave him some pain killers and cleaned him up, nothing broken that I could see. He came in about half an hour ago. But he'll be OK.'

'Good. OK...I'm sorry Alex.' Her shoulders relaxed a little, and she stopped fidgeting.

Alex stood looking at her. 'It's good to see you.'

'You too. It's been a long time,' she said. She leaned forward to kiss his cheek, then wrapped her arms around him. He returned the embrace, and for a few seconds they stood still, silent in each other's arms. He could feel the swell of her breasts through her shirt and smelt her warm breath as it undulated against his cheek. It was too familiar.

'I've missed you,' she said, then stepped back and regained her sense of purpose. 'What's going on Alex? Who bashed him?'

'I don't know, he didn't see them. he just showed up here covered in blood.'

'I was going to bring him here, to surprise you.'

'Well, he certainly did that on his own. You're not staying with Beau?'

'No, course not, we're not together.' She sat down on the couch, reached into her shoulder bag and pulled out a packet of cigarettes ignoring the no smoking card sitting proudly in the glass ashtray. Lighting one up, she paused and looked up at Alex, 'Haven't been together for years. Didn't you know?'

'Not at all.'

'Want one?' She held out the packet to him.

'I gave up. It's the thing to do now, makes you healthy apparently, though the sidewalk coffee drinkers in Melbourne still think it's fashionable.'

She laughed and took a steadying drag on her cigarette. 'Some consolation I suppose. it's good to see you. You haven't changed too much.'

'Neither have you.'

'Twenty years is a long time. You could have called.' said Janice.

'I didn't...couldn't... I had my reasons,' stammered Alex.

'Bullshit. I know what Beau told me, but I'd like to hear it from you?'

'If you've been talking with Beau, then you know. So why are you here?'

'I'm here for Marjorie Beaumont.' She drew heavily on her cigarette. 'She's the only one who didn't run out on me.' The cigarette smoke coiled from her fingertips. She angrily stubbed it out in the pot plant next to the couch, her eyes never leaving Alex. He knew he was guilty as charged. He had his reasons at the time, but facing Janice now, the excuses felt feeble.

'Drink?' Alex gestured toward the scotch bottle as he retreated into the kitchen.

'Nah. Never liked that heavy stuff. Have you got a beer?' It was a half conciliatory gesture, and Alex went to the fridge. Janice walked out to the veranda to take in the night view. Alex brought two beers out for them. She lit another cigarette, the silence between them broken only by the soft sound of the surf breaking.

'So how are you really?' he asked her.

She was silent for a moment,

'I'm good. I got a whole new life in Byron now,' she said with a hint of pride to her voice.

At that moment, Beau appeared from the hallway, shirt and shorts hanging off his skinny frame. His hair was plastered over his forehead, hiding the grazes, as he dabbed at the bruising under his eye with a damp towel. He dumped the empty beer bottle in the sink and walked over to give her a kiss.

'Janice! I thought I heard your voice'.

'Hi Beau,' she said. 'Been in the wars again, have you? You all right now?'

'Don't want to talk about it. All good now Jan. Fuck I'm hungry, do you have anything to eat in here?' There was no acknowledgement that anything was amiss, it was business as usual. He opened the fridge, shook his head, then began to open and close the kitchen cupboards. The old Beau was back.

'Downstairs, there's a decent Mexican joint still open, I had a burrito from them earlier. It's dark, put my cap on and pull it low, they won't know who you are. There's a bottle shop around the corner as well.' Alex said.

'You want anything?'

'No, I'll be right.'

He retrieved his wallet. 'Anything for you Jan?' he called as an afterthought, not really waiting for an answer as he went out the door.

'Typical.' Janice shook her head as she settled back into the couch.

'You guys definitely not together then?'

'God no. We did try to get back together for a bit, but it didn't work. When I met up with Beau again a year after you all left, he was living in a farmhouse outside of Byron Bay, doing some odd jobs for the vet who lived down the road. We lasted a few months together, but it was not easy... Beau wasn't earning much and didn't want to, anyway. I got some bar work at Strop's pub in Byron. Beau told me all about what happened on that last night, and the pact you made without me. I sort of forgave him.' She glanced up at Alex,' I haven't forgiven you though. Anyway, with Beau and me, it wasn't really the same anymore. It was a big enough surprise to find out he wasn't dead. I think when someone is dead, like Beau was for me, you change in the way you think about them, you can't go back to what it was, you can't live on memories.'

They were quiet together, a companionable silence.

'You know, we did OK for a couple of months, but we'd changed, grown apart...and the farmhouse was old, it had no running water, and I was pregnant, it was no place to bring up my daughter.'

Alex looked up sharply. 'You have a daughter?'

'Yeh, Elizabeth...Beth, I named her after Beau's mother, her middle name, for all she did for me. She's all I've got. What about you?

'I'm married...no kids.'

Janice looked quizzically at him, 'You sound like you're not in any hurry?'

'Not yet. Why did you move into town?' He twisted the conversation back to her.

'I moved there to have Elizabeth, but Beau wouldn't be in it...he thought it was too dangerous for him, that he'd be recognised. He said he had to stay anonymous, he wouldn't even contact you.'

'We'd made a pact,' Alex explained. 'No one was to know he was still alive, and we would go our separate ways, wouldn't see each other again. It was safer that way.'

'How do you think I felt back then?' She turned her fierce gaze on Alex. 'Police come to the door to tell me that Beau had drowned. I tried calling you, but you didn't answer, you left for Melbourne without even coming to see me. You didn't trust me with your little scheme, your plan didn't involve me. Pretending he had drowned, and he wasn't dead at all. Left me all alone to deal with it. You arsehole.'

Alex opened his mouth to object but quickly closed it. That wasn't the first time he had heard that today, Megan had accused him of being the same thing that morning.

'Well, we fought a lot over that, but we fought over a lot of things, like he was always quizzing me about who I talked to, who I saw. He was paranoid about being found and arrested for his role in the Herman bombing...still is.'

'It's still an open case,' said Alex.

'As if that excuses you both.'

'I'm sorry,' Alex said lamely.

'Fuck off Alex, twenty years too late.' She leaned across the table and grabbed his arm, her voice bitter with recrimination. 'I don't know what happened to Beau tonight, but I don't want that shit anywhere near me or Beth. She's all I've got. I'd lost Beau, I'd lost you, I've lost Marjorie, That's enough in one lifetime.'

She stood facing him, her voice softened. 'You could have found me easily Alex, it wouldn't have been hard. You've had twenty years to do it. I didn't change my name; I wasn't hiding like Beau. '

Alex had no comeback for that either. He was as guilty of neglect as Beau had been.

'You could have rung, found out how I was,' she said softly, all the anguish going out of her. She looked at Alex with her green eyes. He could think of nothing he could say, she was right.

'Tomorrow will be difficult enough as it is, so don't let it be any harder,' said Janice. She wrote her number on a piece of paper from her bag and handed it to him. She picked up her shoulder bag and headed toward the door. 'We'll talk in the morning; I'm going home now before I say anymore.' She called over her shoulder.

Alex watched her leave. He had plenty to think about.

Out to sea, on the horizon, the inky night sky flashed briefly with a thin ripple of lightening in a bank of low cloud. It was too far away to hear the thunder, but it was ominous, like gun flashes, the prelude to an awful battle. Skerries of wind blew cigarette ash around the perimeter of the verandah and threatened to swirl it inside. Alex slid the door half closed at the drop in temperature.

When Beau returned, food in hand, he grabbed a beer from the fridge as he passed by, slumped into the folds of the couch and immediately began to unwrap his burrito.

'Where's Janice?' he asked, muffled by a mouthful of lettuce and chicken.

'She left, couldn't wait any longer for the burrito you were not going to get her.'

Beau merely grunted; the sarcasm was lost on him.

'What did you talk about?' He asked between mouthfuls, 'Bet it was about me.'

'You, me, her. We had a lot to catch up on'.

'You still like her, don't you?'

'Well, I'm not sure you do.'

'Ah, we get on all right, but it's all over between us.'

'I didn't know you had a daughter?'

'I didn't want one.' Beau studied his half-eaten burrito as if it held the meaning of life. 'To be honest, I'm not sure she's mine.'

'Jesus.' Exclaimed Alex, 'You better stop there before you say something you might regret.'

'I don't regret anything mate. My life has been shit since I left here. Janice turned on me, I had to change my name, I live in a farm shed and now my mum's died. How much worse can it get?'

'Don't go all morose on me Beau.'

'Fuck off! It's easy for you to say, you aren't the one they're still looking for.'

'No! But don't forget if you go down, I do too, so don't give me that. As far as I know, the Police aren't actively looking for you at the moment, so don't give them any reason to start.' It was time for Alex to take control. 'Tomorrow, for the funeral, you're going to keep your head down. Did you bring anything to disguise yourself?'

'I've got some glasses.'

'Shit. Look, keep my shirt, the old Beau would never wear that, and the cap. Wear sunglasses, OK? Tomorrow, take my lead, that way we might all get through this in one piece.'

'It's not your mother that's being buried,' he objected.

Alex softened, 'Yeh, I know. She was a good woman, your Mum. I saw Villi Tanoa today. His family thought a lot of Marjorie too.'

Beau leaned back deeper into the couch and closed his eyes. He appeared to be full of burrito and beer, and all the fight had clearly gone out of him as well.

'I'm glad the old man is already dead, before her. He deserved to go. Not like Mum,' Beau murmured.

'You're right about that.' Alex concurred. 'You can stay here tonight, won't be safe going back to your unit. We'll get you sorted out in the morning before the funeral.'

Beau responded by dragging his legs up to stretch out on the couch and waved at Alex to go away. It was like him all over, quick to anger, and just as quick to drop off into oblivion.

'It's good to see you Alex,' he growled.

Within minutes, Beau was asleep, his regular snores working their way around his swollen nose. Alex wasn't remotely tired; he was in a swirl of emotion. He turned the lights off, stepped outside and collapsed into a plastic verandah chair before checking his phone for messages from Megan, but there were no new ones.

Alex looked back inside. Beau was snoring softly on the couch, he pulled the sliding door closed and searched the register on his phone for Debbie Marcello, his researcher on *The Cold Cases*. Alex had lured her from the State Library with the excitement of developing content for the TV industry, she was a terrier, a hell of a researcher, he never regretted that recruitment. The phone only rang twice before she picked up.

'Debbie? Its Alex,' he said.

'What? You've only been gone a day and you're pestering me.'

'If I told you that I had a swim this afternoon, and the water is beautiful and warm, would that be cruel?'

'Yes! It would. It's raining down here,' Debbie replied.

'It'll probably be like that here tomorrow. Look, I want you to do something for me. Some research. It's not for the next seasons shows, it's more for me...personally. Can you find me anything on a David Burton, in northern New South Wales, region around Byron Bay and Murwillumbah area? It would be from 1981 onward. There will be no record of him there before then. Got that so far?'

She repeated the details back to him.

'He may also be under the name of Dennis Beaumont, but not likely, the first strikes you will get for Dennis Beaumont are that he is wanted for questioning over a murder investigation. He's missing, presumed drowned in a boating accident off Nerimbah, during a storm. His body was never recovered.'

'Oh... now that makes it interesting. Is this the same guy as the David Burton that we are talking about?'

'Yep. Look, we will keep this between us for the moment. If anyone asks, just tell them you are looking into a branch investigation for me. And can you also add a Janice McKenna to that as well. Same years, and probably the same area, but focus on Byron Bay township.'

'That's no problem, Alex, I'll get back to you when I've got something.'

'By the way, Dennis went by the name of 'Beau'...Dennis 'Beau' Beaumont. It's his mother's funeral I'm going to tomorrow, and if you find something before then, let me know. Oh, and try Condong Bowls Club with those names as well.'

'Do I get extra pay for this?' she asked.

'Consider it a love job for now, OK? But I'll see what I can do.' He signed off.

Alex sat watching the moon glow on the water, replaying the conversation he had with Janice tonight in his head. He realised just how deeply she had invaded his conscience. It may have been twenty years, but he hadn't let her go.

And then there was Beau, already in some sort of trouble. He tried to plan how they would get through tomorrow but was distracted by the distant clouds flashing again with intermittent lightning against the night sky. The rock wall lights blinked red and green at regular intervals, pinpricks of white light darted toward the harbour entrance, local fishermen making a late-night run to shore. Alex let his eyes wander back and forth across the glittering tableau, taking in all those moments lost in his move to Melbourne. He closed his eyes and tried not to think of Janice.

Later, when the wind had kicked up more, and woke Alex from his slumber, he left the verandah and went to bed but sleep still eluded him till the early hours.

Chapter 6

The morning light showed the true colours of the bruising on Beau's face. His cheek was puffy and blue with small areas of broken skin. His breathing was regular, and he seemed comfortable enough, so Alex left him just after dawn. At the convenience store he rifled through the shelves, filling his arms with cheap painkillers, some betadine and a tube of haemorrhoid cream that he thought might work on the bruising. What haemorrhoid cream was doing on the shelves of a store that sold hot dogs and newspapers, Alex had no idea. He ordered, croissants and two takeaway coffees, and while he waited, he checked the use by date of the cream to make sure he wasn't about to make Beau's condition worse.

On the footpath, Alex realised the convenience store was on the site of Barrett's old supermarket. It had long since gone, buried under an eight-storey unit complex fronted with takeaway cafes and resort wear boutiques. Such were the changing times.

Few people were about this morning. The weather had changed, it was mostly overcast with patches of blue revealed between light rain squalls. It was still humid, although the wind was stronger, from the east and whitecapped the small waves in the bay. Heads from a few early morning swimmers bobbing up and down near the lifeguard tower in the rising swell. Alex ducked from one awning to another back to his apartment, the theme music from *The Cold Cases* echoing around his brain, only today it didn't annoy him as much, today it sounded appropriate.

In the apartment Beau was sitting forlornly on the couch.

'About time you got up. I come bearing coffee,' said Alex, as he dumped croissants on the bench and placed a takeaway cup in front of Beau.

'Jesus my head hurts.'

'Lift your shirt and give me a look.'

Beau pulled his shirt up over his head to reveal a cluster of purple bruises around his ribs. It wasn't an easy task, and he struggled to stay in that position. Alex leaned down and poked one, Beau jumped in pain.

'Yep. They are a bit tender. Here's a bandage if you want to strap yourself up.' He passed Beau the coffee as he pulled his shirt down. 'More pain killers. And I found you a cream for your bruises. Don't read the label, just rub it into the skin...trust me, I'm a trained professional.' Alex smirked.

'What's this? Haemorrhoids! He didn't kick me in the arse, you know.' Beau stood and joined Alex at the double glass doors where they could both view the bay. They looked in different directions, yet both were assessing the size of the surf, wind direction, speed, angle, it was instinctive, born of childhood imprinting, knowing how the weather affected waves.

'Not looking good,' said Beau. There was no clean line to the breaking waves, the conditions were confused.

'Bigger lefts in front of the clubhouse, bit of a peak over there.' Alex pointed further down the beach where the undulating sandy bottom pushed the waves up into a peak that broke in one spot first, before the rest of the wave walled up and could be ridden left or right. 'But that easterly has got into it, swells too straight out in front.' He nodded at a wall of foam broken all at once, 'Close outs!'

'You still surfing?' asked Beau.

'In Victoria? Torquey and Bells Beach? Its freezing down there. I can't stand the cold, even in summer. But that's what they made wetsuits for, I guess. What about you?'

'I used to go down a lot when I was living in the hills outside Byron, but I'm at Condong now, the track is pretty shitty. Too hard going all the way to Kingscliff or Fingal for a surf, only to find out it's blown out by South Easterlies. I can't tell from my place what it's going to be like till I get there. But if you don't use it, you lose it, so I go when I can.'

'You've got a car though?'

'It's a heap of shit. I keep getting bogged every time it rains. I've got a shed in the cane fields I rent off an old bloke. I keep an eye on his irrigation equipment and give him a hand with the odd job, in return for cheap rent. It's pretty good, no one knows I'm there. Suits me, anyway.'

'Sounds nice, bit of peace and quiet to yourself.'

'I could do without it! Sick of getting rained in.'

Alex switched tracks. 'How did you figure you would run this today? At the funeral.'

'I dunno.'

'I think you should stay in the shadows, see who turns up, any cops or whoever's watching. I'll go in first and see if there is any problem, then wave you in. If it looks dodgey, we could try again later.'

'I don't want to miss the service.'

'Better than being arrested. Look, I don't think the cops will be there, it's been too long, they will have forgotten. Who arranged the funeral anyway?'

'Wasn't me. I have no idea. It was Janice who put me on to it, told me that Mum had died, and St Paul's of North Nerimbah were doing it. She said it was being looked after by the Parish priest, at the church, seems like Mum went to that church a lot after the old man died a few years back, I didn't bother coming to his funeral.'

'You didn't think to reunite with your mum then?'

'She was better off without me, but she meant a lot to Janice.'

'Yeh, Janice told me that last night.' Alex switched tracks again. 'She said you didn't last long together when you met up again.'

'She didn't like the farmhouse in the hills, got a bit too isolated for her. I thought we were doing OK, but then she wanted to move into Byron township because she was four months pregnant. God, that was news to me.'

'You mean you didn't know?' Alex exclaimed.

'How am I supposed to? I don't know these things unless someone tells me.' Beau reacted sharply. 'I think she was seeing someone in town anyway. She was getting secretive, not telling me when her shifts at the pub were, you know.'

'And now you have a daughter.' Alex pointed out.

'Beth's nearly twenty by now, but I don't get to see her much. Janice keeps her at a distance.'

'She said you keep them at arm's length as well. You didn't give her an address when you left. She said she only recently found out you were living in Condong'.

'Janice wanted to bring her up by herself, didn't want to see me much, and that was fine by me. I would have helped if I could,' said Beau.

'What about now?'

'I get by. Mum probably had some savings, and her house will be worth a bit,' he said with optimism.

Alex was sceptical about Beau's real understanding of his predicament.

'Mate, you got to think about this. If she had a will, you probably aren't in it, because you are supposed to be dead. The sale of your mother's house will go through the public trustee, unless you step forward.... but you can't do that. If you let them know you are alive, you'll have to prove it is you, her son. In the searches, it will show up that you were missing, presumed dead, and still a person of interest in a murder case. And that, my friend, will get you referred to the Police.'

'So, I don't inherit Mums house,' he said, disappointedly.

'Not at the moment.' Alex continued, less harshly. 'Did you ever let your mum know you were alive?'

'Who! Mum? No. I never let her know, and I don't think Janice ever did. She said she wouldn't do it; it would be up to me to ease her pain. I guess over time, I just let it ride as it is, it seemed to be the easiest way.'

'I don't think I could ever do that, leave my mother wondering without contacting her,' mused Alex.

'Yeh. But you did that to Janice.' Beau reminded him.

'Shut up Beau,' retorted Alex. 'Finish your coffee and I'll take you back to your motel to get your gear.'

Alex swung the hire car into the far end of the motel parking lot, deliberately driving it around the side to park away from the entrance. Behind them, traffic flowed brusquely, spraying water from the tyres onto the footpath. Grey clouds moved and skated in the distance, releasing bursts of light rain that the wind would pick up and fling against the car.

The Breakers was an old-fashioned motel, built in the seventies when white concrete stucco was popular, but now the grand sign out the front was chipped and faded. The rooms were spread out in a line away from the front office, facing the bitumen carpark and the main road. Small tin tables and identical plastic chairs were arranged on the concrete apron in front of each unit. The site was ripe for development as soon as tourists had finished with the retro feel, and desired more upmarket dwellings.

Unit 7 was closed. Beau walked slowly to the door, sticking close to the wall. He knocked softly, standing back and to the side, Alex directly behind him. There was no response. Beau quickly slid the key into the lock and went inside. Alex wiped at some dried blood on the door frame as he went in, then closed it behind him. He held up his palm toward Beau, pointing at the blood.

'Is this yours?'

'Very funny! What a mess.'

The room had been well and truly turned upside down. Beau's clothes were strewn over the floor, The bed pushed on its side and the sheets pulled back. A check of the bathroom showed his toiletries scattered over the tiles on the floor. He stood still, looking around forlornly.

'They've turned me over.' Beau remarked, a sense of hurt in his voice.

Alex gently touched his arm.

'Come on. You can stay with me again tonight. I'll sort this out while you get dressed, and have a shave, you're going to a funeral.'

He watched Beau grimace in pain as he retrieved some clothes from the floor on his way to the ensuite.

There was not much else to do in the motel room after the bed was put back together and the bedside draws righted. Alex stuffed Beau's cloths into his bag then pulled back the rear curtains to let some light in. Behind the back fence the houses stretched away to the west, the last remnants of sugar cane fields being showered with squalls. The heavy clouds were moving rapidly above, smothering any glimpse of sunshine. Appropriate, he thought. The extra light showed up the small blood patches on the carpet inside the door and dried smears of blood on the wall beside it. Alex turned away. How deep did he want to get involved with this? Beau had led him into trouble many times before, and here it was happening again. He didn't need this right now; he had enough of his own problems.

'That's better mate', Beau said as he emerged from the bathroom, wiping a towel over his face. The bruise on his cheek was still evident but not as blue as the night before, but the change of clothes and dark glasses would suffice to keep him from casual recognition. But who wears dark glasses when it's raining?

Alex looked back out the front window. 'It looks OK from here, grab your stuff and let's go. You are one messy man.'

'Don't be such a wuss, you weren't the one who got bashed. I'll just be a second more. Close those curtains will you.'

Beau had regained some of his bravado. He locked the main door and took a chair and butter knife from the kitchenette into the bathroom. He placed the chair beneath the air vent in the centre of the ceiling, stood on it, and unscrewed each corner of the grill. When he finished, he pulled it away and reached deftly with his fingers up into the hole, removing a small plastic bag. The air vent was screwed back in place. Beau shoved the packet in his pocket, nodded at Alex as they left, locking the door after them. Nothing more said.

In the car heading back to Nerimbah beach, Alex finally broached it.

'I thought you said you didn't bring any drugs with you, that they weren't looking for drugs in your room.'

'Well, they didn't get them, did they.' He laughed. 'It's only enough for a few joints, I think I deserve it, don't you?' He produced the drugs and held them up for Alex to see.

'Not in the car Beau'.

'No, no. Fair enough.' He put them back in his pocket.

Alex was quiet. The drugs were not the issue, it was the added complications Beau brought with them, brought to every situation. He glanced across at Beau as he drove, the disapproval must have shown on his face.

'What's up you?' Beau questioned.

'They wouldn't have bashed you for a few joints. It had to be more than that. Are you sure there's not something else? '

'What, don't you trust me?'

'No mate, it's not that...'

'Then what is it? Think I'm hiding something?' Beau's hostility bubbled to the surface. 'Easy for you to stay in Melbourne, under your own name, TV producer, house, wife, money. Think I didn't want to look after Janice and Elizabeth? Think I don't want those things? Well, where is it? I don't have it; I don't have anything!' He said angrily.

'Heh Beau, that's not it. That beating you got last night, that was not just putting you down to search your room. They put the boot in when you were down as well...I know, I've seen it, Melbourne pubs are rough. I've seen what those bastards do when they get you down...and what they did to you, that was personal. Do you owe anyone money, or drugs? I want to know; I'm in this too.'

'No. I don't know who it was or what they wanted. I don't care. It wasn't me.' He protested. 'I've got nothing.... I just came up to say goodbye to my mother,' he said quietly.

'OK. OK... we'll get it done.' Alex backed off. 'We'll see your mum off properly, today.' They drove on in silence; each lost in their own thoughts.

They reached the top of Georges Headland, the bay stretched out before them, long untidy lines of grey surf were beginning to roll in, pushed from behind by the repeated squalls. The local radio station was giving its warnings about the approaching low, and what it would mean for the holiday makers, few of which were on the streets.

Alex parked in his usual spot, though there were plenty of parks to choose from in this weather. The men ducked under a restaurant awning snapping with the wind. Café owners along the front were busy relocating tables and securing clear vinyl wind breaks to the pavement with straps. Alex glanced out to the horizon, and thought they were being optimistic, it wasn't too bad now, but his gut feeling was that the windbreaks weren't going to be enough.

In the apartment, rain pattered against the balcony glass, the wind was much stronger on the 7th floor. Alex could barely see the beach through the glass and going onto the balcony was to get very wet.

Alex took his time changing into his coat. It hadn't gone the way he thought it would since he arrived. There were so many new elements in play. Seeing Janice was a jolt to his emotions, he had to face up to the fact that she was still as alluring to him as she had been twenty years before, only now she had a daughter, and he was nervous about meeting her. Doing the maths in his head put her at just the right age. He didn't have any of his own children. He and Megan had talked about it, but got no further than talk, they had avoided the issue by mutual consent. Now he felt small pangs of guilt that the desire for children had risen again, and it was seeing Janice that prompted it. He shook himself further into the suit coat, settling the shirt wrinkles inside the arms.

Beau was still infuriating. He was clearly somebody's target, no idea who, he was pretty sure it was not the police. If they knew where he was staying, they would have picked him up, not beat him up, unless it was Sergeant Cooper, that corrupt bastard. He hadn't heard back from Debbie in Melbourne yet, so there was nothing further to go on there.

'Beau!' He said to himself and shook his head. He was still his mate. There was plenty to remember, forgive, and forget about their friendship. He would do his best to get him through this day, he could do that, he was in familiar territory. He could see beyond the chaos, offer quick solutions to problems, for good or bad, and let the natural momentum of a situation carry it forward, dealing with issues as they arose. That was his style, he did it for a job. Never halt, never stop, never over centralize the problems, let them unfold naturally wherever they fall, and deal with them as they come, he was good at that, it happened often enough on set.

Dressed in a neat grey suit coat over black pants and boots, he emerged, refreshed. He knew what he had to do for Beau and Janice, and for himself.

In the middle of the loungeroom, Beau stood in his crumpled shirt and pants, no fault of his own.

'Is that what you're wearing for the funeral?' he asked Beau.

'I didn't plan on being bashed up.'

' 'You'll be fine. You got your cap and glasses?'

Beau nodded.

'A drink before we go?' Alex asked.

Beau sighed and nodded again. Alex poured them a scotch.

'We could both do with this.' He raised his glass in salute. 'To your Mum.'

'To Mum.' Said Beau.

Alex poured him a second.

'You're not having another?' asked Beau.

' 'Not at the moment. I had enough yesterday.' Alex looked at his watch.' Its time.'

Alex marched off down the hallway. Beau finished off his drink with one tilt of the glass and followed behind.

Chapter 7

Alex drove slowly along the main road from Nerimbah Beach, Beau leaned forward in his seat and peered through the rain on the windscreen looking for the turn to Bulagul Street.

'Is that the church ahead? Bigger than I remember it.' Beau was right, the church was much newer than the low block one that Alex remembered. Now it had a tall, white cross atop a stylised spire, the main building of two-story white brick showing above the solid green hedge to one side. Alex slowed the car, thinking fast.

'I'll drop you just before the church, wait over there, at the back, out of the rain.' He pointed to the rear entrances of a set of shops that backed on to the church, their doorways littered with cardboard boxes, now sodden and piled up against the wall. 'See, you can get through that hedge at the side. I'll wave if it's all clear.' He lined up the turn into the back of the carpark.

'Thanks.' Beau was quiet, staring straight ahead.

'Don't come till I signal you.' He repeated, 'Even if the service has started, if there's a problem, wait. I won't forget. I'll get you in somehow', Alex reiterated. It started to rain again, the wind drumming against the side of the car. 'At least this will keep everyone inside for the moment. Wait under that awning.' He stopped the car and pointed to a spot at the rear of a Lock Smiths shop. Without a word, Beau left and darted toward the alcove, while Alex moved off, into the church carpark next door. He found a park in the few spaces left out the front.

Alex headed toward a group of people congregated in the church doorway, but by the time he skirted the deeper puddles the downpour had soaked him. Just like Melbourne weather. He angled over toward Janice standing in the protection of the main archway.

'What a day for it.' He greeted her.

'You're a sodden mess. Where's Beau?' Janice asked.

'Close by. It'll be all right, I've got it sorted.'

Janice raised a questioning eyebrow at him.

'I'll bring him in when it's all clear.'

'How was he this morning?' She asked.

'Getting back to his old self, in more ways than one. His bruising is going down. He'll be alright.'

'I know what his old self means.' Janice stepped to the side and gestured behind her, 'This is Elizabeth'. Her daughter was tall, dark haired like her mother, with a thin narrow face, dressed in dark jeans and a black top with coloured bead necklace to lift it.

'Elizabeth.' Alex held out his hand. 'I'm Alex, nice to meet you.'

'Hi', was all she said. She gave his hand a perfunctory shake. She affected a youthful disposition, the kind that young people exude to say that this wasn't their first choice in being here, but they deigned to attend because they must. Alex could see how she was nearly 20, but he thought her pout made her look younger. She clearly didn't regard the solemnity of the occasion in the same way as Janice did.

He glanced over the hedge.

'We should go in,' he said as he ushered them inside ahead of him.

The chaos of the weather outside was a stark contrast to the austerity of the church and quiet whisperings of the small group of elderly women in the aisle leading to the front podium. A smallish coffin of polished wood stood on a pall before the alter. There were a dozen people scattered around the first few pews. Alex recognised a few of Jeff Beaumont's old fishing buddies from the neighbourhood, but it was mostly women. Behind the raised dais, a large glass window above gave view to the tempest brewing outside, water running in rivulets down the pane.

Alex led the three of them to the third row from the front, settling into the hard timber benches. He recognised a couple of the parishioners, Joan Barrett, who used to own the supermarket,

Cathy's mother, no longer looking as youthful as she once was. She would had to have retired by now. Next to her was old Pru Anderson, who lived near the Beaumont's, three doors down if he remembered. He could only think of her as old; she was old when he was 20, and it seemed like nothing had changed. He nodded to them, Joan smiled, then turned back to her conversation. A side door to the right opened part way, and Alex could see the Priest in his white robes checking his watch and looking at the congregation numbers, before disappearing back inside and leaving the door slightly ajar, his shadow moving about the vestry.

'Where's dad?' Elizabeth whispered to her mother.

'I don't know. Alex said he's coming.' She turned to him. 'He is here, isn't he?'

' Yeh. He's just outside. I'll go get him'. Alex twisted in his seat and gave a cursory glance around the church. 'Bugger'. he exclaimed. He quickly turned back to the front. Seated in the back left corner was an older man, he recognized him straight away. It was Cooper. He wouldn't still be a policeman, thought Alex, so what was he doing here? He doubted that he was here to say goodbye to a fellow parishioner. Alex turned his head slowly and studied Cooper in his peripheral vision. It was definitely him. A dark blue anorak couldn't hide the fact that he was older, a little wider and certainly not as much hair as he used to have, but he hadn't changed that much. And those eyes, the aura of menace that they emanated, he was looking directly at the three of them.

Alex was thrown into confusion. He definitely couldn't bring Beau in now. He looked searchingly at Janice, as if she would supply some marvellous way out of this mess. Janice put her hand on his arm.

'What's wrong Alex?' she whispered.

'Cooper's here,' he hissed.

'Where?'

'Don't turn around. Back corner. Blue jacket.'

'What's he doing here? You are sure it's him?' She whispered.

'I'm sure.'

'What are we going to do? What about Beau?'

Alex shook his head, too many unknowns, but there was one constant in all this, thought Alex, Beau will not be walking through those front doors to attend his mother's funeral today. How to get him in without being recognised.

He turned to Janice, 'I'll just be a moment.' He rose to his feet, skirted the front two pews, heading for the front corner of the church, and marched straight through the vestry door, closing it behind him.

'Excuse me, Father.' Alex called to the priest.

'Can I help you?'

The priest was young, small in stature with a high pitched heavily accented voice. Vietnamese, Alex guessed. This was unexpected. In Melbourne the Vietnamese had a strong presence, but Nerimbah was a small coastal community, it didn't have the same cosmopolitan make up as the cities. Alex imagined some of the elderly parishioners would have trouble understanding the full nuance of his intonation.

'Father...?' Alex inquired with a questioning lilt to his voice.

'Nguyen,' he replied.

'Sorry. Father Nguyen, I don't want to hold you up, but I have a request. A very close friend of Mrs Beaumont can't get here right now, the weather, flooding near Gympie you know.' Alex tried his best not to lie to a priest in a church vestry, the truth was being stretched, and it was true, there was a bit of flooding near Gympie, but it had precious little to do with Beau. 'Perhaps when he arrives later, if the service is finished, can he still come and say goodbye?'

'Of course. There may be some time before the undertakers come. I think that would be OK.'

'I'll let him know when he comes.'

Alex hurriedly left the room and headed for the front doors, skirting Janice and the main seating down the centre of the aisle. Janice followed him with her eyes, twisting in her seat till he was out of sight. Alex marched passed Cooper, avoiding any eye contact and staring straight ahead. Coopers head turned to watch Alex, but he didn't acknowledge him either.

Outside, Alex danced over the puddles, holding his hand above his head trying to protect his eyes from the rain. At the hedge, he waved his arm till he had caught Beau's attention. Beau darted over and began to shuffle through the hedge. Alex threw his hand up to stop.

'Wait. Cooper's inside,' Alex hissed. 'You can't come in yet.'

'Shit Alex. Come on, he won't know me.'

'No. Not yet. He's watching everyone.' Alex pointed to the small door at the side of the church giving access to a side room. 'Over there, after the service. I'll let you in there. Wait for my call,' said Alex.

'It's my mother's funeral mate,' pleaded Beau.

'It's too risky Beau. You'll be recognised. Cooper will know it's you. Wait for my signal. I've got it organised.'

Beau pulled back, let the leaves of the hedge return to their shape, and shuffled back to the Lock Smith's awning. Alex turned back to the church. He deliberately kept his eyes down as he took his seat back next to Janice in time for the service to start. Janice raised a questioning eyebrow at him.

'All set. Beau will come in later. Private.' He whispered.

The service was relatively short. It mostly dwelled on the terrible burden of Marjorie losing her only son Beau to the sea at such a young age, and how she had turned to God seeking solace in her time of need. Evidently, she had taken a strong position in the church parish, displaying a generosity of spirit that resonated with Janice. Little was said of the loss of her husband four years earlier. Janice cried. Elizabeth didn't. Alex wished Beau had been able to hear it, but reflected on his own relationship with his mother, which, while it was solid, could have been better. The elderly parishioners nodded in agreement for most of the service, even throughout Father Nguyen's high-pitched rendition of The Lord is My Shepherd. But it was a fine send off for a fine woman, that was clear.

At the end of the service a parish elder solemnly wheeled the coffin into the side room, while Father Nguyen led the congregation toward the front entrance. Alex left Janice, marched back down the aisle and quickly followed the coffin through the door.

An older parishioner had just settled the pall and turned to face Alex.

'You're not meant to be here,' the elder said, not unkindly.

'I've talked with Father Nguyen, it's a special arrangement.' He pushed past the elder, unlocked the outside door and opened it to the elements. Across the access driveway, beyond the hedge, he could see Beau, fidgeting in the rainy mist. He waved for him to come.

'I don't think this is right!' The elder moved to shut the door but Alex stood in his way.

'It'll just be a minute,' he said, holding his ground.

Then Beau made a sudden appearance at the door. He stepped inside the room, shaking the rain from his hair and wiped his wet hands on his jeans.

'Jesus, I thought you'd forgotten me.' Beau blurted out.

'I couldn't bring you in the front way, too many old faces.'

'Who are you?' asked the elder.

'It's alright, he's meant to be here,' explained Alex.

Beau stepped forward, quiet, solemn, staring at the casket. The coffin filled most of the small room, there was hardly enough space for the three of them.

'This isn't right, I'm getting Father Nguyen.' The old man moved toward the door. Alex grabbed his arm and pleaded.

'Please don't. It's his mother.' He gestured toward Beau.

The old man slowed. Alex released his arm. He stood at the vestry door as he digested this new information.

'I didn't know she had another boy.'

'She didn't. There was only one son,' said Alex.

He turned to look at Beau, still not quite understanding what was happening here.

'But Beau died. He was lost at sea. He was mixed up with drugs, and murders. Police after him. We all know the story. Broke her heart.'

'Not all of it was true,' Alex retorted.

Beau was silent, still staring intently at the casket, the discussion floating around him, he was the centre of it, but not a part of it.

The elder shifted his gaze from the casket, to Beau, to Alex and back again. 'So, that's Beau?' he deduced. Alex nodded. 'He's not drowned after all?' He stared intently at Beau, trying to discern a family resemblance, a recognition.

'No. He didn't drown. And now you know. But no one is to know he's here.' Alex's eyes silently pleaded with the elder for understanding.

The old man was quiet, Beau's fate hanging in the balance.

'No one is to know Beau is here. It's too dangerous for him if the authorities find out.' Alex reiterated.

The elder sighed.

'Who am I to judge what goes on in this building? There's enough of that already. A man's got a right to say goodbye to his mother in peace,' the old man said. 'She was a good lady your Mum.' He reached for the door and turned back to them both. 'I'll not dob him in, but I won't deny it either...if I'm asked.'

'Sir, I wouldn't expect you to lie.' said Alex.

'You're right, I wouldn't lie... but then I don't expect to be asked. Sorry for your loss Beau. The undertakers will be here soon. I'll stall them if I see them, give you some time.' He spoke with some sympathy in his voice as he quickly passed back into the main church and was gone.

Beau leaned over and placed his hand on the casket top, drawing some solace from the touch. He murmured his own farewell to his mother. Alex waited quietly, listening to the patter against the glass, a quiet echo inside the room of wind pushing at tree branches, a muted call of nature. Aware of the time, he opened the outside door, breaking the reverie. Beau looked up at Alex, and without a word more, stepped outside into the elements.

Alex closed the door and locked up behind him. By the time he made his way to the front of the church, few of the congregation remained. The parish elder was busily talking with Mrs Barrett, Janice was quietly in conversation with Father Nguyen while Elizabeth was pretending to be somewhere else. She didn't acknowledge Alex at all when he appeared. He looked around for Cooper, but he was nowhere to be seen.

Alex broke in on the conversation, 'Father thank you for a lovely service, but we must get out of this weather.'

'Did your friend arrive in time?' Father Nguyen asked.

'No. He couldn't get here for your service, He's had to make other arrangements', Alex explained. He looked to the elder standing next to the Father and nodded to him.... and got a nod from him in return.

He made his platitudes, and steered Janice around the side of the building, toward the rear carpark. Beau appeared from the hedge, wet and dishevelled. Janice quickly enveloped him in a hug while Elizabeth stood close to the wall, under the eaves. Alex felt he was intruding on a private moment and looked away.

At the end of the drive, an old yellow Ford was parked under the acacia in the corner of the parking lot, the driver watching them, making no move to start the car or leave. The wind smeared the windscreen with drizzle and fallen leaves. The undertaker's van suddenly appeared at the front end of the drive, startling them all. Beau shuffled back into the hedge, pointing for Alex to pick him up from behind the adjacent shops. Janice and Elizabeth splashed their way to her hire car, while Alex strode back to the front car park.

As he passed under the portico of the church, Janice's car pulled up next to him, she wound down her window and held her hand out to Alex.

'Thank you for today. For Beau and us.'

He held her hand briefly and squeezed it in return. 'Let's go to the surf club for a drink, there'll be no one there this time of day. Beau will be fine.'

'Sounds good. We'll head home first; Elizabeth wants to change into some dry gear.' She moved off and turned left onto the main street. As Alex opened his own car door, the yellow Ford drove slowly past, blinkered left, and followed Janice onto the main road. But Alex didn't notice any of this, he sat at the wheel and sighed with relief, funerals had a way of slowing one down. It had gone as well as could be expected and Janice was thankful. If he hadn't been so self-congratulatory, and more aware of his surroundings, it would have saved them all a lot of grief later, but Alex was too busy trying to find a radio station for the weather update.

Chapter 8

The wipers beat rhythmically on the windscreen as Alex drove from the church. Beau was understandably quiet.

'You alright?' Alex asked.

'I was able to say goodbye to her...and that's all I wanted.'

'It was a good eulogy.' He went on to recount what had been said, but he didn't think it was getting through to Beau too much. He largely sat looking out the window, lost in thought, and nodding to himself at times. Alex eventually left him to his thoughts and concentrated on the driving. At the beachfront intersection waiting for oncoming traffic, he could see Beaus old bungalow up on the right in the distance between the houses. On impulse, he swung across the oncoming traffic and turned down the avenue where the ambulance station used to be on the corner. It wasn't there anymore, it had made way for a set of offices upstairs, and a bike hire and coffee shop on the ground floor.

Alex slowed as he passed. Next to the office block was the vacant land where Herman's house once stood. It was the only spare block in the street, surrounded on three sides by tall timber fences, with a rusty chain link fence facing the road, valiantly keeping intruders and plastic wrappers at bay. Beyond the fence, the rain flattened the wispy grass heads giving it a peaceful, unkept park like appearance. Beau and Alex knew better.

'No one's built on it yet,' Beau remarked.

'You don't build on a grave.' Alex replied. He wondered how many people around the area knew what had happened there. Nothing more was said as they drove by. In the distance was the Beach Shack bungalow, and Alex increased his speed, eager to leave the past behind.

Much had changed in 20 years. The bungalow was still there, but around it was now six pack apartment blocks. The new style of white stucco render giving them a Mediterranean appeal, but the washing hanging on the small verandas lent it more a touch of the backstreets of Naples. Alex pulled over in front of the bungalow. The front door was partly boarded over and padlocked; plywood covered the lower windows. The fibro walls were cracked, and mouldy, and tall grass grew through gaps in the ramp leading up to the verandah. They sat in silence. Memories of a past life left to rot with age.

'Come on. Want to take a look?' asked Alex. They darted up the ramp to the small verandah that was still offering somewhere dry to stand under the flat roof. A corner of one of the boards had pulled away from the window where kids had tried to break in. The house was a remnant of a bygone era. In its heyday, it was the epitome of a late 50s style fibro beach house, full of life, sand and beach towels drying on the railing. Alex had loved visiting Beau and Janice here, where simple childhood had been left behind, replaced by surf, sex, alcohol, and drugs. Beau had never taken that step beyond that, he was still in limbo, that's what Alex had loved about him, not a care in the world. Beau used to say that there was plenty of time to become an adult, till then, there is surf. It was an enchanting proposition to Alex who had just finished his three years at Uni. But that was then, and Beau wasn't saying much today. Times had changed, Beau had changed, and reality was much more complex than either of them had thought it would be. Beau squatted down to look through a gap in the fibro, then turned back to Alex.

'Can't see much. Some old furniture piled in the corner. Not ours. Toilets smashed.' He changed angle.' Kitchens a mess too. No-ones lived here for a while.'

'Just waiting for the right developer.'

'The price of progress.' Beau sneered. A sweep of wet wind across the deck drove them back to the car. At least the front seats of the car were dry.

'You ever came back here? I wouldn't want to come back here,' Beau mused. 'This place has lost it. They're knocking down all the old stuff, putting up more units. I wonder why they haven't built on Herman's block yet either? Too much development, not like in our day. We had it good then. This was a great house... look, you can still see the writing on the wall, that you and Janice did in felt pen.' It was true, faint but still legible against the faded paint next to the door...*The Beach Shack*. They wrote it together one night after too many drinks. Alex hadn't realized it at the time, but that was when he had started to fall for her.

He looked across at Beau. What happened between him and Janice didn't affect their friendship then, and it shouldn't now, as long as Beau never found out about it. Not that Beau would care, too much had happened since they had split. Alex had his own life and a marriage, a bit shaky at times, maybe more than shaky at the present. He pushed that thought to the back.

'I came up once to help my parents pack up for their move, but that was only for a couple of days.' explained Alex, 'Otherwise, Melbourne has been it. After I helped you get away, I didn't come anywhere near the house, or Janice.'

'She was pretty pissed off that you didn't contact her. She told me you must have left the coast straight away after that night. You did, is that right?'

'Two days after I took you south, I left. Couldn't be helped. Janice just had to tough it out for it to work.'

The rain thrummed on the car roof, the drumming adding weight to their shared deceit.

'Do you think about it much?' asked Beau.

'I did... I do...sometimes.' Alex corrected himself.

He didn't tell Beau of his dream the night before. He hadn't had the dreams for a long time, but last night it had come back to him. He knew why. It was never resolved, it was a part of his past that stayed with him, like most things, but this memory had morphed into a dream, one that had recurred often in the months after the explosion. Last night, it came back as clear and disturbing as ever. A blue grey egret walked the water's edge of a calm, shallow lake, inland from a distant sand blow that cut into a hill, leading to the ocean beyond. Strong winds whipped at the distant sand, roiling it into the air, blotting the sun and turning the sky orange. The egret turned to Alex; it had the face of a young girl. He reached out with his hand to warn the egret, but a wall of sand raced across the lake behind her, obliterating her in an envelope of stinging swirling grit that began to bury him. He fought it, he tried to reach the egret, but the sand shifted under his weight and no matter how hard he scrambled upward it sucked him down deeper, his nose clogged, and his breathing laboured, his mouth filled, ...and then he would wake. No one needed to know about that. He turned to Beau.

'The story keeps coming up in the papers every few years. They found you guilty in absentee, apparently you were getting what you deserved. If only they knew half of it.' They sat in silence for a while before Alex continued.

'You'd think that after twenty years, someone would have figured it out, but they haven't. My researcher keeps at me to do a Cold Case episode on it, a one-hour special. I tell you Beau, it's a pretty good story, and all my crew can think about is a month's paid vacation filming in warm tropical Queensland.... mercenary lot. I keep turning them down.'

'You wouldn't do that would you, make a program about what happened?'

'Of course not. I don't think I could do that to you... or me. I think I've betrayed enough of my friends as it is. The police have nothing new, but Cooper is still around, he was at the funeral, and he's still dangerous to you Beau. Without you, all they've got is me and Janice, and I'm not saying anything, it would be you they would be after.'

'Jan said nothing then, and she isn't going to say anything now.' Beau said proudly.

'We owe her. We treated her pretty badly. She didn't deserve it.'

'You said yourself; we had no other way, she had to be convinced I was dead, that's what you said. And we did. '

'She still didn't deserve it.'

A gust of wind buffeted the car, rocking it slightly as they sat outside the bungalow, the wipers pushing hard to clear the windscreen. Alex remembered the weather was just like this twenty years ago, when he arrived here home from Uni, and met Janice for the first time.

PART TWO
CHAPTER 9

Nerimbah 1980

'Welcome home mate, what took you?' Beau yelled from the verandah of the beach bungalow. Rain drummed on the flat tin roof, overflowing the gutters and splashing a deep groove line in the grass along the edge of the awning. The fibro had been newly painted a pale yellow and hibiscus patterned floral curtains in the windows gave it the beach charm.

'Up yours!' Alex grinned, calling out from the offside window of his battered Peugeot. He had driven across the front grass and nudged the nose of his car under the shelter of the awning. In the carport to the side was parked Beaus bright yellow Holden Monaro, wide shouldered and powerful like its owner. Alex opened the car door in the rain and sprinted through the puddles up the ramp, on to the verandah. The door was held ajar for him against the lashing rain. As Alex squeezed past Beau, it slammed shut behind him.

'Welcome home, what took you?' Beau repeated. Alex ignored him and shook his body to get rid of some of the water.

'This weather is shit. To think I came back to this! What a hole!'

'It's only been raining since this morning. What's your problem!' Beau pointed at the fridge, 'Beer?'

'Of course!'

Alex wiped at his clinging T shirt and took in the bungalow. A seagrass matt filled the lounge room floor, and the shabby cane couch just inside the door faced two TVs stacked one on top of the other against the far wall. There was evidence of another hand at work, bright coloured cushions on the couch and easy chair, and a new red lampshade covered the hanging light. The black turntable and sound system looked new, perched pride of place on the concrete block and timber plank bookcase. To his left, the open plan kitchen revealed dishes stacked high in the sink and empty bottles along the bench. The dank, musty smell came from the salt damp that always pervaded beachside shacks, from wet towels and boardshorts on the floor, to the salt air moisture hanging in the curtains. The push out windows were closed. Rain pattered on the glass, and gusts of wind swept across the pane every few seconds, rattling the roof with intensity.

Beau levered the tops off two beers and passed one to Alex.

'Cheers!' He said.

Beau flopped into one of the aluminium chairs around the small kitchen table, and kicked at another, indicating a place for Alex. He pushed the magazines and ashtray to the side with his arm. Although Alex and he were both twenty-one, Beau was tall and muscular, with a broad handsome face framed by long unkempt blond hair. He was always bigger than Alex, and in many ways, his confidence made him seem even more so. He had a slow, languid gait that reflected his nature, a stark contrast to Alex's wiry frame of unsettled energy. They had been friends all through high school, but it had been three years since Alex left for university, he wondered how much had changed in that time.

'When did you get back?' Beau asked.

'Just now. Drove straight through. The car is full. I packed up the flat after the last lecture. Had to drop some gear off to Uni, say goodbye to some friends, and with that...' Alex slugged at his beer, '...I have completed my study, and will just await Christmas and the results.' He leaned back on his chair and smiled with self-satisfaction. 'I'm a free agent.'

'So, what are you going to do now?' Beau was always straight to the point, He hadn't understood Alex's desire to study, it had never been on Beau's radar. *'I surf, I drink, I fuck, therefore I am*" was Beau's mantra, the closest he got to a philosophical future. Beau was the epitome of living on the Coast, in the here and now, a freedom of unleashed action without consequence. After all, to Beau, the coast was God's own country, and why would you think of going anywhere else. But Alex had left and come back. He was a different beast.

To say he was more thoughtful or far reaching than Beau was unfair to their friendship, though it may have represented how they were viewed by the rest of the world.

'I don't know what I'll do yet.'

'Have you got a job to go to?'

'I've applied for some, in Sydney and Melbourne. Mostly Media, some photography, that sort of thing. You got to start somewhere. I should hear something back soon. Till then I'm here to earn a bit of money, catch up on some surf, see you, all the things I've missed out on.'

Beau laughed bitterly. 'You mean you spend three years at university, and you don't have a job to go to. Pretty shit three years I'd say!'

'It doesn't work like that Beau, there's no work for me here, on the coast. Can you see any studios? Have you seen any ads in the paper? Building, Real estate, trades, but no film or TV jobs. Besides, this place is a cultural backwater...you're living proof of that.'

'Fuck off. If this place is so beneath you, why did you come back?' said Beau, leaning forward, jutting his jaw out at the insult. When he first told Beau that he was going away to Uni, Beau just said he was missing out on life, he couldn't conceive of ever leaving the coast.

Perhaps Alex had gone too far in calling it a backwater, but he had changed over the last three years, and the coast was now a stepping stone to something bigger. He couldn't afford to end up staying.

'I came back to see if you're still alive.'

Beau burst out laughing, reached behind a pot plant and brought out a battered biscuit tin, it was where Beau kept his dope, he had seen it once before when he was home from Uni on holidays.

'Well, I am...still alive that is.' Beau turned to constructing a joint with all care and attention, lit it, drew in deeply, and passed it to Alex. It had been a while since he had any and was unused to the sweet rich smoke. He coughed and spluttered, trying to catch his breath, Beau laughed as he took another puff. The smoke drifted lazily around the two of them as they sat silently in companionship, letting the effects meander through their consciousness. Outside the rain kept up a steady thrum on the roof. Alex unfolded himself from the chair and sauntered across the room to the record collection, picking up a copy of a Dire Straits album, turning it over, trying to concentrate on the writing. Beneath it was a Uriah Heap cover, adorned with elaborate wizardry art of the 70s, typical Beau, a stark contrast in design and music to the flat red cover he held.

Alex turned back to Beau.

'You know, I had an art lecturer who told me that if you take drugs while you paint, its cheating. Original thought only comes from a clear mind. I thought he was full of shit. He didn't just tell me once, he told me all the time. I think he was stoned when he told me that.'

'Well, was it true?' Beau asked lazily.

'Wouldn't know, couldn't afford to find out. I was flat out buying food, let alone beer or drugs.'

'You going to see your olds while you're home?'

'Yeh. I'll go see them tonight; I need a bed and somewhere to leave my stuff. It's all in the car, everything I own, except a few things at my folks' place...and my board.'

Beau took a deep drag on the last of the joint, carefully stubbing out the last remains in the ashtray. 'Stay here, there's the couch, we never use it. You can sleep on the couch whenever you want. I don't mind; Janice won't mind'.

It was the first time Alex had heard her name, he looked quizzically at Beau, raising his eyebrows. Beau nodded behind his shoulder at the bedroom door.

'She sleeps in the afternoon. Works late nights at the pub, so uses the afternoons for a catch-up sleep before the next shift.'

'How long have you been...?'

'Most of the year. You haven't met her yet, have you?'

Alex shook his head. Beau hopped up from his chair and sauntered to the bedroom door. He softly opened it and leaned inside.

'Heh Janice, come out and meet Alex. Time to get up anyway.'

He waited a few seconds, then repeated himself, only louder.

A muffled reply came from inside. Beau left the door ajar and went over to the fridge.

'She'll be out in a minute. Another beer?' Alex nodded and accepted the bottle as the bedroom door opened wide.

Janice was a total surprise. She was tall, as tall as him, dark haired with intense green eyes that fixed directly on Alex. He knew the kind of girlfriends Beau usually accumulated, surf chicks, blond, tanned, brimming with health and mischief, but Janice was not one of those. She was dressed in her work clothes which Alex thought suited her, a slim figure in a simple white shirt and black skirt. Her lightly golden skin hinted at a Mediterranean background while her short dark hair pulled back behind her ears, gave her a fresh determined look. Very professional he thought.

'I've been listening to you for the last 10 minutes.' She marched over to Alex and held out an authoritative hand.

'Hi, I'm Janice.'

'Alex.' He held her hand, cool and firm.

'I heard. God you're loud Beau!'

'You had to get up anyway,' he retorted.

'Beau and I are old school friends.' Alex offered as explanation.

'Well, Beau and I are new friends...with benefits.' She laughed self-assuredly. It seemed to be a natural response, then she turned to Beau, a tinge of resignation in her voice.

'Can you drop me down to the pub...in this rain'. She turned to Alex to explain. 'I'm in the front bar most nights, but there's a band on tonight, *Jo Jo Zep and the Falcons*, so they'll switch me to the main room about eight. Come down later for a drink.'

'I've got to get going, see my folks now I'm home. Haven't seen them for a while, and they'll be waiting. They're old.' Alex felt it important to tell her that, as if that was an explanation in itself.

She smiled.

Beau unfolded from the chair, grabbed the car keys off the table and propelled Janice toward the door. 'I'll be back soon, stick around.'

'Nah, I'll finish my beer. Be gone by the time you're back. You working tomorrow?'

Janice coughed in a mock choke.

'Not till later,' he replied.' Early surf if it clears up?'

'I'll dust the board off and pick you up. Have a good night, Janice!' he called, as she disappeared out the door. He saw her turn to say something, but Beau blocked her view.

'Lock the door on the way out', Beau called as he closed it behind him.

Alex stood for a moment, listening to the rain, enjoying the quiet, and come down from the drugs. He lit a cigarette and slowly wandered the room. He felt the couch, the thin cushions on a cane frame were a little damp, but serviceable. He was intrigued by the two TVs, till he noticed only the top one was plugged in. Above it was an orange macrame lampshade. He stopped again to peruse the record collection stacked neatly on shelves of pine planks on concrete blocks to get them up off the floor. It was nearly all Beau's taste in music as far as he could tell, though he wouldn't know what Janice liked.

There were small adornments to the room that had come from her, little touches of femininity, though it was predominantly Beau's place, as if Janice had not yet committed fully to its decoration or upkeep. Her personality spoke of a sense of order and determination, but the room didn't reflect this. It was still Beau's beach shack.

Alex picked up his beer, emptied the dregs into the sink, and pushed the bottle into the already full carton of empties next to the back door. He looked at the open bedroom door, then out the kitchen window. He stubbed out his cigarette and sauntered round the house to the bedroom.

He lingered a little, letting his eyes adjust to the darked room, it was quieter in there, heavy curtains blocked light from the window above the bed. Alex hesitated a little. Clothes were strewn over the floor on one side of the bed and draped over the ruffled bedsheets. Magazines were piled next to the bedside lamp, Cosmopolitan and Surfing World. He couldn't resist a quick look at the latest one. A long thin foil dropped from the centre pages onto the white underwear lying next to the bed. Feeling even more like a thief, he quickly replaced the foil back into the magazine, put it back on the pile, and retreated to the kitchen.

He collected up his things, looking around for one last time and left the bungalow, unsure if his feelings were of betrayal or envy. He closed the door quietly behind him.

Chapter 10

Alex pulled into the gravel carpark next to the Nerimbah Beach Lifesaving Club. The clubhouse was long overdue for a coat of white paint. No doubt the building would be renovated soon as the popularity of lifesaving clubs was on the rise. Stretched before it, the ocean was brown and largely uninviting. The weeklong rain had muddied the surf, the river flushing out into the bay, fanning out from the rock wall northward along the shore.

The surf was strong, imposing. It was easy to see the powerful swells marching in around Bayman Headland, a southeast swell driven from strong winds that began in the Tasman Sea a week earlier. The clouds had cleared, and the morning sun light lit up the wave top spray. A slight westerly offshore kept the bay flat between the sets and pushed against the waves as they broke on the sand banks. Perfect for an early morning surf.

Not a lot was said between them. Both Alex and Beau had done this many times before, a familiar routine. The rhythmic scrape of wax over the fibreglass boards, a struggle with the leg rope, locking the car and hiding the keys up inside the chrome bumper bar. Looking out from the carpark, the glassy swell peeled left from in front of the clubhouse. It wasn't overly large, but at five foot, the ground swell gave each set a hint of menace as it impacted into the shallower water, throwing up a wall of sandy broken foam.

'Lefts! On your backhand. You won't see it coming today, you'll get drilled.' Beau chuckled, referring to Alex's stance with his back to the wave.

'Typical goofy bullshit, eat my dust.' bantered Alex as he straightened up, board under his arm.

Beau laughed and pointed to the smaller peaks further down the beach toward the river mouth to where the waves were smaller. 'Kiddies over there', he said.

Alex said nothing in response as he sprinted down the beach into the surf. He pushed his board over the smaller broken waves, a northerly sweep tugging at his legs. He ducked into the first larger wall of foam, feeling that rush beginning to accelerate his breathing. The water was waist deep, swirling and pulling at him as he waited for the set to finish breaking. Be patient, a lull will come soon.

Each set had three waves, the first was a teaser, the second often larger and the best formed best, while the third was often larger again, but it broke into the dirty water of the first two waves. Alex was hit by the walls of foam, nearly driving him off his feet, but he pushed back against it, and slid on top of his board, paddling hard, aiming for the horizon, making the most of the break between sets to paddle out past the impact zone.

Ahead he could see the beginnings of a set looming. He kept pushing, breathing hard, arms pumping, till his board rose up an unbroken wave and punched through the lip as it feathered and began to break. His board fell through air to slap on the back side of the retreating wave break. Twice more Alex repeated the mad dash, until he was out the back, behind the break.

He pulled his legs up either side of the board to straddle it and catch his breath. looked left then right, decided on his position at the take off point and paddled over to the first point of the break. Beau popped up next to him, not breathing nearly so hard.

On the horizon, swells were forming as they entered the shallower waters of the bay. They began to stand up taller and become defined as rows of moving hills. The sun reflected off the surface, making it difficult to see where each wave would break. The colony of surfers bobbed up and down in the deep green, hands shielding their eyes in unison, until, like a flock of like-minded birds, they slid back on to their boards and jostled for position at the take-off point. Alex knew of no other place he would rather be.

It was the first wave in the next set. Alex turned and stroked into it, but immediately knew he was in the wrong spot for the take-off. The wall rose up as he pushed to his feet, but the westerly wind held him in position too long, he was too slow to get upright, his front foot too far back. The board hung in the lip. Alex was half in position, when the wave took over the point in time when control passes from the surfer to the forces of nature.

The lip threw Alex and his board into thin air and followed him down to the shallow waters below. It drilled him into the sandy mush. He was swirled, and tumbled until the force of water released him, and he broke the surface spluttering for breath. Brown foam slapped at his face; his leg pulled sideways by the leg rope tethering him to his board, held tight in the grip of the swirling water.

He ducked under two more waves that broke in front of him, but each time, he was pushed closer to shore, his feet scrambling at the sand beneath, until he retrieved his board in the waist deep water and started all over again.

His second wave came when he and Beau paddled for the same take-off point. He got inside of Beau, closer to the highest point, and Beau pulled back from the contest, giving Alex a clear run at it.

As the swell rose and the wall formed, Alex swung the board around toward the beach and launched into the peak just as it began to break. It was steep. He angled left.

The board dropped from under him again, but this time, the control was with Alex. He pulled his feet up under his body and found the familiar position this time. He took the drop, his back to the wave, the side rail of his board bit into the wall of water and held him in position as he hit the bottom. He pushed down hard with his back foot, forcing his fin to grab and carve in a bottom turn that nosed the board left, back up ward, and reversed a spiral into the shallows.

Behind him the wave broke. Ahead of him a wall of water curved upward and beckoned to pitch him over the falls. He pushed the board higher up the wave, once, twice, three times he drove the board up and down the wall, generating speed, to stay ahead of the break, its lip pitching just above his head. Sand and foam sucked from beneath him, the breaking wall reaching out for him from behind, but he was too quick.

Time slowed; he was aware of each droplet of water that whisked past his face. Ahead a surfer was ducking under the wave, but it didn't matter to him, he was in total control. For those few moments in time, he was weightless, no sense of speed ... until the whole sandy brown mess collapsed on top of him from above. It had caught him and drove him into the shallow waters of the break, held him down just long enough for it to re-establish itself as to who was boss, and then it released him. Alex broke the surface and let out a primal 'whoop', a shout that proclaimed to the world his victory, and all the joy that came with it.

He surfed for another two hours, lean and hungry for more, until he figured it was time to come in.

Chapter 11

In the carpark, Alex shook himself dry, rubbing the last of the water off with his towel. The surf was beginning to drop in size as the tide retreated, and wind swung around more southerly, chopping at the surface and affecting the quality of the ridable waves. He strapped the boards to the top of the car and turned to Beau.

'I'm starved. Time for breakfast at Barrett's?' suggested Alex.

'Thick shake across the road is closer.'

'Nope. I want the supermarket. We can take it home to eat at your place on the verandah. Will Janice be home?'

'Sure,' said Beau. 'But she'll be sleeping off work. She didn't get in till late last night.'

Alex reversed out of the car park and pointed the car toward the river esplanade, past the ice works to Barrett's supermarket in the distance. It wasn't really a supermarket like the ones in Brisbane, Nerimbah was too small for that, but locals could get most things they wanted there without having to go to Dunoonan. What drew Alex to Barrett's on the river was their fresh baked hot bread and cold lime milk sold in the glass bottle. Alex strode through the front doors, heading for the cold cabinet.

At the checkout he recognized a young Cathy Barrett on the register. She glanced at him as he strode past, and Alex was suddenly aware that he was barefoot and still dripping seawater from his boardshorts.

He had known Cathy from school as the younger sister of a guy in his grade. Alex noticed she was nearly as tall as he now, despite the 3-year difference, her long sandy hair framed clear brown eyes and a young innocent face, but she was now at an age where young girls had grown to young women and liked to be noticed.

Armed with his purchases, he sidled up to the front counter, placed his goods down and smiled. 'Hi, you'd be Cathy Barrett if I remember right.'

She smiled back at him and pulled at her work apron to flatten out the crease over her breasts. 'You're Alex Holmes. You went to school with Paul, my brother.'

'Yeh, Paul, where is now?' He didn't wait for an answer. 'You'd be in Year 12 now yourself, or have you finished?'

'I just finished last year. Thank God for that!'

'Bet you're glad it's over. What are you going to do now?'

'God, I don't know. Everyone asks me that,' she blurted, exasperated.

'Sorry,' remarked Alex.

'I might go to Uni yet, but I don't know. I'm working here for now.'

'Do yourself a favour, get out while you can,' joked Alex, mimicking a deep movie star voice. 'But seriously, your parents still own the store, don't they? Been here a while, haven't they?'

'Yep!' she answered... 'and so have I.' She dropped her eyes and moved to ring up the purchases. She appeared a little self-conscious that she was still behind the counter at her parents' grocery store, while the rest of the world awaited.

Abruptly Mrs Joan Barrett bustled in behind the counter, an air of protectiveness to her. Dark hair was piled on top of her head, a tall woman and an imposing figure for someone over fifty. Her slim lean frame came from many hours of hard work running the business.

Alex appreciated that, he had seen the same in his own mother, and he deferred to it. 'Hi Mrs Barrett. Nice to see you again.'

'Alex Holmes! 'She looked Alex over. She was clearly struggling to replace an image of a gangly 17-year-old adolescent she once knew with the Alex standing before her now. 'How is your Mum? I haven't seen her for ages.' She smiled.

'Fine thanks.'

'You've been away at Uni, haven't you?'

'Till yesterday. Just finished three years. I'm back for the summer, waiting for some work offers from down south. How's Paul going?'

'He's done very well for himself in the Air Force, still at the academy. He'll finish next year, then get his posting. Cathy is interested in going to Uni, aren't you dear.' She nodded at Cathy and smiled at Alex again, seemingly to draw him into further conversation for Cathy's benefit more than hers.

Alex shuffled a little way toward the door, bread and milk in hand. 'I must get going, just had a surf with Beau. He's waiting in the car.'

Joan Barrett went still. 'You mean Dennis Beaumont?'

She tilted her head to the side and glanced at the door leading to the car park. She turned back to Alex, her forehead creased, eyes narrowing. Cathy stood next to her, still looking directly at him, clearly unaware of the change in atmosphere.

'Yep. The surf was good after yesterday's storm. '

'I'm sure it was,' she stated flatly.

At that moment, Beau appeared at the automatic doors, looking left to right, obviously searching for Alex.

Mrs Bennett frowned when saw him and visibly stiffened. She moved ever so slightly to angle herself in front of Cathy – the smile lines were gone.

'You have everything!' It was not a question; it was a command. Clearly, it was time to go.

'All good, thanks Mrs Barrett", said Alex.

Joan Barrett stood still, looking directly at Beau, locked onto his eyes; everything about her reeked of an open challenge, daring him to come any closer.

He didn't.

'I'll say hello to my mother for you,' Alex called to her as he turned away.

'You do that.' She didn't turn her head; eyes locked on Beau.

'See you round, Cathy,' Alex called, smiling at the young woman.

Her head poked out around from behind her mother's shoulder. 'You too Alex.'

He walked to the door and raised his eyebrows at Beau as he left.

Behind him, he could hear Mrs Barrett issuing instructions for Cathy to go to the back of the store and get a mop and bucket to clean up the water Alex left while standing at the counter. She would stay and man the register, no doubt, standing guard.

'What the hell was that all about?' Alex asked Beau when they were both back in the car. 'I thought Mrs Barrett was going to crack a fit when you showed up. What did you do to annoy her?'

'Nothing!' Beau stated.

'Did you do something to Cathy?' Alex asked.

'Nope. Would have liked to though,' he mumbled in reply.

Alex didn't believe him. The drive home was strangely quiet. Alex kept glancing at Beau, unsure of what had just taken place in the supermarket. When he turned into Gulin Avenue and parked in front of Beau's shack, he put any reservations about what had just transpired at the supermarket to the back of his mind, he was more intrigued with Cathy. She certainly had changed, and he didn't mind the way she had looked at him either.

Chapter 12

Alex ripped at the top of the crusted loaf of bread, allowing tendrils of hot fragrant steam to escape. The bread was soft and gooey, bound in a hard crust. Nothing compared to an uncut loaf of hot bread and cold lime milk after a surf. Alex and Beau ripped at the loaf alternatively, stuffing handfuls of it into their mouths, passing the milk back and forth to wash it down. It was a ritual that bonded them since they were 15 years old at High School together and it had never lost any of its pleasures.

'Better than sex,' grunted Beau.

Alex nodded his head appreciatively in agreement. They leaned back on aluminium chairs, both feet on the rail of the Beach Shack. It was only a small house, a fibre cement bungalow on short stumps. A flat roof angled out over two sides. There were no stairs at the front, only a ramp leading up to the small verandah and front door. There was little room for a table, but it faced the morning sun and soaked up the warmth.

The grass stretched before them to the road where Alex had parked, partly on the gutter, partly on the grass, the surfboards were still strapped to the roof of the Peugeot. Puddles of water from yesterday's rain glistened in the sunlight waiting to be soaked up by the sun. A small unkept garden stretched below the kitchen windows, tufts of grass circled the low concrete stumps, and the big corner block was long overdue for a grass cut, it was a rental house after all.

'There were more guys in the water this morning. More than usual.' Alex remarked between mouthfuls.

'Get used to it. Lot more people here since you went away.' Beau turned to face Alex. 'The place is going berserk, there are new estates out the end of Jermu Street, and the whole of North Nerimbah is exploding. I hate it, but at least there's plenty of work...stacks of it...building everywhere. A lot of new guys in town. Good for business. Reggie reckons it's never been better.'

'Who's Reggie?'

'A bloke...a mate of mine... You might remember him, Reg Bishop, but everyone calls him Reggie, tall guy, about twenty-five, reddish hair, bit like yours. Lives next door to Mum and Dad along Boar Road. I've been getting a bit of work with him.'

'What's he do? Is he a builder?'

'God no. Reggie wouldn't be caught dead doing that, or he might have been once, but not now. No... I drive for him ...for his business, you know, like a courier, pick up's, drop off's, different jobs, he pays me well.'

'How long have you had the Monaro? Alex nodded to the two-door muscle car in the garage.

'Since I've been working with Reggie.'

'Shit he must pay well; my Peugeot is a wreck.' Alex looked at the familiar mustard coloured 504 crouched at the footpath. The panels were dinted and scratched from years of student carparks. The shiny Monaro was a stark contrast to his old, tired 'rust bucket'.

'What have you got to do to get one of those?' asked Alex, pointing at the Holden.

'Stick around and you'll find out.' Beau ripped at more bread, stuffing it into his mouth, chewing ferociously till he swallowed with an exaggerated gulp.

'I mostly work around the coast, but lately, more stuff in the country, out the back of Kenilworth,' he said between swallows of bread and milk. 'Sometimes I do drop offs in Brisbane. Every month Reg and I go fishing, the outer banks, near Florette Shoals and Dinnan Rocks in his boat'.

'Catching much?' Alex asked.

'Yeh. A shit load when the weathers good... specially at night. Snapper, mackerel, Jew fish...'

'That would be alright. What sort of boat has he got?'

Beau chewed thoughtfully on the last of the bread. 'A twenty-footer. Fibreglass, with a small half cabin wheelhouse up the front. A work boat. Two 80's on the back. But he gets a bit funny about taking other people out, so I wouldn't ask.'

'I wasn't going to,' said Alex.

'Well don't. Just so you know!' Beau retorted.

'You could put in a good word for me'.

'Leave it alone will you. Anyway, haven't you got a job down south?'

'Not yet. But I will soon, just waiting on a couple of responses to my application. Till then, I could do with some work... anything really. Labouring? Driving, like you?'

'You could try Forrests. Their foreman Lynton knows most of the 'subbies'. He'd know someone. You could try Villi Tanoa he might need a deckie on his boat.'

"Yeh, Villi's a chance. But he might want someone with more experience on the boats, and he goes out a week at a time. I'm not missing out on the surf. Something casual would do, I'm not going to be here long. You said there was lots of work around. What about your mate Reggie?'

'He won't have anything. It's a bit of a closed shop with him, with what he does. What about your dad? He'd have lots of work, wouldn't he?' Beau suggested.

'No chance. He told me long ago that no son of his was going to end up painting houses. He works alone anyway, always has. What about your dad? How's he going?'

Beau didn't respond at first, as if he hadn't heard the question.

'The old prick hasn't worked for years. Still hitting the turps. I see him a bit when I drop round to see Mum, but I don't stay long, too hard these days, I can't stand being around him. You remember when I put a couch in the shed downstairs in Year 12, and they found me in there with Maureen? Well, it hasn't got any easier since then. They think I just surf and smoke dope all day.' He laughed bitterly. 'Which I do!' He laughed again. 'They came around here once, in the afternoon, and Janice and I were in bed. That didn't help either. Fuck 'em. I don't live in the 50's like them. And I'm not going to end up a useless old drunk like him.'

Alex remembered the Beaumonts as decent people, bit like his own parents. Jeff Beaumont, the old man, may have had issues since his car accident put an end to his working life, and it hit the family hard when there was no regular income. He could be abrupt at times, but Jeff Beaumont had always been civil to Alex. He looked at Beau, perhaps the faults weren't entirely one sided. He'd never heard him talk about his parents that way before, and he remembered Mrs Barrett's reaction earlier. Outwardly he was still the freewheeling Beau, but Alex could tell that deeper down, something was not quite right.

Beau turned to Alex. 'Do you want a coffee?'

'Yep. I can make it for us.' Alex shuffled his chair back, making a move to go inside.

'No, Janice will do it.'

'I thought you said she'll be sleeping in?'

'Nah. She'll be awake by now. Heh Janice!' He yelled. 'Coffee!'

Alex made to get up, but Beau reached across to his shoulder and pushed him back down.

'Stay there, I said she'll get it.' He yelled again.' Janice!'

A muffled voice came from inside. 'Yeh, I heard.'

'Alex wants a coffee...and I'll have one too,' he called over his shoulder.

'I don't need it that bad,' Alex said. He turned away, once again unsettled. Up to his left in the distance came the sound of heavy steel caterpillar treads, and the banging of metal on the bitumen. A large flatbed truck and excavator were pulled up on the road.

'What's happening there?' Alex asked.

'Forrests are putting in a set of units, eight storeys so they say.'

Alex leaned forward to get a better view. He could just make out the two-storey ambulance station in the distance, the excavator disappeared from view behind it. Alex frowned, still looking up the road. He was drawn to the Ambulance station, only part of it was visible above the row of roofs, but there was something about it. He was silent for a while and closed his eyes. A bead of sweat ran down his forehead as he struggled to recall where he had seen this before.

His mother had always hinted that he had a second sight. He thought he could control it, break into the vision and consciously know what was about to happen next. His eyes were screwed shut. He searched his current déjà vu, but could only visualise his father, sitting quietly next to him on a wood bench, dressed formally, in a suit, a sombre occasion. His father...looking down at him. He was reaching out with his eyes as a father would to his son, a mixture of composure and compassion. In that look, he was teaching Alex how to behave in the face of adversity. They sat together in a church... at a funeral. Alex opened his eyes. He tried to reach back into his vision but see no more. The spell was broken. Alex looked up and opened his eyes to the present.

There were sounds of movement behind him. Janice appeared and gave Beau his coffee, then edged past Alex's chair and placed a coffee on the veranda rail in front of him.

'Thanks. Pull up a chair.' He reached across and dragged the spare chair away from the wall, retrieving the towel that was draped over it.

Janice dropped into the chair beside him, and in a world-weary voice greeted the boys. 'How was the surf?'

Beau didn't respond, so it was left to Alex to answer, though he didn't think she really cared what the answer would be.

'It was good, big and clean. How was work?' Alex asked her.

'You don't really want to know.' She sipped at her coffee.

Alex stared at her profile, the morning sun darkening her eyes in shadow, highlighting a fine nose. Her lips were thin, a little drawn Alex thought, the fatigue of the nightly grind at work coming through. She pulled her dressing gown up around her thighs to let the sun warm her legs. Alex let his eyes flicker down to the side, to take in her slim calves.

'God! The idiots at the bar last night. Jo Jo Zep was playing, and you could barely hear yourself think. Everyone was shouting so loud I got my orders mixed up...and got blamed for it. And then you wake me up early.' Her voice had a gravelly undertone that he found appealing. 'That new manager is a...I don't know. Beau, you've met him!'

'Yep, he's a prick.' Beau said. He glanced back up the road where the growl of the excavator intruded on their morning coffee.

'What's' going on up there?' Janice had leaned forward to look past Alex.

'Forrests have started the new units. Eight storeys. They got the land cheap and pushed it through Council in record time.

'I thought the building limit was three,' said Alex.

'That got changed, like it always does by the developers, in the pockets of the Council up in Dunoonan. What do they know about the coast? Bunch of crooks.' exclaimed Beau.

'They can't be as bad as the white shoe brigade from the Gold Coast.' Alex pointed out.

'Don't you believe it. Bloody southerners coming in with all their money, pay off the council to build what they want, corrupt bastards. Wrecking our beaches. And it's not the council's job to give in to them. They're supposed to represent us; they're supposed to listen to us. We are the locals, not some city southerners. It doesn't matter what we want, they bribe the council to get what they want and ride over the top of all the locals.'

'But locals never want change Beau.' said Janice. 'You've got to have change. It's a natural order of things. Without it you stagnate and never grow.'

'What do you know, you're not a local,' Beau snapped. 'They bribed the council. You watch, all those holiday houses next to the fire station will go, knocked down for another eight storey block of units, probably ten storey by next year. That's change for you Janice.' He spat in disgust.

Alex was surprised. 'How do you know all this?'

'Reggie told me. He and Roy Conlon know all about it. Council gets paid off to approve anything the developers want. Roy told me how they put the screws on them to vote the right way, and if they don't, watch out! You know Vince Rogers, been in Council for years, lives at Georges Head, he stood up to them. He voted against development and woke up the other day to find his dog Trevor had been poisoned. Dead.'

'And you believe that shit Beau?' questioned Alex.' Everyone hated Vince's dog. Trevor was a mongrel; he'd bite anyone who walked past his yard. He was doing that when I was here three years ago. I'm surprised the dog's lasted this long.'

'Maybe so. But Roy pretty much told me that's what went down. Conlon's' smart! He knows everything that's happening on the coast. He's got a house in Brisbane, comes and stays with Reggie when he's up here. He knows the council's town planning, who works for all the developers and how they swayed the council to change building heights to stay the same as the Gold Coast.'

'I don't know if we need that type of competition,' said Alex. 'Did you ever work for Forrests?' Alex asked pointedly of Beau.

'Don't need to.' Beau told him.

'Phhh! Beau doesn't know how to work!' Janice scoffed.

Beau and Alex both laughed, but as Beau threw the dregs of his coffee over the veranda, his eyes showed that the joke was more of a barb in disguise.

'Got plenty of work with Reggie!' Beau quipped.

'Reggie!' Janice spat out in disgust. 'You spend more time with Reggie than you do with me!'

'Yeh, but that's my work, he pays me!'

'For what?' Janice leaned forward, staring intently at Beau. There was a sudden change in atmosphere, the second time it had happened that morning.

'Lots of things.' Beau pushed back on the defensive. 'You get your money your way, and I get my money my way. It's still the same money. We've been over this before. You don't need to know what Reggie does.' Beau obviously tried to ease the tension by drawing them all into the same predicament. 'Not even I know what he does all the time.' He pointed up the road to the excavations. 'That's what we should be worried about. Southerners coming in taking our jobs. They're the real crooks...the bloody mayor and those big bastards at the top.'

'I didn't say you were a crook', said Janice. 'I just don't trust Reggie!'

'Your problem', Beau retorted.

At that point, the crump of falling masonry and a plume of fine grey dust burst upward from behind the Ambulance station. It triggered something in Alex, an unwelcome familiarity with the scene, but he couldn't place it, and in the back of his consciousness, he knew he didn't want to. He wasn't always comfortable with his visions, he didn't know why, but when it was like this, he avoided digging any deeper for meaning. It confused him, he didn't like it, he couldn't explain it, but he couldn't avoid it either. He looked once more at the chocking dust cloud in the distance, then turned to Janice trying to deflect his unease.

'Why? What's wrong with Reggie?' he asked.

'Nothing.' She shook her head, conversation closed. Janice stood up abruptly, took the empty coffee cups and went inside.

'Don't worry about her', said Beau. 'She's just tired from last night. Mate, I'm going around to Reggie's to drop off a board cover. Come and meet 'the Reg' in person.' Beau grinned and playfully punched Beau in the arm.' I'll just get some dry gear on'. He went inside brushing breadcrumbs from his chest hair.

Alex stayed on the veranda, letting the sun dry the last damp from his board shorts. From inside the house, he could hear raised voices. Beau's was the loudest, while Janice's voice was quieter, more conciliatory in tone. He couldn't hear directly what was said, but when the door opened, and Beau appeared, he neither looked back nor said goodbye to Janice. The door slammed shut behind him.

'Come on.' Beau said as he headed for the car.

Chapter 13

When Beau and Alex drew up at Reggies house, Beau made a point of driving up on the grass and parking next to the front steps, in full view of his father next door. Jeff Beaumont looked up from his boat, a tall bottle of beer in hand, staring intently at his son. Beau made a show of opening and slamming the car door shut. With an arrogance of familiarity, he strode up Reggies front stairs, not once looking in his father's direction. Jeff Beaumont followed Beau's movements with his eyes. Alex trailed behind, a little unsure of how to proceed, after all, he had known the Beaumonts from long ago and he had no beef with them.

'Come on, stop fucking around.' Beau slung the comment over his shoulder and marched through Reggies front door without knocking. Alex said nothing but nodded in Jeff Beaumont's direction, acutely aware of how this tableau was playing out. There was only a cold, silent stare in return.

Reggie's house was next door to Beau's parents, where North Nerimbah meets the inlet past Dunns Point on Boar Road. It was inland from the beach and overlooked Bibings wetlands, the name originally coming from the local aboriginal dialect meaning *tea trees*, and there were plenty of those ringing the shallows The wetlands were really a tidal swamp, from a time long past when the creek ran around Dunsborough Point into the river. At different times the wetland swamp flooded. Storm water would push into the basin and the levels rose, flooding the soccer field next to it and the houses that lined the road. This was where Jeffery and 'Marjorie Beaumont lived, and where their son, Dennis 'Beau' Beaumont grew up.

Most of the houses along Boar Road were like the Beaumonts, two-storey 1950s weatherboard on tall timber posts, with ant and termite capping between the first and second story. The top story had a loungeroom, kitchen, three bedrooms, bathroom, with a set of stairs leading diagonally from a closed in sunroom to the ground below. Under the house, owners parked their cars and stored their boats but nothing much else in case of flooding. Twin tub washing machines sat on small concrete slabs next to old beer fridges and small sheds built underneath for gardening tools and extra storage, enclosed with vertical timber slats for privacy.

At the top of the stairs, Alex paused and looked down at the large fiberglass boat under Reggie's house. It had two powerful outboards on the back and an expanse of aft deck space behind the wheelhouse. The boat was resting on a duel wheeled heavy trailer with a metallic green Ford F100 ute parked next to it. A lot of money tied up in that rig. He followed Beau inside.

'Reggie? You home? Got someone for you to meet,' called Beau.

Alex didn't know what to expect. It was anything but. The front living room was clean and clear of clutter, a neat lounge and two easy chairs bracketed a new model TV and large record player, speakers and tape deck. A white shagpile rug covered polished floorboards. The hallway was bright and airy with newly framed music posters on the walls.

Walking down the hall, each of the bedrooms were neatly made up, windows open, letting in fresh air and light. Decorated with standing lamps, geometric rugs and sparse side tables, it was a stark contrast to Beau's Beach Shack. Reggie was in the kitchen, nursing a large cup of coffee, the smell permeating the room...

'Reggie, meet my mate Alex, remember I told you about him. Just back from Uni, the poor idiot.'

Reggie turned to face them both and stuck out his hand immediately for Alex to shake. He was as tall as Beau, but much slimmer. Alex grabbed his hand in return; he was strong and wiry. His red hair topped off a slightly mottled skin. A doctor once told Alex that with his hair and skin he should be chasing long haired cows across the heathers of Scotland, not burning his skin in the hot Australian sun. If that was the case, then the same applied to Reggie as well. His complexion was mottled with peeling skin from his latest foray into the surf. This was something Alex was familiar with, but he'd been away from both for so long he appeared anaemic by comparison. He would soon change that.

'Alex!'. He greeted him, a voice fast, and clipped with intensity. 'Beau told me you were coming around. You guys want a coffee? A drink?' He didn't wait for an answer, but reached across the table for his smokes, took one out and lit it, then offered one to the boys as an afterthought.

'Smoke?'

'Thanks Reggie,' Beau said. He reached across and struggled to extract one from the packet still in Reggie's hand. Reggie raised his eyebrows at Alex, gesturing with the packet for him to take one as well. Somehow to accept a smoke from Reggie made him complicit with whatever Reggie and Beau were up to together. He wasn't ready to enter that alliance yet.

'No thanks,' he said.

'Don't smoke?' asked Reggie as he gestured for Beau to use the lighter on the table.

'Just had one.' Alex looked around the kitchen. 'Nice place.' It was more a conversation opener, rather than any real appraisal. It was a neat and tidy Laminex kitchen, typical of 1950s design, but needing a makeover. The back door was open to let in the little breeze there was. Reggie pushed back the lace curtains at the kitchen window to help clear the smoke, Alex could see straight across the gap between the two houses at the window in Beau's bedroom next door. He leaned across to the window and looked down. Below he could make out Jeff Beaumont between the timber slats fiddling with his boat and Marjorie Beaumont hanging up washing on a line under the house.

'Been here a few years now. Beau lived next door, that's how he came to work for me. Speaking of work, we're going out for a fish again on the 18th? It's a Tuesday night, you in?'

'Of course.'

'I'll see you before then anyway. Pick you up as usual. Should be good weather. There's no room for you Alex, sorry.'

'Beau mentioned that.'

'Did he now?' Reggie raised an eyebrow at Beau. 'Anything else he mentioned?'

Alex butted in before Beau could answer. 'Only that you might know of someone who needs some work. Labouring, cleaning. I'll have a go at anything. I need the money'.

'Everyone needs workers. There's plenty around. Go see Forrest's, they'll have something. There's a new building going up at the end of Beau's street. They're also doing roads for the council and need gangs. New estates and things, a lot of it council work.'

'Thanks. I'll do that,' said Alex.

Reggie sipped at his coffee, all three of them still standing.

'I brought round that Board cover you wanted.' Offered Beau.

'Good. Are you around this arvo?'

'Yep. Probably,' Beau replied.

'Got some stuff to drop off to Steve Henderson on the way. If you're going past.'

'Yeh. I can do that.'

'I'm heading down to Brissie now, taking Roy for lunch, at the Newstead pub, at Breakfast Creek. Ever been there?'

'No. Not at all,' Beau answered.

'Great food. I'll shout you and Janice a steak there some time.' A short sharp car horn intruded from outside. 'There's Roy now.' Reggie splashed his coffee dregs in the sink, rinsed his cup, dried it and methodically put it away in the cupboard. He stubbed out his cigarette butt and emptied the ashtray in the bin, washed and dried the glass ashtray. He put it away as well. Ignoring them both, he disappeared into the second bedroom off the hallway and reappeared with a small double handled sports bag which he handed to Beau.

'This is for Stevo,' he said, handing the bag to Beau. 'I said you'd be around sometime this afternoon, so he's expecting you. Nice to meet you Alex, don't let this bugger lead you astray. How long are you home for?'

'Probably till just after Christmas. I'm expecting some job offers from down south, to start next year. But I'm after some work till then.'

'Well, go see Forrest's like I said. I'll see you around.' He waved his hands, herding them back down the hallway. Meeting over. On the small landing at the top of the stairs Reggie closed and locked the door behind him. Below, there was a new car in the yard, a silver Ford Fairlane, big, angular and powerful, an imposing automobile. Leaning against the bonnet was Roy Conlan.

Meeting him for the first time, Alex could only marvel at the similarity of the man to his car. Both exuded the same aura of power and singularity of purpose. Roy's shoulders were huge in comparison to Reggies or his. Beau might have been a match in size and strength, but in a contest of menace, Roy was clearly streets ahead. He was dressed in tight fitting slacks, leather shoes and a collared sports shirt, open at the neck to show off a gold neck chain. His hair was dark, thick, and swept across his tanned forehead. Alex couldn't see his eyes; they were shielded by large amber sunglasses.

'Heh Roy, this is Alex, he's Beau's mate..' Reggie called, as he led them both down the steps, out on to the lawn.

Conlan straightened up and extended his hand. 'Nice to meet you. I didn't catch your last name.' He had a distinctive American accent that elongated the 'r' in a deep timbred voice that made the word 'your' sound like a growling bear.

'Holmes,' said Alex as they shook hands, 'Alex Holmes.'

'I'll remember that.' He swung toward Reggie, 'Are we right to go?'

'Sure thing Roy,' said Reggie as he hopped into the Fairlane's passenger seat.

'Pleasure to meet you, Alex... and Beau, that cigarette, don't leave it on the front lawn will you. Good to see you boys.'

'Yeh, you too Roy.' called Beau. Alex said nothing as he watched the two men drive away. He looked at Beau and was reminded of their time at school together waiting outside the Deputy's office after another roasting for playing up in class. Dismissed! That was the word Alex was searching for. They had just been dismissed.

'Beau, your old man is just over there.' Alex pointed out.

'Yeh, I know.'

'You don't want to see him? Say hello?'

'Fuck him.'

'Your mum is under the house too. I should go and say hello. Come on.' Alex made to pull at Beau's shirt, but Beau shrugged his hand away.

'You do what you want mate, I'll wait in the car, but not for long.' Beau retreated to the Monaro, lit a cigarette and flopped down behind the wheel, staring out across the park at the wetlands.

Alex ambled across the two yards separating the houses, stopping in the shade of the Beaumont's garage, next to the stairs.

'Heh Mr Beaumont, Mrs Beaumont. How are you?' he called out.

Jeff Beaumont straightened from leaning in the boat and appraised Alex with suspicion. Marjorie Beaumont looked around at him and placed her washing basket on the twin tub.

'Just dropped in to say hi, Beau's waiting for me,' said Alex.

'He doesn't wait for anyone,' growled Jeff Beaumont. 'What do you want?'

'Don't be so rude Jeff, Its Alex ...Beau's friend from school.' Marjorie admonished.

'Yeh. Well, he came here with Beau,' he grunted. 'He can leave with him for all I care. That's enough for me.' He turned his back on Alex and leaned into his boat. Five years ago, he had thought of this house and the Beaumonts as his second home. Behind him, a car door slammed, and the Monaro's big motor exploded into life. Alex heard Beau revving the motor as he drove over the front lawn, and stopped on the road, the powerful motor burbling in wait.

'I used to love coming here,' Alex stammered. 'You always looked after me, I just wanted to say thanks... anyway.' Alex stood there, remembering the coolness of the concrete floor under the Beaumont house in summer. He was 14 when he first started coming over after surfing with Beau. There were always neighbours around discussing fishing, while Jeff held court over bottles of XXXX beer, late into the afternoons. Every so often he would hobble over to the fridge for a new beer, sometimes offering one to his friends, sometimes not, but he always knew exactly how many beers he had. Beau would sneak the remains of half poured bottles and the two boys would share it behind the back fence. The fridge was still there, and so was the boat.

'That's OK Alex.' Marjorie looked at her husband, then over his shoulder at her son waiting impatiently on the road.' She stood next to her washing, quiet and resolute.

'I'm sorry, I'd better go,' said Alex.

'That's OK Alex, I understand,' Marjorie Beaumont repeated forlornly.

He waved to her and turned back to the street, trotting across the lawn to the car, opened the side door and slumped into the passenger seat.

'You could have waited a bit longer,' admonished Alex. There was no doubt what Beau thought of that, he gave the motor full throttle drowning out any further conversation, speeding off in a burst of blue smoke and a cacophony of gear changes. Alex also remembered once when Beau was caught stealing a whole bottle of beer from the fridge, there were bruises on both his arms and legs the next day. Beau often showed up to school with bruises on his body, but he wouldn't say anything. Beau was like that; his problems were his own and no-one else had to know. Beau accelerated onto Boar Road and left his old house behind.

Chapter 14

Beau slowed the Monaro down as he turned into Wongai crescent in the heart of Nerimbah, coming to a stop outside a tall two-storey hardwood house, not unlike the one he'd just been in. Fishing nets were draped over crossed poles, and an old mullet boat sat forlornly on a rusting trailer in the garage.

'Steve's place.' Beau announced and reached behind him for the sports bag on the back seat. Alex made to open his door, but Beau gripped his arm. "No mate. This is not for you. You don't need to come up.'

At first Alex didn't understand, he knew Steve Henderson from his school days, he was in a year above. His father was a fisherman with his own trawler, and it looked like Steve was following in his footsteps. Alex was keen to connect with his old mates and looked up through the windscreen toward the top of the stairs.

'Why not?' he asked.

Beau paused for a second, "This is my life mate, not yours,' he quipped.

With that, Beau released his arm, retrieved the bag and was out the door before Alex could protest further. He watched as Beau bounded up the stairs knocked at the door, turned and looked down at Alex. Alex nodded back. The door opened and Beau disappeared inside.

Alex knew the area well; it was nestled into the big bend in the river. Everywhere in Nerimbah was only a few streets away from the river. Most of the houses were old fishing shacks, piled high on stumps in case the river flooded again like it did in 1930. Everyone remembered the floods, even though few had been there to experience it. Small towns were like that. Fishing glued the families together, they shared the hard work, the long absences at sea, the riches, and more often than not, the tragedies. The children grew up together, often following their parents into a life on the sea. Steve's parents lived down at the river, two blocks away. Rusting boat gear and old work utes littered the back yards around him, but Alex knew that appearances could be deceiving, fishing boats and licences were not cheap, and hundreds of thousands of dollars were tied up in the trawlers moored at the river. He wound the window down and was immediately assaulted by a mosquito, one of the joys of living here.

The door opened at the top of the stairs, Steve Henderson appeared, followed by Beau. Steve was still tall and lanky, he waved down to Alex, then retreated inside. Beau skittered down the steps to the car, throwing the sport bag onto the back seat.

'That's done for the day', he said and playfully punched Alex in the arm. 'Now for some lunch. Let's go to the pub, my shout.' Beau started the car, whistling tunelessly to himself as they wound their way around the backstreets till they found a park behind the Nerimbah Beach Hotel.

They chose a table close to the front of the beer garden, only a low stucco wall between them and the footpath, beyond was the top of the dunes and the ocean. It was mid-week, and there were few patrons at the hotel, mostly tourists. Alex got the beers while Beau ordered two T Bone steaks from the short order cook at the grill inside.

Their beers were half finished and the meals placed in front of them before Alex broached the subject.

'Did you tell Stevo that I was waiting in the car back there?' remarked Alex.' I could have come up to say giddday.'

'No, you couldn't. '

'Why?' Alex asked.

'It's not your business.' Beau said shortly.

'And you do this for a job?'

"Shit yeh, pays well.' Beau reached into his pocket and half revealed a roll of $ 50 notes held together in a rubber band for Alex to see, then he pushed it back into his pocket. 'Beats working for a living. Think of me as a courier, I move Reggie's goods around the coast and get paid for their delivery and take my cut. It's not for everyone; there are risks you know.'

'I'm sure there is. How did you come to work for Reggie?

'Do you really want to know?'

'Probably not. But it all got a bit awkward this morning with you, Reggie, and your parents next door, and no one saying anything.'

Beau chewed on a mouthful of steak, deep in thought, before he answered.

'I used to see Reg all the time, from my window. He moved in next door at the end of year 12, round Christmas, just before you went away. You know, my bedroom is directly across from Reggies kitchen. Anyway, he used to bring girls home on the weekend, and you know...'

'What, were you perving on them?'

'No, never saw anything. But in the mornings, they'd have coffee together and stuff. I could see them from my bedroom through his kitchen window. It always looked so good, you know, like they were having a nice time. And Reg would dress up, he had money, and good nights out and such. I really wanted that; you know?'. Beau buried his steak in a mound of gravy and chips, scooping it up to his mouth before washing it down with a mouthful of beer.

'Bullshit Beau, you never wanted for anything. Girls hung around you like bees to a honey pot at High school. You knew everyone.' Alex waved his arm wide, as if embracing all the riches that the coast had to offer.

'Do you remember that time we nicked off from school in Grade 12, went surfing and came here to the beer garden instead of going to the cross-country run...sat in these same chairs!' Beau reminisced.

'...and you brought the beer cos you looked old enough...'

'... and that bastard Mr Delucia, "Da Loony" we called him, from the Science Department sprung us...'

'...and what was he doing out of school anyway? Nicking off like us?' chortled Beau.

'Jesus, I got a pasting from the Deputy over that.' Concluded Alex.

'I didn't. He didn't yell at me at all,' said Beau quietly. 'He told me there was no point, I was a lost cause already. Said I should leave school and get a job cos I'm a waste of space. Fuckwit. What did he know. He was as bad as my dad; always telling me I was fucking useless. He said I was a dead weight, just living off him. God, I hate him, hated them both.'

They fell silent, Alex concentrated on finishing his meal, acutely aware that Beau had changed direction.

'Get a fuckin job, he'd say. We didn't have much money, heh. But it was Mum who told me stay at school.'

'You could have gone to Uni,' remarked Alex.

'Bullshit. You don't know anything. You had to have money to go to Uni.' Beau pointed out.

'There was no fees Beau, didn't cost anything, only money for rent and food.'

'I wouldn't have been much of a student anyway. Why leave here? You said so yourself.'

'You could have got the marks to go to Uni if you wanted.'

'What for? It didn't matter if I got good marks or bad, it meant nothing to my old man, he beat me up anyway. Mr Big Fucking Fisherman,' Beau sneered. 'Mum works her arse off, and he spends it all on beer and boats. There was always enough for a new tinnie, but nothing for us. You never knew that did you? You probably thought we were doing all right.'

'No, I didn't know,' said Alex.

'No one did. I don't tell people my problems. He wanted me to quit school in year 10 and go labouring, just so I could pay him board to buy more beer. The payout from his accident didn't last long, that's when Mum started her second job. She used to pack shelves at the supermarket in Dunoonan two nights a week. Kept telling me to stick with school, to be something. And you were part of that.' He pointed a chip ladened fork in Alex's direction. 'She liked it that you would come around after school. "*You stick close to that Alex*", Mum would say, "*he knows what schools about.*"

'Bullshit Beau, you were smart enough to get good grades. You didn't need me.'

'Nah Mate, I had no reason, but you always knew you were going somewhere... I don't know where, but you kept trying to drag me along with you.' Beau finished his beer in a long gulp. 'It didn't work, I'm still here, but I loved you for trying.'

'Heh, you still can if you want Beau, you don't have to stay here.'

'That's something rich boys would say.' He smiled to show there was no malice in it. 'No mate...I'm made for this place. Sun, surf, drugs... and Janice. Besides, look at the car I've got, heaps better than your shitbox. Nah, here suits me fine. Have you heard anything about a job yet?'

'Nothing in the mailbox, but it's coming.'

'So is Christmas!' It was an old joke, and with that, Beau stood and indicated that lunch was over, he had obviously said more than he was comfortable with, and it was time to go.

Chapter 15

The drop off to Stevo that first afternoon set a pattern for many drops that Beau did over December. Alex was not stupid about it; he knew Beau was delivering drugs. Beau would turn to him and wink, 'Just this one.' But it was never just one with Beau. The drops were quick and efficient. The recipients were nearly always home. Steve Henderson was like many of Beau's customers, locals about the same age, renting units or beach shacks in the area, working as fishermen, in building or bar work. Alex would often see them in the surf, sometimes they nodded and shared a few words, other times there was no recognition at all. Beau seemed to get on well with most of them, his easy manner and laconic wit kept the business relationships on a friendly basis.

Alex rarely saw Beau arranging deliveries or pickups on the phone, it was like magic, and hardly anyone came to the Beach Shack looking for a deal or to settle accounts. Beau told him he warned all his contacts to steer clear of the house, that he didn't want anyone hanging around, or for Janice to be any part of his business. Alex liked that about Beau, but thought it was a bit naive to think that she would be in the clear if anything went wrong.

To his credit, Beau never asked Alex to drive his own car for a drop off or pick up. It was always in the Monaro. Beau would break in as they were on their way for a surf to explain that he just had to do a drop off on the way. It wasn't as if a bright yellow Holden Monaro didn't draw attention to them as they drove around Nerimbah, but the boards strapped to the top lent an air of innocent purpose to their movements, at least he liked to think that.

The Beach Shack had become his second home, the couch was thin and worn, it wasn't that comfortable, but it was Janice who made up for it. In the early mornings Alex would wake to the sound of her making coffee, her own ritual that started the day no matter how late she came in the night before. Alex would rise and join her on the verandah to talk or just sit in companionable silence, watching the sun come up, before she went back to bed to catch up on more sleep. Alex would grab his board and either rouse up Beau to join him or head off for a surf by himself before work.

The days took on a regularity that Alex found appealing after the uncertainties of the past three years as a student without an income. For most of December, Alex worked solidly with a bitumen paving company sub-contracted to the Forrest's group. Reggie's contact had worked out. When they needed extra hands on a job, Alex was it. Shovelling 180-degree hot mix bitumen in and out of hoppers and off the back of trucks. It was hard work, but Alex's suntan and complexion darkened considerably. His skin peeled from sunburn and his body began to take on a lean, hardened look.

Initially he dropped into his parents place out on the road to Dunoonan each day, to check the letterbox, looking for replies to his job applications with the different media companies. Twice he was rewarded with replies, but it was only to say that the positions had been filled by applicants with more experience.

As December wore on and his dejection rose, his visits to his parents' house dropped off to twice a week to check the mail, and collapse in front of TV, a home cooked meal and a soft bed. He placated and abused their generosity without giving much back.

It wasn't long before Alex's life on the coast began to take on a languishing rhythm of its own.

Janice worked most nights of the week, leaving Alex and Beau to go to the pub, and meet up with mates. Once a week Steve Henderson and whichever of his various flatmates came with a carton of beer and they would all play cards, listen to music on the turntable, drink and talk in a fug of sweet smoke and bongs. Other nights they went to bands at the North Shore International Hotel, or in the Playroom where Janice worked.

Most nights by the time she got home after midnight, Beau was passed out in the lounge chair, and Alex was comatose on the couch, listening to a Pink Floyd album stuck in a needle groove that repeated the same guitar riff over and over. Janice would cajole Beau to wake up and shuffle him off to bed, turning off the lights and stereo as she went. Some nights she and Alex stayed up on to the deck where they would share a joint and she would unload her angst from work, or from living with Beau.

Her relationship with Beau was often tumultuous. A mixed bag of care, concern and chaos. She had come to the coast to escape her parents. Though she never told Alex what it was she was escaping, but it had left her bitter. She told him that when she and Beau moved in together, he was the perfect tonic for her to be able to repair her life. She said he exuded a strength and confidence that attracted her to him in the first place.

Alex also recognized that she was her own woman, with her own strengths that often clashed with Beau's, their lives fluctuating dramatically. Some nights their arguing in the bedroom kept him awake and other times he couldn't sleep for the sounds of their love making, dull echoes through the walls, or the rhythmic thumping of the headboard. He would toss and turn on the couch, trying to block out the sound.

He dropped in to see Cathy Barrett at the supermarket and arranged an afternoon date together at the pictures, it was a harmless enough request. Mrs Barrett was looking on, and out of the corner of his eye he could see her nod to Cathy with approval. After all, not a lot can happen in a picture theatre for the afternoon matinee of *The Blues Brothers.* He assured Mrs Barrett of that It was a musical comedy, it would be fun and full of funky music and zany appeal, at least that's what the reviews said. Cathy would be going with her mother's blessing, but it wasn't the picture theatre where he was taking her.

Chapter 16

It was the Sunday afternoon session at the Nerimbah Hotel, and the tables in the beer garden were packed with local bodies. Music belted out from a band inside at the bar, and the tin chairs of the beer garden were filled with local surfers, fishermen and female brown bodies in tank tops and shorts. Cathy sat next to Alex, sipping at a wine cooler, their thighs squashed hard against each other which was just fine by Alex. Beau and Janice sat opposite, just as cramped, but none of them seemed to mind, the view was worth it.

Earlier at the bar, Beau ran into Gordon Wallace, who steered them to a table at the front of the beer garden to meet his cousin Andy and wife Jill. A seat at their table that overlooked the ocean was too good to pass up. It was noisy, the floor was raw concrete and the furniture cheap and hard, but there was no doubting the view of the bay was spectacular.

After introductions and the obligatory salute with beers, Alex took a closer look at Gordon's cousins. Andy and Jill were both in their early thirties, brown, fit, with an air of knowledge and worldliness. The conversation ebbed and flowed around the weather, the football, and surfing.

'Andy's got a board factory,' Gordan remarked in between drawing a mouthful of beer. 'Shapes and glasses his own boards.'

'More like a shed', said Andy.

'Which ones?' asked Beau.

'Island Time Boards You know them?' replied Andy.

'I've seen a few of them, mostly swallow tails, two palm trees on the front.'

'That's them.'

'How long have you been making them?' Alex asked.

'About five years now. I got into it after I got home from Vietnam. I didn't want to live in Sydney anymore, so I came to

Queensland instead. Did a year shaping for some local boys on the Gold Coast, then started out on my own up here. I've got a shed out past North Nerimbah. Come and have a look sometime. I'm there most days, though when it feels a bit like a proper job... or it all goes to shit...I go on a research and development tour to try out some new shapes, mostly down at Angourie.' He chuckled and drew a long swig at his beer.

'What's Angourie?' Cathy asked.

'Not what!... where!' said Alex. 'Angourie is a headland down in northern New South Wales, in a National Park. Near Yamba.'

'I've heard of Yamba, never been there though,' said Cathy.

'Janice came from down that way, didn't you.' Beau offered. 'Well, her parents live near there anyway.'

Janice nodded. She didn't elaborate further but turned away to look back at the band playing inside.

Andy was enthusiastic. 'If you haven't been there, you've got to go. No one around, only a few locals. The ranger doesn't mind if you camp there, as long as you can't be seen from the carpark. You should take Cathy camping down there.' He nodded at Alex. 'She'd love it. Great surf off the point. Gets a bit sharky around dusk. Gordan was with me when that Noah popped up and scared the crap out of us, Jill was throwing a fit from the carpark.'

'God yeh. Shit it was big,' murmured Gordan.

Cathy's eyes were wide.

'That's not helping.' Offered Alex, who in his mind was already packing the tent with only one sleeping bag for he and Cathy.

'You've been there haven't you Beau?' Gordon asked.

'I was there last year with a couple of mates, Reggie Bishop and Roy Conlan. We took the boards. Good waves, we were the only ones out'.

'Was that Roy Conlan, the Yank? Big bloke, dark hair, always wears sunglasses. I didn't think he was into surfing!' said Gordon.

'So, you do know him. He doesn't surf, doesn't even like the water. Roy had business in Yamba, so we left him there and Reg and I went on to Angourie,' explained Beau.

'That would be right. From what I know, he's into other stuff.' Gordon sniggered.

'What do mean by that?' snapped Beau.

'Look, I haven't met him, I only know about him from what people say.'

> 'And what's that Gordon?' Beau stared directly at Gordon, daring him to go on.
>
> 'American bloke, he was in Vietnam they say, stayed on here after the war...bit dodgy, you don't want to cross him they reckon.' Gordon replied.

'Who reckons that?' Beau challenged.

'Just saying!' Gordan backed away.

'Who's this Conlan?' Andy butted in.

'You wouldn't know him. He's a bad bastard, that's all I've heard.' said Gordan, ignoring Beau and staring directly at his cousin.'

'I knew of a Conlan in Vietnam, had the same reputation. If it's the same one I'm thinking of, he was a bit of a phantom in our area...bit of a mystery man, big bloke, always in dark glasses... his name was Conlan too.' Andy remarked.

'Do you reckon it's the same bloke?' asked Beau.

'Don't know. Could be. I didn't know him, only heard about him. I was a Nasho in the 4th RAR. This bloke was with the Yanks, supposedly working intelligence in Phuoc Tuy Provence, same place as us.'

Jill interjected, 'They don't want to hear this Andy, it's all stuff in the past.'

'I want to hear this.' Interjected Alex.

'So do I,' said Janice. 'Go on Andy.'

Andy paused to collect his thoughts, then continued.

'A lot of this is only conjecture, rumour. A company from the 3rd RAR went into this village called Long Khanh, I was in the 4th, we were a blocking force with some American 1st Cav units to the east. Apparently, this guy from U.S Intelligence kept showing up at our HQ looking for prisoners. Anyway, the ones we had were a wretched lot, we mostly handed them over to the South Vietnamese army, but this yank wanted us to hand them over to him for interrogation. His name was Conlan. Word was he would interrogate them, then finish them off with a grenade stuck to them.' Andy shook his head in disgust. 'A lot of the Yanks were good blokes, but our CO said he wasn't one of them.'

'That's awful,' said Janice.

Andy's voice switched to a light-hearted banter.

'I don't know if he was the same bloke you're talking about...probably not. But todays a good day, look at it, the suns out, we're having a beer, swells looking good, what's not to love? Who wants another?' He unravelled himself from the chair, and headed toward the bar before anyone could say no.

Alex hadn't met many Vietnam veterans before, and he had his own thoughts on the war. The moratorium marches were famous, and the returned soldiers like Gordon often shunned. Uni lectures kept referencing the war in all forms of media, particularly as studies in propaganda. Alex couldn't help but feel that somehow, people like Gordon had got a bum deal in the call up and on their return. He leaned across to Jill.

'Andy was a Nasho?'

'Yes'. She said. 'Conscripted in 1970. I didn't know him then. Did his tour. He said it was mostly boring stuff, but I don't believe him. He came home in 1972 full of plans. That's when I met him. But really, he was a bit fucked up then, if you know what I mean.

That's the first I've heard about that American bloke. Making boards is good for him, great business too.' She looked up as Andy approached, 'We're thinking of starting a surf school,' she said loudly, drawing Andy to her.

Andy plonked four beers onto the table and re-joined the conversation, picking up on Jill's pitch.

'Yeh, a Surf School. Think of it guys,' he said,' all these young kids wanting to learn to surf, needing surfboards. And I can make them, increase the volume a little, less sharp lines, rounded nose so they don't stab each other, it'll make it easier for them to learn on. Bring it into school as a sport. They've already started it in some schools down south.'

'How would you do that?' asked Cathy, 'They didn't do it at Nerimbah High.'

'Start with their afternoon sport, offer it as an elective, like golf or swimming, off site, at the beach. You know, Senior kids first, but the young kids will soon catch on and want to do it. Make up a curriculum of instruction, how competitions work, beach conservation, first aid, tourism, all that sort of thing.'

Beau sneered; he couldn't see the upside of the proposal.

'The surf will be full of grommets, kids crowding the break, getting in the way. I'll have to go to Angourie for a wave for myself.' He growled.

'Come on Beau, you're like all the blokes round here, you can't see the possibilities. Good business to be had from these young kids.' Andy raised his glass spread his arms to emphasise his cause. 'Maybe even get international students coming here to learn. Here's to kids crowding the break...on my boards'. Andy joked and saluted with his beer held high.

Jill leaned across and whispered to Alex.

'Tell your friend not to mention that Conlan bloke again.'

Alex nodded agreement, then raised his glass to Gordon.

'Good luck Mate,' he called.

Alex turned to Cathy, pressed his thigh further against hers and smiled. She smiled and pressed back. This movie date was definitely a success. He caught Beau's eye before he drank, Beau shook his head and drained his glass, he was probably thinking of the future of surfing, and he obviously didn't like it.

Chapter 17

The next night, Beau went fishing as had been arranged with Reggie. Alex surfed a glassy swell that afternoon with Beau. The wind had dropped from the southeast to nothing. The humid air settled on the water, flattening the left-over lumps, till the ocean was a mirror glass at sunset, with small, easy peeling waves in front of the rocks at north Nerimbah. He and Beau took wave after wave, they surfed until dark, and an easy walk home. Beau was skittish, he had the wrong board, not enough wax, his leg rope got tangled, the surf hadn't relaxed him at all. They shared a takeaway hot chook and chips from the fast-food joint around the corner. Beau ate silently and was wiping the grease off his fingers when they heard Reggies F100 pullup outside with the boat trailer clinking behind. Reggie hit the horn twice.

'Shit, he's early,' said Beau.

'Last few chips.' Alex held up the box to Beau, 'Want them?'

'Piss off, they're cold.'

'Didn't think you'd notice,' Alex laughed. He watched on as Beau retrieved an old Balmain football jersey from the bedroom. With a 'See you later,' he was out the door and trotting down the ramp toward Reggie.

Alex finished his beer while reading an article from a Surfing World about the Smirnoff Pro in Hawaii. He scooped up the leftover chicken bones and chip crumbs from the table in one hand while reading from the magazine in the other, he smiled to himself, men can do more than one thing at a time.

The door suddenly opened, and Janice walked in, startling him.

'Take away chicken for dinner again huh?' she remarked and dropped her bag on the kitchen table.

'I thought you were at work?'

'I was, but there was a mix up in the schedules and they're trying out a new girl. So, a night off.' She flopped into the chair and reached for her cigarettes. Alex threw the magazine onto the couch and picked up his wet towel and boardies off the floor.

'Not staying?'

'No. I figured I'd sleep at home tonight; might check my mail in case anyone ever decides to employ an out of work film maker. As if that will happen!'

'Don't go yet.' She looked directly at Alex. 'Stay and have a ciggie with me, I've been meaning to ask you something. '

Alex immediately felt the humid night, the small of his back was sticky with sweat. She lit up her cigarette.

'When are you leaving?' she asked.

Alex was taken aback. He was confused at first, he thought she wanted she wanted him gone.

'I'm sorry, I didn't realise I've overstayed my welcome. I didn't think it was a problem. I'll give you and Beau some space and stay at my parents' place from now on'.

Janice froze for a moment, then exploded in laughter. 'No... No. I didn't mean that.' She leaned across the table and put a hand on his arm. 'I mean when are you going to Melbourne? You can't stay here on the coast waiting for it, you must go where the work is, Alex. You stay here much longer, and you'll never leave.'

Alex sighed and became aware of her cool touch.

'I haven't got a job yet, but probably February.' he replied. 'That's when all the media companies are preparing their scheduled filming for the year. Did you want me gone?'

She was coolly surveying him, no movement, something was bothering her.

'No, stay here as much as you like, it's a nice distraction,' she said.

She sat back and was quiet for a minute. Alex drew on his cigarette, letting the smoke slowly exhale. He wasn't going to initiate the next move; it was up to Janice.

'You've known Beau a long time, haven't you?' She already knew the answer to that, so it was an opening that Alex wasn't expected to respond to. In chess, this was like pushing a pawn forward one space at the start, no threat in the move, no idea where it might lead, yet.

'Yeh. We grew up together, you know that.' A simple countermove, guarded, it meant nothing.

'Was he always like this?' A second pawn had been thrust forward. More definite in the approach.

'Like what?' Alex countered. Giving nothing away.

'Has he changed at all for you?'

Alex knew exactly what she was talking about. He leaned back; this could get interesting. The Beau that Alex had known was freewheeling, full of abandonment, carefree, smiling all the time and floating around the tensions of everyday life in an aimless pleasure-seeking wander. But of late, he smiled less. He was surly at times, and short in temper, demanding. He clashed with Janice often. It was something he hadn't expected of Beau. But Alex had said nothing of this to Janice.

'Nope. Still the same Beau. Bit fatter maybe.'

Janice was silent as she drew down on her smoke and stubbed it out fiercely in the ashtray.

'Bullshit!' she spat. 'That's bullshit Alex, and you know it.' The queen had found a way between the two pawns and now fronted the attack on the open board. She was expecting a response. Alex was not yet ready to commit.

'What do you mean?'

'You know what I mean Alex. Some days he's great, other days, he's lost it. He snaps at me, big mood swings, doesn't tell me where he's going, does fuck all around the house. I didn't sign up for that.'

Alex nodded slowly in agreement but said nothing.

'When you came home, he was happy for a bit. We were having a good time together, all of us. But the last two weeks...I don't know...like today. This morning, he woke up shitty and had a go at me over the dishes. He's going fishing with Reggie tonight, he's had all day to do the dishes if he felt that way, and he gives me grief about it. He's always edgy when he's going fishing with Reggie. When he gets back, he's in and out the car, slams doors, I can't say anything about Reggie or fishing, or what he does, or I'm the world's worst.' She was running over her words and pushing toward the inevitable conclusion.

'Reggie.' She shook her head.' Fucking Reggie and his mate Conlon. I know what they do, and I don't like Beau when he's around them. And that Conlan, I don't trust him. There's something about him. Am I right Alex. Tell me I'm right.'

> Alex finally relented and pushed his all-knowing bishop out on to the board.

> 'You're right. He isn't the same. But then neither am I....'

'Is he in trouble?'

'Not that I know of. I would have thought you would know if he was.'

'It's not the same anymore, we don't share everything except a bed anymore. I think he has secrets he keeps to himself. You'd tell me if he did, wouldn't you?' she pleaded.

'He's my friend, you both are. I'm not playing favourites here.'

'I know he's your friend. I just wanted someone to talk to, that's all.' She stood up and moved toward the kitchen 'You're good to have around Alex, you're smart, you're good for us both... you'd tell me if he was in trouble.' She stopped and leaned into Alex and kissed him on the cheek. Alex turned his face to hers, and she kissed him again, but this time on the lips. She broke it off and stood up, placing her hand on his shoulder, preventing him from rising. There was no sense of betrayal. It was a simple kiss, and it would go no further, they both knew it. But a kiss can change everything.

Janice continued into the kitchen, fussing at putting the jug on with her back to him. Alex gathered up his things and went to the door. As he opened it to leave, she turned and faced him.

'Sorry Alex. That wasn't fair, just don't get in too deep.'

Alex knew what she meant; it wasn't her she was talking about, it was Beau, and Reggie, and Conlon. He had been wondering the same thing himself. It was hard to hear it said, hard for him to admit what he had been thinking himself, that Beau had been leading him down a path that had not been of his own choosing.

'I hear things at the pub.' She went on.

'What do you mean?' Alex paused at the door.

'I mean, the police are getting interested. Stevo was stopped the other day, and his car was searched.'

'I've seen his car, I wouldn't want to have to search it,' Alex interrupted.

Janice chuckled, then continued.

'But seriously, they didn't find anything. Cooper got him for a busted taillight, that's all. But Steve thought there was more to it than that. Cooper kept asking about Beau. If he'd seen him recently, if Beau had been to his place or been out fishing with Reggie. Why would he ask that?'

'I don't know. Who's Cooper?' asked Alex.

'Senior Sergeant Cooper. He's been transferred into the Dunoonan Drug Squad. But if he's sniffing around, then it won't be long before he's on to Beau. That's what I'm afraid of. I'm scared that Beau is in this too far and it's Reggie that's doing it. You're his friend, can you do something?'

'I thought you didn't know what Beau did.'

'Don't be stupid. Nothing easier than drugs. Beau's always looking for an easy way to make money. I've always known, but lately its changed. I think he's in deeper than he wants to be, I think he's scared of them, especially Conlan, and he takes it out on me.'

'Beau is his own man, Janice, nothing much I can do.' It was a lame response, a coward's reassurance, and Alex knew it.

'That's not much help Alex.' Her sarcasm arced across the gap between them.

'I don't know what you want from me Janice', he retorted, the tension flaring. Perhaps the kiss was an empty promise. It was childish, he knew. Alex stepped out on to the verandah, into the dark, feeling shitty at her, at what she was asking of him. Perhaps he was just as shitty with himself, knowing what he should do but not owning up to it. Deep down, he feared Conlan too. He was halfway down the ramp when she appeared in the doorway the light silhouetting her. He couldn't see her face, but it didn't matter, he was sulking and done with talking with her for the night.

'Alex, wait!' she pleaded. 'You know Beau. Don't let him do something stupid. He listens to you. He always said you were the smart one. No street smarts and not much good with the chicks, but smart enough to stay out of trouble.'

Alex relented,' Not much good with the chicks huh?'

'His words...not mine.' She closed the door and let Alex find his way to the car in the dark, more confused than ever.

Chapter 18

Alex pulled up to the shack the next morning to pick up his board. Reggies Ford F 100 was parked in the driveway. As soon as he turned the engine off, he could hear Reggies' berating voice carrying clearly across the front lawn from the verandah.

'Don't give me that, you lost a quarter of our catch last night. You bumbled the hook and were too slow getting it all in. Conlan was furious when I told him.'

'You didn't have to tell him,' Beau complained.

'Of course I did, it's our business, and he's half shares in the boat. It's a big business and we must turn over stock to make it pay.'

'I'll make it up to you next time.'

'How are going to do that? Even if you worked for nothing for me for the next two years you couldn't pay back what we lost last night. And what about our customers, we can't supply the stock we've promised, they lose business, we lose money, it's a loss all round. Do you want Conlan and me to cover the losses from last night because you can't do your job?'

'It wasn't not my fault you kept backing over them, the prop chopped them to pieces, I couldn't bring it all in.'

'Bullshit. It's not the first time you've stuffed up Beau, you'd be lucky If I take you fishing again.'

Beau bristled, and stood up on the balls of his feet, clenching his fists. 'I told you; I'm not taking the blame for losing the stuff.'

'Well, someone will. It can't happen again Beau. Your neck is on the line.'

'So is yours Reggie,' snarled Beau.

'That might be so, but remember this, I won't be the one who they come after. Business is like that Beau; you need to understand that. In business there is a hierarchy of blame when things go wrong, it always stops at the bottom, and you are on the bottom, and you're on your own.' He glanced over his shoulder and saw Alex at the base of the ramp. 'You'd know that wouldn't you Alex?' He turned back to face Beau. 'You would have learned that at that University,' he called over his shoulder.

'I didn't study Business,' said Alex.

'You should have,' he sneered,' then you could teach Beau here a few things about how the business world works. What did you learn then?'

'Mateship!'

'Shit,' scoffed Reggie, he turned to face Alex, a smirk forming at the corner of his mouth. 'You're too smart for your own good, you know that?'

'I was told that last night.' said Alex.

'Maybe you should come and work for me.'

'No chance of that.'

Reggie rubbed his face and turned back to Beau, a decision had been reached, a warning given, the confrontation with Beau was over.

'Beau, I like you, I really do, but we can't keep losing product, or else we'll begin to think something more is going on.'

'Yeh, I get it,' said Beau.

'Do you? Is something going on we don't know about?'

'No!' said Beau. 'Nothing's going on.'

'Well, we can't have any more mistakes. Understand?'

Beau nodded his head.

'I didn't hear you!' demanded Reggie.

'Nothing going on Reggie.'

'I'll pass that on to Conlan, he'll be pleased to know. You better think about how you're going to make up for your mistakes.'

Reggie turned and pushed past Alex, before marching across the lawn and driving away.

Alex stood looking up at Beau. 'What was that about? he asked.

'You don't want to know.'

'I caught enough of it to know that he was threatening you just then.'

'Nah. He was just pissed off. He wouldn't do that. We go back too far. He was just a bit upset over losing some of the packages the other night.'

'You mean the fish.'

'Yeh, the fish... the product...the packages. Janice still thinks we go fishing for real fish.'

'I wouldn't be so sure of that.'

'Nah, she doesn't know we're into large scale supply and distribution now, sounds like fish, doesn't it?' Beau boasted. 'She still thinks I just deal a few bags of dope.'

'By we, you mean you, and Reggie and Conlan... one of them an angry red headed prick and the other a murdering Yank.'

'Don't be like that, we're making some serious money.'

'Really? It doesn't seem to look like it from here. Nice car, but that's about all I can see. Janice is still working all week, and the shack is not exactly the Ritz, is it!'

'What do you know Alex? You don't know the half of it. There's lots of things behind the scenes you don't see. I got it figured out. Plenty is going my way in the future.'

'The way Reggie talks, you may not have much of a future. He doesn't trust you.'

'Bugger off Alex, I work with who I want.'

Beau always fancied that he was good at manipulating events to swing his way, but that was mostly with girls, his friends, lifts to the pub and the like. But Reggie and Conlan were different beasts, and Alex knew it, he just couldn't seem to get Beau to see it too.

'Mate, you've got to be careful You can't trust that bloke. He turned on you quickly.' Alex implored.

Beau snapped. 'I know what I'm doing. I get badgered enough from Janice as it is, I don't need you too.'

'Fair enough...just wanted to say...'

'Just wanted to say what? What are you doing here anyway?' Beau interrupted.

'Just picking up my board. Want to come for a surf?'

'Nope. Had enough of this today. I need a smoke, and you're not invited.' He turned his back on Alex and marched inside, slamming the door behind him.

'I'll see you round then Beau.' Alex called out in a mock salute. He turned away, troubled by the turn of events. Last night Janice had reached out to him for help, and he tried to warn Beau that he might be in too deep, but that didn't end well. It wasn't like Beau to disregard him so quickly. Under it all, he could cope with Beau's mood swings, and even Reggie's veiled threats, but on the few occasions he had been around Conlan, he knew deep down, he was scared of him.

Alex didn't see Beau and Janice in the week leading up to Christmas, preferring to give them a wide berth while they sorted out their own lives. He was too preoccupied with bitumen paving, he finished each day exhausted, preferring the comfort and cool of his parents' house, to the angst he felt from Beau at the shack. The summer days were scorching, shovelling hot bitumen to fill contracts for driveways and tennis courts before the onrush of the holidays.

Christmas came and went in a blur. All thoughts of film jobs in Melbourne had vanished. He didn't even get reject letters in the mail anymore which depressed him to no end. He had no Plan B for the future, and that brought about its own levels of stress. Alex tried to get in a surf with Beau a couple of times, but Beau found excuses to avoid him. Shops and eateries like Barrett's supermarket ramped up extended hours during the festive holiday season, and liaisons with Cathy were few and far between. Their relationship hadn't progressed very far, but Alex hoped to turn that around on New Year's Eve.

Chapter 19

There were not many choices for the New Year's Eve celebrations, he could either bounce from one party to the next or attempt some sort of special occasion at one of the few restaurants on offer. Alex chose the latter and was lucky enough to get a cancellation at a small restaurant next to the ice cream shop on the Esplanade. This time, Alex was taking Cathy to the place he said he was... and more. The apron strings were slowly being loosened.

The restaurant was decked out as a Caribbean smuggler's hideaway, where fishing nets were draped over barrels and melted candles in squat wine bottles cast a dull, orange glow over the intimate tables. It was perfect. Alex tried as best he could to appear comfortable and in control as he led Cathy through the menu.

For her part, Cathy assumed an air of sophistication that was a little at odds with her natural charm, and while she found the cocktails too strong, it didn't dampen her appetite for them. It was that kind of night, they were charged with an air of anticipation, not wanting to leave after the meal, but not quite sure how best to prolong it. It didn't matter in the end.

Inevitably, they finished at the Nerimbah Beach Hotel for the final hours of 1980, and all pretence of sophistication was lost under an avalanche of noise and drunken revellry. Janice arranged to meet up with them to see in the New Year. She said that she had missed seeing Alex and as an afterthought, added that so did Beau.

The jostle of bodies around them in the beer garden forced Alex to grasp Cathy around the waist and press her close. Janice stood directly in front of them both, trying to keep her drink from spilling as patrons bumped and pushed past her. There was no sign of Beau.

'It's more crowded than last year,' Janice yelled above the noise. 'Were you here then Cathy?'

'No. I didn't come here last year.'

'They probably wouldn't have let you in anyway,' said Janice.

'I love your dress', Cathy replied. 'It's difficult to wear white to a place like this if you don't have a steady hand.' Her eyes dropped to the drink stains on the front of Janice's dress. Touché.

'Where is Beau?' Alex intervened.

'Over talking in the corner. It's not as noisy over there.' Janice jerked her thumb over her shoulder in Beau's direction. Alex led Cathy by the hand through the crowd, following Janice as she weaved between revellers. Beau was in deep discussion with Mitch and Ergo.

Mitch Ferguson was about the same size and shape as Beau, while Ergo was just Ergo, Alex couldn't remember his real name. He was thinner, smaller and wired, swaying from foot to foot like a dancing cobra, his eyes locked on Beau. He knew both of them were Beau's customers, they lived above a surfboard repair shop in North Nerimbah, an old two-story weatherboard relic from the 1940's, badly in need of a paint, or a knock down. He hadn't had much to do with them, but occasionally saw Mitch in the surf, he was amiable enough. Tonight though, the conversation between the three was far from friendly.

'Alex, you're here.' Beau observed,' Help me out Buddy. Last Friday we dropped around with the gear didn't we, but you weren't home Mitch. I couldn't leave it at the front door, could I? And there were other customers willing to pay, and they were home, so they got it.'

'But we were there.' complained Mitch. 'Now we got nothing for the New Year. We've lost a lot of money, and it's your fault. You didn't deliver.'

'I did, I told you that.' He turned to Alex. 'You saw me go up the stairs and knock at the front door, didn't you!'

Alex was nowhere near Beau that day; he hadn't seen him for nearly two weeks. He looked at Beau and knew he was lying to them, but he said nothing.

'Doesn't look like that to me,' said Mitch. 'You never showed. Does Reggie know you never delivered?'

'Come on Mitch don't be like that. Alex, you watched me go up. I came back down and said they weren't home, didn't I Alex. You know the rules Mitch'. His eyes never left Mitch or Ergo.

Cathy tugged at his arm signalling for Alex to leave with her. He desperately wanted to walk away with Cathy right now, slide his arms around her waist and nestle in close to the rhythm of the music. He wanted to see in the New Year with the promise of life and love ahead. He wanted to kiss her and smell the nape of her neck, revel in happiness, a world away from the one he'd just stepped into. Then he looked at Beau and knew there was only one answer he could give.

'Yeh. You did Beau. I was there. You guys mustn't have been home.' He lied.

'Bullshit!' sneered Ergo, he poked Alex in the chest with his finger. 'You'd say anything, you're his mate.'

'Don't touch me.' Alex pushed Ego's hand away.

'You're a deadshit Ergo,' said Beau, raising his fist at him, 'Fuck off!'.

Mitch knocked Beau's beer from his hand while Ergo launched himself at Alex with flailing arms. Alex fell awkwardly under the onslaught, lurching backwards and stumbling against Cathy, bringing them both down in a heap. He had no answer to Ergo's pummelling that connected with them both indiscriminately. He struggled to regain his feet, but he was easily knocked back to the ground before Janice swung a chair into Ergo's back. He was aware of a stand-up fist fight between Beau and Mitch, scattering tables and drinks in all directions. His own ribs hurt, but it was Cathy's crying that got his attention the most. He scrambled to his feet and dived at Ergo, sinking his fist into Ergo's abdomen. And then the bouncers arrived.

The car was quiet as Janice drove the four of them home. In the back seat Alex tried to hold Cathy's hand but she pulled away. Her clothes were dirty from the concrete floor, and she nursed a darkening bruise on her arm. They stopped outside the Barrett's house on Jurmar Street. It wasn't yet midnight, and the lights were still on inside. Alex tried to kiss Cathy, but she pulled back, opened the door and walked up the drive, her head hung down. There would be much explaining to do when she got inside. 1981 had started with a different connection than what they bargained for.

Alex slept the night on the Beach Shack couch. In the morning, Beau sat with him on the verandah drinking coffee as if nothing different had transpired for the last two weeks. All was forgiven for coming to Beau's aid at the pub the night before. But Alex was still keenly aware that he got into a fight because of the lie he had told to save Beau's arse.

Ergo had been strung out and itching for a fight, and Beau goaded him into it. Most of Ergo's punches had failed to connect, but those that had were showing a bruise. It hurt when he bent down. He had landed a few hits of his own, but he knew he had been largely ineffectual in protecting himself and Cathy under that onslaught. Lucky Janice used the chair. He shouldn't have got involved in the first place, certainly not with Cathy in tow.

He swallowed his pride and went inside and rang her on the wall phone to see how she was.

'My arm hurts, and my clothes are ruined.' She answered flatly.' I've never been in a fight.'

'I'm sorry about that. How were your parents when you got in?'

'My mother is furious. I wasn't supposed to be at the pub. I tried to explain that what happened was an accident, but she won't hear me. I've been grounded. I'll be working at the supermarket for the rest of the month but not allowed to go out after work.'

'But you're old enough to make your own decisions, lead your own life.' Alex asserted, ignorant of how he sounded. He had choices, Cathy didn't. 'She can't hold you back. If you want to go out, you should go out. You're nearly 18. She can't stop you from going out with me.'

Cathy was quiet and took a moment before she replied. 'It's not just Mum', she said. 'I really like you Alex, but I don't know if I want to be a part of the world you are in. I don't like fights Alex; I don't like drugs. What happened at the hotel isn't what I want in my life.'

'I said I was sorry about last night; it won't happen again.'

'I'm not so sure Alex. You and your friends live in another world. but it's not my world.'

'But I want to see you again. We had a good time together,' he implored.

'Yes. We did. And I loved it, but then we ended up in a fight. I must have some say in where I want to be, and what I want to do.'

'The hotel was good though, until that happened.'

'You mean the fight your friends started.'

'But you can't just walk away from your friends if they're in trouble,' he protested.

'You can Alex. Last night you just chose not to.'

'I said I'm sorry.' whined Alex, as if that would make up for it.

'So am I Alex.' The phone was silent for a heartbeat and then a sigh as she continued. 'I don't know if I want to go out with you again.'

'Don't be like that. Can I make it up to you? What about next week?' Alex was struggling and he knew it, unsure of how to proceed. 'The Divinyls are on at the Playroom next Wednesday night. Sydney band. Female lead singer. Just you and me, no one else.'

'I'll have to think about that.' She relented. 'I'm grounded, remember. I'd have to get past Mum first. After last night, she doesn't trust you anymore, or me for that matter. Ring me on Tuesday Alex, I won't promise anything.' She closed the connection.

Alex hung up the receiver. Not sure if they still had a future.

'And you call that an apology?' Janice exclaimed, leaning against the bedroom door, shaking her head.

Alex shrugged his shoulders, as if there was nothing more he could do.

'A girl like that...Cathy... and that's the best you can come up with? Offer to take her to another pub band to make up for it? She didn't deserve that last night, and you can't even say sorry properly.'

Alex had no answer.

'What are you becoming? You and Beau are a right pair of arseholes.' She flicked away from the doorway and headed for the kitchen bench.

'Don't bring me into it,' Beau protested from the verandah.

'You are in it, the both of you,' She yelled in a fit of anger.' Whatever you're up to Beau, its fucking not right. Tell me what's going on! And you Alex. I asked you to look out for him. Fat lot of good you are.'

'What's up with you today? Beau complained.

'Look at yourselves for that answer!' She grabbed a water bottle off the bench and marched back into the bedroom, slamming the door behind her. Beau turned back to reading his surf magazine.

'Gee, Thanks' mumbled Alex as he shuffled out, bemused with the way events had turned against him. Now he definitely was lost.

Chapter 20

Alex was still mulling over that phone call two days later. He could never have handled a phone call like that when he was Cathy's age, and Janice had admonished him for how he had treated her. Both she and Janice had swept him aside, and it had all started with Beau's lies. He wondered what he could have done differently when the Police pulled him over down Wurung Avenue, not far from the Beach Shack.

There was a single cursory wail of the siren to catch his attention. He looked in the rear-view mirror to see the Police car and a finger pointing to the curb. He turned the engine off and wound down his window. There were two officers in the car, but it was the young one who got out of the driver's side and walked up to Alex. He couldn't see the other cop, but by the size and stillness of his frame, he could tell he was the older of the two. Alex didn't know if this was good or bad, it went through his mind that the older cops, the ones who had been around the coast a while were more likely to kick you up the arse and send you on your way for your indiscretions, that was the urban myth anyway, and he was about to find out if it was true.

'Morning.' A young constable leered down at him. 'You have your licence on you?' There was no 'Please' in his voice.

Alex scrambled around for his wallet and presented him with the card. He scrutinized it closely.

'You Alex Holmes?'

'Yep. That's me.'

He verified the address, and said, 'Just wait here a minute.'

Alex watched him in the rear-view mirror as he walked back to the patrol car, and leaned in the window, reporting to his partner. He knew he had nothing to worry about, he hadn't done anything wrong. The constable returned.

'You realise, you failed to indicate at the last intersection.'

'No, I did. I know I did.'

'I said, you failed to indicate, we were behind you. There was no indicator. Is this car roadworthy? Show me that your blinkers work.'

Alex turned them on, they responded with a satisfactory regular click and flash on the dashboard.

'Can't see anything,' the policeman called from the back of the Peugeot.

'They have to be on.' Alex smarted.

'Step out of the car sir and see for yourself.'

Just as Alex got there, the constable said 'Oh, now I see them. Not very bright, are they. The covers are dirty! You better get them cleaned.'

'Well, they work,' said Alex,' I told you.'

'Would you mind opening up the boot while you are here.' It was a command, not a request. For the next few minutes, the constable searched through Alex's Peugeot. As he searched, he asked inane questions about what Alex had in each of the compartments. He had nothing to worry about from him; it was his partner that worried Alex. The whole time the other policeman sat immobile in the police car behind, watching, not moving. Somehow this was more menacing than the car search.

The constable finished his search with a warning for Alex to get his taillights checked. As Alex went to get back behind the wheel, the constable called out to him.

'Oi, your licence.' He held it out for Alex to collect. 'Where were you going by the way?' he asked.

'To a mate's place.'

'Where's that?'

'Just round the corner. I was nearly there when you pulled me over.'

The constable walked back to his own car, his voice floating across the gap as he reported to his senior partner, 'He's going to the Beaumont house.' Then the engine started, and he heard no more.

Alex waited for them to go first. As the police car swept past, Alex caught a glimpse of Sergeant stripes on a blue sleeve and a face with a ruddy complexion hunkered down under a police cap. The Senior stared straight ahead.

Alex waited till they were well and truly gone before he pulled away from the kerb and drove on to Beau's place.

'Jesus Beau, they knew I was coming here,' he said angrily as he marched up the ramp to the verandah.

'Who did?'

'The cops!' Alex went on to explain how he had been pulled over and searched, emphasising the constables' parting comment to his partner. 'And they did the same to Stevo just before Xmas,' he said. 'What's going on?'

'Nothing', said Beau, he looked furtively away. 'Nothing. Probably just coincidence. Maybe they need their numbers up, new cops in town. Shit, Look who's here now!'

Reggie's Ford F100 pulled into the driveway, Roy Conlan was in the passenger seat. Reggie strolled across the grass till he reached the Peugeot, leaned against the bonnet and crossed his arms looking up at the boys on the verandah.

'Morning Beau, how are you going? Happy New Year by the way.'

'Reg', acknowledged Beau. 'You want to come up?'

'Sure' he replied. He turned back to the car and gestured to Conlan.

Reggie ambled up the ramp, while Conlan marched across the grass. They both made it to the verandah at the same time. At the top of the ramp all four men shuffled around in the small space before settling against the railings.

'Morning Alex', Reggie acknowledged him.

'Morning boys.' Conlan drawled in his laconic American accent. The amber sunglasses never moved, but his eyes took in the verandah and the open door to the kitchen and lounge inside.

Beau offered them the seats in the sun. In another hour, it would be too hot to stay there, but maybe this wasn't just a social visit. Beau brought out a third seat, while Alex hopped up on the side rail, distancing himself from them. He didn't like Conlan, there was a controlled menace about him, and he gave nothing away. After a few desultory remarks about the surf and weather, which Conlan didn't engage in. Reggie turned to the business at hand.

'New Year was hectic heh? Heard you had a fight at the pub?'

'It was nothing. Some blokes got a bit out of hand, you know. Usual stuff, couple of guys looking for a scrap and couldn't wait till after New Year, they had to begin at the pub, and I was it. But no harm done.' Beau explained.

'Who was it?' asked Reggie.

'Mitch...and Ergo.'

'It was Mitch and Ergo started that, did they?' probed Conlan.

'Yeh. Mitch was all fired up over something.' Beau subconsciously stroked the side of his cheek where Mitch's first punch had connected. Alex looked down at his knuckles to see the scabs of broken skin healing, he liked to think he gave as good as he got.

'Why was he fired up?' Conlan queried. He didn't look at Beau, pretending to gaze with interest at the block of units across the road., but the question was arrowed directly at Beau.

'I don't know. Ergo was trying to make a grab at the girls. He was high as a kite. Wouldn't take no for an answer.'

'I heard he was upset over a business transaction.' Conlan ventured.

'No, not at all, they were just being a pricks, especially Ergo. Mitch is all right most of the time.'

Alex stayed quiet. He knew what had transpired and he wasn't giving anything away. He wasn't getting in on this at all.

'Mitch says he didn't get supplied this month, and he blames you,' explained Reggie.

'Well, he doesn't know what he's talking about. Mitch wouldn't know what day of the week it was let alone how much he was due.'

'Are you sure about this, cos he says otherwise. He says he paid you, but you didn't deliver,' said Reggie. Alex didn't move but his eyes shifted to Beau. This was a new twist to the story.

Beau looked across at both Reggie and Conlan. 'I didn't deliver because he wasn't home... I don't know anything about the money.' Gone was the amicability. There was a stillness on the verandah.

'Mitch says he paid way above the going rate last time, and you would fix him up for that by getting him an extra delivery when the new batch came in, only you never did.'

'What?' Beau said indignantly, 'Does he think we're going to give him a delivery for nothing? Not even for a cut price. Mitch has got his head up his arse. I deliver the goods; I pick up the cash for you and take my cut like I always do. They didn't get their delivery last week because they weren't home. Alex was there; he'll back me up.' Conlan waved dismissively at Alex as Beau continued. 'They were probably so off their faces that they couldn't answer the door. Mitch knows the rules, if you are not there for the delivery, I can sell it on to another customer, so I took off and sold it to that mad prick Jonas Tanoa, Villi's younger brother.'

'Mitch doesn't see it that way. He thinks he's been ripped off, and we can't have our regulars thinking they've been ripped off, they create trouble, they might go looking elsewhere for suppliers. Did he pay more than the going rate last time?'

'Of course not. And you still got the money, didn't you? The right amount.'

'Reggie. Did we get the right amount from Beau?' asked Conlan.

'We did,' he replied.

'You're not ripping off our customers are you, Beau?'

'No!' said Beau flatly.

'You're not ripping us off, are you?' questioned Reggie.

'I said No!'

All three stood silent, resolute in their understanding of the situation. Then Conlan turned to Reggie and nodded.

'Ok. I think we're done here...for the moment.' He turned back to Beau and spoke. 'We run a good operation here Beau, I wouldn't want to see it disrupted by misunderstandings with our customers, or conflicts that attract the attention of the Police. That's when it all goes to shit and accidents happen. And we don't want that.'

'We just wanted to make sure,' said Reggie. 'We are sure aren't we Roy?'

'I think so,' said Roy.' What about you Beau? Are you sure?' Last chance!'

'Last chance for what?' exclaimed Beau.

'To tell me if I'm wrong!' growled Conlan.

The verandah was silent. The sound of surf breaking in the distance enveloped them but couldn't ease the tension in the air. No-one moved.

Reggie cut in. 'Tell you what, I'll talk to Mitch, I'll straighten it out with him. But this is on you. I shouldn't have to do this, it's your mess.'

'I didn't start it, but thanks Reggie.' Beau breathed out, 'I don't want to see them right now. Those arseholes better steer clear of me for a while.'

'Reggie's doing you a favour Beau. Just remember who you work for,' reiterated Conlan.

Alex knew he was witness to a well-rehearsed play that had been acted out before between Conlan and Reggie. It was choreographed to test their victim with questions that they already knew the answers to, hoping to trip them up in the exchange. He didn't know if Beau had passed the test, but he sure as hell knew Beau wasn't telling them the truth.

'I'm fishing this week. I'll need you as the deckhand,' said Reggie.

'No problem.' Beau replied tautly.

'Well, let's hope you don't make a mess of it like last time either. You've been running up a few IOUs lately. But we've been over that already, haven't we Beau.' Reggie's voice dripped with condescension, as if talking to a child. Alex could see Beau beginning to bristle again, but Reggie quickly changed tack.

'It's been a big New Year period, and there is fresh product on offer,' Reggie said. 'We're going out Thursday again, and I don't want any problems. Are you OK with that?'

'I'll be here,' replied Beau.

'Good ...good,' he said placatingly. 'Have you figured out a way to make up for the other bungle yet?'

'Still working on it,' said Beau.

'Work harder,' snapped Conlan.

'We'll be off then. Other business awaits.' Reggie drawled at Beau and Alex and made to rise from the chair.

'I'll get myself some water before I go,' said Conlan.

Beau was brisk in his gesture. 'Through the door to the left.'

Conlan went inside, shutting the front door behind him.

The three men left on the verandah stood looking at each other in silence. If the purpose of Reggies visit was to rattle Beau's cage, then he had succeeded. With Conlan inside, Beau reached out to Reggie.

'What's going on Reg?'

'Oh, we're just being careful. Been some funny things happening lately.' As if on cue a police car appeared at the intersection, then drove down the road past the house. All three followed it with their eyes. It slowed imperceptibly as it drew abreast of the verandah, then continued past at the same speed as before.

'Are those the cops that got you earlier?' Beau asked Alex. He turned to Reggie and explained further, 'Alex got pulled over and questioned this morning for nothing. Same as with Stevo and John Wallace last month.'

'Was that Cooper? The sergeant, who pulled you over?' asked Reggie.

'I don't know who Sergeant Cooper is.'

'That was Cooper in the car just now, he's got Sargent stripes on his sleeve.' Reggies voice was thick with sarcasm as he pointed after the car. 'I could see him in the passenger seat. I'd know that fat prick anywhere. He's starting to be a problem.'

Now Alex was spooked, two cop cars in the same morning, the same cops. He jumped down from the rail, opened the door and went inside. Conlan was just appearing from Beau's bedroom, definitely not from the kitchen, and he hesitated when he saw Alex, he clearly hadn't expected to be caught in the wrong place.

'Find the kitchen OK?' Alex asked, his eyes darting to the left where the dishes were stacked neatly next to the sink.

'Yeh, I did.' Conlan replied. He stopped in front of Alex. 'You know Alex, not everyone's cut out to be a fisherman, for moving product. I don't know if Beau has still got it. Maybe we need some new blood in the organization. You can make good money. We look after our own, maybe your little girlfriend in the supermarket won't get hurt next time. Think about it.' He pushed past Alex, and out to the verandah.

As Conlan passed Beau, he slapped him on the shoulder and remarked, 'No more tangled lines hey Beau! Don't want any accidents, do we!' He strode down the ramp without another word.

Reggie hopped up from his chair and pointed his finger at Beau, 'See you Thursday', and followed Conlan out to the car.

Alex stood next to Beau, quietly taking stock of the situation. He closed his eyes and wondered how deep he was in. The head of a crime gang no longer trusts his drug dealing best friend, threatened him, searched his house and told them they are all being watched. If he didn't know any better, the Police had just searched his car and had now seen him in the company of suspected dealers at a house they knew he would be visiting, before he even got there. Alex thought his life was in control, that he could deal with disruption and chaos, but what was happening around him was plumbing new depths. He couldn't help wondering where it was all going.

Chapter 21

It was after one in the morning and the Wednesday midweek band at the Pub had finished at twelve. Chrissy Amphlett was everything they had hoped she would be - a big vocal performer. Cathy loved it, she was flushed and chatting with excitement. Alex had managed to make up for the New Year's Eve indiscretion. They waited around for Janice to finish at the bar before heading for home together.

As Beau wrestled with the door key, Alex waited calmly on the verandah, pulling Cathy in close to him. The door swung open Beau sucked in a sharp breath...

'What the...we've been done over. Someone's robbed the place,' he exclaimed. All four of them crowded in the doorway as Beau switched on the living room light.

The couch was upended, and Alex's few clothes he kept there were scattered across the mat. The stuffing had been pulled from the cushions and spread like snow across the floor. The TVs were face down; the back covers pulled off. Beau strode across and knelt in front of the remnants of his turntable, smashed beyond repair. His records were strewn around the floor in a pile; cassettes and speakers had been crushed under foot irreparably.

' Look what the bastards did. Look what they did to my records? They didn't have to smash my speakers,' he wailed.

Elsewhere, the kitchen cupboards were open and emptied out on the bench, the fridge door was left open. Janice strode past it and disappeared into the bedroom. Alex and Cathy slowly worked their way around the room, stepping over the debris, pushing and prodding as if that would reveal a clue to what had been done.

'Anything missing?' Alex asked.

'How do I know?' Beau snapped. 'Look at the mess. Bastards! Janice, where are you?'

'Bedroom,' she called. 'It's the same here.'

Alex went to the bedroom door; he was reluctant to enter further. The bed had been slashed open, the spring coils were showing, pillows destroyed, and clothing pulled from the cupboards and piled on the carpet. Alex stepped past the bedroom and leaned into the bathroom doorway, the same wreckage here, even the toilet cistern lid had been left broken on the floor.

'Shit.' Was all Alex could remark. 'Money, or anything like that missing?'

'I don't know.' said Beau.

Janice appeared at the bedroom door, 'As far as I can see, your stash is the only thing gone, that and a bit of cash from your draw.'

'If it was only a bag of dope, that's all right then. I can live with that,' said Beau

'Well, I can't. They went through all my things. My underwear, my clothes. Someone's been here going through all my personal things, and you can only think of your precious records and a bag of dope?'

'Not very professional crooks were they. Just kids most likely.' Alex offered.

Janice scoffed. 'And I thought you were smart, Alex.' She sneered, 'You don't slash mattresses looking for a bag of dope. There must be more than that.' She rounded on Beau, formidable in her anger.' What were they looking for Beau?'

'How would I know.' Angry in his reply. He was leaning against the kitchen table, his eyes darting toward the side door, looking anywhere but at Janice.

Alex waved his arms in the direction of the sink. 'Come on Cathy, we'll help them clean up, start with the kitchen.'

'I want to go home Alex'. Cathy stood rigid in the middle of the floor.

'Yeh, why don't we help with the kitchen first.'

'I want to go home now'. She repeated, calm, resolute.

Alex turned to Beau and Janice.

'Look, I'll be round in the morning, help you then. I'll just take Cathy home; she doesn't need to be part of this.' He ushered her out the door and down to his car.

They were both settled, clicked in their seat belts and Alex reaching for the ignition when Cathy said, 'Stop. I don't want to do this.'

'Do what?' Alex asked.

'Us... the fight at the pub, their house smashed up. What if we came home and they were still there? Another fight, or worse. My mother was right. There's always something bad going on around Beau. Around him ...and you and now me. I don't want to be a part of it any more Alex.' She didn't look at him as she spoke, her voice quivered. 'Please take me home.'

Alex had no response, was sick of saying sorry for how things turned out. He offered no apology for Beau, or himself. He turned the key, bringing the engine to life. Nothing more was said on the way to her parents' house. He had failed again. Girlfriends, job prospects, order from the chaos around him, nothing seemed to be working. Cathy said nothing when she closed the car door behind her. Alex drove slowly to his parents' house, lost in self-recrimination.

In the morning, Alex arrived while Janice was in the shower. No real attempt had been made to clean up. Beau was talking to Reggie on the wall phone.

'Heh Reggie, bad news mate' He waved at Alex as he came in the door, pointing at the kitchen chairs.

'What bad news.' Came Reggies voice over the receiver.

'We were robbed last night mate, when we were out.'

'What? Robbed? Do you know who did it?'

'Didn't see them. Everything smashed up, and...they took my drugs and the cash.'

Reggie started to clear his voice, 'What drugs? What cash?'

'That money I owed you, from the bungled last shipment, I've been working it up to pay you back, but some prick robbed us. I still had a deal going for Missy up the range, the last of the December shipment. I kept it here for her, but now it's gone too'.

'You're not making much sense Beau. What deal? You never told us about holding any back for someone called Missy. And you short changed Mitch, he could have had that!

'I told you I didn't shortchange him."

'Roy is going to be really pissed off now, you still owe us that money Beau. Shit, what a stuff up. You're supposed to bring the delivery money round to us straight away, not keep it till you feel like it, and this is why. Someone will roll you. You'll have to work it off again Beau. Starting tonight. Do you have any idea who did over your place? Was it Cooper?' Reggie suggested.

'Don't know. It could have been Cooper. He's been after me for ages. You were here when he drove past last week. I bet he was checking out my place.'

'Cooper. It figures, Crooked prick. We're going to have to do something about him one day soon. You better get your shit together Beau. Fishing tonight, we'll talk about it more then. Be home when I come.' The line clicked dead.

Beau hung up, raised his eyebrows at Alex and smiled, as if he had just landed a fish. Alex went to question him about the so-called money and drugs, but Beau raised his finger to his lips, urging silence. Alex couldn't see why Beau was so calm, the lies he told Reggie were piling up like the wreckage around him.

Most of that day was spent helping clean up the house, broken and torn goods dumped and replaced. Beau left briefly to get a new mattress and locks for the doors. They didn't want to tell the landlord, nor could they go to the Police about the break-in. Beau suspected it was Sergeant Cooper, discussions with his customers all pointed to Cooper being corrupt and trying to score drugs and cash for himself with his constant harassment and standover tactics. Janice was none the wiser for Beau's conversation with Reggie that morning, as far as she knew, only Beau's small personal stash of dope had been stolen. Beau impressed on him that Janice didn't need to know about the phone call or any missing money and Alex didn't give him any reason to think that he knew Beau had lied. But someone had it in for Beau, that was obvious.

Beau changed the locks, and by late afternoon, the house was back in some semblance of order. There was still more to do, but he retrieved his football jersey from the bedroom and prepared to go fishing. Alex finished packing up the last bag of rubbish at the door when Janice spoke up.

'I don't want to stay here by myself tonight, Beau.'

'I'm only going fishing; we'll be back before midnight.'

'I don't like what happened last night. What if they come back?'

'They won't'.

'How do you know? You don't, do you? You have no idea who has done this.'

Beau stepped up to face her and rubbed her arms in comfort. 'Look Jan, it'll be OK. Alex will stay here with you, won't you mate.'

Alex paused, then spoke up, 'Look, I was going to try and see Cathy tonight, maybe make amends, again.'

'Come on', Beau pleaded. 'I thought you said she was a lost cause.'

The truth of it was that Alex was looking for ways to ease back on involvement with the drug business and regain some control, visiting Cathy was just the excuse.

'Come on mate, just this once' Beau pleaded.

Janice countered, 'No! It's not up to Alex. You stay home with me. Fuck Reggie, he can go another time, I need you to be with me tonight.'

'I can't' Beau said. 'It's all arranged. Tonight, is fishing, and that's that.'

'Beau,' she said, sounding out each word slowly, 'I don't want you to go out tonight. I don't feel safe, I want you, not Alex, to stay here with me. Will you do that for me?'

Beau didn't know which direction to take, it was a test, and he had never been very good at those. He looked at Alex; Alex knew that look – Beau's eyes pleaded with him to help like he did all through High School. However, Alex was happy to let Beau get out of his own hole, he could look after himself.

'Shit,' exclaimed Beau, releasing Janice.

Alex saw her rare display of vulnerability and butted in without thinking.

'Why don't I go fishing with Reggie tonight, and you stay here with Janice,' he blurted. 'Besides, I need the cash, and it will give you time to finish getting the house back in order,' he said, trying to justify himself.

'Really?' Beau exclaimed. He glanced at Janice. 'That will get me out of trouble. You'll get paid for it. Same as my share. Just don't fuck it up.' He seemed lost in thought; Alex assumed he was weighing up how to sell this to Reggie. 'You might even get a few fish.'

'But what about Cathy?' Janice asked. 'You'd drop a chance of seeing her again so quick? I don't understand you, Alex.'

'Tell you the truth, I don't know about meeting up with her.' said Alex. 'It's not like I'd arranged anything; she won't answer my calls.' But the truth was not so simple, Alex stood looking at Janice, perhaps the truth lay somewhere there.

'All a bit too hard for you now, is she? Must have been just a holiday fling after all, a bit of low hanging fruit heh Alex.' The sarcasm was thick in her voice.

'It's not like that,' he retorted.

'It is from where I'm standing,' she said.

Beau broke in, 'Well, are you going to do this tonight or not?'

Alex nodded, then said, 'But what about the money you owe Conlan?'

'What money?' Janice asked.

'Nothing. Don't worry about it,' said Beau. 'I'm staying home, aren't I? Isn't that what you wanted?

Janice gave him a withering stare as Beau went to the wall phone and dialled Reggie's number. Alex looked at Janice, but she turned her back on him. He had suggested taking Beau's place tonight more for her sake than Beau's or for the cash, but now he was wondering why he even opened his mouth in the first place. If he was being honest with himself, he knew everything now was a poor excuse for how his life was going. The only surety was that he knew he was a sucker.

Just before dark, Reggie showed up in his F100, towing the boat behind him. Janice said nothing as Alex left, Beau was busy cleaning his precious records, and Reggie scowled as Alex hopped in the front seat next to him.

'What do you know about boats?' Reggie asked.

'I used to sail a lot,' Alex replied.

'Shit. Just what I need...a fucking sailor!' Reggie released the clutch and powered the big ute away from the curb.

Chapter 22

Reggie checked his watch for the third time, then throttled forward. They came up alongside the anchored *Situ Maru*, its silhouette an immense blackness against the night sky, only its bridge lights were showing. The fibreglass boat rocked heavily in the swell, Reggie working the throttles to keep it clear from the ship's hull. Alex tried to stay on his feet as the 20-footer pitched and fell, waves slapped the ship's side then bounced back at them, hoisting the boat skyward then plunging them into the troughs. Alex gripped the boat hook with both hands and braced himself against the fibreglass floor esky, looking up.

'When are they doing this?' Alex yelled at Reggie. 'Do they know we're here?'

'Shut up, anyone can hear us. Watch for the light and keep your trap shut.'

Sea spray showered over the boat as Reggie deftly pushed the throttles forward and reverse, trying to hold station against the ship.

'There.' He pointed ahead, closer to the bow, high up, he could see a pale-yellow light flickering between the side of the ship and the small boat. Bishop pushed the boat forward as they bobbed toward the light. The steel hull was huge and rose above them, threatening to crush them with its blackness.

'Get ready...it's coming.'

Alex looked up, down, to the left, to the right, he scanned his world for what was coming next. Then he saw it. Out the corner of his eye. A bright green glow stick flashed past and disappeared below the surface of the inky black ocean.

'Shit!' he gasped. He leaned over the gunwale, boathook waving about in front of him as he tried to keep his balance. The glowstick appeared, then disappeared again under the side of the boat as it rose with the next swell.

'Have you got it? It's there!' Reggie barked, gesturing forward.

'Hold it steady,' Alex yelled in answer. There was no such thing as steady in the world of a small boat in the open sea. Alex cursed, but true to Reggie's word, the bright green glow stick re appeared a few metres from the boat.

'Where is it now?' Bishop yelled.

'Right. To the right.... Couple of metres.'

'Well fucking get it.' Reggie squirted the engines in a hard right turn, nearly ramming the bow into the ships' side. Alex reached out, jabbing the boathook at the dark mass tied to the glowstick. It was barely floating. He pushed and pulled at the bundle until he finally snagged the rope that crisscrossed the black plastic. A large chop heaved the bundle up the side of the boat then sucked it back into the trough, almost reefing the pole from Alex's' hands.

'Fuck me...hold it steady' Alex screamed into the wind.

'Shut up. Get it in.' called Reggie. 'There are more coming.'

One after another, four more light sticks dropped into the water ahead of the boat. The yellow flashlight above abruptly went out, and the sea around them was plunged into darkness. Working now by the lights of the wheelhouse instruments, Alex brought in first package, the swell now working for him, the boat dropped into a trough just as he heaved upward and brought the dripping package over the gunwale onto the slippery deck. He twisted the boathook free, wedged himself tighter against the icebox, and looked for the next glow stick.

Reggie cursed. The boat had drifted back down the side of the '*Situ Maru*', the glowsticks were scattered ahead. Alex had to admit; Reggie Bishop was good. He had a deft touch of the wheel and throttle, working both to gather in the scattered glowsticks. Alex jabbed and swiped at the packages, losing one under the bow as Reggie compensated for a larger swell, it reappeared on the port side, taunting Alex till he pulled it in. They retrieved all the five packages, now sliding back and forth on the rear deck, their glowsticks bathing Alex in an eery green light.

Reggie finally turned to Alex.

'Get them secured,' he ordered. 'Put them under the tarp. I don't want anyone seeing them.'

Each of the packages was well padded and heavy. They were wrapped in tough black plastic, with waterproof tape strapped all over, and finally bound with rough hemp rope knotted front and back which had made it easier for the boathook to snag. Alex stacked all the boxes under the tarp, wedging them between the gunnel and the icebox. Reggie turned from the wheel to see how it was going, then switched the wheelhouse lights off. He turned the boat toward the west, toward the winking harbour lights of Nerimbah five kilometres away.

Reggie pushed the boat into the southeast chop, the occasional wave breaking enough to send spray over both men. Alex moved up to stand next to Reggie, holding on tightly to the windshield for balance. Reggie reached down between his feet and pulled up a heavy weather jacket, and without a word, passed it to Alex.

'Thanks'.

Reggie said nothing.

The boat droned on in the dark, the vibration and roll lulling Alex to sleep, only two more kilometres to Bayman Heads, silhouetted against the light glow of Nerimbah township behind.

Reggie promptly switched the instrument and navigation lights on, then turned the boat to the north, away from the harbour entrance.

' What!' Alex exclaimed. 'What are we doing Reggie?'

'Not going in yet', he grunted.

'Why not?'

Reggie turned to Alex, 'Got no reason yet.'

Alex thought about that for a moment. 'Reason for what?' he asked.

'Reason to be out here. It's a fishing boat isn't it!' After a pause, Reggie gestured over his shoulder at the deck. 'So, where's the fish?'

'But Reggie...'Alex tried again,' it's a lousy night. We got what we came for.' He offered lamely.

'You do what I tell you.' He flashed in anger. 'We're going to Dinnan Rocks, over there.' He pointed to a dark smudge on the horizon. MinDinnan Island, the locals called it Dinnan Rocks for short. 'We're doing some fishing before we go in, and that's it '. Reggie turned back to conning the boat. Alex felt a cold descend over him. He shivered in his thick jacket, stared forward, saying nothing more.

With a southeast wind coming from behind them the boat moved smoothly through the water, the sound from the motors rising and falling with the swell. Although they both stood in the cockpit, the gap between them had now widened. Alex now knew what Beau meant when he said not to get on the wrong side of Reggie. He was affable enough to be around but on his terms. The easy sway of the hull and droning outboards lulled Alex into closing his eyes.

The change in the engine note brought Alex back to the present. Reggie swung the boat into the lee of the wind between the two rocky outcrops. Alex scrambled forward, lifted the hatch on the anchor well and waited for Reggie's instructions. With a whistle, the anchor went over the side. When Alex felt the tension on the anchor line bite, the bow swung into the wind and Reggie shut the engines down. A new quiet descended. The wind still pushed waves against the rocks, but the sound was muffled by the stunted scrub growing on the larger of the two outcrops.

Reggie turned on the deck lights.

'You know how to fish don't you?'

'Yeah', Alex snapped.

Reggie brushed past Alex and opened the main deck icebox. Inside was packed frozen and thawed fish. The boat rocked in the swells, and the rich smell of bloody fish floated over the deck as the contents slushed around the bottom. Reggie reached into the bin and pulled out a whole mullet.

'This frozen stuff we'll cut up and use for bait.' He gestured at the cutting table, three sharp knives in their scabbards hanging above it.

'The rest can go.' He shone a torch in the bottom of the esky.

'Give it a good clean and chuck that thawed stuff.'

Reggie set to removing the tarp from their drug haul, cutting away the glow sticks and throwing them over the side. Alex bucketed sea water into the esky, pulling out the bungs to let the bloodied water sluice across the deck. He retrieved three whole mullet for the bait table and threw the bits of squid and fish heads into the light of the green glow sticks bobbing around in the water. Immediately small fish converged on the scraps of bait. The sea was reasonably flat in the lee of MinDinnan Island.

As Alex worked, he looked around. The lights of Nerimbah seemed so far in the distance. The bridge lights of the three ships waiting for their pilots were still riding at anchor off Florette Shoals. The Situ Maru where they had just been, was one of them, but he couldn't tell which one from here. The cloudless night sky was a blaze of stars; among them Alex noticed the flashing navigation lights of a Fokker Friendship over Moreton Bay looking to land at Brisbane. The lights of a plane 60 kilometres away over water seemed so much brighter than over land at half the distance. Alex threw the last handful of fish guts over the back and leaned over to wash his hands in the water. Small fish jumped and emerged from the dark to dart in and out of the blood and fish guts floating on the surface.

Alex rinsed his fingers then held them up to his nose, knowing he wouldn't get that fishy smell off them till he was back on dry land.

He tossed the last bucket of water across the deck and turned to the bait table. The black plastic packets of their haul were gone off the deck, pushed down against the sidewall of the boat. In the shadows of the dark, they were barely visible, it looked like part of the boat.

Reggie crossed to the cutting table.

'Bait the hooks like this, see?'

He cut the mullet into sizable chunks, dexterously sliding the bait on to large stainless-steel hooks, with a heavy triangular sinker, attached to hand line reels. He set four lines overboard in the time that Alex had still baited his first hook. They settled down either side of side of the boat to wait, as all fishermen do.

She was only five years old and 12 foot long, but because she was pregnant, she was slightly larger for her age. The pups growing in her abdomen we're giving her a voracious appetite. The colder months of the year had kept her in the tropics, till she finally ventured south. She had followed a whale and her calf, further than she usually went, stopping in an area just off a small island and rock outcrop near shore where the waters were shallow and warm. She had been here before; the turtles were in abundance and there was little competition for them. Her broad flat snout was perfect for nudging turtles off their course, flipping them ever so slightly so she could lazily crush the hard shells with her jaws. She could twist and turn easily in time with a turtle's frantic escape gyrations, so speed was never necessary, an indolent cat with a mouse. Nocturnal feeding gave her the most reward and also caused her the most trouble. The electromagnetic sensors in her snout detected the movements of struggling prey, but only by mouthing it with a great snout and massive jaws would reveal if it was edible. She did discover that boat propellers had no taste, and fortunately, her teeth grew back quickly. That night, fish fighting over the offal thrown from the back of a boat triggered her senses. She spun on her dorsal fin and swept lazily toward the green glowing water in the distance.

It was Alex's line that went first. His spool ran wildly out of control, taking out his line at a rapid rate. He grabbed the line, trying to recover it without cutting his fingers. Ever so slowly, he began to reel in the fish.

'You got a big Jew by the look of it. See how you go.' Reggie smirked and lit a cigarette to watch. He wasn't going to help, and they both knew it. Alex strained, slowly recovering line until suddenly it went slack in his hands. He wound the final few feet of line over the side, but only the head of a large fish remained, the body raggedly sawn off below the gills.

'Shark got that one.' Reggie glanced over the side. 'She's always around when there's blood in the water.'

Alex looked over the side, fishing forgotten. Beneath the last of the glow sticks, a large dark shape moved in and out of the light, the smaller fish scattering quickly into the dark. Alex shone a torch on the water over the back, just in time to catch the shark in a tight turn, lifting her jaws to mouth one of the outboard propellers.

'Shit.' Alex jumped back and made sure that he was holding the gunwale tight. The boat rocked slightly as the shark mouthed the metal prop and the huge flat snout rose up out of the water to get a better bite and pushed the boat around off the wind. Alex could see straight down into a ribbed throat ringed by rows of white teeth. The tiger stripes were apparent, but it was the dark eyes that held Alex in a torchlight tableau, scarecrow figures on a black ocean beneath. The shark released the prop, turned out of the light and slowly tailed away.

Alex stepped back, Reggie grabbed his arm, and he jumped. He gripped hard, spun him around and pushed his face in close to Alex.

'You've seen a lot tonight Alex! You know... you've seen it all,' he snarled. 'You're part of it now. If you decide you don't want to be part of it, like... you want to tell someone about our fishing trips....' He glanced down over his shoulder and pointed his chin in the direction of the dark water.

'You've seen this side of it too....' His voice was low, full of menace, his eyes black, sightless. Alex had seen those eyes before, just minutes ago, looking at him from the water. Then he laughed, released his arm and slapped Alex on the back, reverting to Reggie again.

'That'll do for tonight. Fuck the fish. Bring the lines in. Get the anchor.'

Reggie started the engines and pointed the boat toward the river mouth at Bayman Heads, pushing the throttles forward to beat into the wind for the journey home.

Alex stared ahead into the dark ocean wondering what the fuck he was doing. He was trapped. The boat pushed ahead towards the harbour lights. Spray washed his eyes with salt, his stomach churned, his mouth dry, he wanted to throw up but one glance at Reg told him it would be a bad idea. People like Reggie prayed on weakness, they instinctively use it to their advantage, it's what makes them the predators they are. Alex shook his head to clear his mind of the what if scenarios. He was scared. He knew what was in those packages. It wasn't dope. They were too small, too heavy, each package weighed kilos, padded for protection on the outside, but he could feel the hard rectangular core within. It had to be heroin or cocaine. He was now part of something so much bigger and more dangerous than he had imagined. The threat was real. He was drowning in fear, uncertain of where this would take him, but he didn't want to go there. He held on, wishing himself elsewhere, anywhere but here. Beau had got him into this mess, he'd better help get him out of it...But it wasn't just Beau's fault he was here, it was as much his own, and he couldn't go back.

The engine note changed, the noise subdued, the bow dropped down as the boat slowed into the mouth of the river. The violet blue channel light ahead and the flashing leads of red and green were set against the glow of the town. Reggie lit another cigarette, the flash of light from the flame showed his eyes furtively glancing back and forward along the rock wall.

The waterway was empty, the yacht basin quiet. The boat rounded the corner, ahead was the pilot boat against its wharf, most of the trawlers were out, the prawn season was open in the north. The only noise on the river was the soft burble of the motors and the wind tapping halyards against aluminium masts from the yachts moored in the middle of the river. Reggie turned the bow in to the boat ramp on the corner. That was when a lone figure stepped out of the dark into the carpark light at the top of the ramp. Reggie swore under his breath,

'It's Cooper,' he murmured, switched off the running lights and reaching into the locker under his seat. There was just enough light for Alex to see a gun in its holster fastened to the locker wall next to the safety kit, but he straightened up with only a wallet and his car keys in hand. Alex crawled forward over the windshield to the bow, and slid his legs over the side, scrambling for purchase on the slippery concrete in thigh deep water. When he found his feet, he pushed back and stopped the boat. Reggie shut the motors down. They were home.

Reggie dropped over the side next to Alex. 'I'll get the car' he said and marched off up the ramp. He stopped in front of Cooper who was dressed in civvies, no uniform, lighting a cigarette and drawing slowly on the smoke. They stood facing each other. Alex couldn't hear what was being said, but Cooper was doing most of the talking, gesturing at the boat and the ocean past the breakwater. Reggie patted his back pocket and walked off into the dark. Cooper looked like he would follow him, then turned and strolled down the boat ramp toward Alex.

'You're Dave's boy, aren't you?' he said as he approached.

Alex nodded, not saying anything, intent on staring past him. Cooper stopped next to Alex looking over the bow of the boat.

'Did you get out far tonight?'

'Dinnan rocks,' he replied.

'How did you go?'

'Not much, a few bites.'

'That's not like Reggie. He usually gets a few fish. Dinnan heh? North or south side?'

Alex could hear Reggie starting the ute, revving the engine. The bright glow of red taillights came on. Alex shuffled, willing Reggie to hurry.

'We were on the northside'.

'Right! You were out there a fair while tonight to not catch anything.'

He went to move down the ramp, reaching for the gunwale to look in over the side of the boat so Alex nudged the boat off the concrete edge into deeper water, if he went any further Coopers shoes would get wet. He stopped. Alex made a great show of preparing the bow rope for the trailer.

'Alex, isn't it? You've been away studying, haven't you?'

Alex pretended not to hear it, so Cooper repeated the question.

'You been at University?'

'I'm back for summer,' he answered.

'So how did you end up as a deckie for Bishop? He usually takes Dennis Beaumont out with him, doesn't he?' Cooper flicked the butt into the water.

'Beau's sick.'

'Didn't go out to the Florette Shoals tonight, did you?' He turned and stared straight at Alex.

Alex shook his head numbly. The arrival of the trailer saved him. It squeaked and banged as it was reversed down the ramp, and Alex fussed with getting the boat loaded and not say any more to the policeman. Cooper stood back and waited for them to winch the boat out and finish loading. He wandered nonchalantly up the ramp, lighting another cigarette at the top, waiting. Reggie quickly circled the trailer, checked the boat was on its rollers then jumped up behind the wheel of his Ford.

'Get in,' he grunted.

Alex barely had time to hop into the passenger seat before Reggie floored the motor. The engine roared, and the tyres slipped on the wet concrete as they shot up out of the dark straight past Cooper without stopping.

Alex sighed with relief. He didn't want to look out the rear window at Cooper, he didn't want to look at Reggie Bishop, he didn't want to look at anything, he just wanted the night to be over.

Reggie pulled up outside Beau's house. It was quiet and dark at midnight. He pulled out his wallet from his back pocket, counted out $3000, and dropped it into Alex's lap.

'You know where we were, and what we were fishing for tonight don't you? And we didn't catch anything...if you remember. You're a smart kid Alex...stay that way.'

Alex nodded, he scooped up the money and hopped out. He watched the Ford ute drive away, lights disappearing in the dark, the boat trailer rattling behind it. He was too numb to do anything more but walk up the ramp into the house and collapse on the flimsy couch. He was smelly, damp and afraid. Sleep would come eventually.

Chapter 23

The chink of ceramic cups against a metal sink and the gravel hum of a jug boiling woke Alex. He raised himself off the couch and looked across to the kitchen, still tired from the tension of the night before.

'What time is it? I broke my watch last night, didn't even know it. 'Alex yawned, and sauntered to the toilet, smelling the fishy odour from the bait on his fingers.

'After eight. Coffee?' Beau called. He proceeded to fuss around the sink, moving dishes to one side, looking for the coffee jar.

Alex wandered back into the kitchen.

'You look like shit.' He finished stirring the coffee cups and handed one to Alex as he flopped into the kitchen chair. 'Thanks for that last night. Janice was scared they might come around again.'

'But they didn't, did they!' stated Alex. 'Nothing happened because Cooper was down at the boat ramp.'

'Was he just?' said Beau.

Alex sipped at the hot coffee, sighed and closed his eyes in resolve. He had made up his mind. The money burning a hole in his pocket was not worth it.

'I don't need to go fishing with Reggie again.'

'What?'

Alex opened his eyes and engaged Beau.' I said, I don't need to go fishing with Reggie again.'

Beau stood up and closed the door to his bedroom where Janice was still sleeping. 'Something go wrong?' he asked.

'No! But we didn't catch anything'.

'Yeah right', said Beau. 'You weren't supposed to.'

Alex looked at Beau. 'You didn't tell me.'

' What didn't I tell you?' Said Beau.

'You knew what Reggie was picking up. That wasn't dope, that was smack, wasn't it? There was at least a kilo of heroin in each of those packages they threw overboard. That's 5 kilos of smack we brought back. And you let me go with Reggie to pick it up! I thought we were just going out to pick up some bags of dope. I don't want to be around smack, that stuff kills people, and its serious jail time if you're caught with it. I didn't come home for that. Why didn't you tell me?'

'You wouldn't have gone if you knew.'

'And you still let me go anyway,' accused Alex.

'What are you on about? I did you a favour. You made good money last night. You earned more in a few hours than a month in the hot sun shovelling shitty bitumen.'

'I don't want to earn it smuggling heroin.' Alex said bitterly.

'So what? Smack, dope, it's all the same in this business.' Beau said offhandedly.

'No! it's not!' spat Alex.

'The problem with you Alex, is you think too much. Let your morals get in the way of business, it's called supply and demand.'

'Don't quote high school economics to me Beau. I passed that subject, you didn't.'

'Stop complaining, you got paid, didn't you? You don't have to do it again. It's about time you got your hands dirty anyway.'

'Fuck the money!' Alex spilt his coffee, waving the cup about as he spoke.' I don't want anything to do with it.'

'Too late now bucko! You're in with the rest of us.'

'But what if I don't want to be?'

Alex wanted to hear Beau say it now. To hear him say sorry for the deceit and the bullshit about how this was his life and not Alex's. He wanted to know if the sickening feeling in his stomach would go away. He wanted to shake off the vision of the shark's black eye looking up at him from the dark waters, and Reggies threat of what would happen if he faltered.

'It's just money Alex.' Said Beau

Alex was furious. 'The problem with you, Beau, is you only think about the money. You're blind to what these pricks have got you into. From a bit of dope dealing to full on heroin smuggling, like Conlan. Do you really want to be in business with that? End up in prison, or worse?"

'We won't get caught. Reggie knows what he's doing.'

'Fuck he does. Cooper was waiting for us at the boat ramp. He knew Reggie. He knew me, he knew I was filling in for you, and where we had been. Now I'm linked with Reggie and a boat load of smack too. Fuck Beau. What have you got me into?'

'It's nothing mate. Don't worry about the cop. Reggie will fix him up. It's all OK with me and Janice now, I'll be doing the next drop.'

'How many of these have you done?' Alex asked,

'A few.'

'How many Beau?'

' A few I said. Does it matter?!'

'Reggie threatened me last night, told me I'd end up shark bait if I told anyone what we did.'

'Yeh, he did that to me too at the start. Don't worry about it.'

'Where did you meet this guy. Him and Conlan, they're a menace.'

'He's not what you think. Want a smoke?' he asked and opened a new pack of cigarettes. He lit one up and offered one to Alex. Alex shook his head. Beau drew deeply on the smoke, as if it opened the gates to his explanation.

'When we finished school, I just wanted out, you had left for Uni, and no way I was going to stay at home, the old man was going to kick me out anyway. Reggie moved into the house next door and gave me a job driving for him around the place. Simple as that. Good money for nothing.'

'What were you doing?'

'Just driving. Dropping gear off.'

'Dope?'

'Yeh, of course. Just dope mostly, at the start. That changed around Christmas 78'. That's when I met Conlan. I made a shitload of money when me and Reggie went to Indonesia surfing. Conlon met us there and introduced us to these Chinese blokes. God the surf was good, you would have loved it. Lefts mostly, good for me, shit for you.' He laughed. 'Didn't have to pay for a thing, and the women.... '

'So, what did the Chinese want?' Alex interrupted.

'Well, the Chinese guys had these two surfboards, and we swapped ours for theirs when we were ready to leave.'

'Were they surfing too?'

'God no. Don't be stupid. They just had the gear. They hollowed out their boards and repacked them with smack, fibre glassed the cut and made them look like new. All we had to do was take them home with us. I was shitting myself at the airport, but it was worth it. Conlan has paid me enough for the car, new boards and the rental on this place, I could move out of home, away from the old man.'

'You brought the boards back into Australia on the plane? I couldn't have done that.'

'It was easy. Roy went ahead of us, to smooth the way through customs, I wheeled the boards; Reggie carried the bags.'

And Beau carries the can alone if they get caught, thought Alex.

'It was easy as.' Beau continued, warming to the story of how he made good. 'Roy said it would be simple, and it was. But we only did two more trips like that, Customs were starting to bust people coming back from Asia the next year, so Roy came up with a new plan, picking the gear up offshore from a ship. Bigger supplies, bigger profits. He and Reggie went halves in the boat, the one you were on last night. Tony Cowell used to deckie for them at the start, but he pissed off to New South Wales, so Reggie asked me, and, and voila, look around.' He spread his arms magnanimously. 'All this and Janice. Not bad huh, and I didn't have to go to Uni for it.'

'Does Janice know what you do when you go fishing?'

'She thinks it's still dope. Not heavy stuff.'

'I've got news for you.'

'Bullshit. She doesn't know about the smack. I want to keep that side of the business away from her.'

Alex was quiet. He thought back to the first day he arrived home, finding a foil in the bedside magazine and had to ask.' Have you ever used it yourself?'

'Hell no. I only test it for purity.'

Alex wasn't sure how much of Beau he could believe in anymore. The world had shifted under his feet in the last few weeks.

Janice had woken and appeared at the bedroom door. Her short pyjamas rode up her legs and only one button held her blowse together at her breasts. She ambled past them to the bathroom for a shower, closing that door behind her. Both men watched her pass with the same look in their eyes.

Alex lit a cigarette, leaned back and wondered why he and Beau didn't joke around as much together anymore.

Chapter 24

Two days later Alex rose to his bedroom door rattling under the incessant knocking from his mother. He'd been working hard in the hot sun for the last day and a half, shovelling hot bitumen for a new set of tennis courts. He was home late to his parents' house and collapsed on his bed, leaving smears of greasy bitumen on the bed covers. The job had finished, and he celebrated by sleeping in late.

'Alex... get up. Beau is on the phone and wants to talk to you, he says its urgent.' Alex barely heard her. 'Beau is on the phone', she repeated, only louder, 'He wants you to talk to him right away.'

'I'm coming, don't get your knickers in a knot.'

'What did you say?'

'Nothing Mum, I wouldn't dream of saying anything about your knickers.'

'Saying what?' she shouted through the door.

'Nothing. I'm coming now. You can hear that, can't you,' Alex yelled. He loved teasing her. When he opened the door, his mother stood frowning, looking up at him. She was lively and full of mischief. Trying to match her was a game they both played, but Alex often lost. His only redeeming wins were that she made terrible coffee and Alex used that to his full advantage.

'You're a bit slow today, aren't you?' She observed. 'And Beau sounds very stressed.'

'I love the detective in you Mum, now leave me in peace so I can talk to him.' He kissed her on the top of her head.

'You get on the phone, and I'll bring you some of my coffee you love so much.'

She smiled mischievously, knowing Alex could not refuse her coffee without insulting her generosity. She strutted away down the hallway and finished with a little shuffle dance as she swung into the kitchen. He couldn't believe she had won that round so easily.

Alex picked up the receiver on its long cord. 'Yeh Beau, what's up?'

'You may not have heard. Mitch and Ergo have been arrested. The Police raided their place last night.'

'Heh, good news for once,' applauded Alex. 'Couldn't have happened to a nicer couple of blokes, especially Ergo, I hope he resisted arrest.'

'It seems like he did, and they beat the shit out of him. But this is serious, the word is that they're going for dealing, not just possession. Reggies pretty worried, it's a mess.'

'How much did they have on them?'

'Don't be a dickhead, this is an open line, I bet your mothers listening in as we speak. Just, come down, we need to talk.'

'Yeh, OK. I'll be there soon.'

'Don't rush, I've got a job to do first. But I'll be back in an hour or so. Plenty to tell you.'

Beau hung up before Alex could think of a smart retort. Mitch and Ergo could point the finger directly at Beau, though he didn't know what he could do about it. Alex showered and hastily constructed a sandwich in the kitchen. His mother placed a cup of her coffee on the bench and looked expectantly up at him.

'I've already sugared it,' she said with finality.

Alex looked at the coffee, then looked at her. She held his gaze, daring him to make a smart comment. Instead, he lifted the cup to his lips and blew the hot steam away from the top of the cup, before taking a hesitant sip.

'Just what I needed,' he murmured appreciatively, avoiding any reference to a judgement of taste. 'But unfortunately, I've got to go. You heard how stressed Beau was,' he said with mock severity. 'Thanks for the coffee, Mum.' He leaned in and pecked her quickly on the cheek, before darting out the kitchen, leaving the full cup on the bench.

When Alex thought back on it later, he realised that his life changed with that phone call.

Chapter 25

Alex had parked his car at the Beach Shack looking for Beau, the Monaro was still there but he wasn't home. Janice said she thought he went for a surf. He figured that in this wind he would be surfing up near the north corner off the rocks, so Alex peeled off his t shirt and changed into his board shorts. He nestled his board firmly under his arm, and headed along the road toward the beach, darting along the patchy grass on the footpath.

Ahead was Herman's old rental house, next to the Ambulance station. Parked out the front next to it was a police car, a Falcon sedan, one of the new ones. The door was open, and the familiar shape of Sergeant Cooper sat inside. A panel van swooped past Alex; *Ken Herman Locksmith* painted in bright colours on the side. It pulled in behind the police car.

Ken Herman wasn't a wealthy man, but he was a local and had built up his locksmithing business on the back of all the recent development, including his own holiday rental which he had up for sale. Isabelle and Donna, his two girls spilled out of the car and raced to the front door of the house. Finding it locked, they skipped off around the side. Ken stopped and talked briefly with Cooper, went round to the side kitchen door but immediately returned, calling to Cooper that someone had changed the lock. He retrieved a small tool kit from the car and followed the girls till he reached the side door. In a few moments he had opened the lock and pushed the door wide. Alex noticed that he stood scanning the kitchen inside while both girls tried to squeeze past him, but he held them back.

'Stay here girls, don't go inside yet.,' Alex heard him impress on his daughters. 'I'll be back in a minute, did you hear me, Donna?'

'Yes Dad', she said absently. Both jostling in the doorway.

Ken turned back down the two stairs and headed round to the front to tell Cooper the door was open. The girls had disappeared inside.

As Alex drew level he noticed the policeman, Cooper, was checking the letterbox. He straightened and made to call out to Alex.

Alex stopped and looked across at him, Herman reappeared from the side of the house, walking toward them both. The Policeman hesitated between engaging the locksmith or Alex, not sure which to talk to first, when the front door behind him disintegrated in a shower of white timber splinters, and glass windows disappeared in a purge of grey leaden smoke. The deep crump of the explosion was but a split second behind.

The blast of air and noise reached them both at the same time. Cooper was enveloped in it, staggering under its power, sprawling forward onto his knees. Alex was hit by a pressure wave of debris and stumbled into the gutter. Dust laden smoke settled over him. Pieces of fibro, wood splinters and glass pattered against the roof of the parked cars. The smoke cleared a little and boiled skyward. A terrible silence completed the tableau.

Alex's eyes didn't want to work. Fibro dust was caught under the lids of his eyeballs, and it hurt when he tried to open them. He was aware of a roaring in his ears, any move he made seemed to echo.

He sucked in a gasp of air and coughed as his body came back to life. He forced his eyes open and held up his hands to the light. Glass fragments and splinters were sticking into his skin, giving it a kind of shimmer. He tried to rise, but any movement on the concrete gutter was painful. He took another deep breath and pushed himself to his feet.

Sergeant Cooper lay prone on the path, ten feet away. Herman was on all fours, retching into the grass, swaying from side to side. Alex coughed again to clear his throat and wiped more dust from his eyes. As the smoke began to drift away, he noted that large parts of the front of Hermans house were missing, the windows and door were black holes in the peppered fibro walls. The back of Coopers uniform was shredded and smoking, his head was moving, and his mouth opened and closed, but Alex couldn't hear anything.

Alex knew he was supposed to do something, but couldn't figure out what it was, so he began to pick at the glass bits on the back of his hand. He looked down and saw a little finger. He picked it up, there was a ring on it just above the second knuckle, where the joint ended. He stared at it like it was the most precious thing in the world, which it was. Alex sat down in the gutter and put the finger with the ring on it next to him on the concrete.

'Alex.... Alex...' The muffled voice from the outside world pushed through the fog. Behind him, on the lawn one of the ambos was helping Herman up while a black Doberman was loping around barking excitedly at them. The other ambo was bent over Cooper furiously patting at his back. Cooper still wasn't moving much.

'Alex...'Beau shook him.' I'm sorry...I'm so fucking sorry.' Alex gave no reply but absently plucked at a wood splinter on his arm. He tried to wipe away the fine shower of glass particles on his shoulder, but it didn't work. And in a moments grace, Alex understood what it meant to be deaf.

'Alex, we got to fucking move, man. Get you out of here'. Beau pulled gently at Alex's arm, guiding him to his feet. Alex stood unsteady, but solid enough for Beau to gather up his battered surfboard and lead him away between a growing number of onlookers converging on the chaos of the front lawn. They were long gone by the time the police arrived.

Chapter 26

Alex let Beau help him all the way along Gulin avenue, alternately lifting and guiding him till they reached the turn to the Beach Shack. His body hurt and each time Beau held his arm, it stung, and he pulled it away. The world was a moving silent movie. Pedestrians ran past them in the opposite direction toward the bomb site, but none paid them any real attention. Janice was standing on the verandah, perplexed, till he was close enough for her to see him in this state. Her mouth moved, and arms gesticulated but he heard nothing. Beau threw Alex's board down in the bushes and pushed him up the ramp through the door.

'There's been in an explosion,' Beau gasped from the exertion. 'Alex was in it.'

Janice grabbed Alex and forced him to look at her. 'Where are you hurt Alex, tell me'.

'I'm OK.' He mouthed, swaying back and forth, stretching his shoulders and clenching his fingers in and out as if that would tell him something.

'What happened Alex? What was it?'

'He can't hear you,' said Beau.

Alex stood in the middle of the loungeroom, picking at his ears, trying to make them work. Janice circled around him, surveying the damage to his body. She grabbed his shoulders as he began to sway but came away with glass dust on her fingers. Beau tried to make him sit at the kitchen table, but Janice led him into the bathroom where she stripped him and bundled him under the shower.

Beau let out a nervous exclamation of anger, lit a cigarette and collapsed into a chair, shaking his head, as if to clear an unwelcome thought.

'For fuck's sake Beau, put that cigarette out and get me a sponge and a clean towel.' Ordered Janice.

Alex stood naked leaning against the shower wall, water running through his hair and down his back. Janice gently washed the glass shards and dust off his body; the grey water tinged with speckles of blood swirling around his feet. He squirmed under her touch, the cuts stinging with each wipe.

'Stay still!' she ordered.

'Fuck that hurts,' Alex complained.

'You'll live.' She reached in and turned the shower off. 'Beau, dry him off then bring him out here,' she ordered.

Alex sat at the kitchen table, a towel now around his waist as Janice dabbed at him with mercurochrome, leaving a trail of orange dots all down his left side. Alex predictably winced and jerked under her touch, the sting of the antiseptic a cruel pleasure. In the distance, sirens were wailing in and out, he closed his eyes, breathed deeply; and shuddered. When he opened them, another siren whooped past the house. Alex's world had taken another tilt to the side.

Janice tenderly stroked his arm and forced him to face her.

'What happened to you Alex? How did you end up like this? What's going on out there.'

Alex slumped low in the chair, opening and closing his eyes as he recounted the blast in his head. 'I was just there, just walking by when Herman's house exploded. It blew me in the gutter.'

'Where?'

'Ken Herman's house...next to the ambulance station. Cooper was there too. He got hit by the blast...it was burning him up... Shit, there were little girls playing around the house. Are they OK?' Alex looked in Beau's direction.

Beau's face was ashen, blank, as if he didn't understand the question.

'Beau?' questioned Janice

'I don't know. I didn't see anything, only Alex lying in the street and smoke everywhere. I heard the blast, but I didn't see it happen...I didn't know the girls were there.' Beau stood up and paced back and forward across the loungeroom, looking out the windows every time a siren sped past.

Alex painfully changed into a fresh shirt and shorts, while Janice started cleaning up the debris of Alex's wounding. He took a handful of Panadol and retreated to the couch to lie on his stomach and take pressure off his wounds. For a while he lay watching Janice fuss around the house, wondering if he should go home, till he closed his eyes and withdrew from the world.

When Alex woke, Janice had left for work. The TV was on, noisily demanding attention. Predictably all the news services ran snippets of the story of the bombing. By five o'clock, Brisbane TV was breaking a special bulletin. Beau sat in front of the screen, leaning forward, his elbows on his knees.

> *An explosion at a vacant Nerimbah house has killed a young girl and severely injured her sister. At the time of the explosion, both girls were inside the vacant holiday rental. Also injured in the blast, were the girl's father and a Senior Sergeant of the Queensland Police. All three are being treated at the Dunoonan General Hospital. Police are, at this stage, unsure of the cause of the explosion. A spokesman says it is only early in the investigation and he would not speculate. However, until further notice, it is being treated as a crime scene. All names have been withheld until relatives have been notified.*

The bulletin continued with witness accounts and accolades for the quick response from the Ambos in saving the lives of both the younger sister and the Police Officer who had both sustained life-threatening injuries. The report finished with a plea for witnesses to come forward.

So now he knew. He hadn't told Beau or Janice about the finger, that was his pain. He looked at Beau, something nagged at him, but he couldn't bring it to the front.

It was getting dark, there were no lights on in the shack, only the illumination from the TV and reflected red and blue flashing lights off the windows from passing emergency vehicles. Beau was slumped in a seat at the kitchen table, a bottle of rum in front of him, and a mound of cigarette buts to show that he hadn't moved all afternoon, quiet and brooding,

Alex's body ached and was itchy with pin prick wounds on his left side. His right arm and forehead was bruised where it took the full brunt of his fall onto the road. Little bits of fibro and glass were still making their way out of his hair every time he scratched at his scalp.

Alex sat up awkwardly. 'Can I have a rum?' he asked.

Beau poured him a half a glass, and brought it over to him, then went back to his chair.

'Heh Beau,' Alex mumbled, 'one of those girls is dead.'

'Yeh... I know.'

'I was there,' said Alex.

'Yeh, I know.'

'So were you.'

Beau said nothing.

'Thanks for bringing me back.'

'That's OK.'

'Why were you saying sorry?'

Beau didn't answer. Alex loaded more Panadol in his mouth and drank the rum in one shot, then leaned back against the wall, numbly watching the rest of the news. Sometime later, Beau or Janice must have lay him back down on the couch.

He woke once during the night when all the world was dark and quiet. He had been dreaming of an angry ocean, and as each wave pushed him down, he struggled to push back up against it, until one held him down so long that he hit the bottom and could feel the coral rubbing against his back, he struggled for air, thrashing at the water to free him, it filled his mouth with grit. He couldn't breathe. He woke with a start. His wounds were weeping and sticking to the cushions. He lay in silence for a while, reliving what he had been through that day. It was a long time getting back to sleep again.

By Wednesday morning the news services had exploded with outrage. Names had been released, Isabelle Herman was killed by the blast, Donna her younger sister and Senior Sergeant Cooper were both still in intensive care. Authorities had established that it was a deliberate bomb, fragments revealing it as one or more grenades, most probably set as a booby trap to explode as Police investigated an alleged drug cache inside the house. The tragedy was that it was accidently triggered by the girls playing in the front room. Isabelle, the taller of the two girls had taken the brunt of the blast and had most probably shielded her sister Donna from further injury. The authorities took great pains to establish that the house had been vacant for some time, and Ken Herman, the owner and father was not under investigation for any involvement in the crime.

Special detectives had been brought up from Brisbane and TV bulletins showed them examining all aspects of the ruined front room of the house. A crime scene Police caravan was set up, reporters pointing out that it was the first time it had been used on a crime site. TV footage showed lines of Police scouring the bomb site for evidence, against a backdrop of the shattered front façade of the Herman house.

Reporters spoke of it as an abomination, a threat by the growing power of drug dealers to destroy the fabric of a peaceful coastal community. One reporter described it as the loss of innocence, another as the result of too lenient penalties for the current crime wave. Police were keen to interview various people seen around the house, both before and after the blast, especially those who may have witnessed it. Arrests, they said, were imminent.

Both Beau and Alex would be high on the list of those the Police wanted to talk to. They had no idea if anyone had identified them as being there, but Alex just didn't want to get involved. He was struggling to understand what had happened to him. The little finger with its unicorn ring was burned into his subconscious, he knew now that it must have belonged to one of the girls, most probably Isabelle...the thought horrified him. He could not resolve why he felt like crying.

Janice brought home the Brisbane paper. Photos of the crime scene and reports outlining the damage and eyewitness accounts filled the first two pages. Alex was drawn to a diagram of a grenade on the third page, pointing out its features, and the most likely steps taken to prepare it as a booby trap. The safety clip was removed, A trip cord as a booby trap was tied to the round safety pin. Pulling on the cord would pull the safety pin free, the spring leaver would release with a metallic sounding 'Ping', arming the device for a 4-5 second delay in detonation. It had a 5-10 metre explosion radius. To Alex, it read so clinical, so far removed from his own world...except now it wasn't. It made him feel sick.

Janice said there was hardly anyone at the pub, the bombing was all anyone could talk about, speculation ran wild over who was responsible. The grenade was attributed to either a turf war or an attempt to get back at the cops. For once, opinion swayed in favour of supporting quick police action, and the desire to catch those responsible.

The whole coast was on edge, condemnation of the murder of an innocent girl by drug dealers was universal. Word had filtered to Janice for Beau to watch his back, many of the locals that used his services were only too happy to answer Police questions if asked.

All that day, Beau barely left the house, prowling back and forward, sniping at Janice and Alex. He tried ringing Reggie but got no answer, which only increased his anxiety. He stalked the house, lighting up endless cigarettes, windows and curtains closed in the heat, it stank.

By Wednesday afternoon, Beau was barely talking, and Alex had had enough, the atmosphere was stifling. His cuts needed a good dose of salt water to clear them out.

The surf was small. He lay in the warm water beyond the break, gentle waves washing over his body, cleaning his wounds and massaging away the tension, but not the memory. When he closed his eyes, he still saw Cooper's gaping mouth, the blast, the ambos running through the smoke. But mostly he saw a small finger with a child's ring on the second knuckle. None of that would wash away. The ocean could only heal so much.

That night, Police arrested the first suspects in the Nerimbah bombing. Brett Hamilton, an ex-serviceman was arrested in Brisbane, along with his flatmate Eddie Tran. A stash of drugs, a sawn-off military SLR rifle and three grenades were found at his house. The men had been known to police who confirmed what the reporter had surmised, that both men had been on the coast the day of the explosion, the bombing was drug related, and bomb fragments were from M26 grenades, ex-Vietnam war stock. Hamilton's car had been seen at the Nerimbah house the day before the explosion. Police were running down known associates and interested in a man seen at the back of the house just prior to the blast.

Beau turned away from the television, 'Fuck. How did they know it was Hamilton?' Beau exploded.

Janice perked up. 'What do you mean, how did they know? Do you know him?' She didn't wait for an answer. 'Did you know it was this Hamilton who did it?'

'No. Not really.' Beau backed away. 'I know of him. I've seen him at Reggie's house. He's a mate of Conan's that comes up from Brisbane.'

'How did I not guess that.' Janice spat sarcastically. 'Conlan!' Well, that makes you an accomplice, doesn't it Beau?' She surmised. 'That's just great.' She turned to Alex, 'What about you, are you part of this too?'

'Look at me Janice. What do you think!' Alex pointed at his wounds.

'It's that Conlan again. Every time I hear his name it's trouble. Was he at Herman's house the other day, the one they say was seen hanging around the back?'

'Not him. Wouldn't have been him.'

'How do you know that?' Janice asked angrily.

'They said it on the news,' said Beau.

'No, they didn't'.

'I don't know,' said Beau.' Reggie told me'.

'You said you hadn't heard from him.'

'Leave it will you. Just leave it alone.' Beau spat in anger.

'Your mates are mixed up in this, aren't they? But you're in the middle of it too and you don't know much about what is going on, do you Beau? Where is Reggie now?'

'I don't know. I haven't heard from him or Conlan, they don't answer their phones. I don't know where they are. I don't know anything about that house or that fucking bomb.'

Beau turned away and lit a cigarette, he wouldn't look either of them in the eye. He was lying, Alex knew, from their school days together, Beau never could lie very well, he always looked miserable. It wasn't in his nature. Some people lie out of impulse for self-preservation, or to improve their own sense of worth, but for Beau it was neither of these, it was something else, something new to him altogether, he didn't know if it was fear... or guilt.

'Beau,' Janice asked, 'did you know who planted that bomb?'

'Jesus, what do you take me for?' He exploded. 'You think I'd know that?'

'I don't know what to think,' she said. Janice stood with her back to the kitchen sink, the distance between them growing ever wider.

Beau looked at Janice, then Alex, and back to Janice again. 'You really think I'd be part of that? What about you Alex? You think that?'

'I know you wouldn't willingly harm anyone.'

'Thanks for the vote of confidence mate! I saved you, remember?'

Alex nodded in appreciation and then identified what had been nagging at him.

'Beau, you got to me only seconds after the explosion and you said you were sorry. You weren't on your way home from the surf, were you? You didn't have a towel, you weren't even wet,' Alex was speculating.

Beau said nothing.

'When you picked me up after the explosion, you kept saying you were sorry...Sorry for what? The explosion? You didn't do it.'

'No! I fucking didn't!' Beau said caustically.

'But you knew it was going to happen? Were you already there? Are you the person the Police are searching for?' Janice interjected.

He shook his head back and forth. 'You don't get to accuse me. I didn't set that fucking grenade. I was over at the shop when that thing went off if you want to know.' He bounced up from his chair and pointed his finger at Alex.' Go and ask old Comino if you don't believe me. He'll tell you I was there. Shit, and I thought we were mates.'

'We are. But you're not making much sense. You're fucking hiding something.' Alex was sick of it, he made to leave, scooped up his cigarettes and car keys. 'I've had enough of this. I'm out of here,' he said.

'You don't have to go Alex', said Janice

Beau stabbed his cigarette at the ashtray, 'Where are you going?'

'Back home. See my parents.'

'Yeh, well, go home to mummy and daddy if you want.' He grumbled from the depths.

Alex wasn't expecting that. 'What?' he said.

'You heard.'

'What's up you?'

'You always piss off when it gets a bit tough.'

'That's not fair,' scolded Janice.

'You shut up.' He turned back to Alex. 'Go if you want to, I'm not holding you back.'

'Better than being here, hiding behind the curtains, waiting for the cops to come knocking,' Alex retorted, his anger boiling to the surface. Pent up tension, post trauma release, call it whatever, but he'd had enough of Beau's attitude.

'You and your mates are in the shit,' declared Alex. 'I tried to warn you, but you wouldn't take any fucking notice of me. Get your loyalties right Beau, I've stood by you the whole time, not Reggie, not Conlan, where are they? Those guys are bringing you down. Look at you, look how far it's gone and I'm in it too now, thanks to you. Isabelle Herman, remember that name Beau... We are one step away from being arrested for murder, you know that don't you, Hamilton, Conlan, Reggie, then you, then me. I've been seen with all of you, an associate of fucking murderers and drug dealers,' Alex snarled. 'Thanks for a great fucking summer, Beau...thanks for nothing.' He was angry, bristling in front of Beau.

Beau stepped up, chest to chest.

'Well why don't you just fuck off then. You've been here long enough, sponging off us.'

Alex balled his fist; Janice tried to push between them. She jostled and pulled at Beau.

'You better go Alex,' she urged, holding on to Beau.

Alex turned away and gathered up his few belongings in silence. Beau stood watching him the whole time, fists balled. He nodded to Janice as he went out.

'Gutless prick.' Beau yelled as Alex slammed the door after him.

Chapter 27

At first, his mother had quizzed him about his cuts and bruises, but Alex had run afoul of rocks enough from surfing in the past, that he easily passed it off as a surfing accident. She accepted that and fussed about him appropriately, but his father kept glancing at him as if sizing him up.

He was used to this, his university years had taught him to hide many aspects of his life from his parents, sometimes successfully, other times not. It was harder to fool his dad. But by the Saturday, they had both begun to smell a rat. They knew that in the last two days he had not been his usual self.

Alex had trouble sleeping at night. His dreams of being trapped in a vortex of sand kept jerking him awake in the early hours, and he would roam the house, making cups of tea and willing himself back to sleep. He avoided any conversation about the bombing, even though newspapers lay all over the kitchen table screaming the latest headlines. He was short tempered with his mother, exasperated at any show of concern she had for him, especially when small pieces of glass kept disgorging from a few of the wounds that refused to heal cleanly.

He especially didn't talk about Beau but spent long periods sitting aimlessly on the verandah watching a dusky blue egret that continually patrolled the ponds along the border of their property. It would stalk the edge before chasing insects among the lily pads. He had helped his father dig those ponds and build the stone bridge over them when he was still at school. He would sit and watch it for hours, it reminded him of the lakeshore brolga he had seen in his dreams, the one with a girl's face, a beautiful thing that was enveloped in a dust storm. He was smart enough to know what it meant, but there was nothing he could do about it.

It was the Saturday 'morning News Broadcast from Brisbane that sparked the biggest reaction.

> *Police confirmed more details today in the Nerimbah bombing case. It is confirmed that Sgt Cooper was responding to a tip off from the public which placed him at the scene at the time of the explosion. Attention is now centred on the identity of a man seen near the property both prior to and straight after the explosion on the day. He is reported of large build, thick set, long blond hair, approximately 18-25 years of age. He was dressed in a floral shirt, shorts and thongs. Meanwhile, further drug seizures and arrests have been made on the Nerimbah coast as Police continue their investigation into the fatal bombing.*
>
> *In other news, relatives and friends of 10-year-old Isabelle Herman are gathering on the coast in preparation for the funeral to be held at Nerimbah Lutheran Church, Monday 26 January.*

He knew straight away that they were hunting for Beau. The description fit him perfectly. And if they were after Beau, it wouldn't be long before they were after him. It confirmed his fears. There was no pretence left, he had to find out the truth and only Beau could tell him that. He rang Beau's number, but it was Janice who picked up.

'Have you seen the news tonight?'

'No. I just got in. Beau's not here.'

Alex looked around to see if his parents were close to the phone, but both were in the kitchen, the evening's dishes being washed and dried. He lowered his voice to a whisper.

' Janice, it's Beau. He was definitely at the house before the explosion. They have a full description of him now. Is he there?'

'No, he's out, thank God. I don't know where he went, he didn't leave a note, but I could have killed him the way he's been. We argued after you left the other day, we've barely talked. What makes you think he was there?'

'Police have his description; he was in one of his Hawaiian floral shirts on Tuesday when he brought me home wasn't he? Police said tall, thick set, blond hair, early 20's, wearing a floral shirt. Must be Beau, he's the only person I know who wears those shirts.'

'Could it have been Hamilton?'

'Beau said it definitely wasn't Hamilton.'

'What about Reggie or Conlan then? '

'Reggie has red hair, and he's thin. Conlan's tall, thick set like Beau, but he has short black hair. Neither of them match the description; but it fits Beau.... Straight after the explosion, Beau said he had been swimming, but he wasn't wet, he was dry remember. He hadn't been in the surf. He lied about that.'

Janice was quiet on the end of the line. 'Why would he lie about that?'

'I don't know. That's what I want to find out. He lied to us both.'

'I thought Beau was better than that,' she paused. 'Hang on the line, someone is at the door, that could be him now.'

Alex waited patiently, hearing muffled voices in the distance over the receiver.

'It's the Police.' Janice said and hung up the connection.

Chapter 28

Alex left his parents' house early and drove down to the Herman house in Nerimbah. He hadn't been back to it since the day of the explosion, and he wasn't sure how he would react to the scene, but he knew he had to see it again before he confronted Beau. He pulled up across the road and joined the smattering of early dog walkers who had stopped to view the house. It was a weekend and more people than usual had come to see the destruction of the crime scene.

All the debris had been cleared from the front lawn and the road. Police barriers were erected across the remains of the splintered front door and fibro wall. It was only that terrible gash in the façade that indicated what had happened here. Beyond that, the front room was dark, he couldn't tell if it was in shadow or blackened by the smoke. Small holes had been blasted through the fibro wall, testament to the intensity of the grenade.

He saw his spot in the gutter where he had sat and even looked to see if the finger was still there. He could see where it had been, he knew with a singular clarity the exact spot where the finger had lain, and where he had placed it after he picked it up...and where it had come from. The news hadn't revealed the extent of Isabelle's injuries, but when he saw the shattered wall, he knew it must have been terrible.

A detective pulled up in his unmarked Ford and stepped up to unlock the Police caravan that was parked in front of the house. He turned and looked directly at Alex before he disappeared inside. It broke the spell, and Alex walked away, getting back into his car. He was helpless to understand the sea he was swimming in; it wasn't one he was used to. This one was dragging him under, he was drowning, and he knew Beau was pulling him under.

The knock on his side window startled him. The detective he'd just seen was at his car door, gesturing for Alex to open it. He wound the window down.

'Can I talk to you for a minute?' he asked. 'Would you mind coming over to the caravan where we can have a chat?'

He was of that indeterminate age, older, experienced, with the dark wrinkled skin of a heavy smoker. He noted the stiff long sleeve white shirt and narrow dark tie of a Detective that didn't go well with the temperatures of a Queensland summer. His tone was pleasant enough, and Alex couldn't detect any real concern, but it didn't stop his heart from speeding up a notch. Alex said nothing but opened the door and followed the detective over the road to the caravan.

'I'm Detective Newman, Brisbane CID.' He introduced himself and squeezed into one side of the caravan table and indicated for Alex to sit on the other. He opened a buff manilla folder and quickly scanned the pages. Behind him a thick curtain blocked off the rest of the caravan, and outside he could hear the arrival of other detectives and smell the sweet tobacco smoke that found its way in the door. Alex wished he had one now, but they weren't on offer.

'Thank you for coming in. Let's start with your name. You are?' Newman questioned.

'Alex Holmes.'

Newman made a note in the file in front of him, before resuming. 'Do you live locally?' he asked.

Sometimes, at a house just up the road. Last night I was at my parent's place, they live on the road to Dunoonan.'

'Are you aware of what this might be about?'

Alex nodded.

'Is that a yes, or no?' Newman asked. Alex held his stare and was determined to make the detective work for it.

'I'll take that as a yes?' He scanned a few pages ahead in the file. 'So, you have been staying at a house just up the road, the one rented by a Dennis Beaumont and Janice Mckenna. Would that be right?'

Alex struggled to stay calm, they already knew about him. He nodded. 'Again, I'll take that as a yes,' said Newman. 'Did you witness the explosion here on Tuesday? Or were you in the vicinity when it happened?

Alex stared back, saying nothing.

'Mr Holmes, I need you to answer me.'

'I not sure what you are getting at here, am I a suspect?' Alex asked, trying to sound more in control than he really was.

'I don't know. Are you?' He stared back in return. 'Look, this is an investigation into a crime that led to the death of a young girl. It's serious. Let's not muck around here Alex. A person fitting your description has been identified as being in this location on the day of the explosion, it was only a matter of time before we caught up with you. Just lucky you dropped by today, and... volunteered your time.'

'I thought you had caught the blokes who did it?'

'We have two men in custody at present, others have been questioned, however the investigation is ongoing. This isn't a formal interview; we are talking to everyone who was present in the area to establish a picture of what happened.'

'Fair enough. 'Alex could see no reason to stall further. 'What do you want to know?'

'Were you here when the bomb went off?' He paused, then continued. 'Sergeant Cooper identified someone of your description at the scene, he thought it might have been you, so were you present at the explosion?'

After a pause, Alex relented, 'Yes, I was here. I was passing by.'

'Why haven't you come forward earlier Mr Holmes? Surely you have been watching the news, you know the gravity of the situation.'

'I've been sick,' Alex answered flatly.

'I see.' Newman said, the disbelief barely disguised. 'And why were you here?'

'I was on my way to the surf; I had my board with me.'

Newman glanced down at the notes in his folder. 'It doesn't say that here, no mention of a surfboard.'

'Well, I had one with me. I was on the way to the surf when I walked past, and the explosion knocked me onto the road.'

'What time was that?

'I don't know. I don't remember. I wasn't looking at my watch.'

'Had you arranged to be here at that time?'

'No. I was on my way to the surf, as I said.'

Newman leaned back, tapping his lighter on the Laminex table and looking directly at Alex as he spoke.

'You know, in most arson cases, the perpetrator is nearly always at the scene of the crime, watching whatever he torched burn to the ground. They get their jollies from watching. Is that you Alex? Got your kick from being here when the explosion went off?'

'No way', said Alex, the tone of the interview had distinctly changed,' I was passing by with my board on the way to the surf when it hit me, blasted me off my feet into the gutter, it wrecked my board. I was hit, here and here.' Alex pointed to the cuts and scabs around the left side of his face. He pulled up his T-shirt to show him further evidence.

'Sergeant Cooper saw you watching from the road.'

'He's wrong! I was walking by, I just saw it, that's all.'

'So you've said. Show me where you were standing.'

'I wasn't standing, I was walking by,' Alex repeated.

Newman led Alex outside onto the grass footpath. He tried not to look at the broken house but had to get his bearings. He moved out on to the road, and around to the back of the caravan looking down. The caravan was positioned just next to the spot where Alex had landed on his side. There was no finger there now, but he was sure he could still see it. He blinked and shook his head to clear his vision.

'It was just here.' He pointed down. Most of the road had been cleared of debris, but there was a small piece of white fibreglass among smattering of glass fragments on the rough bitumen.

'There's a bit of my board, where the nose broke off, if you don't believe me.' He looked up at Newman, it was then he noticed two other detectives had moved in close to him, one next to the far side of the caravan and the other to Newman's' left, attentive to everything Alex was saying. They must have been outside the door listening the whole time to his interview, they had him boxed in, if he had wanted to run, he wouldn't get far.

Newsman bent down and retrieved the piece of the fibreglass. He held it up for Alex to see.

'Is this from your board?'

'Looks like it,' said Alex.

He passed it to one of the other detectives, and said, 'I'm going to need to see your board as evidence.'

'Evidence? Do I need a lawyer?'

'Only juveniles get automatic representation Alex. For the moment, you can just answer the questions and assist us with our enquiries...voluntarily. You say you were heading for the surf! We are two streets back from the beach, and the surf is over there.' He pointed in an easterly direction.

'The waves aren't any good there.'

'Where are they good?'

Alex pointed ahead.

'So where were you coming from that you ended up here, on your way to the surf?'

Alex baulked. 'From back there. I knew the waves were better up here, so I came this way.'

'From where Alex? From the Beaumont house?'

He nodded.

'Can you go through what happened for me please?

Alex recounted as best he could what he had seen up to the blast. He had difficulty describing the girls dancing around their father as led them to the side of the house. Newman stood impervious as he went through the details, interrupting him at times to clarify a point, or ask him if had noticed anything further afield. But overall, his story must have rung true to what they already knew. Up to a point.

'Was anyone with you?' Newman asked. 'Sgt Cooper says he saw someone with you. You had an accomplice, didn't you?'

'Accomplice? You make me sound like a criminal.'

'This was a criminal act son. A little girl died. It's a murder investigation. If it wasn't you who was responsible, who was it? Was it the person with you?'

Alex could say nothing. They already knew about him. They knew where he had been, where he was going. They were playing him, trying to trip him up, to confirm what they already knew. He looked at each of the detectives.

'It's been four days since the blast, and you are a key witness who failed to come forward and help us with this investigation. Not very civic minded of you Alex. So, tell me now. Who was with you?'

Alex glanced from face to face of the detectives that ringed him. It wasn't him they were after now, it was Beau. Sweat trickled into Alex's eyes. They stood around him waiting for his answer, sweat running down their necks and staining the collars of their shirts.

'I don't know who you mean?'

Newman sucked in a deep breath; he had clearly come to a tipping point.

'Mr Holmes', he hissed, 'we are piecing together an investigation to find out who was responsible for this murder, and tragic murder it is.'

He leaned closer, his breath and spittle a shock to Alex, driving him back up against the caravan wall.

'We know someone helped you get away, they were seen helping you down the street, in that direction.' He pointed in the direction of the beach shack. 'Funny thing is no one can remember seeing that person coming to your aide in the first place, which means that they were already here, they were on the scene faster than those ambulance blokes, and they live next door.' He gestured at the station, 'He didn't come in a car, and he wasn't from the houses around here.' Newman waved his arm around for emphasis. 'Who else was there? Who helped you? Was it Beaumont, or Reggie Bishop, or Steve Henderson? We know who they are. You've been seen with them. They're your mates... and you're a part of it aren't you, Alex?'

'No!' he protested. 'I'm not' Alex backed hard into the rear of the caravan.

'Bullshit. But you know them don't you. You're shacked up with Beaumont and the McKenna girl, aren't you?'

Alex took his time to reply, 'Sometimes I stay there.'

'Did they plant the bomb?'

'No way.' Alex was indignant.

'If they didn't, who did?'

'How do I know?'

'Was Beaumont just passing by like you, or was he already here?'

The question threw Alex, it was the real question they wanted, but Alex knew the answer already. When he hesitated, it gave them the confirmation they had been looking for.

'Beaumont was already here, wasn't he?' Said Newman.

Alex said nothing.

'I think we can take that as a yes.' He turned back to the other two detectives and said,' I think we've found our man. Beaumont's the one we are looking for. He was here at the time of the blast.

See if he's home yet.' The two detectives turned away from the interrogation and strode to their squad car and headed down the street in the direction of the Beach Shack.

Newman continued exploring minor details, getting Alex to point out where he thought Cooper and Ken Herman were at the time of the explosion. Finally, he told him he could go.

As Alex turned back to his car, Newman had one final question,' Hey Alex, if you were injured, where did you go after the explosion? Because you didn't go to the ambos next door for treatment.'

'I don't remember, I was in shock!'

'I think I know. Doesn't matter. We'll get him. Bring your surfboard into the station so we can formally identify it and don't leave the area without notifying us.'

'Arsehole' Alex mumbled under his breath as he turned his key in the ignition and spun the Peugeot around back to the Beach Shack.

' Shit, shit, shit!' Beau was now their chief suspect, and Alex had just confirmed it in the interview. He hoped he wasn't home when the detectives showed up. He might be a big dumb prick, but he was still his mate, and by rights, mateship counted ...unless you were in love with his girlfriend.

He bounded up the side ramp, pulling open the door. 'Is Beau here?' he gasped.

'He's not here. 'Janice answered. She looked frazzled. 'Detectives have just been around looking for him to take him in for questioning. They just barged in, didn't even knock.'

'Do you know where he is? I want to ask him a few questions myself.'

'He hasn't come back Alex, I don't know where he's gone. We had another row, and he didn't come home last night. Leaves me to hold the fort. The police come asking questions about him, Jonas comes knocking on the door looking for a deal, I'm left to clean up his mess. Fuck I hate this.' She was exasperated. 'Make some coffee will you! No! Something stronger.'

Janice disappeared into the bathroom. Alex had two glasses of rum ready when she re-appeared, her face was wet and eyes red and rimmed with moisture. He motioned toward the verandah, but she shook her head and flopped into the kitchen seat. Her fingers shook as she accepted the glass.

'Sorry Alex. I'm sick of it. It's been really difficult the last two days.'

'What did the cops say?'

'The ones last night were uniforms, young guys, pleasant enough, completing local enquiries about who lived here, where we were on the day, did we see anything unusual? But the Detectives just then were something else, they were coming in after Beau, no doubt about that. I said to them not without a warrant, but that didn't stop them, they still came in and barged around, checked all the rooms. The way they were going on, it was as if Beau was the bomber. Beau might be a lot of things, but he's not a murderer.'

'I've just been down there. One of the Detectives, Newman, grilled me about last Tuesday. They're sure Beau was the person at the house before the blast.'

'What did you tell them?' Janice asked, raising her eyebrows questioningly.

'Nothing they didn't already know. They'd figured it out. Beau had been at the house before the explosion and straight after... I think I confirmed it for them.'

'Not your fault Alex. Beau makes his own mess. But why was he at the house in the first place?'

'I don't know. I don't think he knew there was going to be an explosion. He wouldn't have been at that house if he knew there was a bomb inside,' said Alex. 'But Beau was there before the explosion, he is the one the police are after. So why was he there?'

'Pick up drugs probably. Like he always does, picks up and drops off drugs for Reggie, or Conlan. That's who he works for. It was a job I reckon,' said Janice

'So, they sent him to get drugs from a vacant house rigged to explode?' Alex surmised. 'That doesn't make sense.'

'It does if none of them knew the bomb was in the house. The news say it was an attempt to kill Cooper. What if it was really meant for Beau? And I wonder if Beau thinks the bomb was meant for him. That would explain why he's been acting scared all week. He thinks they were after him. If that's the case, I'd be hiding too,' said Janice. 'I understand them trying to get rid of Cooper, but not Beau.'

'Why not? You know yourself. Reggie and Conlan are pissed off with him, they don't trust him anymore, he's a problem, and Conlan's got a reputation for getting rid of his problems.'

'But Reggie is his mate, it can't be him. Beaus been trying to ring him all week. He wouldn't do that if he thought Reggie was trying to kill him, he'd run a mile instead.'

'Janice, look around you, he has run, he's not here.' Alex gestured at the empty room. 'He is hiding. If not from the Cops, then it could be from his boss.

But Janice intervened. 'The Police said the bomb was a grenade, and they found some at Hamilton's house in Brisbane. They got proof that Hamilton planted the bomb.'

'But the cops want to arrest Beau as an accomplice, because he was the last one seen at the house before the explosion. An accomplice to murder. Shit, if they can pin that on Beau, they'll get Conlan and Reggie, and then I'll be going down too. If Beau was caught; it would jeopardise their whole operation.'

'Maybe they don't want him caught. Come on Alex, think! You're the smart one. Why was Beau at the house the same time as the cops? Did they want him dead, or tried to frame him?'

'I don't have an answer to that. Shit, we just keep going round in circles. Only Beau knows why he was there, and he's not here.'

They finished their coffee in silence, confused, lost in their own thoughts.

'Alex, where do you think Beau is? Why wouldn't he tell me where he's gone?'.

'So that you can't reveal what you don't know,' said Alex.' The Police have been around looking for him. If you don't know where he is, then you can't give him away, even by accident. It stands to reason.'

'You and your reasoning. God, I hate it.'

'He'll be back. I think I know where I might find him, or at least I've got a good idea.'

'He better be back soon, or I may not be here when he does. I didn't sign up for this. If you find him, tell him ... I'd really just like him back.'

'So do I.'

They looked at each other, no more reasoning, no more deduction. They had hit a wall. Alex rose and headed for the door.' I'm going to the funeral tomorrow. Will I see you there?'

'No,' Janice replied. 'I don't know if I could stand it.'

'Neither do I, but I'll still go. It's about respect,' said Alex. He left her slumped in the chair, rum in hand, none the wiser.

It was dark. Alex finished the last of his cigarette and ground the stub into the grass. He had parked up around the corner and walked the last 100 metres to Jeff and Marjorie Beaumont's house. Next door to them, Reggie's house was dark, there were no cars parked under his place, no yellow Monaro on the lawn, and no lights on. But Alex wasn't here to find Reggie. He turned his attention to the Beaumont house; lights were on inside.

As he climbed the steps, his hand brushed over the peeling paint, the edges grabbing at his skin. He never thought that the Beaumont's would let their house go. Not that Alex cared what people did with their house, something the privileged could think about. He knocked on the door panel of frosted glass, lead lined green and red triangles in the centre, and waited patiently till he saw a shadow pass behind it. The door opened.

'Hi Mrs Beaumont, it's me, Alex. Nice to see you. Is Beau in?' It was sing-song, it was merry, it was false, and it sounded as put on as it was insincere.

'Oh, Alex, I wasn't expecting you. Come in...come in,' she repeated, as if already trying to decide what she wanted to say...or not say.

'We don't get many visitors at night.' She took a furtive glance down the hallway. 'Beau's not here at the moment, but come through to the kitchen, and say hello to Jeff.'

Alex remembered the house from the times he came over during the high school years. Jeff and Marjorie Beaumont were 'old' parents then, certainly older than his own. It seemed that modern times had passed them by, they didn't adjust to change very well, and found it hard to relate to Beau, who was headstrong and often in trouble at school. The door to Beau's bedroom was closed.

'He doesn't come home very often now, goes next door instead.' She led him into the light of the kitchen. The kitchen still had red veneer Laminex tops and aluminium chairs, original from the 1950s, the house was first brought by them. On one of the chairs, Jeff Beaumont sat nursing a tall bottle of cold XXXX Bitter, no glass. He nodded at Alex, then turned his gaze back to the racing pages of the paper spread in front of him. Alex had stepped back in time...but he took the lead.

'I was just trying to hunt up Beau, that's all, and wondered if you had seen him at all this week.'

Marjorie went on as if she hadn't heard. 'It's been so long since you left high school, really, only a few years, and we haven't seen you since then. Sit down, would you like a drink. Jeff, get Alex a drink.'

She wrung her hands on the tea towel to dry them, but there were no dishes in the sink.

Alex stayed standing, Beau's car wasn't outside, but that didn't mean he wasn't here or hadn't been recently. Marjorie Beaumont prattled on.

'I haven't seen your parents for a while, please say hello for me.' She changed tack and looked directly at Alex. 'What has he done now?'

'Pardon', said Alex.

'What has Beau been up to now?'

'Ah, nothing Mrs B.' Referring to her as he used to when he was much younger, a familiarity long gone.

'Is he in some kind of trouble? Not mixed up in that awful bombing, is he?'

'No.! Not at all.' Alex lied.

'We just don't see as much of Beau these days; he and Jeff don't get on. And that Janice, his girlfriend, she's a sweet young thing, I don't know how she puts up with him.'

'Neither do I Mrs B,' Alex chimed in good naturedly, trying to keep the conversation light.

'He stops by to say hello every month or so. He was about due again soon. But he mostly hangs around with Reginald Bishop from next door.'

'That prick!' Jeff butted in.

'Jeff! That's not fair, he's done nothing to harm you?'

'He's a prick, and Beau hangs around him like a bad smell. And I know what the bad smell is, and where its coming from.' He pointed in the direction of Reggie's house next door.

'Jeff doesn't get on with Mr Bishop, especially now that Beau goes fishing with him and not his own Dad.'

'Him and his big flashy boat. Useless pricks, the two of them.'

'That's not fair Jeff, Beau comes around when he can, picks up and drops off a few things, and keeps his room neat. But he hasn't been here lately, and not in the last week or so. Especially after that terrible thing that happened next to the ambulance station. Brian Dobson, from the ambulance, said he's never seen anything like it, he had to go in and help that poor little girl. He said there was only...

'Thanks Mrs B,' Alex interrupted,' I was only looking to see if Beau had been by.'

'Oh, yes! But he always went off by himself to who knows where, with that Reggie half the time. He's always looked after himself, not much thought for anyone else, mind you, never thinks about his dad at all. But I expect he wouldn't have gone far. He wouldn't leave here without it.'

'Without what Mrs B?'

'Without seeing me, or his dad. It's very quiet, even next door have gone away. They've gone fishing for a few days, I think. Yes, I think he's gone fishing with Reggie for a few days. But Janice would know. '

'She hasn't seen him either. Can I see it?' asked Alex.

'See what love?'

'His room... he might have left something behind...that he might need.' God that was lame, Alex, you must think on your feet quicker than that.

'Oh, I don't think you need to do that,' said Marjorie Beaumont, decisive.

'Well, if Beau does drop in, or gets back from...fishing, tell him I understand what happened, and I'd like to see him. You'll tell him, won't you.'

'Have you two had a disagreement?' Marjorie asked. 'You were such good friends.'

'Just a difference of opinion Mrs B, that's all. Remember to tell him that. I'll be off now. I'm hoping to see Beau at the funeral tomorrow, if he's around.' Alex turned quickly and headed down the hall, quick enough to catch movement in the shadow under the gap at Beau's door, as if someone had stepped back from it. But he couldn't be sure.

Marjorie Beaumont thanked Alex for dropping by as she closed and locked the front door after him. The outside light helped him navigate the steps down, but at the bottom, in the faint reflected glow, he could see that Reggie's boat wasn't gone from next door. As he walked down the front path, it took all his will power not to turn and look up at Beau's bedroom to see if he was being watched from the window.

Chapter 29

A church wasn't Alex's usual haunt. He grew up with some semblance of Christian faith and spent most Sunday mornings with a whole host of children the same age at the Nerimbah Presbyterian Sunday School, colouring in pictures of Christ and his disciples. That church was small and built of stone tucked in behind Georges Head. It was certainly not like the grand Catholic Church he was in for Isabelle's funeral. It was large, airy and could take a full congregation three times the size of the Presbyterians. But their function served the same purpose. There was no room for inter denominational jealousy, today the congregation was united by Isabelle Herman.

The rows of pews were full, facing a bank of lead light windows above. The light played differently through the density of colour in the opaque glass and bathed them all in dappled light. He certainly missed much of what the priest had to say, but the intent was not lost on him. Funerals, after all were a lament to what was lost, and what could have been. But there was no doubt that Mrs Grace Herman's grief demanded attention, her body rocked gently. Jeff Herman sat straight backed, resolute, holding the hand of his surviving daughter Donna, a small body, still swathed in bandages, sitting between her parents.

Alex struggled to find his place in the depth of feelings around him. He looked around the congregation. The young engulfed in tears of grief, while the parents sat stoic rather than emotional. They understood what the loss of a past and future was, and were intermittently leaning in, to whisper words of solace and comfort to their own children, clutching the hands of the younger ones, rounding up their emotions in the squeeze if a palm, willing the pain to be transferred to them.

Alex felt he was witness to private moments, a voyeur of emotions. His own father gently touched the side of his leg; it brought his attention back to the front. He glanced around at his father, looking into his face. He'd been here before, he knew it, but couldn't figure out when. His mother sat dignified in her empathy and held his father's hand. A few pews ahead, he could see the long blond hair of Cathy Barrett, next to her, Joan and Ron Barrett sitting straight, still. Other families were grouped around the church. Most knew Jeff Herman since he had come to the coast from down south. We had all come from somewhere to be here thought Alex. The Millar's from England, Villi Tanoa and his family from Fiji, the Shannon's and Kennets of the pilot station, the Nerimbah fishing families like the Flannery's, they all came from somewhere to end up here, on the coast, yesterday and today. They were all immigrants in some form or other. He knew these families; he grew up with them, especially the Beaumont's. He caught a glimpse of Janice; she did come after all. She was sitting next to Marjorie Beaumont. ... but there was no Jeff Beaumont, or Dennis 'Beau' Beaumont. Even Senior Sergeant Cooper, covered in bandages and heavily surrounded by police sat at the back, Newman and his Detectives stood just inside the church entrance.

The service was long and full, a tribute to the community who came to farewell Isabelle. The full pews and standing room only were a sign of respect. In closing, four fathers, uncles, friends gathered at the small coffin, each to a handle. The coffin was so small, Alex struggled to keep composed. His father gently held his forearm.

Alex thought churches are an old institution with no real place in the brave new world he thought he was part of, except for today. Today they are for Isabelle Herman. And there will be other days as well. The congregation stood, to honour the collective loss of one of their own. Alex found it hard to recall Isabelle, his memory of her skipping through the grass, yet he was one of the last to see her alive. He was inextricably linked to her. What was much clearer in his memory was her little finger, and her little silver ring with a unicorn and red glass ruby embedded in it.

As the coffin left the church, he looked around one last time for Beau, but he wasn't there, and he should have been. Alex felt the anger well up inside of him. Who's the gutless prick now?

Chapter 30

There was no wake, no soulful reminiscing of Isabelle's life over a beer. Alex hadn't had much to do with death, it was his first funeral, but he was angry. He didn't understand why, but it knotted up inside of him, but he didn't know how it should manifest. The anger of keeping secrets, of lying to keep the reality from the door.

He was in a spiral of deceit with his parents, the very people that deserved it the least. They suffered the brunt of Alex's frustration. The last two days he barely spoke with them when he was home. They didn't deserve it, but he couldn't find a way to stop it either. His mother had felt it was important to show a strong, united family presence at the funeral, so he stood with his father and mother in the church grounds as they talked with each of the Nerimbah families that they knew but hadn't seen for some time. Funerals were a place to renew old acquaintanceships. Alex just wanted to get out of there. He barely said anything to them as he left.

Alex hadn't known any young people who had died, they were mostly old, it didn't really affect him. They were older than the music that they failed to understand, older than the thoughts of love and sex and drugs and waves that corrupted and cleansed at the same time. Death was detached from his youth...until now.

He wanted to find Beau. He wanted to know why he felt so corrupted. He wanted to know why he shouldn't tell someone what he knew, perhaps it would cleanse him, relieve him of the burden of deceit. Police were looking for Beau, and he knew more than any of them what had happened. The Herman family deserved better, Isabelle deserved better, he deserved better.

It wasn't that far from the church to the Beach Shack. He pushed his Peugeot too fast into the corners, the tyres squealed, it wasn't made for this sort of carelessness. He pulled up outside Beau's house, marched up the ramp, he was angry, and he wanted to front Beau.

When Janice opened the door, she said nothing, but swung it wide to let him in. She retreated to the kitchen table where a nest of cigarette butts revealed what her afternoon had been like.

'You're not working?' Alex asked.

'No', she said. 'Not till later. I changed my shift.'

'He's not here, is here!'

'No'.

'Why not?'

'How should I know!'

'He should have been at that funeral today.' In Alex's world, Janice lived with Beau, she shared his life and so shared the shame of his absence.

Janice said nothing.

'He owed it to Isabelle, to their family. Show some respect. Face up to it. '

'Face up to what?' Janice interjected.

'Face up to the fact that he crossed a line. He was there when that little girl was killed. I saw it... I've touched it. If he had showed at the funeral, then I'd know he'd be trying to come back, that he's like me, ... not like one of them... not like Reggie or Conlan or Hamilton. It would show that he only worked for them, and being like them is only temporary. That he's not changed. ... that it's not forever that he's mixed up with those bastards. That he has a plan, to return to normal, to return to the Beau he was. You see that don't you?'

'Yeh. I see that. But its Beau we are talking about here. If he showed up today, he would have been arrested. He knew that. He's not like you Alex. He's not full of moral indignation. This is his kind of world, not yours.'

'If he was arrested today, he could tell them that he wasn't really a part of it.'

'Oh, grow up Alex! He couldn't do that, you told me so yourself, he's in too deep. He is part of it, and he'll go to jail,' she said in resignation, 'and he scares me.'

'What? He threatens you?'

'No. He'd never do that; this is Beau we're talking about. It's what he does when I'm not around that scares me.'

'It scares me too.' Alex slumped into a kitchen chair opposite her, all the anger seeping away from him. 'I don't want to end up like Beau. I didn't come back here for that, mixed up with drug deals and police, bombs and death ... this is so fucked, and Beau got me into it.'

'It's not all Beau's fault Alex. I think he's hiding because he's scared too.'

'Not good enough Janice. Dealing a few drugs is one thing but getting into murder is another. You asked me to find him the other night. I did. He was at his parents' house, hiding in his room. He knew I was there, he heard me, but he didn't come out, and I'm his mate.'

'He's not a coward Alex.'

'Yeh, I know that, but he's not much of a friend at the moment either.'

'No. And not much of a boyfriend either for that matter,' she said.

That sat across from each other at the kitchen table, lost in their own thoughts, letting companionable silence fill the void.

'I guess I was just looking for a lost summer, like the ones I'd missed out on when I went away. I didn't realise that life has moved on and got a whole lot more complicated while I was gone. I can't live like this. I thought I'd just be passing through, should be nothing complicated about that.'

'And Beau has made your life more complicated, has he?'

'Nope. Beau has made it much more, dangerous,' Alex observed, '... you're the one who has made it more complicated.'

Janice was silent for a moment. 'Not Cathy?' she asked.

'No. Not Cathy... it's you.'

She was silent. The shack was quiet, boards creaked, contracting after the heat of the day. Dusk was falling. Alex sat back in his chair, looking at her. He sighed deeply, closed his eyes. It didn't matter what happened from here, he had said all he had to say, the truth had come out about Janice, about Beau, about himself. The truth could be so exhausting.

A chair scraped back. He felt her breath, warm, moist on his eyelids. Next her lips, smoky, pressed gently against his own, no force, but a gentle brush to find a place to settle. Her hands warm on his shoulders. Alex opened his eyes and looked into hers, green, sure, unwavering. Janice pushed her lips harder against his, both slightly open now, accepting the exploration. Alex reached his hands in under her shirt, feeling her warm skin, drawing her to him. She straddled him on the chair, pressing down with her pelvis. His hands worked up her back, stroking her shoulders, till she broke off from her kiss. His hands moved around to her breasts. She pulled off her shirt and helped Alex take off his. She leaned in again, hungry for his mouth and skin, he responded, then disengaged.

They pulled at each other's clothes in the few steps to the couch, leaving them scattered on the floor. Janice spun around and lay back on the covers. Alex leaned over her, pressing his palms into the soft cushions, reaching for her. She sighed as he entered her. He gasped in surprise; he'd been holding his breath. They kissed deeply again and found their rhythm, gripping at each other, grasping at air when they could, until a final release for them both.

Alex crawled up next to her and they lay nestled side by side on the couch drawing breath. It was getting dark outside, the sound of passing traffic swished over the rhythmic ticking of the kitchen clock. The couch was damp from their love making, but neither of them felt compelled to move. They lay in silence, absorbing the heavy night air. There had been something desperate in their love making, but now it was over, he was content to lay with her and run his fingers through the thin sheen of sweat on her skin.

Alex looked down from the cushion at her each time the lights of a passing car lit her body in its soft glow. He was trying to form the right words to say. She glanced up at him, saw his brow furrowed in concentration and nodded to him. Whatever he was going to say was fine by her.

'I'm glad I came here today,' Alex said.

'I glad you did too. I've been half expecting it. I saw most of you in the shower last week.'

'I don't feel remorse you know. I don't feel that I've betrayed him. '

'Nor me,' she said, 'it's OK. I've known for a while that it's not perfect.'

'It looks pretty prefect from here,' he murmured as ran a finger over her breast.

'I'm being serious. Today we needed each other. Don't think this is for ever. I'm not going to up and leave Beau just because we slept together. I can't leave. I must stay here, this is my home with Beau, I have a job, this house, I came here for that and I'm not giving it up lightly.'

'I know that,' he said. 'I certainly don't expect you to. But I had to let you know the truth. Not enough of that has been said around here lately. I think we are all at a crossroads here.'

'A crossroads heh?' She said. 'Maybe just a crossroads for tonight. This is between you and me, it's separate, it's our business. I'm not going to tell him about this. Beau needs me, and if he's going to get out of this mess, he can't do it alone. I owe him that...and so do you. Beau and I have been together for too long. He wasn't always like he is now.'

Alex untangled himself and rose to put on his clothes.

'I won't be saying anything either. I meant what I said, I don't feel bad about it.'

'Neither do I Alex, but it won't be happening again.'

He finished dressing. 'I guess not.'

'Don't be mad Alex,' she reached for his arm. 'Beau's an idiot sometimes and we might be on rocky ground, but we live here, together. You have to respect that.' She picked up her clothes off the floor. 'I think I need something to eat before I go to work, what about you?' she asked.

'I think I need a drink. It's been that sort of day.'

They sat across from each other in companionable silence, Alex sipping at a beer while Janice picked at a leftover sandwich. It was different now, and neither could fathom how it had changed nor what it meant. Janice was lost in thought and didn't look up when Alex snatched up his car keys and left.

The door closed behind him, and he stood in the dark of the verandah. He didn't really feel like going to the pub and he didn't want to stay here. Janice's bed clearly wasn't for him tonight, or any night in the future for that matter, even after they had just made love, she had made that obvious. The couch was a long second best.

A car passed the front of the shack, its headlights illuminating a new Ford further down the road, parked on the opposite side of the street, the driver sitting still behind the wheel, smoking. The red glow of the cigarette waved up and down as he drew on it, then flicked the ash out the window. The only people who sit in dark cars and smoked were jilted boyfriends, or cops on a stake out watching houses. He briefly wondered who this guy was staking out.

'Shit! I'm going home,' he muttered to himself, hoping the Peugeot would start the first time.

Chapter 31

Alex woke in his own bed, the morning sun lighting up the room, still thinking about the sex with Janice from the night before. But what Alex had said to her after was not entirely true, he did feel some guilt. He may have been angry with Beau, but it certainly wasn't a good enough excuse to sleep with his girlfriend. No, that was a different thing, she was as willing as he, but he had no idea how it would go from here, and Janice had made it clear it wasn't going to be with her, but he wished it was. Today seemed a little lighter, part of his burden lifted.

'Any mail for me yesterday?' he called to his mother from the front verandah, stretching his legs out in the sun and sipping at her atrocious coffee.

'Nothing for you,' her reply echoed from inside. 'Are you working today?'

'That's all dried up,' he called back. 'No casual work left. The company is closed till February, and everyone else is on vacation.'

She poked her head out the door. 'Well, aren't we lucky? Now I've got someone to mow the lawn.' She smiled conspiratorially as she retreated inside.

Alex pondered how for the last month he'd been on the back foot, he had come to the coast to regain a piece of that carefree life that he glorified while he was away, but Beau had dragged him into a different world. He had no job prospects, there were the fights, the drug smuggling, police harassment, he had been blown up, and through Beau, implicated in a murder. Sleeping with Janice, his best mate's girlfriend, seemed the least of his indiscretions. Friendship or not, it was time to extricate himself from that world and regain his own life. He collected his camera from inside his bedroom and thought that was as good a place as any to start.

The summer swell had come in, overcast conditions with a light offshore wind. Nerimbah was breaking fast. Head high waves generated in the southern oceans surged around Bayman Headland past the rock wall. Thick lips broke into hollow tubes on the sand with a crump of compressed air. It was heading toward the low tide, and the waves were getting steeper, and hollower as they broke.

Alex used a Pentax K1000.It was his favourite camera, dints and scratches on the metal body the scars of many wild outings. The 200mm lens allowed him to capture close ups as he roamed the shoreline; he flicked between settings with barely a glance down at the dials. Swing the lens, focus, release shutter, wind on, check settings, light and shutter speed, focus again. It wasn't dissimilar to surfing, it was instinct and familiarity. Perfect left handers for a goofy foot. He had loaded with Black and White high-speed film to capture the mood. Surfboards sliced horizontal trails across grey walls of water decorated with marbled foam. Riders hanging precariously in space on dark ominous waves, frozen in time by the shutter release. If only Beau was surfing, his combination of power and recklessness would have provided him with an endless set of frames that he could submit for publication. As it was, he couldn't wait to see the proofs.

'Alex Holmes! How are you doing?' Peter Gollinsky splashed through the surf next to him, holding a film camera mounted high on a tripod. He spread the legs in the ankle-deep water and bent over the view finder of his Super 8.' Haven't seen you for ages,' he said without looking up.

'Hi Pete.' Alex called; he resisted using the old high school nick name of 'Gollie'. 'Nice camera but I think your tripod will be stuffed. 'Alex nodded at the sea foam swirling ankle deep around the legs.

'It's the old man's, he hasn't used it for years. At least it will have rusted to bits for a worthwhile cause,' he laughed.

Directly in front of them it was wild exhilaration, whoops and cries of 'Inside!' preceded an enormous wave that threatened to engulf the line-up. A few jostled for place, until one surfer took the peak and dropped into position on the wall hungrily sucking at him till, he disappeared inside its belly. He reappeared a few seconds later, speed and balance poised in confidence, bursts of spray following him. With a whoop of joy, he flicked out over the back and started paddling back out toward the line-up. By then, Alex and Peter, were back peddling fast, cameras held high, a two-foot wall of foam, the remnants of that last wave was racing toward them.

'Tell me you got that Pete,' Alex yelled when they got to drier ground. 'You got him in the tube?'

'Oh, shit yes!' laughed Pete, 'I got it ...I tracked him the whole way.' He could hardly talk with the excitement. 'What about you?'

'The take-off was vertical, and one of those God's rays was just behind him, a silhouette of him in mid-air. I'll have to wait till I develop it, but I think I got it. That was epic.'

They both glanced at the horizon, judging when the next set would appear. Alex knew he had just caught something special and by the looks of it, so did Pete. He hadn't seen Peter Gollinsky since high school. Though they weren't firm friends, they had shared a similar interest in the arts at school.

'How long have you been shooting film?' Alex asked.

Pete held his camera up for Alex to see. A Nikon R10 8mm, film cassette.

'Stole it from dad's cupboard last year. He doesn't know I've got it. He only ever brings it out at Christmas to make embarrassing movies of the relatives. He won't miss it. What about you?'

'I've shot a few pieces on 16 mm. Short 10-minute docos and narratives. I've transferred them to video tape for editing. Beats scissors and sticky tape.'

'Don't I know it', Peter lamented. 'Video tapes. They're like cassette tapes, aren't they? Magnetic.'

'Tapes are cheap, less than developing film. It's the video players that cost the money, but it makes editing so much easier.'

'I don't think I could afford it. I'm not that serious about it anyway'.

'Look around, only you and me are here filming this, no one else. You don't get much more serious than that.'

'My flat is covered with strips of celluloid as it is.' Peter pointed to the next swell filling the horizon.

'I'll tell you about it later, see you in the car park,' Alex said and waded down the beach to where he felt the angle would suit him better while Peter buried himself in preparing his camera for the next shot.

Alex checked his own settings and looked up. This was where he should be. He shot another roll of film before he ran for the carpark, showers of rain chasing him all the way.

Alex sat in his car, drying his camera with a towel, and rubbing at his hair to get rid of the rain. He looked out at the surf, riding each wave in his mind, and imagining new camera angles and the type of music he would put to Gollinsky's footage if he ever got hold of it. It had been weeks since he'd felt like this.

Pete Gollinsky ran past the front of his car, waved at him through the windshield, and bundled himself into the white VW next to him in the carpark. He noticed a girl already in the passenger seat deep in conversation with Gollinski. She turned to Alex and made signals for him to wind his window down.

'HI. I'm' Steph Moreton, a friend of Cathy's.' She called. 'Nice to meet you, Alex. She told me about you.'

Alex waved back at her. 'Hi Steph. Nice to meet you too', he called back between the cars, the rain squeezing in between the small gap in the side window.

'Sorry it didn't work out. Pete says it should have; he doesn't know why not.' Steph must have been about the same age as Cathy and equally full of vivacious spirit. She seemed genuinely sorry about he and Cathy. Pete leaned across Steph to join in.

'I'm coming back down filming tomorrow if you're still around, Alex. Come and have a coffee with us after,' he insisted.

The wind sprayed more rain into his open window, so Alex hastily wound it up, smiled and waved acknowledgement to them both.

Maybe this was how his summer was supposed to be, meeting with friends at the beach and planning for drinks on the run. He hadn't smiled like that around Beau for the last month. He started his car and backed out, swinging around to drive down the river esplanade and look at the boats. As he passed Barrett's market, he saw Cathy through the shopfront glass, and by instinct, he swung into the car park. Cathy looked up, and saw him, but didn't smile. Two boys sat in the gutter, still wet from the surf, chewing on a cream bun and passing a lime milk bottle between them.

'Food of the gods' heh boys!' Alex proclaimed as he stepped past them.

'Oh yeh. This is seriously good.' The blond one said between a mouthful of dough, cream squirting from the side of his mouth. Alex laughed and recognised himself at fourteen.

He waved at Cathy inside at the cash register. She looked around, there were no customers near, so she stepped up to the doorway. Alex met her halfway. He wasn't sure if he would still be welcome around here.

'Hi Alex,' she said, without offering anything more.

'Hi Cathy. I'm not sure why I stopped, I'm not here to buy anything, only that I needed to see you to say I'm sorry for the way it ended up. The situation can be difficult sometimes, but that doesn't excuse what happened.' He paused, she didn't encourage him, but he thought he saw a slight smile at the corners of her lips. 'I realise now how it must have been for you, and I understand completely. I wouldn't want to get mixed up with me either,' he offered as explanation.

She definitely smiled at that.

'Thank you.' She said quietly. Cathy could have said many things, but she didn't. It only confirmed to Alex why he liked her.

'Look, I'm leaving soon, heading to Melbourne. If you are serious about going to Uni, stay with it. Don't give up on it. This place isn't all it's cracked up to be.'

'Don't I know that! I hung around with you for long enough,' she quipped, then continued in a more serious note. 'I've been accepted for an Arts Degree in Brisbane.'

Behind her he could see Joan, her mother approaching down the aisle, trouble was brewing.

'That's great news. But right now, I'd better go. If you ever want to study in Melbourne, look me up. I mean it.'

'I just might do that.' She looked behind at her mother's approach. 'I'd better get back to work. Thanks for that Alex.' She leaned forward and pecked him on the cheek, then turned back inside; a customer waiting patiently at the checkout.

Walking back to his car, he passed the two boys still in the gutter, silently smirking. They had heard it all.

'What are you looking at?' Alex scolded them. 'Get back in the water where you belong.'

'Piss off!' The boys laughed and reached for the last of the cream buns in the paper bag between them. Alex smiled to himself.

He drove to North Nerimbah, the sky was clearing, but the wind had swung onshore by now, the bay water was choppy and uninviting. That didn't worry Alex at all, he had other things on his mind. For the first time in ages, he felt clear headed, regaining some control of his life. He didn't have a job in Melbourne yet, but he knew that it was time to go.

He wanted to clear any misgivings he and Janice may have about last night. He really did feel for her, from the first time that they had met. It had pained him to see the way Beau treated her at times, he wanted to tell her that. He also wanted to tell her that he was leaving soon.

Alex pulled into the Beach Shack and bounded up the ramp with a newfound sense of purpose. He turned and stared down the street, looking for the unmarked police car that had been on surveillance the night before, but it was gone. With a sense of relief, he knocked once and opened the door. The first thing he noticed was Beau sitting calmly at the kitchen table rolling a joint.

Chapter 32

Beau was reading an album cover propped up against a bottle as if it was all normal. He give out a business-as-usual impression, he barely looked up. It was a far cry from the previous week when he had prowled the loungeroom, hiding behind curtains, furtively pulling them aside every time he heard a car go past. Alex looked at Janice, she gave no indication that yesterday had been any different or anything unusual had transpired between them, but her skin was pale and taut, her eyes hooded, her lips a thin smile as she nodded a greeting to Alex.

'Hi mate. How are you?' Beau said, as if nothing untoward had happened in the past week. There was no acknowledgement that he had been missing for days, or that he was nervous about the police at the end of the street.

'How come you're here? Where's your car? The cops are sitting just outside,' Alex said exasperated.

'The Monaro's still up at the farm and Reggie dropped me off in the street behind. I came in the side door, no one can see from the street if I come over the fence. If they don't know I'm here, then they have no reason to come knocking.'

Alex was not so forgiving, he sat down across the table from Beau, silent, waiting for Beau to look up, waiting for an explanation.

'Thanks for looking in on Janice while I've been away. They tell me it's been pretty crazy around here; the cops even came looking for me. Janice saw them off, didn't you?' He reached out, hoping she would step into his protective embrace...she didn't.

'That's not what I want to hear Beau,' said Alex.

'I've been up at a shed in Kenilworth, it's a good setup out there, over 500 plants. It's a great set up really, wouldn't mind trying that myself. Maybe down near Byron, you know, up in the hills. Not as risky as that other stuff off the boats, bit more organic.'

'That's not what I want to hear either Beau.'

'Well, what do you want to hear then?' he jeered, raising his voice. 'That I'm sorry for calling you a gutless prick?

'That would be a start,' said Alex.

'Yeh. Well...sorry. Alright. I was bit tense last week, and it all got away from me. But it's all good now...now that it's all quietening down. Everything's OK.'

'Fuck mate, I don't think it's all OK.'

'Well, it is. There's been a change in plans. I've been talking with Reggie. He and Roy are going to wind up the offshore operation here, there's a new supply route opening up. We've got one more shipment coming by sea and its worth top dollar in the current market.'

'Jesus, said Janice, 'listen to yourself.'

'Everything's coming back to normal, you'll see,' said Beau.

'Except for Isabelle Herman.' Alex retorted.

'What's wrong with you?' Beau reacted angrily.

'She had a funeral Beau. On Sunday. And you weren't there.'

Beau's face changed ever so slightly, at first his jaw moved around without any sound, as he searched for the right words to use.

'I wanted to go to the funeral, really, I did. But I thought about what had happened, and decided it was better to lay low. Cops were there anyway.'

Alex was disgusted.

'You should hear yourself mate! Have you got any feelings for that girl?'

'It wasn't my fault. I didn't plant the bomb.' Beau tried to defend himself.

'That's not what the police think,' said Janice. 'They're still looking for you.'

'Have you been listening to the news at all?' asked Alex.

'No. I've been out in the bush, no TV reception,' he said.

'Beau, you were identified at the Herman house before the explosion, and after, when you helped me. The cops have you as an accomplice to the bombing, which makes you an accomplice to murder.'

Beau's face was ashen.

'Why were you at the Herman house before the explosion Beau?' asked Alex.

Beau put his unlit joint to the side and reached for a cigarette instead. He wiped his hand across his forehead, composing his answer, wiping a thin layer of sweat from his forehead.

'No lies this time, Beau.' said Janice. He glanced up at her before he spoke, all his previous bluster deflated. He looked at Alex and then toward Janice, and then down to the tabletop. He tapped at the Laminex with his finger as if listing off the steps to his actions.

'Hamilton said I was to unlock the door,' he recounted. 'The side kitchen door, to make it easy for Cooper to get in and retrieve the drugs.'

'What drugs?'

'Hamilton said they were setting up Cooper by planting drugs in the house.'

'But it wasn't drugs, it was a booby-trap,' exclaimed Janice.

'I didn't know that...I know that now. I thought there were just drugs stashed in the house, and Cooper was going in to get them, and when he came out, I'd ring Hamilton, and he would tip off the cops about Cooper and he'd get busted for possession. It was to be a stitch up of Cooper, to get rid of him from the coast. Reggie and Conlan reckon he's crooked, muscling in on the operation. Getting him busted would take the pressure off us. That's why I was there. I told you I'd been surfing, but I hadn't, I'd been watching from the phone box at Comino's store, waiting for Cooper to show up and get the drugs for himself. That's why I saw you get hit by the explosion. That bomb going off was just as much a shock to me.'

Alex screwed his eyes shut, he could see Ken Herman's house, with the policeman, Cooper at the letterbox and two girls skipping around the side... Cooper was there before Ken Herman pulled up.

'So why didn't the plan work? Why didn't Cooper go in the house when he arrived? Why call a locksmith?'

'He couldn't get in,' whispered Beau. 'The door was locked.'

Alex looked quizzically at Beau, 'I thought you said you unlocked the door?'

'I did,' he insisted. 'I did. But it locked again when I left.'

'I'm not following Beau. How did the door lock itself?'

Beau paused before answering.

' I was inside when Cooper showed up. He wasn't supposed to come that quick. Hamilton was to wait till I rang him the first time to say I had unlocked the door, then he would call Cooper, tip him off about where he could find drugs. But I guess he jumped the gun. Cooper nearly saw me, I panicked, dropped the key, and as I left, the door locked after me. That's why the locksmith was called...' Beau's voice petered out.

Alex finished it for him,' ...and when Isabelle Herman went into the front room, she triggered a grenade that was meant for Cooper. All you had to do was unlock the door. Why did you go inside? The house was empty. Why did you go in the house Beau?'

Beau refused to lookup.

'The drugs. You went in for the drugs.' Janice accused him. 'You went looking for an easy score. You couldn't help yourself, is that right Beau?'

'I don't know, I just thought there were... that I could get some for myself before Cooper arrived, they wouldn't miss it. But Cooper came early, he nearly caught me inside.'

'If you had done what you were supposed to do, and just unlock the door, Isabelle Herman would still be alive today, and Cooper would be dead instead. The Herman girls were only there because the door needed to be unlocked again. '

'It wasn't supposed to happen that way.'

'No Beau, it wasn't,' said Alex harshly. 'God, they stitched you up didn't they.'

Janice turned away and shook her head in disbelief.' How could you be so fucking stupid,' she said.

Beau flashed in anger, pushing to his feet, the chair tipping on its back.

'Don't call me stupid...you haven't had to fucking live with it.' His face screwed in anguish. 'You didn't kill Isabelle Herman.... I did. I must live with that... It was me. I fucked up and she got killed because of it, so don't you judge me! You think I don't judge myself...do you?' He thrust out his jaw, wet with tears.' I think about her every day, every fucking day, so don't shit me off with your 'holier than thou' attitude for not going to the funeral Alex.' He picked up the chair and sat back down on it, dejected. 'Fuck me it hurts,' he growled in anguish.

The room was quiet, the only sound of water dripping in the kitchen sink from a broken tap. Janice stepped over to Beau and squeezed his shoulders. He reached up and squeezed one of her hands back. He wiped the back of his other hand across his eyes.

'The plan was good, and it should have worked,' he said in finality.

'Beau, since when is killing a cop a good plan?' Janice asked quietly.

'Hamilton said specifically that it was drugs. They were only out to get Cooper busted, put him away for messing with us.' He re-explained.

'What a bunch of liars! You say Hamilton sent you? Why wasn't it Reggie or Conlan?' asked Alex.

'It was Hamilton. He was staying at Reggie's house. The other guys weren't around; they were out at Kennilworth. They didn't know Hamilton had put a grenade in there instead.'

'How convenient,' sneered Janice.' The two of them out of the picture, with alibies no doubt. Where's your alibi Beau?'

Alex continued, 'Beau, whether it was Cooper or not, you were going to be an accessory to murder. What part of that is not a set up?

Beau sat looking at him in stoney silence, Janice stood wide eyed, Alex elaborated further, his voice louder.

'So, why did they set you up, lie to you? Because there is no way Hamilton would have set you up without the nod from Conlan, or Reggie for that matter. You work for them. What have you done that's put you on the wrong side of those pricks?'

Beau didn't answer, but there was fear in his eyes, and Alex couldn't read if it was fear of them, or fear of the truth. People fight or flee when confronted with fear. Beau had already tried fleeing by hiding out in the hills. To fight was to admit to the truth and face it head on, engage with the enemy, and hope you come out on top. But Beau adopted a third option, to freeze, do nothing.

'I don't know. I haven't done anything. They can't prove I've done anything. Maybe we should wait and see.'

'Beau, you are an accomplice to a murder. And because you are, so am I, by association. When the police come knocking at your door, they will arrest you, then they will come looking for me. They've already done it once. I'm in the shit because of you, and unless we can find a way out of this mess, I'll go to jail, where you will already be!'

The three sat in silence, each digesting what Beau had revealed, and what it meant for them. Beau was the first to speak.

'So, we leave. Simple as that. We get out of here while we can. If the cops were serious about getting me, they would have staked out mums' place as well, but they haven't. We'll leave just as soon as I've done the last fishing trip with Reggie, that's in four days, the 16th.'

'You mean you're going fishing again? After everything that's going on?' Alex asked.

'Conlan said it will be the last haul, so we have to go on the 16th, no other date.'

'I don't want to you to do this anymore Beau.' said Janice. 'Please listen to Alex, he knows.'

'He doesn't know everything Jan, I'll make it the last one, it'll set us up, I promise.'

'I want it to finish now Beau. No more fishing. No more Reggie or Conlan, I don't trust them. Let's get out now, together.'

'Come on Janice, I trust Reggie, he's all right. One more haul and it's all over.'

'I don't want to wait around here. I think want to leave now, go south.'

'Well, why don't you?' Beau's stubborn streak kicked in. 'You don't need me; you can go when you like, I'm not stopping you. Unless you'd rather go with Alex instead.'

Alex held his breath, wondering if Janice had told Beau about them.

'That's not even funny,' She said, looking from Beau to Alex and back to Beau again.' I want you to come with me Beau, we go together.'

'Well, I'm not. I'm staying... until the 16th.' Beau sat back in his chair, a satisfied look on his face. 'For now.'

Alex paused before he spoke. 'You wait around here any longer for it all to go away, and you're sunk. If you take off, head south now, you might have a chance. A girl was murdered, a copper was nearly killed, even if Cooper is crooked, he was one of their own. The cops won't stop until everyone who was involved is in prison.'

'You don't know that;' said Beau.

'Sit around waiting and you'll find out.'

'I'm staying here.' drawled Beau.

Alex looked at Janice, but she looked away.

'Think about it Beau, sitting here thinking it will all go away in time won't be enough, you have to find a way out of this now.'

Beau stayed silent, resolute in his stubbornness, convinced he was following the right path, but Alex knew the dilemma they all faced, fight, flight, or freeze, and the last option would end in disaster.

The overcast sky did nothing to lower the humidity. Alex sat behind the wheel of his battered Peugeot, lit a cigarette, and pondered his next move. Flight was easy, he should drive away now, he owed either of them nothing. Leave all that in the past, fly, disappear, start a new life in Melbourne, stuff them. His summer had come to an end. He turned the key and the engine whined into life.

He shook his head; he wasn't equipped for this. He looked across at the Beach Shack once more. Beau was a stubborn dickhead at times and Janice was way too loyal to him, let alone how he felt about her, but he couldn't leave either of them. 'Fuck. What am I doing?' he said out loud to the empty car, thumping his hand on the steering wheel in frustration. He knew he had chosen to stay and fight.

Chapter 33

Alex went on the attack. His instinct told him that Conlan was the real force behind the organization, and he was by far more dangerous than the others. Hamilton from the Brisbane end might be in jail, but Conlan was still free. He had to convince Beau that Reggie and Conlan were out to get him, and he was sure that Hamilton would never have set up Beau without the OK from Conlan, he just needed the proof, and Reggie would supply that.

He waited patiently in his car on Boar Road, where he could see the roof of the Beaumont house, and the lights on in Reggie's house next door.

Boredom was setting in, he was almost going to give up when the lights went off at Reggie's, and a few moments later, headlights came on, and Reggie's F100 appeared at the end of his drive and turned away down the street: two figures silhouetted in the front seat, Reggie and Conlan.

Alex left his car around the corner and walked from there. He didn't know if he could find it, but surely it would be in Reggie's house. He skirted the streetlights and worked his way in the dark around the back of the house, and slowly climbed the rear steps, till he was at the back door. All was quiet and dark inside.

He took a flat screwdriver from his back pocket and tried it in the wooden casement windows. They didn't move at first. He readjusted the angle further along the sill till it moved a little, careful not to chip any of the paintwork. He'd done this once before to get into his flat at Uni and cracked the glass. He was no master breaker and enter, nor was he a thief, but he reminded himself that there was much more riding on this now than anything he had done before.

The window gave some more; he gripped the edge with his fingers and slid the screwdriver up until it found the catch. He wriggled at it, the widow was twisted, the glass at breaking point, he could feel it, flakes of painted putty began to shower his hands. This wasn't good. All at once, the catch released, and the window sprung open. Beau sighed; it still wasn't going to be easy. He levered his body up and over the sill, sideways through the narrow gap until he was hands down on the floor, bringing the rest of his body through the gap.

He straightened and realised he had no torch. He had lost it somewhere from the car to here. Some burglar he thought. Stupid. He tried the first three kitchen draws to see if Reggie had a torch. He didn't, but he found paperwork instead, notes, a calendar, and bills. He held them up into the ambient light from the windows, but there was very little to help him, he could barely read it, he wouldn't dare turn a light on. He looked around the kitchen, neat, tidy. Who was he kidding, Reggie would hardly leave an account of what Beau owed him in a kitchen drawer, it had to be hidden somewhere. 'This is no good, get the torch', he muttered to himself. He closed the drawers and retreated to the window, squeezing himself through the gap in reverse.

Below him, shafts of bright light suddenly lit up the concrete, heralding the unmistakable sound of a car pulling into the driveway. 'Shit' Alex nearly panicked but stayed calm enough to close the window behind him and stay where he was. If he ran down the stairs now, he would be lit up like a Christmas tree. He crouched behind the door on the small landing, waiting for the headlights to go off. Behind him, shadows of the wooden slats alternated with strips of light on the backyard grass.

The engine stopped, and a car door opened. Reggie's voice could be heard clearly.

'Do want another pack of smokes as well?' Reggie called to Conlan.

He didn't hear the reply. The lights were still on, Alex couldn't move. Suddenly the headlights went off, and the yard was plunged into darkness. Alex waited. Footsteps crunched the path and thumped up the front stairs till they stopped at the door.

Alex didn't hear anymore, he crabbed silently down the back stairs, trying to stay in the dark. Crossing the yard was no good, too open, Jeff Beaumont's fence was close, luring him, but he would cross Conlan's vision to get to it. No good. He looked at the garden shed under the house to the right of the stairs. Upstairs, lights went on as he heard Reggie's footsteps moving over the floorboards. Residual light silhouetted areas of the back yard and side fence.

Alex moved quickly to the shed door, slid the bolt and ducked inside, crouching on the concrete, it smelled of oil, petrol and grass clippings. Between the missing slats of the shed he watched for any movement. He knew he closed the window but wasn't sure he had put the papers back in the drawer. Too late now.

Conlan opened his car door, lighting up the front seat as he smoked, waiting for Reggie. Through the slats Alex could just make out the gleam of metal on the ground in front of the car, his torch. He stretched forward to get a closer look between the slats and rolled the old Victor mower to the side.

He looked up at the house again, the lights retreated one by one inside, Reggie's footsteps striding purposeful to the door. Once again, the house was in darkness. Reggie trundled down the front stairs and back to his car, threw a pack of cigarettes on the front seat, then everything lit up again, the car reversed out, and they were gone.

Alex breathed out and sat back against the shed wall. He eased the mower back into position, loose electrical tape sticking at his fingers from underneath the cutter deck. He leaned forward and used the Victor as a handhold to help him get up; it rolled again under his weight. This must be what it feels like to be sixty, he thought, uncertain on your legs and your bowels ready to give way at a moment's notice. He pulled at the electrical tape tangled in his fingers, it stretched but wouldn't release.

On impulse, he lifted the front of the Victor to find the snag. The house next door shed enough light for him to recognise it when he saw it. He had never held one, but he knew what an automatic pistol looked like. It was one of those American ones, not a revolver, but a rectangular shaped automatic with a magazine in the grip. It was taped to the mower blades under the cutting deck so it wouldn't come loose, but it had, and some of that tape was stuck to his fingers. Secured against the other blade, was a grenade.

He froze. It was a green orb; oval shaped with a shiny round pin and a spoon shaped handle. The letters M26 and 'fragmentation' were written on the side. He slowly lowered the Victor back onto the concrete. 'Shit' he said, and he backed out of the shed to go home, carefully closing the shed door behind him. How deep was he in this? How deep was Beau. These bastards were killers. He had had enough of Reggies house for one night.

Chapter 34

The next morning Alex stood remonstrating with Beau, trying hard to convince him of the facts.

'But the grenade is there, Beau, it's under Reggie's mower. It's taped there with a pistol. It's proof, they set you up. It was a grenade that killed Isabelle Herman, and Reggie and Conlan have one.'

'Doesn't prove a thing.' said Beau. 'It could have been Hamilton's; he could have hidden it, and they don't know it's there.'

'Come on.' Alex pleaded. 'It's Reggie's house and mower and Conlan is a proven killer from the war, he knows grenades. Here I'll show you how they hid it.' He led Beau round the side of the Beach Shack and pulled the mower out from under the house, tilted it back and pointed out where and how the tape had attached the weapons, then he pushed it back under the eaves. Beau said nothing, disbelief still in his eyes.

'Beau, you've got to cut them loose, get out of here. It's proof they are dangerous. They've got a gun, I've seen it before, on the boat when I did the pickup last month. That gun was taped with the grenade, so it must be theirs.'

'I know he's got a pistol. Reggie showed it to me; he keeps it for sharks.'

'Bet you he didn't show you the grenade? You don't keep them for sharks. It's not *Jaws* you know.'

'Mate, I believe you. So, there's a grenade,' said Beau,' What do you want me to do about it?'

'Ask them what it's for. Ask them if they had anything to do with the bombing.'

'Fuck off, I'm not doing that. But I do need to see them about my car.'

'You've got to finish this, Beau. At least see the grenade. Seriously, the only way to prove it to you how dangerous these bastards are, is if we go round to Reggie's now. I'll keep them talking, you duck into the shed and have a look for yourself, then tell me you're not convinced.'

Beau agreed and begrudgingly followed Alex to the car. Alex for his part was putting on a far braver front than he let on to Beau, he was petrified. If the thought of being near that grenade again wasn't enough, it was the knowledge that they were going up against Roy Conlan, trying to out manoeuvre a man that Alex knew in his heart, had already outsmarted them all.

At Reggie's house, the ruse went off perfectly. Beau used the excuse of dropping off his jacket into the boat downstairs next to the mower shed before going up to talk with Reggie and Conlan about getting his Monaro back. When he joined Alex at the top of the stairs, there was no reaction, Beau played his part perfectly. Reggie and Conlan were inside the sunroom and gestured for the boys to join them. The Monaro was still at Kenilworth, and after Thursday's drop, they would go up to get it. Beau broached his concerns about the weather. The forecast was not favourable at all; strong winds and seas were predicted from a tropical low-pressure system marching its way down the Queensland coast. Conlan said it was full steam ahead on Thursday night. It was to be the last shipment, and the weather was not going to hold it up. Beau would go 'fishing' with Reggie no matter what, there could be no delays. Beau accepted this and it was all very amicable until he departed from the script.

'Heh! Look,' he blurted out, 'seeing as this will be our last pickup in the boat, how about a bonus. I'm a bit worried the cops are going to ping me as an accomplice to the bombing, and It's only a matter of time before they show up again. They keep harassing Janice when I'm not there, and who knows what she's likely to say. Me and Janice might head south after this trip and start up my own operation near Byron. I wouldn't want things to blow up like they did here.'

Beau said all the wrong things. Alex had no idea where this had come from, and he kept staring hard at Beau, willing him to shut up. He noticed that Reggie and Conlan were looking at Beau equally so, but he'd seen that stare before. He'd seen it out on the boat when the shark came up to look at him.

Beau continued, oblivious to the reactions. 'Or...maybe instead of a bonus, I do the pickup on Thursday for free, and we cancel what I owe you. What do you say?' Beau stood with his arms out, as if he was doing everyone a big favour by emphasising this revelation.

Conlan glanced at Reggie, who returned the look with a slow nod. 'Yeh. All right Beau,' he said, 'We'll think about that.'

'I mean, it's been pretty wild round here, Hamilton's in gaol for that bombing and the cops are still looking for us, maybe it's just time for us to move on.' Beau offered tentatively.

'Sure. I understand.' Reggie smiled.

Conlan chimed in.' And tonight, why don't we all meet at the pub for a last drink together. We can talk about your proposal then. We'll call it your renumeration package. You too Alex, 8 o'clock? We'll make it a good night, bring Janice.'

'Yeh sure Roy. We can do that. Janice is working there tonight anyway.' offered Beau.

'Perfect. See you both then. Don't be late.' Conlan stared at Beau before dismissing him with a wave and turned back to Reggie.

Alex couldn't bundle Beau out of the house quickly enough, down the stairs and into the Peugeot. It had been sitting in the sun outside Reggie's house, and the seat covers had begun to expel all the aromas of spilt coffee and milk from the last few years. Beau quickly lowered his window to let the hot air out. Alex didn't bother; he was fuming.

'Well, I think that went alright.' said Beau.

'You've got to be fucking joking!' Alex admonished him.

'How did you think it would go, smartarse? Seemed all good to me. Nothing to worry about.'

'Nothing to worry about?' Alex exclaimed, parroting Beau's remark. 'Why did you say that stuff? You just reminded them that you owe them money, and you're not going to pay it back before you clear out and start a rival drug business with Janice, who, according to you, can't keep her mouth shut around the cops. You already owe them and now you've given them even more of an excuse to get rid of you. Why don't you just paint a target on your back!'

'We'll know how well they took it tonight when we meet for a drink.'

'I don't think they'll take it well at all. Did you see them smiling? Like a pair of fucking crocodiles. What about the grenade? Did you find the grenade under the mower?'

'It wasn't there.'

'What do mean?'

'It wasn't there. Nothing.'

'The mower was gone?'

'No. The mower was there, but nothing underneath.'

'Shit!' said Alex, how to get Beau to believe him that he was in danger.' Beau, these guys are hard core crims, you are not a crim. I don't think you know what you are doing because I don't.'

'I know exactly what I'm doing. It's a good deal, they know that. I can handle Reggie and Conlan, I'm made for this.'

'But you're not like Reggie and Conlan.'

'I know that... I'm Beau! And don't you forget it.' He laughed and playfully punched Alex on the arm. 'I got this! Now let's get the fuck out of here.'

Chapter 35

The front bar at North Nerimbah hotel was quiet for a mid-week. Normally the Wednesday night supported a local band, but there was none playing tonight. It was windy and had started to drizzle rain outside which would have kept all but the locals at home. Steve Henderson and Brian Flannery were breasting the bar, chatting with Janice when Alex and Beau came in. There were not many in the room, business had taken a downturn since the bombing, and only a few drinkers had begun to return during last week. They had a choice of tables, but Beau chose to breast the bar till Reggie and Conlan arrived.

Janice moved across to the taps and poured two beers for them. Smoke curled from the ashtrays while a bit of Bob Marley reggae escaped from the speakers set into the ceiling. Beau was confident about the upcoming meeting with them, he felt like he was in control, that this was his meeting to direct, but Alex, quietly nursing his beer, knew better.

It was nearly eight o'clock, Beau shouted the next round of beers and was looking for a table when Steve Henderson detached himself from the bar and strode over to him, blocking Beau's path.

'Roy Conlan's out to get you, you know Beau,' he said.

'What do mean? I'm meeting him here.'

'You've got to get out of here.'

'Did Alex put you up to this?' he asked suspiciously.

Alex shook his head. He was standing next to the two of them and listening in intently.

'You know me. I'm telling you this because we're mates. You're a marked man. They are after you and you've got to get out of here, not the pub. I mean the Coast.' He reiterated. 'You know too much...and you owe them too much.'

'How do you know that? Are you telling me this so you can take over my job?'

'No...it's just rumours you know. I heard rumours, and Conlan doesn't like loose ends.'

'Jesus Stevo, is that all? I'm meeting them here tonight to sort it all out,' he said in disbelief.

'Come on Alex.' Beau slapped Stevo on the shoulder as he nudged past him, heading for a corner table. Alex raised his eyebrows at Steve Henderson and followed Beau.

An hour later, Reggie and Conlan hadn't shown, and Beau had clearly come to the realization that he was now a loose end. Beau's mood had changed, all his optimism had gone.

'They're not coming are they. There's no goodbye drinks, no bonus, no deal,' spat Beau.

'Stay cool Beau, maybe they were held up.'

'Bullshit. I'm out of here.' He went to stand, but Alex grabbed his arm and pulled him back down.

'Beau, I want to make sure. If they show up and say they accept your offer, then it doesn't matter if they give you some bullshit story as to why they are late, we will have nothing to fear. It'll be over, and we get to leave cleanly. Don't spoil it by not being here if they come.'

'But you don't believe they are going to do that, do you?'

'I just want to see if we can all get away from this without anyone getting hurt. Otherwise, we must think of another way out.'

'What do mean another way?'

'Beau, you're dealing with Conlan and drugs, guns, grenades, you name it,' he whispered. 'You, me, Janice, we can't just sit around and hope it will all settle down. It's just a matter of if we can get out peacefully or they are going to stop you from doing it.'

'Jesus you're a morbid prick.'

'You know I'm right.' They finished their beers in silence.

'What's the time now?'

'Just before ten.'

'They're not coming, are they?'

'No, they're not. You know where you stand now Beau.'

'Bastards,' he said. 'So, what do we do now?'

'Fuck, I don't know.'

They left before Janice finished. She waved them off, saying she would be home later, there was always cleaning up to do, and to come and get her if it was still raining.

They ducked and weaved around the cars; rain squalls rattled the trees lining the road home. Few cars were out, their lights reflecting off the wet roads, wheels hissing as they passed.

Alex parked the Peugeot around the side, out of the wind. Beau raced around the front to open the door, Alex followed under the awning, skirting the puddles and the mower left out in the rain. Inside they shook the water off as Beau flopped onto the couch.

'What's our next step mate? You've got to help me, and Janice get out of this'

Alex started making a coffee, filling the jug and preparing the cups while he thought. After a few minutes he answered.

'You pretend tonight was not an issue. You do the drug pickup trip tomorrow night, and then you pack up the house and you leave. Don't push for a bonus, don't quiz them. Take what you can get and leave while you can in the next few days. If it turns out otherwise, we will have to deal with that as it happens.'

'Yeh, like grenades under the mower!' he scoffed.

'They were there I tell you,' Alex protested.

'I believe you,' Beau said, like he didn't believe him.

'And then if they weren't taped under the mower...they would have...they....'

Alex put the cups down. 'Where's your torch Beau? I need a torch.'

Beau pointed to under the sink. Alex strode out the side door into the rain. He pulled the mower back on its rear wheels and shone the week light under the cutter deck.

'Heh Beau! come out here,' he called.

Beau appeared at his side, looking over his shoulder at what Alex was shining the light on.

'Fuck!' was all Beau could say.

Alex leaned around and pointed at a grenade that had been taped to the mower blades. Same as at Reggie's, only this one was rigged to explode. Alex shone the torch on the pin and handle. He had seen enough episodes of Combat on TV to know how they worked. A piece of cord tied to the safety pin led to the mower drive shaft. When the mower was started, or pushed forward, the cord around the drive shaft would tighten, pulling the safety pin out, releasing the spoon lever to fly free and arm the bomb. Five seconds later, the blast would destroy the mower and shred everyone within five meters with shrapnel and petrol. They stood looking at the same type of bomb that had killed Isabelle Herman only two weeks earlier.

'See. I fucking told you those bastards had a grenade. Now do you believe me? It's rigged to blow up, look, the cord is tied to the safety pin, it'll pull out if we start it.'

'What do we do with this?'

'I don't know, but now we know why they didn't show up at the pub,' said Alex.' They were here rigging this up.'

'I'll push it over to the fence, get it away from the house.' He grabbed at the handle.

'No! Stop!' shouted Alex 'The blades might turn or catch on something and pull the pin. Fuck!!!'

Beau turned around in confusion and fear at what might have just happened. he was shaking, his shoulders were slumped, his life had spiralled out of control, the truth had finally taken hold.

'What do I do? We can't go to the police.'

'No, we can't. We cut this thing off, very carefully, and put it in a hole. You got any holes?' Alex asked.

'No!'

'Well, go and dig one, can you?'

Alex tilted the mower fully back on its handle and propped the torch. He studied the booby trap carefully. Drops from the awning soaked his shirt as he squatted next to the mower. The patter of rain in the gathered pools around him became overtly loud. He shook and wrung his hands, trying to steady them.

'Shit! Shit! Shit! What am I fucking doing?' He carefully untied the cord from the mower shaft. Then he unwound the tape, careful not to tug at the string, releasing the grenade from the cutter deck. He used the cord and tape to secure the spoon handle, wrapping it around the egg-shaped body of the bomb. Beau was standing over him, silently watching.

'Put it in here.' Beau said, holding out an old ice-cream can.

'Were you there the whole time?' Alex asked.

'Most of it.'

'Brave but stupid!' He rose to his feet and placed the grenade gingerly into the bottom of the tin.

'Same about you,' said Beau. He put the lid on and held the tin as far away from him as he could and marched over toward the fence.

Beau lowered the can into the hole he had dug, a temporary grave for it. He filled it in but avoided stamping the soil down, leaving a little mound of dirt to mark the spot. Both trudged inside, the enormity of the truth weighing heavily in their steps. They dried off and changed into fresh T shirts. Alex lit a cigarette and stood silently looking out the window at the corner of the yard where the grenade was buried and took a deep sigh.

'That would have killed me or Janice, wouldn't it?' said Beau. 'How did you know it was there?'

Beau joined Alex at the kitchen window. 'I saw the mower was out from under the awning, it wasn't like that yesterday, I'd put it back under the awning, someone had moved it.'

'No. I mean how did you know that Conlan or Reggie had booby trapped the mower?'

'You should have known that after your speech today they would come after you, mate. They've been trying to stitch you up all along. You know too much, and you pretty much told them that you're more trouble than you're worth.'

'It would have killed me if I started it up. It would have got Janice; she likes to do the mowing sometimes. It would have killed her.... What do I do? This has gone so bad. Help me, Alex.'

Alex sat quietly, and let his mind float through the possibilities, giving over to his reasoning. Beau always had trouble with this, he lived in the moment, in the here and now, relying on his size and presence, but he was increasingly lost and turning to Alex for a way out. Alex let the confusion and adrenaline seep out, slowly forcing calm over the top of the chaos. Alex had grown up fast in the last few weeks, but he hadn't figured it would be this way.

Beau waited expectantly.

'Beau, it's like this. Before the booby trap tonight, I thought we might have found a way to get you out of it with Janice, and they leave you alone. It would have cost you a fair bit of money, but now that's changed. They want you dead mate, and even if you leave now, tonight, they'll come after you. They'll keep after you and Janice until you are gone, or Reggie and Conlan are, whichever comes first...the cops will sweep up what's left, and that's me. You know too much to let you go, and like I said at the pub, I think we have to fight our way out now.' Alex paused, 'So I have no idea yet. Why don't you come up with something?'

'I'm not the smart one, remember. Janice tells me that nearly every day.'

'Yeh, well, there's something that still doesn't add up yet. It'll come to me. Where is Janice by the way? She's not in yet.'

'She must be walking home.' said Beau.

Alex looked out the open door at the light rain blowing on to the deck.

'Are you going to get her?'

'I don't have a car, remember.'

Alex retrieved his keys from his pocket and threw them to Beau.

'You do now'

'Get out. I'd be dead before I was seen driving that heap of shit,' Beau said without humour in his voice.

'That was closer than you think.' Alex smiled but got no reaction. 'Well, I'll get her then.' The drive would help him think, it always did. He headed for the door, turned to Beau and said, 'We won't say anything about the grenade to Janice either'.

'No, that wouldn't be a good idea.'

'In fact, keep everything normal, don't reveal anything to Janice yet. Don't want to scare her.'

Beau just nodded as Alex went out the door.

Alex sat in his car at the pub, waiting for Janice to appear. The main lights were off in the hotel, the bright red *Nerimbah Hotel* sign was extinguished. He couldn't see movement inside, but that was nothing new, the girls were often still working in the storeroom late. Alex rolled a smoke and shuddered. Finding the grenade had pushed him into a new realm, they were all in direct danger from Reggie and Conlan now, they had to find a way to fight back.

He wound his window down a crack to flick out the butt and let some air in. The sound of the surf echoed from the beach on the other side of the dunes only 100 metres away. Wild ocean spray swept across the car park, swirling under the road lights and battering Alex's car from the side. The pub had been here a long time, perfectly positioned to overlook the ocean. Alex remembered when he and Beau would try to get into the nightclub underage. Trawler lights on the horizon, bobbed and disappeared in big swells and atrocious conditions. No wonder so many of them went overboard or were lost, never to be heard of again. A germ of an idea began to form in his sub conscious.

The Manager appeared at the Service door, locked it behind him, and made his way across to his own car. Alex started his up and drove over to pull up next to him. He wound down the window.

'Heh mate. Is Janice still in there?'

He looked up from his car door.

'No. She left a while ago, dunno where she is.' The manager said nothing more as he got into his own car and drove off. Janice was right. No concern, he really was a prick, thought Alex.

He turned his Peugeot around, and began a slow drive back to the shack, retracing the route Janice would have taken in the dark. He nearly missed her. The soft glow from a light inside a Thai Takeaway shop revealed her standing under its awning, arms clenched tightly across her chest, trying to stay dry. It was just around the corner from home. Alex pulled in and flicked the passenger door open.

'You're soaked!' Alex stated the obvious.

She said nothing when she got in, she didn't look at him or talk on the short drive home.

When he pulled up, she merely thanked him and went inside. Alex was even more confused. By the time he had joined her in the kitchen, she was feigning tiredness and was going straight to bed, barely acknowledging Beau.

He slept fitfully on the couch that night, he tossed and turned. He re-lived disarming the bomb repeatedly. He thought about Janice and the new threat to deal with. The world was closing in on him fast, he was drowning under the weight of it and Beau wasn't much good at helping him. He lay awake for hours, formulating plan after plan, tossing, turning, running scenarios through in his head, each one getting more implausible than the last, till he reached the only conclusion that would help them... Beau had to die.

Chapter 36

Alex woke to the rattle of wind and rain against the glass above his head. He had no idea what time he went to sleep, but it didn't matter, no amount of rest was going to prepare him for today. Janice shook his shoulder again and gestured with a coffee cup, an invitation to join her with one. He squirmed around, tangled in the sheet until he sat with his legs over the side of the couch and smiled at her. She signalled that Beau was still sleeping, and if they kept quiet, this coffee tryst was for he and her alone.

Alex pulled on some shorts and stretched, watching the shape of Janice's body silhouetted behind her kimono. The weather outside was miserable. Their usual spot on the verandah was out, too wet. Inside the shack, there was precious little space to move out of voice range from the bedroom, so they settled at the kitchen table.

'Sorry about last night. Did you sleep well?' He lowered his voice to a whisper.

'Not much. How about you?' She replied in the same tone.

'Same.' He said, sipping at the steaming coffee, a bitter brew to bring his senses awake. It had been a while since just the two of them shared a morning companionable coffee, it brought back all the pleasure he felt just being in her company.

'Miserable day,' she remarked absently.

'Shouldn't last longer than another day or two. Keeps the tourists away.'

'Your parents going to miss you?' she asked. 'When you go to Melbourne I mean.'

'Of course. They're just like anyone else's. Dad is like Dads everywhere, life goes on without too much excitement, though he'd tell you different. Mum's the centre of the family as you would expect. She'll miss me. What about you?'

'My mum doesn't miss me. She doesn't even know I'm here. I never told her. I don't want them to find me anyway. Beau is all I've got for the moment...and you.' She took a long, blowy sip from her coffee, '...but I don't know for how long, do I?' She finished.

Alex glanced sideways at her, conscious of his betrayal with Janice. 'Is that because of us, the other night?'

'No. I'm OK about that. It's something happened at the pub last night. It's got me worried. Beau doesn't tell me everything now. You've seen how he's been since the bombing. It's not been the same between us since then, and he's hiding something. Do you know what it is?'

'No. I don't. But I'd tell you if I did.' He lied, thinking of the grenade in the back yard.

'You know how he likes to think he's got Conlan, and the others covered, that he knows what he's doing, but he doesn't! Beau's just not smart enough, look at all that's happened to him in the last month. Conlan is after him for some reason. If they are gunning for him and he tries to go up against them, he'll get hurt, he's not a real crim like them.' She glanced at the bedroom door, then looked back at him. 'And here they are, going out fishing again tonight, pick up more drugs, in this weather. Haven't they got enough? It doesn't make sense. Fuck I wish we could just leave.'

Alex didn't respond. He had lain awake all night thinking the same thing, wondering why he stayed around, frustrated that the only way out that he could come up with involved betraying Janice.

'Remember the other night?' she said, 'You promised me you would look out for him.'

'I am. It's why I'm still here, but don't go putting more faith in me than I think I deserve,' he said.

'But you're smart enough Alex. You'd find a way to get us out of this mess, I know you can.'

There was a subtle change in their relationship. For a fleeting moment, Alex wondered if she knew what power she held over him and was using it. When he had looked into her eyes, she knew he wouldn't say no. A slight smile creased her lips. He fell for it every time. There would be no fanciful escape to Melbourne for Alex yet, no avoiding it, only acceptance.

'What do you plan on doing?' she asked.

He didn't answer. He couldn't tell her. If he did, he would have to lie. He looked out the window, the weather was foul but workable, he hoped it would hold and not get worse, just long enough for the fishing trip to still go ahead, and for Beau to drown.

Chapter 37

It began with a phone call to Reggie while Janice was out. Alex schooled Beau in how he should approach it. No accusations, no recriminations, just keep it normal, and make sure they were still going fishing.

'Where were you last night? We waited for you'. Beau asked Reggie over the phone.

'Sorry mate, we got held up Roy's car wouldn't go. We'll go for a drink another time'. Reggie's voice squawked back through the receiver. Beau held it slightly away from his face so that Alex could hear as well.

Beau covered the mouthpiece. 'Bullshit' he mouthed silently to Alex.

'Are we still fishing tonight? The weather is fucking awful.' Beau asked loudly.

'Of course, there's no choice, we have to go tonight. No delays. Conlan's coming as well,' said Reggie. 'We could do with an extra set of hands. He won't like that, but it will have to do. See you at six as usual.' Reggie ended the call.

Beau hung the receiver back on the hook and turned to Alex.

'Fuck! Why is he coming out? Conlan hates boats, he can't swim for shit. He wouldn't come out in the boat tonight unless the world was about to end.'

'Then why is he coming tonight?'

'Reggie said he needs another set of hands, but he'll just get in the way, throw up all the time, probably end up overboard,' said Beau.

Alex looked questioningly at the wall phone and back at Beau, replaying the conversation in his head, till it dawned on him.

'I know why Conlan's coming,' said Alex. 'He's not the one going overboard, you are. That's what Reggie needs the extra set of hands for. They're going to dump you overboard. They want to pitch you over tonight. Why else are you all going out in this weather? They make doubly sure, either the grenade or drowning, it gets the same end.' Alex pointed at the window where the casuarina branches were swaying and flicking against the glass. 'What the fuck did you do to them that they are coming after you so bad?' asked Alex.

'Stop accusing me of shit. I haven't done anything to them.' Beau arced up. 'It's all right for you, you're not the one they are trying to get rid of. I haven't done anything. Why don't we just leave, pack up and go. Disappear?'

'Because they want you dead Beau, the booby-trapped mower proves that, so you have to give them 'dead', or they'll keep coming after you. You know too much. Conlan going out with you tonight just confirms what I thought, they'll turn it into a fishing accident. I thought about this last night. They want to get rid of you, so we must make sure they do. This could work for us. There's no way around it Beau, you have to die tonight, you have to drown like they want.'

'Are you fucking crazy?' he exclaimed angrily as he pushed at Alex and stepped back.

'Better than getting blown up. Hear me out. When you are out going for the drop tonight, you must drown. It's the only way so that they don't come after you again. It's going to be you or them. They want you dead, so we make sure you die, you get to drown, or at least they will think so.'

Beau looked at him, aghast at what he was proposing.

'It'll be rough tonight, but you have to go overboard before they push you over. If they get hold of you first, you'll be unconscious when you hit the water, or have a bullet in you and a huge lump of chain wrapped around your legs. You have to pretend you've gone overboard first. Fall over the side, slip on the deck, jump, I don't care, they just must think that it was an accident that you went over the side and drowned in the storm. Just make it convincing.'

Beau stared in horror at Alex, not yet understanding where this was taking him. Alex went on, relentless in getting it all out before Beau could object further. 'Now for the hard bit, you have to swim to Bayman Headland. I'll pick you up from there, in the top carpark...and then I'll help you disappear. They won't see or hear from you again because they'll think you drowned, and you'll be safe, Janice will be safe, and I'll be safe.

'So, if I'm dead, Conlan stops coming after me, and the cops will stop looking for me too.' Beau began to understand the reasoning.

'That's the end result...I hope. I'll drive you down south of the border tonight, somewhere like Kingscliffe, plenty of desperados down there, you'll fit right in. I should make it back before dawn, no one the wiser.'

Alex was pleased with himself, an avalanche of plans that came together as he spoke, and he had no idea if it would work, but at least it was a plan. Beau would be taking a huge risk in trying to swim in the middle of a storm, but perhaps that was his path to redemption.

'Don't tell Janice anything,' Alex said. 'She has to think you are dead as well. You have to disappear without a trace. You become a fisherman presumed drowned in the storm. You disappear,' he reiterated. 'It's the only way they will stop coming after us all is if you're dead.'

'Why have I got to die? Why don't I just use the grenade on them in the boat tonight, get them first?'

'Do you honestly think you could kill someone in a rocking boat with a grenade, and not blow yourself up too?'

Beau sat down and stared vacantly out the windows, then looked up at Alex with hooded eyes, 'Wouldn't be so bad, would it? What if none of us come back?'

'That's not what I meant Beau. Accident or not, you're not a murderer'.

'What makes you think I'm not.' He paused, his voice wavering. 'I'm already responsible for one life... I may as well be responsible for three...what we did killed that little girl, Isabelle. I could take that grenade out and kill Reggie and Conlan, some justice for her,' he murmured. 'If I don't make it back, well, perhaps that's justice.'

'You can't think that way Beau.'

'Well, I fucking do. It's all I've thought about since it happened, how she died...and I did it, I fucked up at the house, The cops think I done it...I did do it.'

Beaus' remorse was as palpable as it was real. Alex finally understood his friendship with Beau, it was there all along, the belief in the innocence of the inner soul, it was why they had become friends in the first place, for this very moment in time.

'No!' said Alex firmly, 'You don't do that. You are not a murderer. You didn't kill her, you didn't plant the bomb, they did... Hamilton, Reggie and Conlan are responsible for that...they murdered her. You don't get redemption by becoming one of them. Disappear and let the police work out how to get them. If you don't, they are going to get rid of you first.'

He pressed on, raising his voice. 'So, we stick with the plan. Look at me, stay focused, you have to become dead tonight. Dive overboard in the dark. And when they come in without you, who are they going to notify? The police? Are they going to tell the cops that they lost you overboard while they went out to pick up a drug haul? Not likely. The cops might suspect something, but when they come around to tell Janice, she must believe you were lost at sea. She will be shocked; you can't fake tragedy. Whatever you did to them that started this whole mess stops there. Even if the Police bust Reggie and Conlan, it stops there, they can't get at you if you are dead.'

Beau sat quietly, taking in all that Alex had said, and came to his own conclusion.

'But what about Janice?'

'If you are dead, they won't touch her. They don't need to. You are the link in the chain. As long as you are gone, she can't be touched, and neither can I.'

Beau was quiet as he digested it all. 'Janice will be back from the shops soon.'

'She mustn't know. Do what you always do before a fishing night. Tell her you are going pack it all in and leave next week, except you won't be coming home.'

'So, when I disappear tonight, it will be the last I see of Janice too?' The realization hit him.

'That's up to you. In the future that could change, but for this to work now, everyone has to be convinced that you are dead, Janice, the cops, Reggie, Cooper, your family. If anyone finds out different, those bastards will come after you again.'

'You sure this will work?'

'Do you have a better idea?' asked Alex.

'My best friend wants me dead, what's not to like. So, I guess this will be it. My last day here. I should go and see my mum today then.'

'You can't give anything away.'

'That's easy, the old man will be home. I don't say much to either of them when he's there.'

'I'll have spare clothes and a bag for you tonight, nothing from here. Any cash, give it to me this arvo when I'm round before you leave.'

'This better work', Beau said.' You better be right!'

'The only way I could think of mate. Just don't go over the side tonight wearing your big jacket, you'll go straight to the bottom.'

'I should put it on Conlan and push him over instead.'

'Nice thought. Put some chain in the pockets. Stay cool. By tomorrow morning it will all be over,' Alex said with a confidence he didn't have. 'And Beau, there's two of them and only one of you on that boat. They'll be primed for action. Don't try to be a hero and change the plan.'

Beau nodded his understanding, but Alex was not sure, no plan survives the first engagement with the enemy, and if ever there was a loose cannon, Beau was it.

Alex spent the day at his parents' house, packing up the gear he was taking to Melbourne and spent an hour in the garage chatting with his father, helping him clean out paint pots. He finished with a cup of tea with both his parents, and an assurance that all was good, and he would be leaving for Melbourne on Saturday. Under the surface, he was crawling with anxiety, and wondered if Beau was holding it together, he had no idea.

> 'Are you alright Alex? Everything is OK?' His mother asked, her intuition coming to the fore.

'Sure mum. Just a little tense about the move. I'll be here Friday night, for dinner, cauliflower and melted cheese?' He fobbed her off with the desire for his favourite dish. She smiled, and he left before she prised more out of him.

Later that afternoon, at the Beach Shack, he made coffees and smoked endless cigarettes as Beau prowled the house. Beau slipped Alex two huge rolls of money while Janice wasn't looking. More money than Alex had ever seen before.

'There's more where that came from.' Beau whispered. The admission startled Alex, but he thought nothing more of it at the time.

It was just on dark as Reggie pulled up outside the house, the boat on the back squeaking under the brakes. He blew the horn. Inside, Alex was looking at Beau to see if he could carry it off. Beau turned and gave Janice a long kiss, then hugged her, holding on tight. Footsteps thumped up the ramp, Reggie pulled open the front door, holding it against the wind that threatened to pull it from his grasp.

'You ready?' Reggie scowled.

Beau broke off his embrace and turned to Reggie, his face serious, resolute, he was ready.

'I'll see you later Janice,' Reggie called.

Janice just stared back at him. Beau followed Reggie out the door, turned and nodded to Alex.

'Tonight!' He strode down the ramp to the ute and slid into the bench seat of the Ford next to Conlan. Conlan neither turned nor acknowledge them as they drove off.

Janice turned to Alex. 'This is ridiculous. Why did you let him go. Look at the weather.'

'It'll be alright. At least the rain has stopped and Beau's a good swimmer.'

'Why would you say that?' She asked.' He's going to pick up drugs, not surf. What was Conlan doing there? He doesn't usually go with them. Somethings not right. Do you know something I don't?' She was wound up, tense, perceptive.

'It'll be fine Janice.' Alex reached out to touch her arm in assurance, but she sprang back.

'Don't piss me off Alex! You and Beau have hardly said anything to me all afternoon. You've been avoiding me. What's Beau and you been up to? You're hiding something, I know. Conlan told me.'

'Conlan? What's he got to do with it? You hate him.'

'Conlan picked me up from the bar, just as I left work, and told me he'd drive me home...It wasn't a request, he showed me a gun in his waistband. He put me in his car and drove me to Georges Head Park...'

Alex wasn't sure he wanted to hear the next part of this confession.

'He didn't touch me like you think, but he said that seeing as Beau wanted out of the organization, it will be best for everyone if I tell him where it all is now. I said I had no idea what he was on about.

He said if I knew where any of the missing stuff was, no one would get hurt. If he got it all back today, nothing would happen. What's he talking about Alex?'

'No idea, but I can take a guess.'

' He said Beau and I were in too deep to just walk away. If we want to walk away, he wanted something in return. He said that he and Reggie had been watching me for a while, he knows when I'm home alone, when my work shifts are. He knows when Beau goes up to Kenilworth and leaves me by myself.' She was pale, looking at Alex for an explanation.

'Why didn't you tell Beau he threatened you?'

'He said this was just between him and me. If I mentioned it to Beau, there would be consequences. If Beau came around, he would be waiting for him. He only wants me and the stuff, or Beau gets hurt. I just want this last trip to be over with and we can think about getting out.'

'So Conlan says Beau has been ripping him off, and he thinks you know where it is.'

'But I don't. If I knew where it was, I could tell Conlan, or give it back and it would all be OK'

'Not a chance,' said Alex. Whether they get the money and drugs back or not didn't matter. They don't want Beau around anymore; they don't trust him, then they're coming after Janice. Conlan and Reggie want her for themselves.

'No Janice, it wouldn't be OK. It was never going to be OK. You're in big danger. I wish you'd told me this earlier today. Did he mention a mower?

Janice stood looking at him bemused. Alex shook her shoulders, 'There was a bomb in the mower. Did he mention not to touch it?'

'He didn't say anything about that. Only to get him the stuff Beau owed him, the stuff he had hidden. Do you know where it is?'

'I've got no idea.' Alex wrung his head in his hands. It had escalated in a direction he hadn't thought of. Janice was now a target regardless of what happened tonight. This will only end if Conlan and Reggie are gone too. Beau can't do it, he couldn't, but maybe the Police could.

Alex ran out into the rain, tripped and fell scrambling in the dirt next to the fence. He dug with his fingers until he hit the tin, brought it up and rubbed off the mud sticking to it. Back inside he put it in the sink and prized the lid off.

'What's that? 'Janice gasped,

'A grenade', Alex replied. He lifted it out gingerly, and held it up, checking the safety pin was in and the handle compressed. The smooth steel orb was cold and wet; he wrapped the grenade in a tea towel as if that would protect him.

'When were you going to tell me about that? What are you doing with it?'

'I can't explain now, I'm sorry', but I am going after Conlan and Reggie like you wanted. I'm going to pin the bombing on them with this.' He held up the grenade wrapped in the tea towel. He didn't hear her reply, he was out the door and, in his car, before she could ask him anything else.

Chapter 38

Rain smeared the windscreen as Alex pushed the little car recklessly over Georges Head and down into Nerimbah beachfront road. Across the bay, he could just make out the red and green marker lights at the harbour entrance, barely visible in the squalls. At Florette Shoals, ships rode unsteady at anchor, he could barely see them. They were kidding themselves if they thought they could do a drop and pick up on a night like this.

He slowed as he drove passed the Pilot station houses, till he could see the boat ramp ahead.

Reggies green F100 and empty boat trailer was the only one in the carpark. Alex turned off the road and parked in the dark. He skirted the light post until he came level with Reggies ute. He tried the door. Of course it was locked. How stupid could he get. He can't break the window and hide the grenade inside, it would look like a plant. The rear tray was empty, a grenade rolling around in there was too easy to find, and if Reggie and Conlan got back before the cops showed up, they'd know he'd been there and would come after him.

Alex had to hide the grenade in the car and stop it leaving the boat ramp before the cops showed up. He looked down the rear wheel of Reggies Ford. Cursing that in his haste he had forgotten to bring a knife, he settled with pushing twigs in the tyre valve to let it down, but after a few minutes, he had barely noticed any change in the pressure. Too slow. He looked at the tea towel bundle at his feet. If he can't flatten the tyre, perhaps he could blow it off. That would slow them down and definitely attract some Police attention.

He quickly dried off the grenade the best he could. He clenched his fingers in and out to stop the tremors, staring intently at all the parts of the firing handle. Was he really going to do this?

If Beau can jump off a boat into that sea, then I can do this. The car springs behind the back wheel were a perfect place to wedge the grenade. He gently made a loop with the cord and measured enough to tie it to the inside of the wheel rim and loop back securely through the safety pin. He checked that it was holding secure and there was space for the spring handle to release. When Reggie reversed the trailer down to the ramp, the string wrapped around the back wheel would tighten and pull the safety pin out of the grenade. Hopefully it would blow the wheel off or at least shred the tyre and cripple the car. This would leave Reggie and Conlan stranded with an exploded tyre, a boatload of drugs, and a missing crewman at the end of the spit when the Police arrive. Alex thought of it as poetic justice after the same booby trap had been set on the mower.

He straightened up and hobbled back to his car, wiping water from his face, pondering what he had just done, wondering if it would work. There were a lot of 'ifs' in his plan, and these were dangerous adversaries if it didn't come off. He shook his head, how had it ever come to this? He desperately wanted the night to be over.

It was a 20-minute drive back around the river, over the bridge, to Bayman Heads. If all had gone to plan, Beau should have swum ashore to the rocks by the time he got there. Jesus that surf was huge. He wondered if Beau would be coming ashore alive or dead.

Alex wound his way down the cliff track from the carpark, slipping and sliding on the wet gravel. Rain lashed at his face as he gripped shrubs either side of him trying to stay upright. Lightening illuminated the void below, but more so allowed him to glimpse the terrible ocean ahead, the source of the thunderous surf and spray whipped up the cliff face. Waves as tall as trees smashed the breakwater below. There was no sign of the boat, only white water mounded and lumped into a maelstrom of peaks and troughs. How could Beau survive swimming into shore in this? What a stupid idea to think that this was a plan that would save him. It would kill him more like it.

Alex tripped and fell the last few feet onto the sand, breaking his fall with his hands outstretched. He rolled on his side and reached for the torch in his back pocket. The beam illuminated the wet rocks in front but couldn't penetrate the spray dashed over them. He turned it off and tried to adjust his eyes to the darkness. He stumbled across the rock shelf, keenly aware of the strength of the water washed across it with each passing wave. He scanned the surf around him, shutting out the roaring of the waves breaking, listening for any voice, flicking the torch on and off, looking for a body in the waves, looking for Beau, but there was nothing.

The self-doubt washed over him as he roamed the rock shelf back and forward piercing the murk briefly with stabs of torchlight. In the end, it was Beau's head that gave him away. A round white face at the edge of a torch beam swung across a moving wall of black water before it disappeared as the wave dashed itself on the rocks.

Alex surged across the rocks toward where he thought Beau would come ashore, stabbing the torch beam ahead of him. He'd lost him. No. There, washed onto the platform then sucked back out. Beau was offering no resistance, his arms twisted lifeless in the roll. Alex dropped the torch and grabbed Beau's collar just as he disappeared under the foam again. He slid over the rock trying to get purchase with his free hand but was pulled off the shelf by the retreating wave and sucked into the deeper water with Beau.

He pushed off the rocky bottom, determined not to let go of Beaus shirt. The next wave smashed them both against the boulders. Beau was wrenched from his grasp, Alex tried to get some purchase, but it was slippery, and another wave drove him forward wedging his leg between two rocks. The surge sucked back, and Alex drew a breath, but couldn't pull his leg out. The next wave covered his head and twisted him deeper in the crevasse. He couldn't break free; the pressure was keeping him wedged in and he barely drew breath before the next surge. He was failing fast.

Beaus' arms suddenly wrapped around him and hoisted him back into deeper water, the power of the next swell washed them both up onto the rock shelf again. This time Alex dug his fingers into a crack, and he held them both as the water receded. He gasped and pulled at Beau till they got to shallower water, washed and sliding across the rock shelf till finally they made it to the sand. Beau coughed and spat water, so Alex rolled him on his side and let it dribble out. He lay back himself and sucked in air, wheezing and gulping, restoring life to a body that suddenly felt very heavy.

'Jeez you're a heavy bastard,' gasped Alex.

Beau continued to splutter; he could barely see him in the dark.

'I suppose you want me to thank you?' Beau croaked.

'Not a chance.' Alex felt the cuts and loose skin under his fingers, his body pulled and torn.

'The car is up there.' He pointed up to the top of the cliff.

'You can go if you want. I'm staying here for a bit.'

'Come on fuck ya.' He helped Beau to his feet and shifted his arm under his ribs, helping his exhausted friend. They stumbled their way around the rocks and sand to find the track that led up to the carpark above. It was a long climb in the dark.

In the light of the carpark, they sucked hungrily at a bottle of water between them. Alex passed Beau a towel as he leaned heavily on the bonnet, sapped of energy. The wind on the top of the headland was noisy and pulled ferociously at them, Beau dabbed the blood from his forehead and stripped off to change into the dry clothes Alex gave him. He scrambled for some dry things of his own.

'How did you find me?' Beau asked.

'Had to use a torch. Your big boof head gave you away. Otherwise, I wouldn't have seen you at all. Where's the boat?'

'Out there somewhere, on their way to the drop if they're still afloat.' They both looked out to sea, where the ships should be swinging at anchor, but could see nothing, no lights, nothing. Another squall was coming.

Beau cupped his hands to light a cigarette and sucked the smoke in hungrily.

'Did I say thanks for that?' he said.

'No, you didn't.'

'Where's the torch?'.

'Dropped it to save you.'

'I owe you a torch.'

'It was yours anyway.'

'Oh.' was all he said. He pulled hard at the cigarette again. Both men stood leaning against the car savouring the companionship of survival.

'That's the most stupid thing I've ever done,' revealed Beau.

'I don't think so, I've seen worse,' Alex replied.

'Huh' Beau laughed, life restored. 'That was the dumbest plan, nearly killed me. Just dive overboard you said, make it look like an accident, and swim to shore. What idiot suggested that? Reggie is just as stupid for taking the boat out tonight. You should have let me just go around to their place and grenade them today. It would have been easier than swimming ashore in that.' Beau pointed out to sea.

Behind them, down at the harbour, the boat ramp suddenly exploded in light and noise. Beau and Alex leaned over the cliff edge to look down at the commotion on the other side of the river. Car headlights illuminated Reggies Ford F100 ute, shouts were heard and flashings of blue and red burst into life. An engine revved. A burst of bright white lit the boat ramp carpark, followed by a loud sharp explosion. Cracking sounds preceded a dull crump, and a ball of orange and black flame mushroomed out from around Reggies ute.

'What was that?'

'The grenade,' said Alex.

'Look, that's Reggies truck, it's on fire.' Beau pointed down to it.

Below them, the flickering orange flames silhouetted a figure in the front seat of the Ford, the flames had engulfed the rear of the flat bed and were curling around the cab.

'That's Reggie in there. Why doesn't he get... For God's sake, get out of the truck Reggie,' Beau implored.

Alex stood in silence, stunned, watching from the carpark above as the flames engulfed the cab fuelled by the strong winds carrying with it the black smoke and the pops and cracks of exploding glass. One of the figures was darting in, trying to get close to the cab where Reggie was still propped behind the wheel, but he retreated in the face of the heat, shielding his eyes, unable to do anything further. Then Reggie disappeared behind a wall of swirling smoke.

Beau was transfixed by the grizzly tableau below. 'Fuck. Was Conlan in there too? Did you see him?'

Alex couldn't answer, he didn't know, he couldn't look, he had turned away, horrified by the enormity of what had happened. Close to the burning wreckage the police lights flashed blue and red through the smoke, one of the figures kept circling the flaming pyre, while the other stood at the door of the police car, radio in hand.

'What were the cops doing there?' asked Beau.

'I called them,' whispered Alex.

'What did you do that for? Look at that...'Beau pointed down at the carpark. 'That wasn't in your plan, was it? I think Reggies a goner, and probably Conlan too, burnt to death. Jesus Alex, what did you do?'

'I didn't think it would do that.' mumbled Alex. 'I only wanted to slow them down. I rigged up the grenade to blow off Reggies back wheel, stop them from leaving so the cops could get them. ...I didn't mean for the petrol tank to go up...shit, it blew up the petrol tank. Why didn't they get out?'

Beau grabbed Alex by the arms and forced away from the edge. 'Did you blow them up? Tell me mate, come on...' Beau led Alex back to the car, out of sight from below. 'You blew them up didn't you!' Beau started to smile. 'You've got balls Alex, I didn't think you had it in you. All our problems solved. Yippee!' Beau danced a little jig from foot to foot in celebration.

Alex tried to shake off what he'd done.

'No. All I did was tip off the cops about Reg and Conlan at the boat ramp. I had to, they were going to hurt Janice, tonight, when they got back.'

'What do you mean?' Beau was suddenly serious.

'Janice told me.' Alex let out a deep sigh, he was coming down now, the enormity of it all weakening him, weakening his resolve. 'She'd had a run in with Conlan. We should go and see her, tell her she's safe now.'

Beau straightened. 'We can't do that. It's not in your plan. There will be cops everywhere after this. Their place, my place. We can't risk it, we stick to your plan Alex, cops are still after me, I'm supposed to have drowned remember. I have to disappear; it still has to work.'

'But I killed Reggie and Conlan. I rigged that grenade, and they burnt to death.' Alex was anguished.

' No. You didn't... you didn't do it. I did,' said Beau.

Alex looked blankly at him, not understanding his friend.

'I did it. Whatever happened tonight is on my head, not yours? Whatever it takes, if we get busted, you blame it all on me, understand? Promise me that.' Beau stood firm, tall, resolute... faithful. 'Alex, you promise me that I will take the blame for whatever happened to Reggie and Conlan.'

'I can't do that,' said Alex.

'Yes, I can. You got me out of this mess so far. Mate, you've stood by me and Janice this last month, among all the crap that's been going on when you could have walked, but you didn't. I told you once before, I'm Beau Beaumont, I'm made for this shit... you aren't.'

Alex stood silently weighing up the meaning of their friendship. Beau knew it, and now Alex knew it. He nodded solemnly, aware of what his friend had now taken on for him.

'And I thought you were a 'piss ant' Uni boy, and you go and take out a drug ring. Balls of steel! Let's get out of here before anyone sees me.'

Rain swept across the carpark, forcing them to seek shelter in the car. As they dried off and lit cigarettes Beau turned to Alex.

'Let's go to Kingscliff so I can start a new life. On the way you can tell me everything about what you did tonight, so I know what to say if I ever get arrested.'

'You won't get picked up.' Alex said, more confident than he thought. He turned over the ignition and looked across at his friend.' Did you see the boat at the ramp?'

'Nope,' said Beau.

'Wonder where it went?'

'Don't care. I'll see Janice again, won't I?' Beau asked.

> 'That will depend on how long you want to stay dead, I guess.'

Beau sat quietly in the passenger seat, wound down the window and threw out his cigarette butt.

'I dived off you know,' he admitted proudly.

'Bullshit! I bet you fell out,' said Alex, laughing.

For the sake of them all, it was time to leave Nerimbah behind. He turned the Peugeot around and accelerated down the hill. They would have plenty to talk about on the long drive south to Kingscliff.

PART THREE
CHAPTER 39

Nerimbah 2001

The Nerimbah Surf Club was an impressive building, floor to ceiling glass had been built the length of the front wall facing the ocean and gave patrons a spectacular view of the bay. It was as good a place as any to go for a wake. Beers in hand, Alex chose a table away from the main area, though it didn't seem to matter so much, there were few guests in the bar, they were young and wouldn't recognize Beau. A look out the window was reason enough to keep most people away. The dark clouds swirled around the headland, sweeping rain across the front.

'Jesus its wild out there. No wonder no one is here.'

'Cheers, to your mum.' Alex held up his beer glass, in honour of Marjorie's funeral that morning.

'Cheers.' Beau returned,' thanks mate.'

Beau stared into his glass while Alex gazed out at the wild ocean, an endless vista of interest. It always had been, the surf, the weather, he never tired of looking at it, always gauging the possibilities, firm in the belief that he could always predict it. A couple of brave souls, boards under their arms, sprinted down the beach, and tackled the ugly waves. The teens raised their boards to launch over the walls of tumbling foam but were easily picked up and thrown back against the shore. It didn't dissuade them, they kept trying. When he was young, he wouldn't have given up either.

'She went all religious after the old prick died you know.' Beau started out of his reverie.' I heard about it from Janice. She told me, must have been in contact with mum, or someone from up here. I don't know why she put up with him for so long?'

'Who? Your mum? Perhaps she knew all along he wasn't right and just lived with it.'

'When I left home, moved in with Janice, she kept my room the same as the day I left. I'd drop in every month or so, pick up a few things. But my room was spotless, same old bed, same old rug, even the same posters on the walls. I bet it's all there today. She wouldn't have touched it after I disappeared. I wouldn't mind going there today.' He looked at Alex.' Maybe later? We can go round, have a look? Tell me more about the wills and stuff about the family home? What happens to her estate?'

'Really, I don't know much. Have you got any aunts or Uncles? I didn't see any at the funeral today.'

'There was an uncle in Adelaide. Don't know much about him, Richard... Rodney...something like that, on the old man's side. He probably doesn't even know Mums gone. He mightn't even be alive either.'

'I think it goes to the state if there is no relative, I'd have to check it out. It can't be you, because you don't exist. Own up to the house, and you own up to a murder twenty years ago.'

'But I didn't do it,' said Beau.

'But the cops still reckon you did. Cooper has said as much all this time. Keeps bleating about it in the papers. He identified you as one of the Gulin Street grenade bombers. All that stuff is still around in some police file, waiting for the likes of Cooper to identify you'.

'But I didn't plant that grenade, you did.'

'Keep your voice down. We all know Hamilton did, he was tried for it.'

'Not that one,' whispered Beau, 'the one that killed Reggie.'

'He died in a shootout, they said. It wasn't the grenade.'

'Yes, it was, we were there, remember, he went up in a ball of flame'.

Alex gulped at his beer, spilling a bit down his front. He didn't want to be reminded of that at all.

"But the point is,' said Alex, 'that the cops aren't looking for me. They still believe you are an accessory to Isabelle Herman's death, and Cooper has placed you in the thick of it all. He just can't find you, and it must stay that way. If you come alive again, they'll pin everything on you, and then me. You remember that Whiskey Au Go Go fire? They found the blokes who did it 30 years ago, but they're still hunting for more culprits. They claim there were more involved, that they didn't get everyone. Cold Cases stay open forever. I know, I've built a TV show around it. Some of these retired cops, like Cooper, never give up.'

'You're only worried about yourself!'

'Of course, I am. But you should be worried too. We've come this far by being careful, we need to stay that way. So, no stupid ideas. No breaking into your mother's house and leaving windows open for the neighbours to see.'

'I don't need to break in, I know where the key is. I guess it would still be there.'

'Really?' It was Beau's house, his mother, his memories, who was he to deny him a chance to settle his own life. 'Look, maybe we can go and take a look later when it's a bit darker.' Alex conceded. He looked across the room and saw Janice. 'Here they are.'

Janice and Elizabeth came into the bar area and walked around the tables to them. Alex made to stand, but Janice waved him back down. She leaned over Beau, and gave him a short squeeze around the shoulders, shook off her wet jacket, before flopping into the seat opposite him. Elizabeth kissed Beau on the cheek, ignored Alex and sat down opposite him.

'This weather,' said Janice. 'God it's wet. Great view.' She switched tack. 'It was a nice service, Beau; you would have liked what they said about her.'

'Yeh, Alex filled me in'.

'Marjorie Beaumont was a beautiful person. I haven't been to many funerals, or churches for that matter, so I don't really know the difference between a good one and a bad one. I didn't even get Elizabeth baptised. But I think that service did her justice.'

'You went to that Buddhist place behind Mullumbimby.' Elizabeth added tartly. 'That's the closest thing you've come to religion Mum.'

'That wasn't for a funeral. I guess I haven't been very religious, hard to be when you have a daughter to raise by yourself.' She looked at Beau pointedly, then back to Elizabeth.

'Not my fault. I'll get some drinks,' said Beau taking the opportunity to escape to the bar. Retreating from any further scrutiny.

'Should he be doing that? Showing himself?' asked Elizabeth.

'I think the risk here is minimal Elizabeth, the bar staff are too young to remember the past or notice much of anything for that matter.'

Elizabeth bristled. 'Just because they are young doesn't mean they don't know anything. Just because we weren't around in your 'good old days'. Besides, they were hardly good the way mum described it. Look at what happened to Dad.'

'I didn't mean it that way,' retorted Alex. He turned to Janice. 'She certainly has your fire in her.' He observed.

'That's so condescending. I don't know why Mum likes you so much.'

Alex was taken aback, he'd never thought of himself as condescending, but maybe there was some truth in it. He held up his hands a in a gesture of surrender.

'I'm sorry Elizabeth. All I wanted to point out was that I doubt he would be recognised here.'

'It's easy for you to say, He's not your father, is he? He takes all the risk coming here, it's not you they're after, nothing's going to stick to you.'

She was fierce and eloquent, aiming right at Alex. He wondered what had set her off. He glanced back at Janice, but she just raised her eyebrows at him.

'You're on your own in this one,' she said.

Alex sucked in a deep breath with resolve, 'I don't know how much you know of the past Elizabeth, but I assure you, there is plenty that could get flung around that would stick to me, and your mother for that matter,' He said in a conciliatory tone, but when Elizabeth's eyes showed no response in backing down, Alex hardened his voice. 'If you think for a second that I don't understand the risks involved in this weekend, then I suggest you get Janice to spell it out for you. Your father is no saint, but a jail is no place for him or me. It's no coincidence that we are here, we all chose to be here this weekend, we know the risks as much as anyone.'

She huffed and turned her head away from Alex, defiant and dismissive.

Alex continued.' But now that we are here, and paying our respects to Marjorie, I suggest we just enjoy a drink together, for Beau's sake.'

'Sure. For Dad's sake.' Her voice was thick with sarcasm.

'Beau has been my friend for many years, long before you showed up Elizabeth, long before even your mother was on the scene.'

'Yeh? Well, what did you do for him...for Dad? If you're such good mates, why didn't you do something for him, or for Mum? She says its 20 years since she saw you, what have you done in all that time that wasn't just for you?'

It was a good point, and cut straight into Alex's conscience, but he was growing tired of her angst.' It's complicated Elizabeth, ask your mother.'

'Why? Because I wouldn't understand? Am I another stupid young person? I understand enough to know that you and dad both abandoned Mum and left her to fend for herself. Mrs Beaumont was her only friend, and now she's dead, and you are all back together again, like it's all forgiven.'

'That's not true. Alex knows more than you do about what's going on here.' Janice waded in.

'Why are you defending him? I know enough that I don't want to sit around here listening to you three saying sorry to each other all afternoon and playing 'remember when'. That's boring.' Her angst was palpable.

Beau arrived with glasses of beer and wine, unaware of the direction the conversation had taken.

'I got you girls a wine, hope that's OK with you Elizabeth?'

'I don't want a drink. I'm going home.' She stood, pushing her chair back.

'In this weather?' remarked Beau.

'Yes Dad, in this weather!'

'I'll drive you.'

'You don't have a car.'

'I'll take you then', said Janice, 'or Alex will.'

'I don't need anyone to take me. There's plenty of shops on the way, I'll make my own way back to our place. You can sit here and get drunk if you want to.'

'You can't go out by yourself in this. Alex said this weather will only get worse.'

'I don't care what Alex said.'

'That's enough Elizabeth. If you really want to go, then go!' snapped Janice.

'I will. Why don't you have a few more drinks like you usually do and make doe eyes at him while I'm gone.' She pointed across the table. Alex wasn't sure if she meant him or Beau.

'I'm not eyeing anyone.'

'You could have fooled me,' she jeered.

'Just go. Be at the apartment later,' said Janice

'Maybe I will, maybe I won't. But it's my choice.' She had the last word, swung away and marched out of the bar.

Alex wisely held back on any reflective judgement and had another sip at his beer. He raised his eyebrow at Janice.

' 'She's been like this ever since I said we were coming up here for the funeral and we'd see her dad again.'

'What? She's angry with me?' asked Beau.

'What do you think? She's young and wants to blame someone for her life. Of course, she blames you. You left us. Alex just copped the brunt of it as well. I've been copping it for years; I'm used to it. It's about time you pair had a taste of it'

Alex dismissed it with a wave. 'That's OK. There is some truth to what she said though.'

'What? Sitting around talking about the good old days, or the bit about Janice staring at you,' guessed Beau.

'Neither. Apologising to each other for what we did,' remarked Alex.

'I'm not sorry.' Beau looked at both of them.

'We've been over this. I don't want to talk about it anymore.' Said Janice, directing her dismissal at Beau.

The afternoon was going well Alex thought, exactly as they left each other 20 years earlier, not knowing what was in each other's heads. The Nokia in Alex's pocket rang, he fished it out, saw who was calling and excused himself. He left Beau talking adamantly about why he had to leave and move to Murwillumbah. Janice was unresponsive, ignoring him as she surveyed the surf. She had heard it all before.

Alex stopped in the corner away from the table and answered the phone.

'Yes Miss Marcello. I presume you have an excuse for not getting back to me earlier,' he said good humouredly.

'Don't Miss Marcello me, you smart arse.'

'Sorry Deb. What did you find out?'

'I didn't get back to you earlier because the New South Wales police don't answer their phones after five. Anyway, I've got what you wanted; I think. Firstly, there is plenty of stuff on Dennis 'Beau' Beaumont. Exactly as you said, missing presumed drowned.... Lots linking him to the drug trade and a bombing, and the death of a little girl, Isabelle...'

Alex interrupted, 'Yes, I know all of that part.' Hearing Isabelle Herman's name again still affected him.' It's David Burton, after January 1981 that I was interested in.'

'OK. Nothing for a while. House rental in Coopers Shute Road, near Byron, owned by a Dr. Adrian Thomas. Local vet. Burton was picked up for driving without a licence near Mullumbimby in '84. He disappeared off the charts for a long time after that, no rental records I could find, and didn't reappear till a few of years ago. In 1996 he was picked up for a disturbance at a house in Reynolds Street, Murwillumbah. He was caught urinating in the access lane behind it. Suspected drug party going on according to the report, but he didn't have anything on him. Misdemeanour offence for urinating in public. Got off with a warning.'

'Anything else?'

'Well, a year ago, 16th April, Burton was admitted to the Murwillumbah hospital. He was found bashed in the carpark of the Condong Bowls club. Late night Manager found him as he was locking up. He said Burton was a regular, so he drove him to the hospital himself rather than wait for an ambulance.'

'Here's where it gets messy because Burton didn't want Police involved, and he abused the Manager for driving him in. Very appreciative is David Burton. Incident report stated Burton didn't see who had bashed him. His car wasn't stolen, and get this, nothing was missing. His wallet was still in his pocket with cash in it. The Manager said he's never heard of it before. A few young guys like to roll the drunks every now and then, hassle them for money, but this was different. He'd been knocked out from behind with something hard, not a usual punch up, those are the manager's words.'

'And the manager had no idea who it might have been?'

'Like I said, no police involved beyond an Incident Report, so there was no reason to enquire further. The Manager said he hadn't seen Burton since that night, and he is a bit careful about locking up late at night after that. Nothing more till you asked about him yesterday.'

'That's great thanks Deb. Was it only yesterday I rang? '

'What about Janice Mckenna? You wanted to know about her. '

'Shoot,' said Alex as he looked back toward Janice. She appeared to be stone walling Beau as he gestured and pointed at her. 'Good old days' not a chance, he thought. He turned his attention back to the phone.

'She has no records of contact with Police. Her lease of a duplex in Byron Bay started in mid-1981. Various leases show she probably lived there continuously since. Do want the addresses?'

'No. I don't need them. What about work?'

'She applied for a business number and leasing arrangement on a clothing and gift store in Byron, seven years ago. It seems to be moderately successful. She hasn't gone under anyway. I can give you a current real estate value. But I don't think she's that liquid. There is evidence in the last few years of late payment of bills, electricity, registrations, Council fees, you know the kind. '

'I got it. Um, What about her daughter, Elizabeth?'

'Right... Born Byron Hospital...attended...'

'I'm more interested in the last few years.'

'Let me see.... High school wouldn't release any of her records, understandable, so I rang one of her teachers, and found out she was a bright kid, but often in a bit of trouble in her senior years, nothing serious, just rebellious. The teacher knows Janice, and they would often liaise. She has worked in a bakery since she graduated and is thought of as a good employee by the boss. He says Elizabeth was hoping to get into the media industry at some point, but like so many kids in Byron, the place is just too good to leave...his words.'

'How did you get all this?'

'You pay me to get it, not to tell you how I do it. But let's just say that I'm now good friends now with a teacher in Byron Bay whose got somewhere for me to stay for my next holiday there. Look, I've got heaps of detailed notes here, tell me which ones you want, and I can fax them to you.'

'No Deb, I think that's enough for now. The details can wait'.

'One last thing, Mrs Marjorie Beaumont's funeral that you went to today. Apart from the local paper, I also found the notice through a red flag in a search engine reference for David Burton. I was the second person who had accessed specific information on him in the last week.'

'Shit! How did you find this out?'

'You pay me for my particular skills, I go where most researchers don't, and the only people who use that particular search engine are either police, or people wanting to hide from the police.'

'You're telling me that the Police are interested in David Burton?'

'If you mean David Burton or Dennis 'Beau' Beaumont, then more than one are...and not necessarily the police, there are others around with less savoury backgrounds. For someone who has been missing for 20 years, he's attracted a fair bit of attention in the last week. Is David, or should I say Beau with you up there, for his mother's funeral?'

'I'm not saying anything. But this weekend has turned out different in more ways than one.'

'It'll make a great story. Can I start a loose script outline now? A background synopsis for a mini-series?'

'NO!' Alex exclaimed,' Not at all. Collate those papers and research sites in one place for the moment. No one's to see it. When I get back, I promise I'll fill you in on it all. But this goes no further, understand. Keep working on that Somerton man mystery in Adelaide till I get back. It's got the makings of a great program one day.'

Alex flipped the phone closed, he had to shut down Debbie Marcello quickly, she was a very smart researcher, but also a great gossip, and his was one story that could go no further. He turned back to the table to rescue either Janice or Beau, whichever one looked like they needed it.

Chapter 40

Alex stopped to watch the TV above the bar reporting flooding on the local news. Kids with boogie boards were wading through two feet of water over the soccer fields near Dibing estuary, courtesy of the rising tide. Why weren't they at school? He must be getting old. Flood water was starting to back up on the main roads, and the graphic listed the various road closures to a backdrop of cars and trucks spraying arcs of water as they passed. He turned away from the bar and ambled over to the table.

'Are you guys hungry? Do you want to get a bite here.'

'No. I'll go and meet Elizabeth later. We'll get something near the motel. A bit of shopping will give her time to cool down.'

'You didn't want to drive her over?'

'She's a big girl; she's used to getting around by herself on public transport. She regularly tells me that she doesn't need me, or anyone for that matter, and reminds me that she's mostly grown up looking after herself. '

'That wasn't my choice,' said Beau. 'You moved to Byron, not me.'

'Let's not start that again Beau.'

'Byron's a hole, not like it used to be. Pubs are full of backpackers and rich southerners on holidays now.'

'So what? It's been a good place to bring up Elizabeth, not too big, has a hospital. It's changing, but what place isn't? Look at here? Get real Beau, times change, places grow up, people grow up.'

She shot that last comment directly at Beau. Time hadn't changed Beau's perceptions; he still resisted progress of any kind. She turned to Alex for understanding.

'The shop does OK and Elizabeth is working at the bakery, most days. She starts early, which she hates, but usually gets the afternoons off to go surfing. Despite what you saw this afternoon, we do get on well enough, she's still young. She's happy there, and I'm not leaving anytime soon.'

'What about you Beau?' Alex asked. 'Are you leaving anytime soon?'

'Hope to. I'm getting sick of the shed in a cane field. Every time there are storms, I end up flooded in.'

'That must be why you don't have an address where I can find you.'

'I don't want an address. Suits me fine. When we going to see mum's house?'

'Not till later, we wait till its darker I think.'

'I'm heading off.' Janice put her empty wine glass on the table. 'I want to be home for when Elizabeth gets in, beat the storm. She's a good kid, really. Just a bit confused at the moment.'

Janice stood and collected her jacket.' I'll probably stay in tonight; the weather is shitty. But tomorrow, Ill drop around to see you in the morning. Are you leaving to go back tomorrow, Beau?'

'Probably. I could do with a lift to Murwillumbah, beats going by train.'

'I'll think about it.'

'Come on, give me a break. The least you could do is give me a lift back.'

'Despite everything between us Beau,' said Janice, 'I am truly sorry for your mother. I don't know if she deserved you.'

'That's a bit harsh.'

'Not really Beau. Have a think about it. You can help him with that too Alex. You're no saint yourself. I'll see you both tomorrow.'

Alex watched her sway between the tables as she left. There was a silence between them as they digested what she had said. What was it about Janice that always made her right, Alex thought. She was living proof that he needed a moral compass through life. His wife, Megan used to provide that, but he wasn't so sure that she was still operating as one. He admonished himself for the way he watched Janice walk away, which proved he was probably looking in the wrong direction. He turned to the ocean instead.

Out to sea, a strip of white water rippled the horizon of grey ugly seas. The waves were now breaking at Florette shoals, which meant the swells were beginning to top 5 to 6 metres out there. The strong winds pushed wave tops like white sharks' teeth in every direction. Half a surfboard was pushed around in the foam at the base of the rock wall below where he was sitting. It's owner staggered out of the surf, raised one arm to his friend further up the beach and held aloft the bottom half of his board, a sheet of fibreglass flapping where it had been torn in two. The time for surfing had passed, the conditions had changed to one of survival, and he was celebrating. The glass panels in front of Alex shook.

'Reminds me of that night.' Beau shuddered.' If I'd seen it in the daylight, I wouldn't have gone out that night with Reggie even for the best of reasons. Lucky it was dark. I had no idea what I was getting into.'

White spume laden swells swept across the mouth of the river to batter against the inner rock wall.

'Jesus, look at that. The pilot boat is trying to get back in,' exclaimed Beau.

They looked out to sea, past Florette Shoals where only two ships were left lined up at anchor waiting for a pilot to be delivered before they could enter Brisbane to offload their cargo. They looked solid platforms from here, but both of them knew it was an illusion, they had been up close in rough weather, and those ships were pitching and bucking, far from stable in these conditions.

'I would have thought they would refuse to go out in this.' Alex remarked.

'Must have been desperate. Watch this, he's going for it.'

While they talked, the Pilot boat, a powerful 60-footer with a flush deck and enclosed cabin worked around and through the breaking white water near the entrance. It was waiting for a lull in the sets. When it came, a belch of dark exhaust signalled a thrust of the bow bursting through a steep swell, then spiralling down into the trough between the crests.

The boat shot forward and roared toward the entrance. He nearly made it, but the next wave hit his stern just before the boat found the safety of the lee behind the rock wall. The wave delivered a massive blow that tipped the boat on its side. As it was held in the balance perched on the top of the white water, Alex could see the whole deck plan, as if looking from above. The stern was skewed toward the inside rock wall. More diesel exhaust spewed forth as the engine fought to recover. The boat righted, just meters from disaster and shot into the safety of the river mouth.

'Shit that was close.' Alex exhaled. He didn't realise how much he had been holding his breath, willing the boat to make it. He turned to Beau. 'If I remember right, you told me you had dived overboard that night.'

'What are you getting at?'

'That last night, out on the boat with Reggie and Conlan., you said you had dived overboard, but I reckon you must have been washed off the deck, no sane person would have jumped overboard into that willingly.'

'How do you know? You weren't there,' Beau retorted.

'You did, didn't you?' Alex's tone jumped with the revelation. 'You did get washed over. You told me you had dived on purpose. I thought that took guts... stupid, but gutsy. It didn't happen that way at all did it? You got washed off the deck.' Alex chuckled good naturedly.

Beau looked defiant.' I don't really remember. Dived, fell, whatever. Doesn't matter now.'

'I was thinking about that,' said Alex.' Their boat must have got swamped, a small boat like that, because Reggie ended up at the boat ramp not long after you came ashore without it, so his boat must have gone under soon after you went over. Either that or he bailed out on Conlan and left him by himself, but Reggie wouldn't have willingly left the boat. I wonder if Conlan chucked him overboard.' Alex drummed his fingers on the tabletop as he divulged his theories. 'And then they caught a shark with bits of a life vest and Roy's ring in its gut. But they never found him or the boat. Bit like you Beau, only he got eaten and saved the Police arresting him for conspiracy to murder over the Herman bombing.'

'What a way to go. And Reggie got his too, thanks to you Alex.'

'I told you; I didn't mean that. He wasn't supposed to die.' Alex protested.

'But he did, and we got away. Come on Alex, he and Conlan were going to feed me to the sharks that night. What happened to them doesn't matter, they both deserved to go, it saved my skin, and Beau Beaumont ceased to exist that night, David Burton has taken his place, and I'm in the clear.'

'Don't be so sure of your new identity, Beau. My researcher in Melbourne found you in a day. She's linked your two names together and knows that David Burton is really you. She knows where you are now, and where you've been for the last 20 years, and she's not the only one looking for you.'

'What? Are you checking up on me?' scolded Beau. 'But who cares. If anyone figured it out, they would have gone to the cops by now. I didn't kill those blokes, really the only thing I've done is change my name.'

'Now you're being stupid Beau,' admonished Alex. Beau bristled and went to say something in retort, but Alex ploughed on,' We've been over this. You are still wanted in relation to a murder; you can't come back to life now. But someone thinks you have. They've been looking you up on the internet. You got rolled last night, and I'm not so sure that's not related to this. You got bashed up the same way in Condong last year.'

'How do you know about that?'

'Like I said, my researcher knows her stuff.'

'Does she know about the smuggling? About Reggie and Conlan?

'No. She doesn't know anything about that side of it. She doesn't know anything about how you were hiding drugs and cash from them, and how they wanted it back,' he said pointedly. 'But Janice did.'

Beau looked confused.

'Conlan threatened to do her in, and more, unless you gave up the money and drugs that you were hiding from them. Did you know that?'

'I wasn't hiding anything of theirs.' Beau protested.

'Are you keeping up that charade? You were screwing them over Beau, and they wanted it back, so they went after you, and Janice as well.'

'Doesn't matter now, does it. They're both dead,' reflected Beau as he took another sip at his beer. 'Besides, the money's not there. It's gone.'

It was Alex's turn to look bemused. 'What do you mean?'

'The money, the drugs, it's gone. I couldn't find it.'

'Where did you hide it?' asked Alex.

'At Mum's place, in a false panel behind my bedhead. I came back just before Elizabeth was born and got in when no one was around, but it was gone. The wall space was empty, nothing. That's why I want to go back again. Today. Now that mum's no longer there, I can have a decent look around.'

'How much did you have hidden there?'

'I had three kilos stashed from the pickups. I'd tell Reggie not all the packages made it to the boat, but I did get them all, I just kept a few for myself and told him that they were lost at sea. I sold some off, skimmed off some deal money as well that they didn't know about.'

'But they did know about it Beau, that's why they came after you. That nearly got you killed. Was it still there before you disappeared?'

'Yeh. That's where I got some of the money from to give to you.'

'You must have had a fair bit; two fat rolls of cash if I remember, thousands. You told me there was plenty more where that came from. What did you do with it?'

'There was plenty more...once. Enough to set me and Janice up when the time came. But when I came to get it, it was gone.'

'Well, it couldn't have been Reg or Conlan, they were in the boat with you that night, so who might have moved it?'

'Cooper. I bet,' snarled Beau. 'But I want to make sure.'

'So, we go and search your mum's place when it gets dark. See if there's anything still there. If there is, money only! No drugs. Tomorrow, you pack up and go home to Murwillumbah and resume being David Burton living in a cane field for a while longer.'

'And you and Janice get to go back to your happy families, is that it? And the best I get is a shed in a cane field by myself,' he said bitterly.

'It's not like you to feel sorry for yourself.'

He looked up at Alex. 'What about you? Whining all the time about not meaning to kill Reggie. Pretending to be Mr Perfect, don't get your hands dirty. You planted that grenade in his car, that makes you responsible, so get over it.'

'I'm not a murderer'.

'You just keep telling yourself that Alex. We both were... back then. Plenty of skeletons in the closet.'

'Stop now Beau.'

'And what was it with you and Janice anyway? Did you have something going for her...behind my back?'

'You're my mate. I wouldn't have done that.' But he had done, Alex thought to himself, hypocrite and condescending, all in one day. 'All I'm saying is that perhaps it was a good thing we split apart when we did, because it worked out for the best.'

'Not the best for me, was it?' Beau pointed out.

'I think she was going to leave you anyway Beau.'

'If she was going to leave me, why did she come down to Byron?'

'Might have had something to do with the fact that she was pregnant to you.'

That stopped the argument in its tracks. The bickering was really window dressing for a stressful day. Beau looked in the big mirror on the far wall, and saw himself hunched over a beer glass, next to his best friend.

'She doesn't like me much you know,' he said, referring to Elizabeth,' And I'm her father.'

'She likes me even less.' said Alex. The conversation had moved on to more secure grounds, mates again

'Yeh. She's pretty feisty. What about you? Are your kids like her?' asked Beau.

'I haven't got any,' replied Alex. His mobile phone buzzed and vibrated across the tabletop. 'That'll probably be Megan now'. Alex answered it, but said nothing, he only listened.

'That wasn't Megan, that was Janice,' he said. 'Elizabeth has disappeared.' He shut the phone and looked at Beau.

Chapter 41

The wipers beat heavily against the pounding rain. Alex had to concentrate as he pushed the hire car up the road leading to Georges head. The front left wheel would dip into overflowing gutters and engulf the car in liquid silver, momentarily blinding them both until the wipers pushed the water aside and allowed Alex to see the road again. The radio was espousing warnings about the dangers of driving, minor flooding and a high tide pushing river waters back upstream of both Nerimbah River and the Dibing Creek wetlands. They both had to yell over the drumming on the roof to make themselves heard.

'She said that when she got home Elizabeth wasn't there, but the room was trashed, like yours had been, and there was a note on the table, addressed to her and you.'

'What did it say?'

'Only that they had Elizabeth. I think there is more, but Janice didn't say.' Alex swerved to avoid a car parked half off the road, deep in water, hazard lights flashing. 'Shit this is getting worse. Where is her place again?' Alex asked. He slalomed the car around depressions of water, the car buffeted by the wind. Few people were on the road, no one walking the streets.

'It's close to the front. Turn up here and take Wurung Street, it's up high, near the shopping centre.' Beau pointed to the left. They passed a carpark awash with water. Last minute shoppers risking being caught in rising floods.

'Alicante Apartments, you can just see it ahead.' The block was new, three streets back from the esplanade. 'There it is, number 6, first floor, there's Janice in the doorway.'

It was a newish unit, not dissimilar inside to the one Alex was renting, however, like Beau's place the night before, this one had also been trashed. Janice stood next to the kitchen bench and held out the note for Alex. He was acutely aware that it was he she handed the note to and not Beau. It was written on old exercise book paper. The handwriting neat, unhurried, planned...

The girl in exchange for the money and drugs. Beach Shack. 7.pm.

Alex looked at Janice and Beau in turn. It was not lost on either of them.

'This has to be someone we know,' he said. 'Cooper or Mitch Donald or his fruit loop mate, Ergo. He always blamed you for their arrest, said you dobbed them in.'

'Could be. What about the *Beach Shack*? They would have to have known that it was our place,' said Janice.

'We can't go to the police with this,' said Beau.

'I want to,' snapped Janice. 'They've kidnaped Elizabeth. We've got no choice.'

'If we go to the cops, we are all undone.'

'I know that' she said.

' 'What about the other part, the money and drugs?' Alex looked at Beau, it was time for him to admit he had it and use it.

Beau looked searchingly from Alex to Janice, and back again. 'It might still be in Mum's house somewhere,' said Beau, 'We can find it.'

Janice shook her head. 'It's not there Beau. She burnt it.'

'What?' he exclaimed.

'She burnt it. Don't waste your time looking for it. Marjorie thought you were dead, we both did, so she got it out of the wall and burnt it. She told me so. We have no way to get Elizabeth back unless we go to the cops. We have nothing to trade.'

'She burnt it?' gasped Beau. 'Why did she do that?'

Janice huffed, 'She told me she knew all along what you were doing, hiding drugs and money in her house. She let you keep doing it because you wouldn't come around otherwise. When you were pronounced missing, lost at sea, she got it out and burnt it. It was evil and it had taken you away from her. And if the Lord ever brought you back to her, he would provide, not some drug dealer like Reggie'. There was bitterness to Janice's voice, sentiments that weren't his mother's alone.

'Hell.' Beau slumped back on the bed.

'She knew you were dealing Beau.' Janice continued. 'We both did. You fucked off and left us both alone, no wonder she confided in me. She even took Reggie burning to death as a sure sign of what to do with the drugs.'

'But Reggie didn't burn to death, he was dead before it went up.' said Alex.

'You wish.' said Janice. 'That doesn't matter now, we got no time for this, so it's no use looking for something that's not there. We've got nothing to trade; we have to go to the police.'

'Who has taken Elizabeth? Who are we trading with? It could be Cooper. He's the only one who knows the whole story, from when we were here twenty years back,' said Alex, still trying to find a way.

'Or Ergo, or Mitch. They might still be around.'

'I bet whoever bashed me the other night, they were looking for the stuff.' Beau surmised.

Janice was exasperated, 'Cooper or whoever has got Elizabeth, and we haven't got anything to trade for her. Stop wasting time.'

'Trade or not, if we go to the police now, we go to jail for something we did 20 years ago. You know that don't you,' said Alex.

'We can trade him his life.' Beau drawled cautiously.

'What do you mean?'

'I know where we can get a gun,' he revealed. 'The Beach Shack, under the floor. I hid a gun there a long time ago.'

'A pistol?' Alex queried.

'Shit no. A rifle, a .22. I got it as part payment for a deal once. It's up in under one of the joists in the shack. It could still be there.'

'It wouldn't still work, would it?'

'Don't know. But at least we'll have a gun.'

'Have you ever fired it?'

'No.'

'Any bullets in it.'

'The bloke said there were three in it when he gave it to me.'

'Have you ever fired a gun before?' Alex asked.

'Slug guns when I was a kid. I don't have to fire it, just point it at him and force him to let Elizabeth go'.

Alex shook his head. 'If you are going to point a gun at someone, you hope it works, otherwise you'll only be bluffing.'

'They won't know that. Can you think of anything better?' said Beau. 'Bluffing is fine. I told you once before Alex, I'm made for this game, you're not. I love you like a brother, but you're too soft.' He gripped Alex's shoulder and turned to Janice. 'And this is my daughter we're talking about.'

Janice looked imploringly at Alex, willing him to come up with something better, but this was now Beau's gig, it was simple and relied on a confidence that only he could muster.

' Whatever happens tonight, it's on me. You've trusted me before Janice, trust me again, I'm made for this.' Beau smiled wickedly.

Chapter 42

Alex swung the rental car up onto the grass, the headlights illuminated the rusty carport, water dripping through the holes in the roof and pooling on the dirt. He drove across the grass and parked around the back of the Beach Shack, unseen from the road. Janice twisted around from the front seat to face Beau in the back.

'You reckon you know where the rifle is?'

'I can find it if it's still there.' Beau opened the rear door and darted in under the awning. They watched as he crouched down and wormed his bony frame between two stumps, disappearing under the house.

Alex and Janice tried pulling ply from the front door, but it wouldn't give. They sloshed around to the side door ramp and tried their luck at the kitchen door. The rotten timber frame gave way as they pulled and shook it. A strong gust of wind reefed the door from their hands and slammed it open. Cyclone Cliff had well and truly taken hold. A brief lightning flash lit up bare floors, and some broken furniture stacked against the far wall. They stepped inside out of the rain. It smelled of rotting damp and mould, all the good times of its past life long gone.

There was just enough light from the streetlamp across the road for them to see each other and move around safely inside. Water dripped from a leak in the roof on the lino floor in the bathroom, setting up a persistent patter. Janice slid her finger over the kitchen bench, leaving a trail through the dust as Alex moved across to the front windows and peered out over the top of the plywood.

'Is Beau still under the house?' he asked.

'Think so.' Said Janice as she glanced toward the kitchen door then drifted toward her old bedroom.

'Headlights,' called Alex.

Janice moved across to join him at the window, peering through a gap in the ply nailed to the opening outside. The car mounted the gutter, drove across the grass and parked just out of view behind the carport.

'Now they're gone. He's early,' said Alex looking at his watch.

'Where's Beau?' she whispered. Alex moved to the far wall, and slid the curtain back from the widow, he could just make out the car around the side. The next flash of lightning showed that it was empty.

Too late, Alex turned to the kitchen. The door was pulled open. In the doorway stood a figure. It looked like Cooper, only bigger, more thick set, menacing, a pistol in his right hand.

'Hello Janice, Alex...long time,' Roy Conlan said. He stepped inside, the door slamming behind him. Conlan looked around the room. 'Where's Beau?' he asked. He pointed the pistol at the bedroom door.

Alex was the first to recover. 'Not here. He's still at his parent's house getting what you wanted.'

Conlan surveyed the room, came in, pulling the kitchen door behind him and walked to the bedroom. He pushed open that door, nothing. The bathroom had no door, inside were cracked tiles and a broken wash basin next to the toilet.

'I'll wait. I've been waiting 20 years as it is. I can wait a bit longer. You two sit.'

'Where's Elizabeth?' Janice blurted out.

'She's safe,' he replied calmly. 'On the floor.' He gestured with the pistol.

They both crouched down low.

'Sit!' he commanded. They both settled awkwardly on the timber floor.

Conlan put the gun down on the kitchen bench and reached into his pocket for his cigarettes. He set about lighting one in an odd way, the flame revealed he only had a thumb and forefinger on his left hand. The rest of his fingers and the palm of his hand were missing, leaving only a knot of scar tissue. He retrieved the pistol.

'You looked surprised when I came in. Didn't know I was still alive, did you?'

'No.'

'Huh. Like that for everyone. You all thought I'd been eaten by a shark or drowned. Roy Conlan gone, just like Beau. Nearly did, lost a few fingers that night.' He held up his hand, the cigarette pinched between his thumb and forefinger the way fashionable Europeans liked to smoke. 'A fucking big shark got them before some fisherman in his boat pulled me out of the drink. Wonderful man, a real good Samaritan. I thanked him by keeping his boat.'

Alex wondered what happened to the fisherman, but he could guess.

'Hello Janice. Nice to see you. Did you miss me?'

'Fuck off Conlan.'

'Oh, So bitter. You weren't like that last time we met. A back seat can be pretty cramped but I'm still keen if you are.' He smirked.

Alex looked at Janice. 'It doesn't matter,' she said.

The kitchen door flung open, slamming back on its hinges. Beau stood in the door frame, covered in mud, an apparition from the bowels of the underworld, a very dirty rifle held high, pointed at Conlan.

Conlan had spun around at the noise. He didn't get his gun up, but left it half raised, pointed at Beau's groin. Alex stood quickly, helping Janice to her feet.

'Where's Elizabeth?' Beau yelled, his eyes ablaze, rock steady, focused on Conlan. Conlan in response was rapidly calculating his odds and said nothing in reply.

'Where's Elizabeth?' Beau repeated.

'Not here.' he drawled. 'Where's my money and heroin?'

Beau wasn't used to tense stand offs, the mud made his hands slippery, and he had to keep reapplying his grip on the gun.

'You give me the gear; you get your daughter.' said Conlan.

Beau's eyes flickered from Conlan to Janice. Not sure what to say next, how to take the stand off to the next step.

Conlan smiled, 'Or she could be my daughter,' he added. 'I knew Janice too you know.'

For a few seconds, Beau looked confused, then his eyes swung across to Janice, which was exactly what Conlan hoped for.

Beau looked back at Conlan, but it was already too late, Conlan had lined the gun up on Beau. When Beau pulled the 22's trigger, the firing pin didn't even drop, it made no sound, the trigger and breech were rusted solid. Conlan didn't flinch, he sighted the pistol and shot Beau.

The impact crumpled him. He grunted in pain and dropped sideways out the door, slipping off the wet ramp, landing in a twisted heap to the side. Conlan moved into the doorway, kicked the rifle away, and waved the pistol around until he found his target point, then he steadied the sight on Beau's back.

Alex hit Conlan with a shoulder charge. It was too high to do any damage, but it pushed him out the door, the gun exploded, and his shot went wide. Both men tumbled down the slippery ramp, Alex atop the larger Conlan, their legs tangled as they slid to the bottom.

Conlan smashed the butt of his gun into Alex's forehead, stunning him and opening the skin in a gush of blood. He tried to bring the gun round to bare, but Alex leaned back and lashed out with his foot, hitting Conlan's shoulder, spinning the gun out of his hand, away into the dark. Conlan responded with a flurry of kicks and punches to Alex's body. He tried to bring his knees up to protect himself, but Conlan's foot drove into his abdomen, exploding the air from his lungs in searing pain.

It ended when Conlan disengaged and crawled away. Alex could barely move, blood was streaming into his eyes, behind him he could hear Beau groaning as the rain kept pattering into his face.

Alex shook himself off, got to his knees and looked around. A brief flash of lightening revealed Conlan disappearing around the side of the house. Behind him Beau writhed on the grass, Janice was hunched over him, pressing down on his upper chest, the rain washing away the blood as fast as it was appearing between her fingers. Alex slid in close and pulled her hands away to see the wound.

Beau groaned and winced under his touch. It looked closer to the shoulder than the middle of his chest.

'Fuck that hurts,' Beau groaned, coughing, and spitting phlegm. There was no blood coming from his mouth, so maybe the lungs weren't punctured.

Alex pushed her hands back over the wound and leaned away to topple onto his back, letting the rain wash the blood from his eyes and clean the mud from the wound on his forehead. He reached down to feel if any of his ribs were broken, sharp pains where he rubbed at them, but it was bearable. More than anything, he wanted to lay back down close his eyes.

'Alex! Alex!' Janice shook his shoulders, leaning over him.' Elizabeth... Conlan's still got her.'

'Shit!' Alex exclaimed, turning his head to look at Beau, knowing that he desperately needed a hospital. Beau looked back at him and smiled, his grimacing smoothed out and for a brief moment the Beau of old returned.

'Alex, please.' Janice implored, her hands back pressing on Beau's shoulder wound. He looked between Beau and Janice, fraught with indecision. It was Beau who broke the stalemate.

'She's my daughter,' he pleaded.

Alex nodded, and rose unsteadily to his feet, gasping at the pain in his side.

'You stay with Beau, get an ambulance. Where's your phone?'

'I don't know.' Janice cried.

'I'll follow Conlan. I'll find her. You find your phone,' he shouted, 'and ring the Police.'

She looked at him and nodded her understanding of what that would mean for them all. Elizabeth would be safe, Police could get her back, but they sacrifice everything, and Beau would go to jail.

From behind the carport, a Ford skidded across the grass till it hit the bitumen. It was Conlan. Alex watched the lights trail down the street as he staggered around the back of the house to his own car.

Chapter 43

Alex tried hard to keep up with Conlan. Every now and then, the wipers revealed a hint of smeared yellow with red taillights ahead as Conlan pushed the car through sheets of spray.

Alex rubbed at the broken skin on his forehead, felt a stinging loose flap, and wiped watery blood from his eyes. Conlan was heading for Nerimbah boat harbour, that would be the only reason why he hugged the coast road south. Alex knew there was no way to get ahead of him. In the cyclonic conditions he had to satisfy himself with tailing Conlan.

He swung wide on the corner of Jermu street and ploughed into a pool of water where the old ice works used to be. The car slewed left over the gutter, tearing the wheel from his hands, bringing it to a stop. A sheet of muddy water waved across the bonnet and up onto his windscreen, then receded. The engine stalled. Ahead, Conlan's taillights disappeared into the murk. Alex tried repeatedly to restart the car, the starter motor whining as it tried to ignite the engine. On his fifth go, it caught, spluttered, and finally roared into life. He franticly reversed out of the water and searched ahead for lights. Nothing.

Jermu street followed the river esplanade down to Mullu crescent, where the road finished, and the river narrowed into mangroves and tidal flats. The area was a dead end. If Conlan was driving out, he would have to pass Alex, and he would see him.

Alex drove slowly along Jermu Street, looking left and right, searching for Conlan's car among the houses and riverfront lots. His wipers beat franticly in a losing battle against the rain. It was dark, the headlights revealing swirling leaves and windblown flotsam. All the houses were shut tight, slivers of light showing where they were battened down against the storm. There were streets to his right where Conlan could escape to, but his instincts told him to keep left, follow the river, look in the driveways.

Behind the riverfront houses the trawlers and yachts would be straining at their moorings in this wind. As he drove further inland, the river shallowed, less affluent houses, more gaps, more midges. There, between a house and a shed, the pale glow of an outside light showed the boot of a yellow car.

He reversed up out of sight, jumped out and sprinted down the side of the house, stopping at the car, it was Conlan's yellow Ford, he recognised it from the funeral today, parked under the tree. The house at his back was quiet, empty, no lights on inside. Ahead came the sound of an outboard being pulled into life. He worked around the car, tapped on the boot and investigated the back seat. Nothing. On the river he could see a torch arcing ahead of a small dinghy spluttering through the rain toward a houseboat moored just off the bank. It was Conlan. Alex watched him pull up to the boat, tie off the dinghy and go inside. A feeble light came on between the curtains in the side window. This was where Elizabeth would be.

It occurred to Alex that Conlan now knew there was no hidden stash of money or blocks of heroin for him. There was nothing to trade Elizabeth for. Maybe he would just leave her and melt back into the darkness from where he came. But he was a vindictive bastard, it wasn't in his nature to just walk away, he didn't leave behind loose ends.

Alex looked back down the driveway to his own car. It was just him. There was no one else. There would be no Police, that would take too long, it had to be now to get Elizabeth. Alex took a deep breath to steady his nerves and slid over the bank into the river.

The water was remarkably warm compared to the rain that pounded his head. He breast stroked hard against the current, his ribs protesting all the way, till he reached the back of the houseboat where a small metal ladder dangled in the water. The buffeting of the wind against the hull disguised his movement as he climbed aboard. Through the gap in the curtains, he could see Conlan moving about the small space inside, packing cloths into one of two bags on the centre table. Elizabeth sat on the bunk, her arms and legs tied together, swivelling her head from side to side as she followed Conlan's movements. Alex could see no weapon; it doesn't mean there wasn't one, but he would have to take the chance. He tried to formulate a plan, but he had nothing. His mind was blank, so he pulled open the sliding door and stepped inside.

'Fuck...it's you,' said Conlan. Alex stood just inside the door, he looked at Elizabeth, her eyes were wide with panic.

At first, Alex didn't know what to say. Finally, he pointed toward Elizabeth.

'I can just take her with me, you know. Nothing more said,' he offered lamely.

There was silence, Conlan didn't react.

'There's no money or drugs, you know that. We can just leave, and you can go as well.'

'Not going to happen,' growled Conlan.

Without warning, Conlan launched himself at Alex, his left hand outstretched, driving his muscular forefinger at Alex's face. It connected just below his eye into the soft part of his cheek, punched through the skin and Alex tasted the blood in his mouth. His head snapped back as Conlan's body slammed into him, barrelling him back through the open door onto the small aft deck. They tripped over the mounted outboard and tumbled into the river.

When Alex's head broke the surface, Conlan repeated his attack. His deformed hand was a formidable weapon; the gnarled finger was a solid ball of muscle that jabbed at Alex's face with far more penetration than a closed fist.

Alex was losing the battle fast, he was already gasping for breath, his ribs constricted, flailing his arms, trying to move away from the onslaught, but Conlan was relentless, following him, jabbing at his eyes with his hand, and pushing his head under with the other. He gasped, pushed and beat at Conlan, but it wasn't working.

Alex had one option left, he tumble turned under him, and swam down deeper, grabbing Conlan's leg and dragging him under. He held on hard and pushed himself deeper. Conlan struggled and kicked at Alex, connecting with the top of his head and shoulders, but he refused to let go. They both began to rise to the surface, Alex brushed past an anchor chain and grabbed it, wrapping his legs around it to keep them both under, his arms gripping on to Conlan.

Conlan's struggles began to spasm, his body scrambling for the surface, but Alex didn't let go. He could feel his own chest begin to pulse, he resisted the urge to open his mouth and head for the surface himself, but he knew he could outlast Conlan. His brain screamed for oxygen; he was dizzy. He screwed his eyes tighter, and air began to squeeze past his lips in short bursts as his lungs spasmed. When he could take no more, he didn't care, he released Conlan's leg and searched blindly for the surface.

He broke through, gasped and coughed, wanting to throw up, sucking in oxygen and rainwater, till his lungs began to settle and he lay back in the water floating face up. The rain was cold on his cheeks. Conlan's body bumped into his, but when he pushed at it, there was no resistance, he was face down and slipping below the surface.

The current had taken Alex far from the houseboat. He was exhausted. He bobbed past another moored boat, grabbed at the anchor chain, weakly holding on against the current and rested before he struck out for shore. It took all his remaining energy to swim to the riverbank. He lay on the sand clutching his sore ribs, trying get back enough energy to return to the houseboat.

When he staggered in through the back door; Elizabeth was laying on the floor next to the bunk, curled into a ball. She started to cry. He found some scissors and cut at her bindings, then sat down beside her and held her close. They were both coming back from the brink.

Alex woke with a start. He had closed his eyes only for a second, but it hadn't helped. He was weak and barely able to get up, Elizabeth helped him.

'Where's that man?' she asked.

'He's gone.'

She was quiet for a few seconds. 'What do we do now?'

'We get off this boat.'

He looked around and shook his head to clear some space in it before he began to think what needed to be done.

'Elizabeth, is any of your stuff here? Did he bring any of your things with him?'

'No. Nothing.'

Alex looked around. 'Straighten the bed and throw those bindings overboard,' he said. Alex was trying hard to concentrate. He unpacked Conlan's bags and stuffed those clothes back where he thought they had come from. The scissors were returned to the drawer and he picked up Conlan's car keys from the table.

He pointed to the door, looked around one last time, turned the light off and followed Elizabeth out on to the back deck, locking the glass slider behind him. He looked thoughtfully at Conlan's keys, then threw them overboard.

'Help me with this will you?' He pulled the dinghy around till it was side on to the deck. Elizabeth made to get in, but he held her back.

'No! I want to sink it.' He pulled one side of the dinghy up until the opposite side had dipped into the floodwaters. The current did the rest, rapidly filling the dinghy with water and ripping it from their grasp, it had sunk to the gunwales. Alex let go the rope, and it disappeared into the dark.

'Can you swim to shore?' he asked.

'Of course.'

'Then you can help me, I'm done.'

He lowered himself into the river one last time and started for the shore. Elizabeth easily caught up to him, grabbed his shirt and kicked by his side. The silt on the bottom never felt so good under foot.

Elizabeth sat wrapping her arms around her knees in the passenger seat. He leaned his head back against the car's headrest and closed his eyes in relief, the warm dry car cocooning them both.

It's not easy to kill someone, he had warned Beau about that once. Now he understood his own warning. In the safety of his hire car, through his closed eyelids he saw Conlan's body again. Reggie's death didn't count, that was an accident, it was distant, the result of misadventure. Conlan was another matter. His was deliberate, and he couldn't have got any closer. If only the shark had done it properly in the first place. He had purposefully ended a man's life. He opened the door and leaned out, the taste of bile tingling his cheeks, he prepared to throw up.

'Who was he?' Elizabeth broke into his silence.

Alex hung out the door, the bile retreated. He sat back up and faced Elizabeth.

'His name was Roy Conlan.'

'He was an American, I heard it in his voice. He knew you.'

'From a long time ago.'

'Why did he kidnap me?'

'He's been after your father for a long time. He was just using you to get to him. '

'What did Dad do to make him do that?'

'You can ask him yourself, or your mother.'

She was silent.

Alex had to ask.' Did he do anything to you, like...?'

'No. But he was creepy. I think he wanted to.' Gone was the defiance of earlier in the day. Her next question was more of a childlike observation.

'Did he drown?'

'Yes.'

'You, did it?'

'Yes'

She leaned back in the seat and closed her eyes.

'Thank you.' she said quietly.

They sat in companionable silence. He looked across at her. She was Janice's daughter, but he could have been her father as much as Beau was. He shook that thought from his head. She had Beau's eyes; he was sure of that. Alex started the car and headed for home.

Chapter 44

The shack was still in darkness when Alex pulled up next to the ramp. Janice appeared at the side door and walked tentatively down the ramp. Elizabeth had barely opened the car door when Janice wrenched it open and pulled her daughter from the front seat. She stood holding on to her in the rain, Elizabeth hugged her just as tightly in return.

'How's Beau?' Alex called across from the driver's side, sliding his hand back and forth around the seat and floor looking for his mobile.

'He's alive.' said Janice.

'Is dad hurt?'

'He was shot. He's inside,' she replied.

Alex gave up on the phone and headed for the kitchen door. On the floor a stub of candle flickered a feeble light, enough to see Beau lying with his head propped up by dirty old cushions. His eyes were closed. His bloodied shirt had been bunched up and placed over the wound in his upper shoulder, above the heart. His breathing was deep and regular.

Janice came in behind him. 'I couldn't find my phone, couldn't go anywhere or get help, you took the car.'

'Dad,' cried Elizabeth. She pushed past Alex and dropped to her knees beside him.

Beaus' eyes opened briefly, he winced a little smile, then closed them again.

'Conlan shot him,' Janice explained for Elizabeths benefit. 'We've got to get him to a hospital.'

'No hospital.' whispered Beau. 'I'll be OK. Where's Conlan?'

'He's gone.'

'Good.' He closed his eyes again.

'Is there an exit wound?' Alex asked.

'In his back. The wound is quite small. I've covered that too.'

'Great,' said Alex. 'Help me get him up. Elizabeth, go open the back seat, we'll slide him in there.'

Beau groaned in pain as they lifted him on to his side, blood oozed out from under his shirt, it wasn't as much as Alex would have thought. But then, all the gunshot wounds Alex had seen were only on TV, and that medium was known to exaggerate.

'If we don't do the hospital, we can take him to my unit,' said Janice. 'It's on the first floor. I've got painkillers and antiseptic ointment in my bag. We'll try that first. If it doesn't work, then the hospital, OK?' She looked at Alex for agreement. He nodded, and they manoeuvred Beau down the ramp and into the car.

Janice took over as soon as they had him in the bathroom at her apartment. She stripped him down to his underwear and washed off the mud and blood. Beau was conscious but moaning objections. Elizabeth was keeping him upright, perched on the edge of the bath, while Janice washed both sides of the wound. The bathroom was a mess, but they all crowded in to inspect her work.

'I'm sure the bullet went straight through. I don't think it hit any bone. Its clean.'

'If he doesn't get an infection from under that stinking house, all that mud.'

'Alex, hold Beau.' She retrieved some tablets and antiseptic gel from her toiletry bag on the sink. 'Elizabeth, clean cotton shirts in my bag, get some.' she ordered.

Beau took the pain killers while Janice finished wiping at the dribble of blood still oozing from the wound. She crushed up two Flagyl tablets, mixed it with antiseptic gel and pushed it into Beaus wounds with her fingers from both sides. He squirmed and sucked in his breath.

'Will that work?' Alex asked.

'No idea, but I'll try anything,' Janice said as she used Elastoplast to bring the wound together and bound his whole shoulder tight with her shirt. She used another shirt tied tight as a sling, to raise his arm high across his chest.

They helped him to his feet, put a towel round his waist, and led him out to the sofa where he lay back. His breathing was starting to ease, and some colour returning to his face. He slid into a light sleep. The real danger now was from infection, and they would know by morning if they had successfully held that at bay.

Alex made coffee while Janice dragged Elizabeth off to the shower and some fresh clothes. They were away for a while, murmurings coming from the bedroom, until Janice appeared, alone.

'He didn't touch her,' she said.

He handed her a coffee. 'Elizabeth told me that.' He was quiet for a minute. 'What about you? Did what Conlan say was true?'

'Jesus, no. He didn't, he just said it to stir up Beau. But he threatened to once. I'm glad he's dead. He is dead this time, isn't he?'

'Yes.'

'How?'

'He drowned. Fell out of his dinghy. At least that's what I hope people will think when they find him.'

'Jesus, here we go again.'

'I'm getting used to making people disappear, 'he said tiredly. 'Christ, listen to me, like I'm some sort of seasoned hitman.'

He was silent as the implication of what he had done that night returned.

'I've never killed anyone before. Never even hurt them, apart from pub fights, and I was never very good at those.'

'I know. I've seen you in action.'

'I'm not ashamed of what I did. Conlan was an evil bloke, he was a killer. He wasn't going to let Elizabeth go. He would have killed her and me, but even then, it doesn't feel right.'

Janice reached across and touched his arm. He pulled away.

'It's OK. I'm OK,' Alex said,' I'll be glad when I get back to Melbourne, it's safer there.'

'Is it over Alex?'

He thought about it all for a minute and nodded. Perhaps that included how he felt about Janice as well.

'Yeh! I think it's over. If Beau gets through this OK, we at least go back to how it was before.'

'I don't want to go back to that,' she said. 'I want to move on. I have Elizabeth, I have my business, I have my life. You have your life and Beau has his.'

'Fair enough. I'm not going to argue. I'll come by in the morning, see how he is. If he's OK, he won't be fit to travel anywhere by himself.'

'Not like he is now, no. I'll drive him to Byron with me. I know some natural healers there who will help look after that wound and any infection. He can stay on their farm, out of the way. I'll see how he is in the morning, but if he's running a fever, we may have to take our chances with the hospital.'

'If that's the case, you clear out, and I'll take him.'

Janice looked at Beau and felt his pulse. 'It's strong, I think he'll be fine as long as there is no infection.'

She walked over to Alex and hugged him.

'Thank you, Alex, for Elizabeth, and for me.'

There was no kiss this time. It really was over, all of it. He released her and ducked his head to sniff at his damp clothes.

'God, I stink.' He pulled out his car keys and headed for the door.

'Not to me.' She called after him.

'Bullshit.' He chuckled as he left.

Chapter 45

During the night the cyclone had crossed inland to the north and had largely blown itself out on the coast, the sun was trying to split through the clouds. The smell of damp foliage was everywhere; leaves splattered his hire car. Alex had checked out of the apartment and threw his bag in the boot. His mobile phone chirped. It had been lying on the back seat all night and only had one bar of battery life left. He flipped open the screen and saw it was Debbie Marcello.

'Miss Marcello, this had better be good.' he said with a false sternness to his voice.

'You know me, I just couldn't let it go. I kept working at it yesterday, and bingo.'

'Bingo what?'

'I'd delved further into the attack on David Burton and found a record of interview at Murwillumbah Police station that David Burtons name was referenced to. A cane farmer on the Condong-Murwillumbah Road had complained to the police that he had been threatened by a bloke who wanted to know where a David Burton lived. He told him that he didn't know who he was talking about, but the guy wouldn't take no for an answer, pushed him around a bit and threatened to 'mess him up', his words. Apparently, it scared him enough to report the incident to the police.'

'Go on.'

'Anyway, this guy was quite distinctive, tall, spoke with an American accent, and only had two fingers on his left hand. It was only a reference, was duly recorded, no further action to be taken unless there was a second contact. I don't know if that helps you or David at all.'

'Yeh,' drawled Alex, 'would have helped yesterday, but not anymore. Thank you for that. I'm just about finished up here.'

'How was the funeral? Did it all work out the way you thought?'

'Ahh, yes and no. But it makes a good story. I'm just heading around to see the others now. I'm booked on a flight back later today, but I won't be coming into the office till tomorrow. Your inquisition will have to wait till then.'

'And Megan rang in this morning, wanting to know if I knew where you were. You hadn't answered your phone all night and she was worried.'

'Really?'

'She sounded very concerned Alex.'

OK. Thanks Debbie'.

He ended the call and checked his screen, four missed calls, all from Megan last night. He'll ring her from the airport. He snapped the phone shut and leaned over and wiped leaves from the windscreen. When he opened the driver's door, water dribbled from the inside panel. Alex brushed at the seat covers, shifting more leaves and twigs. Everywhere inside was wet. He wiped at the seat, and flicked water off his fingers.

'Doesn't look like you'll get much deposit back from the hire car people.'

'It certainly is a mess.' Responded Alex as he straightened up and looked into the face of Senior Sergeant Cooper.

The policeman had certainly aged, his face was blotched from too many years in the sun, his hair was streaked with silver, and he had affected a stooped posture where apparently grenade shrapnel had injured his lower vertebrae long ago. He leaned against the other side of the car to ease his discomfort.

'That was some storm last night Alex. Fortunately, Cyclone Cliff crossed at Bundaberg and didn't come any further south. It would have made a terrible mess here if it did. As it was, some poor soul drowned. They found his body early this morning in the river. There easily could have been more.'

Alex stood still and just looked at Cooper.

'The bloke that drowned, turned out to be Roy Conlan. You remember him? He supposedly died 20 years ago, taken by a shark by all accounts... the same night as your friend Dennis Beaumont was drowned...by all accounts.'

Alex was wary, not sure where this was going.

'Fascinating,' he said.

'Funny thing is, this Conlan shows up in the harbour today and he's definitely not been in the water 20 years...twelve hours more like it. Seems like his dinghy tipped in the storm trying to get to his houseboat, and he drowned. Would you know anything about that Alex?'

'I wouldn't know Mr Cooper, you tell me, but then you're not a policeman anymore, are you?'

'Let's just say I'm a concerned citizen.'

'I've listened to many concerned citizens in my time.' Alex made to get in the car behind the wheel. 'Most of them crackpots.'

'Perhaps this week Roy Conlan was not the only dead person to come back to life? It's been twenty years since Beau disappeared, hasn't it?' Cooper was playing with Alex, looking for a bite, so Alex bit.

'I don't think much at all Mr Cooper. All I know is that since the day Beau disappeared, you've been blaming my friend for everything bad that's happened on the coast. That's past news, I don't need to hear any more.'

Cooper pursed his lips, as if coming to a decision.

'Alex. I was never after Beau.' He relented. 'Conlan was always the target. He ran the whole drug operation on the north coast in the 80's. He was a mean bastard. Your mate Beau was too minor to be a serious player. It was Conlan I was after. He murdered the Herman girl, caused so much grief to her family. But If I could rattle Beau, I knew Conlan would be close by. I was never interested in Beau, it was Conlan's links up the chain to Brisbane and Singapore we were all after back then, not some local surfer like Beau. And then you showed up as well, I first thought you were the new brains in the organization.'

Alex stood, one foot in the car. Now he was interested.

'You were just a minor player Alex. Expendable. In 1981, Conlan was getting ready to go. The offshore drug hauls were at an end. Yeh, we knew about them. North Queensland by plane was the new way, and Conlan was cleaning house before he left, Reggie and Beau had to go. But both in one night, and then Conlan, now that surprised everyone.'

'Reggie?'

'We got tipped off about that last offshore drug haul. We knew they were out, even in that storm, so waited for them to come back. But only Reggie Bishop showed up. He pulled a gun at the boat ramp... we finished it. He was dead before Conlan's grenade got him.'

'But the papers didn't say that.'

'Nope. We didn't tell them everything. All three dead, two of them by misadventure.'

'But you couldn't know that Beau would drown.'

'Ever hear of an Anthony Cowell? He used to go fishing with Bishop before Beau came along. He disappeared. Word was that he left here for Northern New South Wales after a fishing trip with Bishop one night. He was never seen or heard of again. But his parents suspected otherwise. That's when I started to take an interest in Bishop and Conlan's activities. Similar case to Beau don't you think?'

'I'm not sure what you're getting at here?'

'We never found Cowell, and we didn't find Beau, so I started watching Miss McKenna. She was honestly shocked that Beau had disappeared, or she was an incredibly good actress. But my gut feeling was that she honestly thought Beau had drowned. But when you went to Melbourne a couple of days after, it left the drug network open for a takeover. I wondered if she wasn't as innocent as I thought. She could have been the new drug queen. If Beau was still alive, he would meet up with her again. So, twenty years on, when she comes up for the funeral, guess who also shows up, you...and then low and behold, Conlan, a man everyone thought was already dead. And I'm betting Beau's not far away either. Would I be right in guessing that?

'Beau's dead, Mr Cooper, It's a nice story. I've been here for Marjorie Beaumont's funeral, to pay my respects, and now I have a plane to catch.'

'The airports flooded I'm afraid; You won't be going anywhere.'

They stood facing each other in the car park. Cooper sizing Alex up.

'Beau's mother, funny thing there. She paid the church in cash for her funeral before she died. $10,000. Lot of cash for a lonely old widow on a pension. Yesterday afternoon, a mate of mine, still in the force, attends a break and enter at the Beaumont house. The neighbour gave a description of the burglar; she bore an uncanny resemblance to Janice Mc Kenna. Would you know anything about that?'

'I know nothing about that Mr. Cooper. If you'll excuse me.' He collapsed into the front seat, his pants squishing in the damp, shaking his head in disgust.

Cooper tapped on the passenger window. He reluctantly lowered it.

'Phew, this car smells like it's been in the river.' He reached in and plucked a mangrove leaf off the passenger seat. 'Conlan's drowning saved me the trouble. My back still aches from the grenade wound, but it's nothing compared to the wound the Herman family have felt every day since losing Isabelle twenty years ago. Sometimes justice is served outside the law Mr Holmes, but I guess you know that.' He paused. 'Oh, and give my regards to David Burton won't you.'

Alex burst out laughing. He threw his hands in the air in surrender.

'Somehow, I think I needed to talk to you earlier. I tell you what Cooper, if I ever do a Cold Case episode on this, I'll look you up.'

Alex closed the window and drove away. Cooper knew everything. He was a strange ally. He hadn't got all of it right, but he got most of it.

Chapter 46

Alex drew up next to Janice's unit. The door was open, and Elizabeth was bringing a bag out to their car, stepping around puddles in the bitumen. He sat and watched her from the front seat. Her hair was free and cascading around her shoulders. She moved with a skip in her step, showing no sign of her physical ordeal the previous day, more than could be said for him, his muscles felt like he had been worked over by a Turkish masseuse. He hopped out of the car called out a greeting. She looked up from the back of her car and smiled. That was the best response he had had from her yet. It was radiant, the petulant sneer had gone, for now.

'You're looking fit and healthy,' he said. 'No sign of the drowned rat from last night.'

Her smile faded quickly, perhaps he wasn't out of the woods yet, it's not wise to compare a young woman's appearance to that of a wet rodent. She turned and walked back inside, leaving Alex to wonder who else he could insult today. He sauntered over to the door and peered in. Beau was sitting at the table, his arm bound tightly with a sling around his neck, gone was the grimace of pain seared on his face from last night.

'Heh mate,' he called, and raised a coffee cup to his lips. He was still quite pale and certainly moved stiffly. Janice appeared from the bathroom, throwing her toiletry bag into a small suitcase on the couch, zipping it closed, the last of her gear. She looked up at Alex.

'I went out early this morning to the 24-hr chemist, got some stitches, bandages and more antiseptic powder for Beau. He's recovering well, fair bit of bruising around the wound, but nothing that handfuls of pain killers won't fix. Most people would overdose on what he's taken.'

'He's not most people Janice! I didn't know you could stitch wounds?'

'I do all my own sewing now, always had to. He'll be alright. I've got his stuff all ready to go.'

'Apparently the airport is still flooded, so I won't be flying out today, I'll rebook my apartment. Are you still right to take him?'

'Do I get a say in this?' he complained.

It was easy to bypass Beau in the plans.

'No. I'll take you with us, you're recovering quick enough. I've sorted it out with my friend, you can stay with her a week while she watches for infection, their farm is only a short drive out of our way.'

Beau winced in pain as he stood, emphasising how much he really did need care, but Janice gave him no sympathy.

'You'll be right Beau, stop your whinging.'

'Don't see why I can't stay at your place.'

'No, Beau, you can't! I'll drop you at the farm, and after I've settled Elizabeth back in Byron, I'll come up and see how you are going, but that's it.'

'I ran into Cooper at the beach this morning.' said Alex. All three stopped what they were doing. 'He was waiting at my car.'

'Elizabeth, take my bag out to the car please. We'll be out in a minute,' said Janice.

Her daughter began to protest, but Janice held up her hand and pointed to the door. She looked from one to the other, but no one said anything more. She shrugged her shoulders, picked up her mother's bag and left.

Beau snarled, 'What did that prick have to say? Did he recognise you?'

'He did. But it's pretty good news Beau. You're not wanted any more, he was after Conlan all along, you were just bait, you and Janice and me. He was after you to get to Conlan. He even thinks the grenade in Reggie's car was set by Conlan. Apparently, you weren't the only one Conlan wanted to knock off that night, Reggie was in the firing line, as well.'

'I don't believe that. Reggie was a good bloke, he was smart.'

'Jesus Beau, these guys were crooks, they're dead and you're not, so who are the smart ones? You've been given a reprieve; the cops aren't interested in you anymore.'

His eyes lit up. 'I can claim Mums house now. Sell it, make some money.'

'Not so quick, there is a difference between the authorities not looking your way anymore and you sticking your head up to tell them where you are. Not everything will hold up to police scrutiny.'

'But I'm in the clear.'

'Not likely. What about now? How do you explain a gunshot wound?'

'He's right Beau. You can't come back yet. You're not going to risk that. I won't let you.' Janice chimed in.

Beau bristled. 'You won't let me what?'

'Spoil Elizabeth's chance at a clean life. Don't you think she's had enough of our world this week already?'

'Beau, being David Burton you have a clean slate; it would be best if you stay that way for a while longer. It'll be few months before the Public Trustee deals with your mother's house. You can come up with a good story by then,' said Alex.

Beau stood deep in thought, his eyes flickering between Alex and Janice.

'And you say Cooper's not hunting for me anymore?'

'Nope.'

Beau nodded, smiled and shuffled out the door with his cigarettes. Janice rinsed out his coffee cup, looked around one last time and made to follow. Alex stood in front of her barring her way. He looked into her eyes; it would register there if he was right.

'So how much was Marjorie Beaumont hiding from Beau?'

Her eyes flicked wide, then returned to normal.

'I don't know what you mean?'

'How much was hidden? Where did she move it to?'

Janice's eyes widened again, strike two. She looked resigned. 'Marjorie Beaumont was a wonderful woman. We became very close. Losing Beau brought us together, we both believed he was gone.'

'Go on,' he said.

'They tried pinning it all on me. They turned the bungalow upside down. They accused me of getting rid of Conlan and taking over the drug ring. They shouted at me. They accused me of everything, and the whole time, Marjorie Beaumont sat holding my hand. She lost her son, and all she could think of was looking after me, helping me to face the accusations. She would always say she didn't believe he was truly gone, and that If Beau ever came back to her, Jesus would provide.'

'And yesterday afternoon? At her house?'

'Yesterday? How do you know?' She quizzed him. 'I guess it doesn't matter now. After I left you two yesterday, I went to her house, and Jesus did provide.'

'She didn't burn the cash, did she!' He stated with some certainty.

'No. She hid it all in those tall ceramic religious statues they buy from the church shops. She had them scattered all over the house. That money is for Elizabeth, for us. Beau had his chances, but he messed up, he always does. Last night I thought I lost Elizabeth. I won't let that happen again.'

'Fair enough. And Beau?'

'What he doesn't know won't hurt him. He's lucky he's alive and has a daughter that he will get to see every month.'

Alex paused, unsure how to ask it, but finally went straight to the point.

'Janice, Elizabeth is his daughter, isn't she?' he asked, seeking certainty.

Janice looked him straight in the eye, 'Like I always said, I wouldn't lie to you Alex.'

He smiled, they hugged warmly in understanding, and he kissed her gently on the cheek. She nodded. Satisfied, he walked out behind Janice, shutting the apartment door behind them.

Alex stood leaning against the car sharing a cigarette with Beau while Janice and Elizabeth settled into the front seats, sorting out their personal space.

'I could do with some gear,' said Beau.

'And I'm sure you'll find some soon, recuperating on a farm outside Byron Bay, the hills are covered in it,' Alex said with a chuckle. Some things never change, though in this case, he could see why.

'There's no need not to see each other now is there?' said Beau. 'I mean, maybe you could come up for a surf sometime, you could help me with Mum's estate'.

'I suppose I could. Do you have any funds to pay a solicitor, on the quiet.'

'No, mate, I don't have that kind of money.'

Alex thought for a moment.

'What ever happened to your Monaro?' he asked.

'Don't know, hadn't thought about it, we never got to bring it back from Kennilworth. Could still be up there in the shed for all I know.'

He raised his eyebrows at Beau. 'That Monaro would be worth a lot of money these days, a two-door classic muscle car, not many miles on it. If it's still on the farm.'

'I don't know, it could still be there. We could find it together. We make a good team,' Beau said, wincing with pain.

'We made a good team once Beau...but we are better just as good mates now. I'll think about it, see you in a couple of months.'

Alex flicked the butt away and they shook hands warmly. He helped Beau into the back seat before he walked over to his own car and watched them leave the carpark.

Later that day, the remnants of the cyclone surf still heaving beneath him, Alex ducked and dived until he was out past the break. He rolled on his back and looked up at the sky. The clouds were still heavy with moisture and looking like they wanted to break at least one more time, but the south-easterly wind was punching holes in the cover, revealing the blue sky above it.

Alex flipped on his stomach and stroked onto a solid wave that launched him into the break, his body bouncing down the face, picking up speed until the wall broke and rolled him in the foam toward the shore. He emerged from the surf, shaking the water from his ears. He felt good, rejuvenated. He dried himself and pulled out his phone from his backpack. He chose Megan's number, thinking perhaps she would like to fly up and join him here. He'd introduce her to Villi Tanoa.

His phone cheeped. It was an incoming text from Beau.

Have you left yet?

'Shit!' said Alex. 'Not again.'

Also by Alistair Hume

About the Author

This is the first book by the author that shares with the reader his love of Australian coastal communities.

The town of Nerimbah is not a real place, though many of its geographical characteristics bear the elements of any number of Australian seaside fishing towns. To help me establish and maintain a geographical identity for my story, I drew a fictitious map for my own reference, filling it with my own place names, some of which are derivatives of traditional languages. The map helped me to keep track of my character's movements.

Alex's story is not based on any real person, though what happened to him could be associated with real events of August 1974 that contributed to the theme of the loss of innocence. There is no doubt that drug crime has had a significant impact on what were once innocent coastal communities, and that has been well documented.

I am indebted to my family, wife Debra, and daughters Anika and Chloe, for their continued encouragement and editorial input. The cover photo was taken by me of the South-East Queensland coastline, and I am indebted to Chloe and Col for adjusting the cover for print. A big thank you to Michelle Perry for her professional editorial assessment and guidance to get a first timer heading in the right direction. My friends are just glad it's over.

www.ingramcontent.com/pod-product-compliance
Lightning Source LLC
LaVergne TN
LVHW091023080826
845145LV00002B/336

* 9 7 8 1 7 6 4 5 8 7 3 2 7 *